As he slid my c... descent with his lips, ~~first padding at my~~ ... brushing the tips of my breasts, then tracing with his tongue the line of my belly until I felt it approaching my most sensitive part – as I felt all this, I say, pleasure entirely overwhelmed me, and soon we two were upon the floor before the flickering firelight, our limbs bathed in a rosy glow, engaged in pleasuring each other to the utmost.

Also available from Headline:

Eros in the Country
the first volume of the adventures of Andy and Sophie
Anonymous

Eros in Town

The Further Adventures of a Lady
and Gentleman of Leisure

Anonymous

HEADLINE

Copyright © 1989 Derek Parker

First published in Great Britain in 1989
by HEADLINE BOOK PUBLISHING PLC

10 9 8 7 6 5 4 3 2

ISBN 0 7472 3199 0

Typeset in 10/10½ English Times
by Colset Pte Ltd, Singapore

Printed and bound in Great Britain by
Collins, Glasgow

HEADLINE BOOK PUBLISHING PLC
Headline House
79 Great Titchfield Street
London W1P 7FN

**For the convenience of the reader
we here record a note of
IMPORTANT PERSONS APPEARING IN
THE NARRATIVE
in the order of their appearance**

Master Andrew Archer, our hero.
Sir Franklin Franklyn, Bart., of Alcovary, Herts, and Brook St, London.
Primp, a servant.
Blatchford, a coachman.
Mrs Saunter, a madam.
Six nymphs.
Mr Chafer, an agent.
Mrs Sophia Nelham, sister to Sir Franklin.
Mrs Polly Playwright, a servant.
The Viscount Chichley.
Miss Moll Riggs, a lady of the town.
Mrs Aspasia Woodvine, sister to Mrs Playwright.
Sam Rummidge, a coffee-house keeper.
Mrs Jopling Rowe, a madam.
Miss Xanthe Holden, a lady of the town.
Miss Rose Stibbs, another.
Miss Constance Moran, another.
Miss Sally Reed, another.
Miss Cissie Minards, another.
Miss Ginevra Briere, another.
Sir Philip Jocelind, an impoverished gentleman.
Lady Frances Brivet, a lady.
Bob Tippett, a Cockney.
Will Pounce, a countryman.
Harry Riggs, a young man.
William Langrish, another.
George Float, a third.
Ben and Tom Maidment, brothers.
Spencer Middlemas, a mature gentleman.

An Uncle to Xanthe.
His wife.
Robin, a servant.
A tailor.
His wife.
Gossage, an apprentice.
Mordan, another.
An Uncle to Sir Philip Jocelind.
Robert, his footman.
Mary, sister to Robert.
John Riggs, brother to Moll.
Mr Ambrose Forfeit, a man of law.
Six mermaids.
Sergeant Gross, a watchman.
Five young ladies of quality.
David Ham, a young person.
Miss Jenny Portland, a *coryphée*.
Miss Pussy Markham, another.
Mademoiselle Louisa Veron, a dancer.
Monsieur Jean Fiorentino, another.
Mr Sam Berensi, a merchant.
Miss Elizabeth Fawcett, a lady.
Miss Penelope Gayley, another.
Miss Rhoda Gosse, a third.
Three ruffians.
Carlo Gaskill, chief of pimps.
Bill, a workman.
Two young postulants.
Mrs Damerel, a county lady.
Lady Curd, a dowager.
The Misses Priscilla and Louise Minuet, young ladies.
Miss Mary Yately, an heiress.
Albert, a footman.
The Honourable Mathilda Yately, aunt to Miss Yately.

Chapter One

The Adventures of Andy

While we had been used to hearing tales of the lecheries of London, it was nevertheless something of a surprise to Sir Franklin Franklyn (of Alcovary in the county of Hertfordshire) and myself to discover that his house in that city was one of the best-known brothels the town could boast.

After a long but not unpleasant journey in the fresh airs of spring, our coach rattled at last down the road from Edge Ware at about eight o'clock of a fine evening, past Tyburn, and finally up to the door of a tall town house in Brook Street, near the elegant new Grosvenor Square. It was a finely proportioned house, the walls of which however were peeling, and the entrance to which indeed seemed a little shabby. But this was not surprising since Frank's father and mother had not, to our knowledge, visited it for the past twenty years, nor as far as we knew had it been inhabited but for a caretaker. Its handsome proportions, however, promised well despite the fact that shutters stood closed at every window and the dust lay white upon the glass, advertising the fact that the casements had not been opened for some time.

We were glad to leap down and stretch our limbs upon the pavement before my friend (for so I called him, we having been intimate since childhood) impatiently rattled out a fusillade upon the door with his cane. After a moment it opened, though only to the extent of five or six inches. In the dark gap thus offered appeared a cadaverous face which regarded us in silence.

'Yes, gentlemen?' enquired the face.

'Well, open up, man!' said my friend peremptorily.

'Certainly, sir; in a moment. But first, who sent you?'

'Nobody sent me, blockhead,' said my friend, over whose shoulder I was now peering.

It did not surprise me that the face showed no intelligence of Sir Franklin's person or rank, for to the best of my knowledge there had been no communication between my friend and the caretaker, and our decision to start for town had been taken of a sudden only the day before, and there had been no time to send instructions to open up the house or apprise its caretaker of our arrival. 'If the beds are damp, a night on bare boards will do us no harm,' Frank had said.

'Ah, well now, gentlemen,' said the face.

'Will you open this door?' demanded Frank, and in an access of impatience (for he was not a man to wait for long upon the convenience of others) he applied his shoulder to the oak, and it only being held by the foot of the doorman there was an oath and a clatter as the man fell to the floor, and we were past him and into the hall.

The house was evidently a most capacious one – more so than its narrow frontage promised, for it ran back for some distance, and thus there was room for a fine, tall hallway, with a handsome stone staircase mounting from it, and doors to left and to right. It was somewhat a surprise to us that candles were lit in the candelabra which hung above, for this seemed a signal of expectation of our presence – which could not have been the case. Even more surprising was the appearance upon the stairway of an astonishing apparition – a large, blowsy woman upholstered, rather than dressed, in a fine collection of satins and plushes, and upon whose head was hair of such astonishing redness that one could only infer a wig.

'Well, Primp, what's all this noise?'

Primp, for that was evidently the name of the door-keeper, was still picking himself up from the flagstones upon which he had landed, and as he did so muttered something about gentlemen and impatience and violence and only trying to protect the house . . .

'Well, gentlemen,' said the apparition, continuing down the stairway towards us, 'Mrs Saunter at your service, and if your impatience is so precipitate I have no doubt we can find something to quiet it!'

She had now reached the floor, and though the light from the candles was dim it was possible to confirm our first impression that this was no housekeeper – or if so, a strange one. Beneath the surprising wig her face was so thick with paste and powder that it cracked, here and there, into thin lines, three curiously shaped black patches giving the impression of holding the whole together, while bright spots of red upon her cheeks matched the scarlet of her lips.

It seemed time to set her to rights.

'Madam,' I said, 'you cannot know who this gentleman is . . .' but a violent dig in the stomach from Frank's elbow took the breath from my lungs, and I was unable to complete my sentence.

'Glad to hear it, ma'am!' he said, with a bow. 'Perhaps we can inspect the house?'

'No refreshment first, gentlemen? Not so much as a dish of tea? But no, I can see that your spirits are too high to be satisfied with tea. Perhaps a bottle of claret while you are at work. Please to follow me.'

She waved a hand, and sailed off up the stairs, which were nobly proportioned though, like the rest of the house, distinctly grubby. Pictures – no doubt of earlier Franklyns – hung askew upon its walls, some uprights were missing, like vacant teeth, from the balustrade, the stairs themselves were chipped and in need of sweeping. At the top, on the first floor, was a roomy landing, and right ahead of us double doors which, I had no doubt, led into the chief drawing-room.

It was a fine room, and the furnishings had once been handsome enough, though of a former age. The shutters were closed despite the bright daylight and the room was lit by candlelight. As far as I saw, the usual sofas and chairs stood about, and had been joined by piles of cushions upon the floor, but my attention to the furniture was incomplete, for my eyes fixed upon the half a dozen young women dressed – or, rather, undressed – in a most lascivious manner, who were using the room as though it was their own. It was a scene such as Mr Rowlandson might have been pleased to draw: wherever the eye fell, a naked limb engaged it – a long thigh scarcely veiled by thin lawn, an arm negligently thrown over the arm of a chair, a bosom the rosy tips of which were palpably exposed, the flesh lit by the mellow, warm light of naked flames. One girl, a charming bosom visible through the drapery which made only a

gesture towards concealment, had a drawing board upon
her knee, and was working at a portrait of another who,
entirely naked, lay face downward upon a pile of cushions,
the sublime contours of whose arse stabbed me with their
beauty. The other ladies were employed in various
negligences – one painting her face, one with a book, one at
darning.

I glanced at my friend, whose interest was no less
palpable than my own, for we were lusty fellows still not
twenty years of age and had not been in the company of
ladies for some weeks – except that of Frank's sister Sophie
who, being like him my friend, was not for common use in
the way of love-making (though when a mood of familial
tenderness turned to sensuality, such was not unknown to
happen, to our mutual satisfaction and the tying of the
firmest knots of friendship between we three).

I half expected a protest from Frank for the scene, however pleasing for a whorehouse, was not one that a man
might expect to find in his own drawing-room, though the
ladies were of a beauty not always to be found in such
places – at least not in my experience, which however – as
readers of an earlier chronicle will be aware – had been
confined to the provinces of England and had not encompassed the capital, to which I was entirely new. But to my
surprise, my friend simply threw his cane to the floor, and
in a moment had thrown off his shirt and was turning his
attention to his breeches.

'Come, Andy!' he said. 'Lose no time! Was it not worth
the journey to be presented with such delights?'

I did not long hesitate in following his example. As I
stripped, the blowsy commander of this company of
trollopes was remonstrating: 'Sir, if you would care to
choose one of these nymphs, I will conduct you to a chamber. Besides, we have not discussed terms.'

But before she was able to complete her sentence, Frank,
now being in a state of nature, and his enthusiasm advertised by his rampant manhood, had thrown himself upon
the equally naked object of the artist's attention and,
pausing only to turn her upon her back and to spit upon his
hand and anoint his tool with saliva, thrust into her with an
intemperance which if at first surprising and even painful

was soon giving her obvious pleasure, for after an initial squeak of apprehensive protest she soon began to buck to his thrusts, her hands asplay upon his buttocks the better to pull him towards her, so that their bellies slapped together in applause at the enthusiasm of their congress (a sound at which her friends could not suppress some envious laughter).

'We can discuss terms later,' said he, pausing for a moment in his ministrations. 'Meanwhile, ma'am, no interruption, I pray!' – whereupon he grasped his lady's breasts, pinching her nipples between his fingers and thumbs so that she squealed from the enjoyable pain.

I was by now divested of covering and hesitated only through a surfeit of choice, until two girls advanced upon me, one fixing her lips to mine, gripping the lower one gently between small, sharp teeth while the other fell to her knees before me, and I felt the softness of her tongue flickering about the tops of my thighs.

Presently, while Frank single-mindedly ploughed his way towards a final pleasurable leap, I found myself at the centre of the five remaining young women, each eager to obtain some satisfaction, for they had obviously been dull without company. One offered to my lips the most delicious nether mouth, to my surprise entirely divested of hair and thus smooth as can be to my delighted mouth. 'Twas my first experience of so smooth a target, and was inexpressibly exciting to me, so that I was scarcely sensible that two more girls were clasping my naked feet between their upper thighs and encouraging me to tickle them with my toes and that two others were guiding my hands over their bodies, a hardened nipple one moment beneath my palm, a smooth posterior the next. From time to time one would bend to kiss my almost painfully distended staff, to take my cods in her hands and roll them enticingly, or to tickle my nipples with their tongues – until, mad with delight, I seized about the waist the girl whose quim I had been pleasuring with my tongue and lifted her bodily upon me, lowering her so that she slid down to embrace my essential manhood like a soft, smooth glove, laughing with pleasure as the plentiful hair which embellished its root came into contact with her own unusual smoothness.

Almost immediately I came off with an excited spasm, regretting only – as the nymphs, I believe, did – my inability to pleasure each one in turn.

I had naturally been for some time unconscious of Frank's doings, he being still preoccupied with his single girl, but now I heard a cry and lifted my head just in time to see his delighted expression as he plunged finally into her from behind, she bending over the back of a chair above us. They must have at some time, unnoticed by me, altered their posture so that they could observe my pleasure and the pleasures of my companions, while still gratifying their own senses.

Exhausted with delight, we disposed ourselves to lethargy while our ladies, with warm towels fetched from another room, ministered to our hot and sweaty bodies, wiping the moisture from our chests and buttocks, and with a gentle delicacy cleansing those parts which a few moments before had been so actively engaged.

After a while, the manageress of the tribe appeared with a tray of wine and we enjoyed a glass while the girls completed their favours. They had not paused to cover themselves, and their postures as they bent and rose were so pleasant that I began to be ready for another bout. My favourite houri noticed, and laid her hand upon me in a manner which would have proved fatal had not Frank shot me a meaningful glance, and rising to his feet drawn on his shirt. In what was for me too short a while, we were dressed and, bidding the nymphs farewell, left the room. At the top of the stairs, our hostess waited.

'You will forgive me, sir,' she said, 'but I must now suggest a gift of twenty guineas for our girls. They were clearly delighted to serve you, but I have the expenses of the house to pay . . .'

'Ah, madam,' said Frank; 'I see the time has come to introduce myself. I am Sir Franklin Franklyn, of Alcovary. I think my name is not unfamiliar to you?'

Speechless, the woman drew back, her mouth falling open. At last, 'Sir,' she said, 'forgive me – I was not aware . . .'

'Clearly,' said Frank, 'but perhaps we could repair to your room of business, where you might enlighten me as to the conduct of this place?'

To cut the tale short, Mrs Saunter told us that the house to her knowledge had been a brothel for the past ten years. She had been approached by Mr Thomas Bidwell, representing himself as the man of business of Sir Franklin, Frank's father, and informing her that he wished to let the house on advantageous terms.

'I was then,' she said, 'running the house in Frith Street of which you must have heard . . . No? Well, you are young gentlemen, but 'twas a famous house, though small – so that I was glad to come here, where there was more room and I could enlarge my stable of fillies. And here we have been since then.'

It appeared that each month no less than two hundred golden guineas was handed in person either to Mr Bidwell or to his representative, and had no doubt made its way into the late Sir Franklin's coffers – which went some way to explain the large sum which the miserly baronet had left, so unexpectedly, at his sudden death. It was also clear that she had heard neither of the old man's end, nor of Mr Bidwell's sudden death, for she had been paying his agent, Mr Higgens, regularly until that very week – something about which, as Frank remarked, we should have words with him.

'Well, Mrs Saunter,' said Frank, 'I mean to live here, so you must vacate the place – and soon.'

Mrs Saunter was not in the least discomfited.

'Well, sir,' she said, 'as it happens I have been contemplating a move to Hammersmith – 'tis all the rage to the fashionable, and I have obtained a lease upon a large house there which I am almost finished fitting out. It will be possible there to offer hospitality not for a mere hour or two, but for an entire weekend. Some gentlemen find that one evening in the company of such girls as I commonly supply is all too short a time, and will welcome the opportunity for a dalliance which will last for some days. You two gentlemen, if I may say so' – and she eyed us with a significant smile – 'seem yourselves to be of such sort, and I shall always be glad to see you there. In the meantime, there is on the upper floor a room which was always kept in readiness for Mr Bidwell when he occasionally spent a night with us. Though, to tell truth his appearance was always less than welcome, for he insisted on three of the girls attending upon him at one time, which on a busy night seriously depleted my profits. Not,' she concluded, 'that you would not be welcome to such comfort tonight, should you desire it, for the evening is uncommon quiet.'

Frank bowed his acknowledgement, and Mrs Saunter led us upstairs to a small but comfortable room with a single, large bed, and in a short time Primp, not in the best of tempers, had struggled up with our luggage, and we had ordered a chop from the establishment nearby whence Mrs Saunter secured food for her clients. This proved excellent, as did the second bottle of claret which she sent up 'with her compliments', and when we had dealt with both, the journey and the events which followed it having proved sufficiently exhausting, we threw off our clothes and were a-bed and asleep without more ado.

I was woken next morning by a soft hand upon my shoulder, and opening my eyes for a moment thought it was still night, for the branch of candles which had lit us to our bed, and which we had extinguished at last, was once more lit and shone upon the face of my nymph of the night before, who was bending over and softly shaking me. But then behind her I saw a streak of white light outlining the shutters of the window, and realised that 'twas day.

Beside me I felt Frank stirring, and glancing toward him saw his own partner of the previous night's pleasantries at his side, and that upon the tables at the bed's side were trays bearing pots of chocolate, cups, and . . . But as I was about to examine the trays more closely, I was made aware that a hand, not my own, was closing upon my prick, piss-proud as often when I awake. Nor did I protest when, throwing back the covers, my lady bent to slip it between her lips, permitting myself the liberty to place my own hand beneath the single garment she wore, to trace the line of her spine down to where it fell into the divide of her delightful nether region.

Though we had not noted it, having been so tired that we could have slept upon a plank's breadth, Frank and I had shared a bed scarce three feet wide, and when the girls, having thrown off their light frocks, attempted together to climb upon it to mount us, side by side, like twin horses in a stable, it was clear 'twould not accommodate them. So with a glance at each other and a wink, as though it had been planned, we rose from our places and, taking each a girl by the hips, threw them across the bed, one from each side, so that as we went about our work my head was next to Frank's busy bottom, while after a moment I felt his girl's hand slipping between my thigh and my accomplice's, rising until it could seize my stones and fumble them, adding a delightful titillation to my increasing pleasure.

Reaching his goal somewhat before me, Frank raised himself and took to slapping my buttocks as they rose and fell beside him, this, together with the continuing ministrations of his lady and the delicious smoothness and liquidity of which my girl was mistress, before long encouraged me to throw out a tribute to the occasion, when as one man we rose and handed the girls to their feet – upon which, without even pausing to cover themselves, they poured us out chocolate and lifted the cups to our lips.

We lay for a short while, until the swift gallop of our hearts engendered by our recent race steadied to a mere trot; then with an oath Frank jumped from his bed.

'Enough of this damned candlelight,' he protested. 'Let us let in some of God's good sunlight!' – and striding to the window, he swiftly threw off the bars and turned back the shutter. For a moment my eyes were dazzled, and then, as they grew accustomed to the light, what a sight met them! The room, which in the dim and friendly light of the candles had seemed pleasant enough, was revealed as dingy and dirty, scarce fit for a beggar to inhabit, with the filthy hangings tattered, the carpets threadbare, and the bed linen, now that it could be seen, grubby and unclean. Thick cobwebs hung from the curtain rail and clustered in corners, while all manner of stains and excrescences disfigured the walls.

The girls had hastily donned their single garments, but even had they not, our disillusion would have been plentifully fuelled, for what could be seen of their flesh was grubby and unwashed, their dresses – if that word can be applied to the shapeless, greying material which now hung about them – equally shabby, and their faces, which had seemed pretty enough by candlelight, betrayed that they were of a certain age, and that the amorous experience of which they were undoubtedly queens had been long and hard in the winning.

They were clearly conscious of our surprise and dismay, for they turned away with a shamed look, and made towards the door.

'Nay, please remain!' said Frank in as kind a manner as he was capable of – and he was always a fellow of the greatest charm. 'Please, ladies, join us in a cup –' and gesturing them back, passed them his own cup of chocolate, a gesture I was happy to imitate, since it could now be seen that the china was cracked and stained, and the liquid within it a purplish grey.

The girls – or, rather, women – sat upright upon the bed as we pulled on our breeches and shirts, and our being clad seemed in some way a comfort to them, for they were soon more relaxed, and Frank began to question them about their accommodation. Yes, they lived at the house, as did their four companions – all in a single room above the drawing-room, which had once, they supposed, been the main bedroom. Mrs Saunter looked after them well – which turned out to mean that they were properly fed, given a small proportion of the money they earned, and allowed a certain freedom which placed them far above the other whores they knew who worked in similar houses, for (they said) 'twas often the case that a girl might be taken in only for a night or two, then thrown upon the streets once more to make her way as best she could.

Both had earned their living from their childhood up by pleasing men, there being no other career open to them except the lowest kind of domestic service; at least whoring allowed them to save a little money for their old age, and to be fairly comfortable the while.

And what of the men who frequented the house, asked my friend? It became clear that whatever Mrs Saunter might pretend, those were of the lowest sort, for some were violent, others escaped without payment, some few were diseased – and seeing our alarm, the girls were quick to assert their own freedom from the pox, though Mally, one girl, had been turned off last week as Frenchified, having been tipped a burner by some seaman from the docks, which she was known to frequent.

Perhaps too hastily for politeness Frank thanked the girls for their attentions and showed them the door, whereupon with a wordless glance at each other we divested ourselves of our breeches and seized the soap, ignoring the coldness and, I fear, pollution of the water provided in jugs for our toilets, and scrubbed our cocks diligently until they were more sore from our attentions than from the first rogering they had done for several days.

Still far from confident we had escaped disease, we then dressed and tidied ourselves as best we might, and were just preparing to leave our room when a knock at the door announced Primp, who begged that we would attend Mrs Saunter and Mr Chafer downstairs.

From the way Chafer made his obsequious bow, Madam had obviously revealed Frank's identity. He was a thin little man all in black, with a continual nervous giggle which he disguised by thrusting a fist into his mouth. It became clear that he, too, had been unconscious of Bidwell's death. He had heard that his master was visiting Frank's father at Alcovary, but since he had done so often before, frequently staying for some time, had thought nothing of his absence and had heard neither of the baronet's death, nor of Bidwell's. Fortunately for us, Bidwell had been sufficiently a tyrant to prevent his agent from attempting any fraud; the rent for the house had been paid into account as usual and, yes, he would in course be happy to accompany Sir Franklin to Coutts's bank, where he could check upon the account and the veracity of his statements.

He was clearly much impressed by being in the presence of a member of the nobility, however young, and backed his way bowing and scraping to the door, leaving us alone with Mrs Saunter. Frank, as he had done upstairs, walked to the window and despite her protests – 'No, pray, Sir Franklin, pray, I have not yet made my *toilette* . . .' – threw back the shutters. If the wreck of what had once been a pleasant room was immediately notable, 'twas nothing to the wreck of Mrs Saunter, who looked desperately around for something to shield her face but found nothing larger than a notebook, which did little to conceal her white-washed visage, heavily rouged cheeks and blackened eyes.

Frank was unfailingly polite – as he was to all whose offence to him was impersonal.

'Will it be convenient for you to leave within the week, ma'am?' he asked.

'In course, Sir Franklin, in course,' she said. 'You must please believe yourself master here.'

'I do, I assure you,' said Frank firmly, with half a wink in my direction.

'And you will remain in your room here?'

'Well, no, I think not,' said Frank. 'We will perhaps take rooms nearby for the while, for there are certain refurbishments . . .'

'But of course,' said Mrs Saunter, 'a gentleman of your quality . . . I am of course all too aware that the place has been let go, but 'twas not my place to speak to Mr Bidwell about it, and as you know your late father never did us the honour to visit us . . .'

No, the income had contented him – and for over ten years, we learned. But we were not inclined to stay any longer than we must, and Primp was soon in the hall with our cases, and opening the door onto the street, where we stood for a moment in the spring sunshine, breathing deeply. Frank's coachman was leaning against the railings nearby.

'Ah, Blatchford,' said Frank, 'you found somewhere to stay, I trust?'

'Very good coffee house nearby, sir,' said the man, who knew enough of his master to engage pleasant accommodation for himself, whether told to do so or no. 'The horses bedded down at the back, sir, all tight and snug. The rest of your luggage to be brought round, sir?'

'No, Blatchford, thank'ee,' said Frank. 'We shan't stay here.'

From his look even at the outside of the building, the man entirely understood.

'Thought not, sir, and emboldened to enquire at the coffee house for rooms. A fine set in Hanover Square to be had for fifty guineas a week, sir. A Mr Plant, at number 14, with the lease. If you would care to inspect?'

Bowing to Mrs Saunter ('Yes, Sir Franklin, honoured, Sir Franklin, will leave within these five days, Sir Franklin, and pleased to see you at any time . . .') we made our way down Brook Street – a noble and wide thoroughfare in which, Frank confided, he was ashamed to see that his was the least cared for of houses – and were led by Blatchford to a handsome square somewhat to the east. Within an hour we had been introduced to a gracious set of rooms on the first and second floors of one of the houses there – drawing-room, dressing room, dining-room and two bedrooms – ('Cooked food available from the Blenheim coffee house, gentlemen, in Bond Street, not two minutes' distant,' advised Mr Plant) – and had taken them for a month.

Ordering up hot water to the dressing room, we stripped and cleansed ourselves thoroughly, then dressed and, feeling more ourselves, strolled out and made a breakfast at the Blenheim, a house catering for single gentlemen, then took a turn westward and into Hyde Park, the new young trees of which were just beginning to green with the spring. We strolled slowly down to the Serpentine and along its brim to the beautiful enclosure bordered on one side by the small gardens of the keeper's lodge, on another by the noble grounds of Kensington Gardens, and on the third by the park wall. There sat a woman with a table and chairs, and glasses for the accommodation of visitors who wished to drink from the mineral spring which filled a marble basin. Children were drinking directly from this bowl, while servants, sent from their mistress's carriages out upon the main road, waited with jugs for their turn to fill with the liquid, a vast quantity of which was cast up into the reservoir.

We turned into the footpath which ran from this enclosure back towards town. I was not the first to remark upon the circumstance of Frank's father proving a brothel-keeper. Frank himself was, he said, not surprised; he was not aware of any family riches, nor that his father had ever worked to acquire a fortune, so the extent of that left him at Sir Franklin's death had astonished him, and he had felt that it must have been acquired clandestinely. He was sure that his mother knew nothing of it and that Bidwell, in making an attempt on her virtue, had thought not so much of marriage for affection as of acquiring in some way a share of the capital.

'Well, Andy,' he said, 'now I have it, and will you be surprised to hear what I shall do with it?'

I could not think.

'What most struck you about last night's adventure?' he asked.

The fact that his father's house should be a brothel, I replied.

'Certainly, but about that house itself?'

'Well,' I replied, hesitantly.

'Were you not surprised by its shabbiness, and certainly when we let in the daylight, this morning, was not your impression one of disgust and horror?'

I was forced to acquiesce.

'And our companions?' he said. 'I was as ready for a fuck as yourself, and will not say that I was not pleased by our reception. But was the sight of our ladies in the light of day not less pleasing than you would have wished? To say nothing of the suggestion that they might be poxed?'

I raised my eyebrow.

'Well,' he said, as we passed the enclosure where cows and deer were already turned out and grazing, 'we shall see what has been earned in such filth and disorder, and then we shall see what *can* be earned.'

My lower jaw must have dropped, for he laughed and slapped me on the back.

'Yes, Andy,' he cried, 'I shall see what a little care and money, a little organisation and thought, can make of the house in Brook Street. I can just imagine the kind of man who has been attending there. If we smarten the place up, engage some girls of the better sort, allow for comfort and guarantee cleanliness – why, whatever my father's scale of charges, we can charge five times as much. I've always believed there was a fortune in fucking, my lad, and now we shall try the question!'

At which he laughed so infectiously that I could not but join him, and in a moment we were leaning against a tree helpless with laughter, to the astonishment of the passers-by.

When we had recovered somewhat, we walked on in silence for a while. The sun was low in the spring sky, small buds were appearing on the branches, the city was beginning to stir – though here, in the park, we could have been in the country. Surreptitiously, I put my hand under my coat-tails and pinched myself. Was I, Andrew Archer, sometime footman, lute-player, childhood friend and now companion of Sir Franklin Franklyn of Alcovary, now to be an associate in a brothel? It seemed so. I glanced towards Frank, and caught him watching me a trifle anxiously, I thought. I grinned at him, and he threw his arm across my shoulder.

'Let us see what Coutts's bank has to say about our funds!' he said, and we turned on our heels and strode off towards the city.

Chapter Two

Sophie's Story

I set off alone on my journey to London, taking not even a maid, and catching the stage coach from Alcovary village – for my half-brother Frank and our friend Andy had driven off a week earlier in the family equipage, taking with them our coachmen. I had remained behind to close up the house, leaving only one servant in residence to care for it during an absence of I knew not how long.

My friends will know from my previous narrative that, despite my relatively slender years, my experience of life had already been sufficiently wide to render such a journey as I was upon – a mere eight hours consumed the fifty miles or so between my home and destination – entirely free of anxiety. And I knew that in the town my own house awaited me – or rather the house which had been the property of my late husband, Mr Nelham, a gentleman whose lack of humanity and affection was balanced by an extraordinary degree of miserliness. Upon his death I found myself heiress not only to a considerable fortune in coin, but to a house in the district of London called Soho, which, it seems, he kept to avoid having to pay the expense of hiring rooms when he was engaged on dry-as-dust research at the British Museum or some similar receptacle of musty documents. While my brother had been unable to discover anything about the property our late father possessed in London, my enquiries had revealed that my own house was small and compact, and in the charge of a Mrs Polly Playwright, whose letters to me had been written by some public scribe, and were signed by a simple mark, but who seemed, for aught I could tell, honest enough.

And indeed it was a cheerful, round, good-humoured face which greeted me when I knocked upon the door of the narrow house in Frith Street at about four in the afternoon;

the face almost of a good country maid, except that it was rather paler, as most city faces are. She made a curtsy and stood back for me to enter, then ordering the carrier who had borne my luggage behind my chair from the White Hart in Piccadilly, where the coach had ended its journey, to set it down in the hall and be quick about it, handed him his one-and-sixpence fare together with an emolument smaller than I would have dared to offer, and berated him for ingratitude when he protested.

It did not take long for me to see over the house, which indeed consisted simply of a set of rooms one upon the other; a kitchen in the cellar; a drawing-room upon the ground floor; a bedroom over the top of this; and a small upper room in which Polly had her residence. She had informed me that the house was barely furnished, and only with old and discomfortable things, so I had sent her money with which she had bought modest but comfortable new furnishings – chosen, I should say, with a taste far superior to that which I might have expected. A bright fire burned in the hearth against the slight chill of the spring afternoon, while food was set upon the table in the drawing-room, for which I was more than ready, and which she served with cheerful application.

I was eager to see my brother and our friend, and the house which had belonged to our father. A brief note had informed me only that 'twas unfit for habitation for the time, and gave a nearby address where Frank and Andy were living. I lost no time in setting out, with Polly accompanying me, and a decent linksman from a neighbouring hostelry to marshal us, for though Polly was perfectly aware of the way to Hanover Square, she let me know that it was best we should be escorted by a man – not in fear of theft or violence, though such sometimes occurred, but lest I should be affronted by some gentleman taking me for 'a common woman,' as Polly put it. By this I took her to mean a whore, but neglected to inform her that I was entirely capable of defending myself if such an incident should occur, for I did not yet know her so well as to realise that no such barrier against complete confidence need exist between us.

Having been seated all day, I was ready to stretch my limbs, and a thirty minute walk was no hardship to me –

first north to Oxford Street and then along it to the westward to a point at which we could march into Hanover
Square, where we were soon knocking at the door of Frank's
rooms.

The affectionate claspings and kissings with which I was
greeted might suggest to the uninformed witness that we
had been parted for a year rather than a mere week, but the
degree of affection between us was such, and a long parting –
as I have previously recounted – so relatively recent, that
we were ever reluctant to be parted and pleased to be
reunited. In no time the claret was flowing and we were telling each other our news and I learnt, to my astonishment,
that they had found my father's house a brothel, only that
week vacated by its whores and now awaiting redecoration –
'And to what purpose?' enquired Frank, with what seemed
a sly grin.

'Why, I suppose you mean to live there,' I said.

'Indeed, you might suppose so,' said Frank, 'but how are
we to fill such a large house, and to profit?'

I thought I saw a wink pass between Andy and Polly, who
had indeed been eyeing each other with mutual friendliness.

'May I guess, gentlemen?' she said unexpectedly. 'Begging
your pardon, ma'am' – (with a bob in my direction) – 'do
you not think of continuing in the same business?'

Frank's jaw dropped before he burst out laughing,
'Indeed you have it, Mistress Playwright!' he said.

'A brothel?' I enquired.

'What's good enough for my father is good enough for
me,' said Frank, 'and I have the notion that a really
superior establishment would be an ornament to the town,
and would be much frequented.'

'Right you are, sir!' said Polly, then blushed and fell
silent, feeling that she had stepped out of her place. But I
am the last person to take a snobbish view, and encouraged
her to speak out.

'You have experience in that area?' I said.

'No, ma'am, not directly,' she said, 'but I know that
many of the gentlemen of the town have a dislike to the dirt
and disrepute of the profession. Many of the girls are well-
meaning enough, but are much taken advantage of by the
pimps, and a respectable place . . .'

We could not but burst out laughing at the idea of a respectable whorehouse – 'Though,' said Frank, ' 'tis what I intend, and can see that Mrs Playwright will be of the greatest assistance to us.'

He poured another libation, and we drank to Polly, who blushed with pleasure and responded by lifting her glass and emptying it in one swallow. Enquiring her history, we found that she had been engaged by Mr Nelham four years previously, when she was sixteen. He had found her weeping on a doorstep down by the river and offered her a position – an uncharacteristic act of charity, as I thought, but more likely inspired by the knowledge that a distressed young female could be engaged at less expense than another.

'And your title is an honorary one, Mrs Playwright?' asked Frank.

'No, indeed, sir,' she responded, explaining that four years previously she had been married by a young sailor of uncertain birth, who had given her his name before a magistrate then 'had me twice in the yard at the back of Newgate, left me, and was never heard of since.' The magistrate seemed to us a problematical fiction, though we did not say so, yet at the memory (and no doubt under the influence of the claret) poor Polly became somewhat tearful, whereupon Andy, whose eyes were more and more attracted to the fullness of her bosom, slipped an arm around her and filled her glass again. And while Frank and I spoke a little more about his plans, which indeed were not yet far advanced, his familiarity grew, so that in a while I turned to see that one of his hands had slipped within her dress to fondle a breast, and his other palm lay upon a knee whence it had crept beneath her skirt while he pressed kisses upon her neck.

I had been sitting with my back to the couple, but Frank, while speaking to me, was affected by the view of their increasing familiarity, for I could now see beneath his breeches a swelling which – as I had discovered when we were still but innocent children – denoted a rising passion.

' 'Tis all very well, Andy!' he said. 'You and Polly leave brother and sister without the means of satisfaction, while you take your pleasure!' – and so saying, passed between the two of them, and began gently to undo the ribbons at the neck of the girl's dress. Her eyes opened wide and turned towards me – but I gave her a smile of approval, for I guessed what was the truth – that she was not displeased by the attention of two such handsome young men, for both Frank and Andy were in that bloom of youth in which every part of them was attractive to the female senses, though one part more than the rest.

It was not long before the girl was entirely naked – a pleasing sight, for though of a generous figure her heavy breasts, sturdy thighs and broad hips were all of a proportion, so that the fullness of her bosom (which on a slighter figure would have been too ample) was entirely apposite. That she was as attractive to the male as to my female eyes was attested by the fact that my brother and his friend had in no time thrown off their clothes, giving her, as myself, ample evidence of their readiness to embody their admiration.

I must confess that the sight arose a certain warmth within me, and leaning forward I laid my hand upon the firm globe of Andy's arse, slipping a finger below in a manner which I knew to be an irresistible signal to him. And indeed, leaving Polly to the ministrations of my brother, he turned to me and, raising me to my feet, clasped me in his arms, and began immediately to unlace me.

I should say here that we had been familiar, in this way, since we were children – and indeed that the adventurous period of my life had begun when our mother had discovered us both a-bed with Frank, in a state of nature, when we were scarcely old enough to perform those acts which we were essaying. However, since our re-union six months ago, after many vicissitudes, Andy had been somewhat withdrawn from me, and while we had made love upon occasion, it was (it seemed to me) only because no one else offered, for he seemed to regard me more as a sister than as a lover – something I regretted, but understood, for Frank and I had ever treated Andy as one of our family.

Even now, it appeared to me that he turned from Polly only because I desired it, and not especially because he preferred to do so, and could not suppress a pang of regret. However, as he slid my clothes to my feet, following their descent with his lips, first paddling at my neck, then brushing the tips of my breasts, then tracing with his tongue the line of my belly until I felt it approaching my most sensitive part – as I felt all this, I say, pleasure entirely overwhelmed me, and soon we two were upon the floor before the flickering firelight, our limbs bathed in a rosy glow, engaged in pleasuring each other to the utmost.

There is something most comforting in the love-making of a partner with whose ways one is familiar, and though our amorous passages were now somewhat infrequent, I knew well those turns of lip or finger which could give Andy most joy, just as he knew how to arouse me to the utmost – his tonguing of my nether part accompanied by a light pinching of my tits with finger and thumb; the caressing of my neck with his right hand followed by its passage along shoulder and arm until it lay over the small of my back, pressing me towards him. And I remembered the delight my biting of the skin of his thigh could bring, the pleasure I gave in stroking the fur of his arse until my fingers slid down to flick at his cods, and finally the joy – almost to culmination – that my lips gave as they slid over the knob of his standing instrument, and then with a gentle motion rose and fell upon it.

Meanwhile, a disparate pleasure was experienced by Polly and Frank, who being strangers could only by experiment discover what pleased each other. A cry of surprise and pain came from Frank, for instance, when the girl applied her teeth rather too firmly to a nipple, and she gave a vigorous shaking of the head as he thrust several fingers into her secret parts – which, it was clear, she preferred to be otherwise occupied, for before long she had forced him upon his back, and was mounted upon him – not yet indeed taking his instrument within her, but rocking to and fro upon it, causing him (evidently) a mixture of pleasure and pain which was at least as gratifying as it was uncomfortable.

Finally, implored by his eyes and hands alike – which latter gripped her about the waist and positively lifted her so that she sank upon him to the hilt – she joined me in being engorged by that delicious flesh which makes us truly women, and we begged our lovers to steady themselves so that we could enjoy some minutes of delight before that moment, alas almost always premature, which signals man's keenest pleasure and (too often) woman's keenest disappointment.

Soon, however, we were urging them to more vigorous movement, our mood changed by the warm caress of sword in scabbard, and we both cried alike, and almost simultaneously, with pleasure as we mounted to our apogee, our lovers proving their devotion by the release within us of their vital juices. And at the moment when we collapsed into a lethargy, what was my surprise to find that I had reached out to take Polly's hand – whereat she leaned over to where I lay, my head now lying upon my brother's flank, and kissed me upon the cheek. In a moment, she realised what she had done, and coloured, but I reassured her with a gesture and we were, from that moment, not only mistress and maid, but sworn companions, however much circumstances might keep us within our stations.

Now Andy, having kissed me upon the lips, drew himself from me and, taking a napkin, wiped me tenderly between the thighs before cleansing himself. Polly, evidently reluctant to move, sat for a while still impaled, until my brother's tool, having done its duty, shrank from her, whereupon she knelt to kiss it before ministering to herself, and we sat together in a state of nature before the warmth of the fire, hand in hand and flank to flank. Then, without asking, Polly wrapped herself in her clothes and called from the window to the linksman that we would need him no more that night, throwing him a coin, and we repaired to a bedroom where one large bed shared our tired limbs, and we spent a welcome quiet night.

We woke next morning all four cramped together in a tangle of limbs – a sensation pleasantly warm and friendly to one who otherwise might have felt alone in a strange city – and I could not but congratulate myself that my first night in London had not been spent in a necessarily lonely bed in Frith Street. Though I certainly did not foresee waking to first daylight to see my brother Frank in the arms of my servant, when she awoke, stretched, and paddled across the floor in bare feet to draw the curtains, her gentle smile towards me, accompanied by an acknowledgement as friendly as it was respectful, showed that she was entirely conscious of our relationship and ready to honour it.

By turns, we cleansed ourselves – in the most luxurious manner, too, for as with most of the houses in the area (I was informed), lead pipes brought water three times a week to a grand cistern in the roof, and while it must still be heated by fires, it was plentiful and fresh, and large vats brought to the bedrooms by a man employed to do so made it much easier to be continually cleanly and sweet-smelling than even our best endeavours had formerly attained.

We broke our fast modestly upon fresh, warm bread from a nearby bakery, and a pot of chocolate (for at that time I much preferred it to coffee, then more fashionable, while the modern infusion of tea was still regarded as vastly unhealthy). Polly returned to Frith Street, where she said she had much to do, and I accompanied Frank and Andy to my father's house in Brook Street, and found it as they had said. Its interior was empty and almost ruined; the furniture had been carted away, exposing tired and cracked plaster, woodwork badly in need of repair and painting, and floorboards often almost split through. After I had been conducted over the house, a knocking upon the door announced the arrival of some workmen whom Frank instructed to repair everything that needed repairing, and to paint all the woodwork white (except that in the large room on the first floor, where there was fine panelling). 'Then,' he said to the chief man, 'I will have further instructions, for my plans will have been fully made.' These he promised to reveal to me when he had properly worked them out; they were to prove, he said, something remarkable.

While the men set to work we strode out that I might see the town – which was a revelation to me for richness and sophistication far in excess of that I had seen in such provincial towns as Southampton or Bristol.

We walked through Bond Street, Albemarle Street, Berkeley Square, Piccadilly, St James's Street and Park, Pall Mall, St James's Square, the Strand, and several other fine thoroughfares. Well-dressed men and women thronged all the streets – many dressed in black (Frank explained that this proceeded from the general mourning for Princess Charlotte, who died some weeks ago). Nevertheless, the show of fashion was remarkable, as was the press of traffic in all directions, for the roll of chariots and carriages of all kinds was incessant. Coachmen with triangular hats and tassels, footmen with cockades and canes added a dignity and even a gaiety to the show – yet Andy informed me that 'twas nothing to the display to be seen in Hyde Park upon a weekend.

Here and there in the streets were lines of hacks, poor worn horses eating out of nose-bags. Sometimes enormous wagons filled with coals, and drawn by great, shaggy horses would lumber by. And on market day, it seems, cattle are often driven through even the most fashionable streets to that part of town where they are sold and all too publicly slaughtered.

It was soon clear that the quarter where Frank and Andy were dwelling, known as Mayfair, was the best and most fashionable, for houses elsewhere were often a muddle of ancient and modern, too frequently huddled together without form, space or proportion. But the shops – the haberdashers, poulterers, fishmongers and butchers. The open squares and gardens, the parks with spacious walks, the palisades of iron or enclosures of solid walls wherever enclosures were requisite. The countless number of equipages and fine horses; the gigantic draft horses. What industry, what luxury, what infinite particulars, what an aggregate!

The men were taller and straighter than the peasantry in the country where I had spent most of my life, and dressed (where they were gentlemen) in the height of style. Altogether, it was a remarkable taste of a city which I hoped soon to call my own.

I said farewell to my brother and our friend in Piccadilly, for, I said, I wished to stroll in the new Burlington Arcade, among the pretty shops with their show of millinery, hats, silks and shoes, tambours and furs, all displayed with the greatest taste and delicacy. The number of unescorted ladies strolling there was somewhat of a surprise to me, my brother having (unless he was unaware of the truth, which I cannot believe) mischievously failed to explain to me that the Arcade, while certainly a showplace for pretty things, was equally one for those ladies whose interest was in acquiring the money with which to purchase them. Nor had he mentioned that most of the shopkeepers there had rooms behind or above their shops which could be hired by the hour for a matter of a shilling or two.

I was soon educated, however, for halfway up the arcade I paused to admire a window of engravings, some of mythical scenes, some of foreign views, and out of idle curiosity, entered and asked if I could look through some of them. The middle-aged woman curtsied, handed me a folder, and showed me into an interior room where there was a comfortable sofa and a table, at which I sat and opened my folder. You may imagine my surprise when I saw that it indeed contained views of antique scenes, in which the gods and godesses were nobly shown, but that rather than being semi-nude, their figures politely disguised by a fold of drapery or a leaf, they were on the contrary depicted not only completely naked, but in eager congress. Here was a Judgement of Paris in which the handsome young god, his manhood joyfully extended, toyed voluptuously with the three candidates for his approval; here were satyrs thrusting their hairy staffs gleefully into the persons of soft maidens or nymphs; here was Vulcan at work while on a bed behind him Mars, clad only in a gleaming helmet, lay between the legs of Venus, one thigh thrown artfully upwards so that his tool could be seen enfolded by her pleasant, eager parts; here was Lotis lying on the ground, viewing with amazement the cloak of Priapus, held aloft by the proportions of a vast Something beneath it, the quality of which she was clearly frightened to try . . .

I had seen nothing of this sort before, and was engrossed in the pictures when a soft voice at my back enquired whether I was at liberty. I looked up to see a young man – younger perhaps even than Frank – dressed in clothes superlatively cut, which fitted him like a glove. His blue coat was single-breasted and set off by a buff waistcoat; his nether garments leather pantaloons, and he wore hessian boots. Round his throat was a huge, brilliantly-white neckcloth of many folds, out of which his chin must struggle to emerge. The picture was completed by a finely brushed beaver. His visage was sensitive and open, and from it sparkled a pair of eyes of intense brightness, vivacity and humour.

'I beg your pardon, sir?'

'I asked, ma'am, if you were at liberty?'

'For what?' I naively enquired.

The boy paused, as if wondering (as he might well have done) whether I was a mere tease, then replied: 'For such pleasures as you witness in those pages.'

While in my life I had many times been approached by men for carnal purposes, the enquiry had never been so forthright, and despite the boy's tender years I rose to my feet with the sternest of rebukes: 'I am amazed, sir, that you should address such remarks to a woman with whose name, even, you are unfamiliar, and whose person surely requires greater respect from one so young!'

This was something of a quirk from me, who could not have been but a year or two older than he – for I doubted that he was more than sixteen or seventeen years old, despite his outward assurance and manner – and he coloured immediately, stepped back a pace, and said: 'Madam, if I have offended you, of course I apologise. It was finding you unescorted in these premises, where . . .' and his eyes moved to a curtain at the end of the room, which, I now saw, was drawn slightly aside to reveal a bed.

At once, of course, I realised the true circumstance, and why the boy had approached me so confidently. Still blushing, he was backing away from me; I owed it to him to elucidate my mistake.

'Sir,' I said, 'I regret my curtness; the truth is that being from the country I was unaware of the reputation of this place, and quite innocently entered it to view some engravings, the nature of which – and I ask you to believe me – were as great a surprise to me as my reaction to your approach was to you.'

The boy removed his hat, revealing a tumble of fair hair.

'Ma'am,' he said, 'please forgive me. I understand now the nature of your response. This place is, I fear, not one for respectable persons such as yourself. Gentlemen, liable, I regret, to appetites foreign to ladies, frequent it in order that such as yourself should not be troubled by our importunities. I beg you, once more, to forgive . . .'

But this was too much! 'Appetites foreign to ladies', indeed! The lad must be taught a lesson.

'Ah, sir,' I said, 'it may be that the ladies of polite London society lack that eagerness of which you speak. In the country, however, it is otherwise . . .' And striding forward, I reached for his lips with my own, and slipped my tongue between them, while at the same time pressing my form firmly against his.

After a moment's surprise, his dark eyes twinkled again, and – whether under the misapprehension that I was indeed a professional lady or believing my words (which were of course entirely true) – he threw his hat to the floor, swept me up in his arms with an ease which betrayed greater strength than might have been supposed, and carried me to the bed, pausing only to close the curtains before undressing first me and then himself.

It soon became clear to me that, while forward in speech, the child was not only inexperienced but entirely without understanding of the fine art of making love. Not for the first time, I pitied the wife whose husband came untried from altar to bed. His was so beautiful a person that my first tribute was to slip from beneath his slim, white body and, falling upon my knees beside the bed, to salute the long, pale wand with the purple tip which stood from a cloud of blond hair below his belly. No sooner had my lips embraced it however, than a deep shudder ran through his body, and I drew back hastily – but too late, for a paroxysm overwhelmed him, the muscles of his slender thighs tightened, and a moan escaped his lips as from his instrument an eruption of liquid signalled the premature extinction of my hopes of pleasure.

He had the grace to blush, and indeed even covered his eyes in shame, but I drew his hands away and kissed him upon the lips; in one so young the juices run almost continually, and in no time he would be recovered. With his handkerchief I mopped at his chest, whence the power of the spasm had thrown the nectar, and, laying myself at his side, gently stroked his body with my hands, then very gradually with my fingers, and finally with my fingernails, flicking at his nipples, which swiftly tightened and were as erect as my own. Against my thigh I felt a stirring, marking the beginning of his recovery, but meanwhile he lay supine, not making so much as a gesture towards my own body, which was crying out for satisfaction. So, throwing my leg across him, I knelt astride his chest and applied my forefinger to that part which most eagerly cried out for friction.

His eyes grew wide, for though he must have played with other boys and been entirely aware of the manner in which they could excite themselves (or each other, as I had observed Andy and my brother at play when together we began to feel the stirrings of warmth in our bodies), it had clearly never occurred to him that women had the same propensity for self-pleasuring. After a while, and with a look at me that seemed to ask my permission, he reached out with his hand and allowed me to guide it so that soon he was giving me a more febrile delight than any touch of my own could raise. After a while I was positively panting with delight, and to my added pleasure felt his hands under my arse, lifting me so that he could reach out with his tongue to touch me where, I would swear, he had previously touched no woman.

Meanwhile I was reaching behind me and gently frigging his own most tender part, which became hard as ivory, so that in a while I could no longer resist and, pushing his shoulders back to the pillow, slid down until I could raise myself gently (for fear of once more depriving myself of the ultimate joy) and slide his staff within me, watching as first the tip, then the perfectly shaped length, slipped into me, and finally my dark hair knit with his own fair. Then, still gently, I began to rise and fall, his flesh appearing, pulling my lower lips to follow its movement, then disappearing again. His eyes caught at mine, and sparks seemed to fly between them as gradually my movement quickened, and I felt him thrusting up towards me, and finally, this time with exquisite slowness, the waves of his pleasure broke within me just as I – roused by the luxury of pleasing him as much as by my own physical delight – also reached the final mark.

We kissed gently, and dressed in silence. He began to fumble with his purse, and then refrained.

'Ma'am,' he said, 'I know not . . .'

I laid a finger on his lips.

'I took great pleasure,' I said. 'You must know that I do not throw myself into the arms of every man I meet; but I am pleased to have given you joy.'

'May I call upon you?'

'Certainly,' I said. 'I have yet no card, being freshly arrived from the country, but –'

He produced a tablet, and at my dictation wrote my name and address.

'And perhaps you have a card?' I said.

He reached into his pocket and handed me a slip of card, bowed, smiled, and was gone. In the shop, I heard from the woman an expression of delight that could only be commensurate with a very considerable emolument. I looked at the card:

THE VISCOUNT CHICHLEY

7 Charles Street, W.

Wenscombe, Buckinghamshire

That, I thought, might be a useful acquaintance, and stored the card safely away in my reticule, bowing with what I hoped was a sufficiently distant politeness to the woman in the shop, who was talking in a delaying manner to a florid man and an equally florid, not very young woman, as – I saw – behind me a girl was hurriedly remaking the bed.

Chapter Three

The Adventures of Andy

Two days after the anticipated but no less keenly pleasurable arrival in town of dear Sophie – and my enjoyable encounter with her admirable servant Mrs Playwright – Frank returned from Brook Street to our rooms in Hanover Square with the news that work was going forward well there. Slapping me on the back, he said, 'Well, my boy, the serious work now begins – we must do a little research into the stock-in-trade of the business into which we are to adventure.'

I had wondered how he was to find the women to employ in Brook Street, both of us being entirely ignorant of the city and of what went on there. I had no doubt that a sufficient number of bobtails existed here as elsewhere and had heard of those parts of the town where they were most readily to be met with. But as to the manner of recruitment, I suspected that Frank must take pot luck, unless we should be fortunate enough to meet someone who could inform us fully on the matter.

'We shall need half a dozen girls only at first,' Frank said, 'and of various shapes and sizes, and I've no doubt our good taste and varying ideas of what's fine in a woman will lead us to success if we follow our noses.'

'Follow our sugar-sticks, more like,' I said, at which we grinned. He advised me to put on my second-best clothing – 'For,' he said, 'we want to appear neither wealthy nor poor, and thus we shall find the girls whose chief regard is for the game rather than the gold.'

I had extreme doubt whether such existed, but followed his example and, dressed in decent but not remarkable clothing, we set forth at half-past six in the evening and made our way first to the Haymarket, which already was thronged, not least by women evidently of the class we sought. The whole street – and Regent Street to the north of it – was brilliant with lights, the shops, cafés, Turkish divans, assembly halls and concert rooms all advertising themselves with a degree of opulence not seen anywhere, I would guess, outside a great European capital. One glance showed the troops of elegant girls rustling in silks and satins and laces, walking in the fashionable crowd. Some were tall, elegant, worldly, with pale cheeks and a haughty mien; others were clearly not long from the country, their cheeks rosy from working in the open air, but now determined to seek what employment they could find indoors.

There were too, it must be said, blowsy old women still occupied long after a lifetime of vice and lack of care had reduced them to wrecks; these offered themselves with a whine for a few pence, and were sometimes to be seen led off by some young punk to a narrow alley away from the main streets.

But it was on the elegant that we fixed our gaze, some of them finely dressed and clearly accomplished in manner, many with the style of a lady, and plainly of education – reduced perhaps by ill fortune to their present straits. Some of these latter, I later learned, were at one time milliners or sewing girls in genteel houses in the city, and perhaps ruined in character by their mistress's husbands, or having quarrelled with their relatives, were reduced to a life of prostitution. Others had been waiting-maids, similarly destroyed either by fellow servants or by gentlemen, and now devoted themselves to a wild life of pleasure.

'Well,' says Frank, 'we can't hunt in couples. I'll leave you now; it's – what – seven o'clock. Let us meet at Fenton's in St James's Street at nine, and compare notes. If you find a likely girl, note her name and address and tell her we shall be in touch – you can hint for what purpose, but give no promise and no address.'

And he made off down the street, where I saw him first eye then approach a girl in a brilliant yellow dress, and after exchanging a word or two, they vanished into a side street.

To survey the crowd at my ease, I entered the Royal Coffee House and found myself a seat near a window whence I inspected the passing crowd. It was not long before I caught the eye of a pretty young girl in a willow bonnet and a green dress which I glimpsed beneath the black cloak she held about her. Walking down the bustling pavement towards the window she held my eye, then paused – it seemed to study the bill of fare – while passing her tongue slowly over her lower lip and glancing sideways at me, for whom her appetite seemed as keen as for the food upon offer on the bill. She had a fine if sallow face, framed by jet-black hair, her eyebrows beautifully arched and the eyes deep and inviting. I rose, threw money upon the table, and left, whereupon she came straight up to me and said in a low voice, 'I believe, sir, that we are to be acquainted?'

'I think so, positively,' I replied.

'You wish me to come to your rooms?'

Ah – I had not thought of that. 'Perhaps, ma'am, you know of somewhere . . .?'

'Certainly,' she said; 'please to accompany me.'

She walked up the Haymarket, catching prettily at my arm, and though at first I felt inclined to shyness, a glance about me told me that almost every man in the street had a similar girl on his arm. We turned into Orange Street, then into some other, and stopped at a small coffee-house the lower room of which was deserted save for a few elderly men at one table, playing at dice.

My siren saluted the owner, who stood behind a table in a white apron idly polishing some glasses.

'Mr Rummidge,' she said, 'may we have the use of a room?'

'Certainly, Moll,' came the reply. And then to me: 'That'll be two shilling, and in advance, sir.'

I fished in my pocket and found the coins, he handed the girl a key and a lighted lamp, and we mounted a narrow staircase for two flights. My friend then unlocked a door and ushered us into a small but decent room whose furnishings simply consisted of a small table with a basin of water and a dish of soap, and a bed the linen of which was passably clean, as far as I could see, though clearly rumpled by previous occupants. Setting the lamp down upon the table, Moll turned to lock the door, and without more ado began to undress – at which there was nothing for me to do but follow her example.

When we were both naked, she approached me and

without ceremony put out her small hand to my cods (how cold but how inspiriting it was!) and said, 'Perhaps you would like to give me some money, ducks?' Her accent, I could not but remark, had suffered deterioration since we climbed the stairs.

Enquiring how much would be her fee I learned that she expected half a guinea, and fetching it from my pocket handed it to her, whereupon she tested the gold with her teeth, smiled, and placed it in her reticule.

'Now, ducks, what's your fancy? A simple buttock ball, a screw up, a throw in my diddeys, or something strange? If 'tis too strange, there may be a few shillings to speak for it . . .'

No, no, I assured her, ordinary congress was sufficient for me – though truth to tell I had no notion what the strange phrases she spoke could mean.

And indeed such was the case, for having wiped me thoroughly she bent her head to my lap and I soon felt the soft warmth of her lips upon me, accompanied by the run of her hands upon my hips and flanks.

Not to weary the reader – for it is ever my wish to avoid the mere repetition of lubricious detail – I need only say that she was indeed mistress of her art, with all that appearance of enthusiasm and pleasure which is a true aphrodisiac (for I have often confirmed that those women who appear to perform the act solely for the gratification of their partners fail to arouse acute delight, and dealing with them is little more satisfaction than dealing with the palm of one's hand). It may of course be that the writhing of her body under my embrace was counterfeited, that the small whinnies of pleasure (like those of a young colt) were mimicked, and that her final explosion of delight, when she clung to me so fiercely I thought my ribs would crack, was a calculated display of acting – but I believed not.

As we lay afterwards upon the bed, she stroked my body with what seemed a loving care, kissing me gently as with the cloth she wiped down my heated limbs.

'Thank you, sir,' she said. ' 'Tis some time since I danced the jig so pleasantly.'

'Nay, Moll,' I said, 'surely 'tis I should thank you,' though indeed I suppose that not every one of her visitors

would have shown the consideration with which I was careful to nurse her to an excitement which clearly pleased her.
There was a pause, for I could not think of the sort of
conversation proper to the occasion.

'You are in a good way of business?' I finally asked.

' 'Tis always spring in this town,' she replied with a
smile, 'though 'tis rare the evening brings me a friend so
charming as yourself,' bending her head to nip the lobe of
my ear. 'I trust we shall meet again.'

'I trust so,' I said. 'Where may I find you?'

'You can enquire here,' she said, 'Rummidge's Coffee
House in Whitcombe Street – Moll Riggs. I'm never far
away, after six, and Sam Rummidge downstairs will take a
message.'

I reached for my note book and jotted down the details.
'Then we shall meet again,' I said, 'I'm sure of it.'

'No doubt,' she said. 'A lad so riggish as yourself cannot
go long without strapping.'

Still naked herself, she helped me dress, handing me my
clothes piece by piece, drawing up my nether garments,
buttoning my shirt – and only then drawing on her own
clothing, which consisted, now that I looked, merely of a
single garment with a cloak thrown over it.

'Well,' she said, seeing my glance, 'a swift unveiling is
sometimes a necessity, and fortunately the winter is now
over and the evenings in this town positively sultry.'

To my astonishment, it already wanted only fifteen
minutes to nine o'clock – in my passion I had lost count of
the time, though my partner had not, for as she made to
unlock the door she said, with a pretty hesitation, 'I remark,
sir, that we have been occupied for some hundred minutes,
which is forty longer than would normally . . .' breaking
off with a little cough. Whereupon I dipped into my pocket
for an extra half-a-crown, with which she expressed herself
delighted.

Having bade her farewell I made my way back to the
Haymarket, and thence to St James's Street and Fenton's
Coffee House, where I found Frank, who greeted me with:
'I have arranged a brine bath for us both.' Seeing me look a
question, he explained that this was a house in which warm
sea water baths could be had for seven shillings and

sixpence – which seemed to me to be an exorbitant price, but since my friend was paying I acquiesced. He explained that sea water bathing was all the rage in town, the water, it was said, being brought in pipes from Brighthelmstone, a resort much favoured by the Prince Regent. Meanwhile, artificial sea water was provided.

'There are,' Frank said, 'several large public establishments – one indeed in St James's Street itself – but I wished to see a smaller one.'

Directed towards the back of the house, we found ourselves in a middle-sized room in which were four large wooden tubs in which water steamed, and climbing each into one of them found ourselves indeed immersed in warm salt water. It appeared the recipe for such a bath was to fill the tank with water and to add to it about as much common sea salt as there is water. Such a bath will keep good any number of years and may be employed in the midst of frost and snow without danger of the bather catching cold. Spluttering from his immersion, Frank asked whether I had not indulged in sea bathing – which indeed I had not, apart from the dip I had had when escaping from the press gang at Portsmouth the previous year.

'Ah,' he said, 'our Prince Regent has made it popular at Brighthelmstone, and now 'tis spread to London, and is said to be mighty healthy.'

'Mostly nonsense!' remarked a voice, and the head of an elderly man, the face much decorated by whiskers, appeared over the brim of one of the neighbouring tubs.

This proved to be the visage, so he informed us, of Major Trumball, of the medical corps of one of our great regiments, and recently returned from a tour of duty in Turkey – where, he said, they ordered their baths better, aided by the heat of the climate and the ready supply of those he described as 'the most amiable bum-boys east of Cyprus, as amorous as a sackful of whores, and in the dark quite as capable of entertainment.'

As to the health-giving qualities of salt water, he exclaimed, 'twas mostly flim-flam, and a fashion spread by 'that fat fool' (for so he alluded to our gracious Regent) in order that he might have excuse to escape to Brighthelmstone with his doxy, one Mrs Fitzherbert – a lady whose name I now heard for the first, but not for the last, time.

'The one purpose 'tis good for is to relax the muscles,' said our new acquaintance, 'and for that purpose 'tis to be commended, but for no other – why, 'tis useless even for cleansing the body, for soap has a great antipathy to salt.'

Somewhat to my surprise, for to be honest the man seemed to me to be a tedious bore, Frank cultivated conversation, asking whether regular bathing in hot, fresh water – even daily immersion – was in his view not a fine thing, and received the answer that 'twas.

'Bodily cleanliness is now much under discussion by our masters at the War Office,' said the major. 'Though 'tis impossible to maintain under conditions of battle, we are experimenting with the installation of machines for dispensing hot, or at least warm, water in barracks, and engaging the men to bath each day in it, and the information we have so far gathered shows that an increase in health runs with cleanliness of body.'

'The pox, I suppose, must concern you greatly when men are stationed in a great city?' asked Frank.

'Indeed, sir, but again, there is much to be done by care. The Spanish gout is punishment enough, and if by example we show ways of avoiding it, we find even the roughest of men in time take care.'

'But how do you do this?'

'The cundum, sir,' said the major. 'I have sometimes wished we could tie each man into one before letting him from barracks, but what persuasion can do, that we essay. And now many of the women of the town, themselves a-feared, use these preventatives, which prove to be a salvation.'

He heaved himself over the edge of the tub, preceded by a large paunch.

'Pleasure to be acquainted with you, gentlemen,' he said, and made off.

No sooner had the major left than the door opened and three women entered bearing large pails of steaming water. Without ceremony they tipped it into our tubs, highly amused when we cried out with the shock of it – for it was almost boiling!

When they had retired, Frank asked how my evening had been spent.

'You mean you found only one girl?' he asked. 'Why, at this rate 'twill be 1850 before we have a crew together!'

So how many had he found, I asked, at which he laughed, and said about twenty – but this merely meant, I found, that he had approached some likely women in the street and engaged addresses at which they could be found. And when I asked how he knew their performances would come up to their appearance, he was at a loss to answer except to say that they would be well tried before their engagement. We begged to differ, then, about our relative activities (though I pointed out that ten or twelve days at the most would, by my method, result in our engaging a full stable of known and tested mistresses of amorous play). But what, I asked, was his notion – the building of a set of baths in St James's?

No, he replied, but in the cellars at Brook Street!

Noting the rage for baths, he said, he recalled what he had heard at university about those of the ancient Romans, and also from travellers of those still in existence in Turkey, and that though some were of gigantic size, others were small and capable perhaps of establishment even in a private, modern house.

' 'Twould have been impossible,' he said, 'even a few years ago, when water was delivered in pails only twice a week or so, but now with the advantage of water piped to the house, it should not be impossible to put it to the use which we are now making of it . . .'

But it would be enormously expensive, I objected.

'Ay – but think of the advertisement!' Frank said. 'The curious would be immediately attracted, and moreover, as I suspected and as the major has confirmed, there would be a great advantage in that both the girls and the visiting gentlemen would be clean, for it is my intention not only that the men shall be protected from dirt, but the women also. My understanding is that there is increasing fear of the French disease, and that a reputation for avoiding it would do us the most good. But,' he went on, 'I have discovered one obstacle to our plans.'

And what was that?

The fact, he explained, that while the law did not prohibit a lady selling her body for gain, nor did it prohibit another woman from organising such sales, it was adamant against any man who made profit from such a business.

'So,' he said, 'we must have a woman to manage the trade.'

We were silent for a moment, both, I suppose, with the same thought, and both hesitant to express it.

'Sophie,' Frank began, 'though I would not hesitate to consult her in the matter . . .'

'I do not care for the notion of her as brothel-keeper,' I said.

'Though,' Frank agreed, 'we know her to be enthusiastic for the game it is somehow a position that I would not care to offer her. But at least we could discuss it, and invite her opinion.'

The water was now beginning to grow cool, so we hauled ourselves from our tubs – I must say with a glow on our skin and very agreeable sensations – dried ourselves, dressed, and made for Frith Street, where we found Sophie absent, but Polly Playwright sitting before a good fire, happy to entertain us to a cup of chocolate. After a while, she enquired of Frank how his plans were progressing, and he opened with her the problem of the law's inhibitions.

'You must clearly put in a Madam,' she said.

'Ay, but who?'

Polly was silent for a moment, then said: 'I was reluctant to let you know of it, for many gentlemen would regard it as a matter of shame, but I think I can introduce you to the right person – someone of considerable experience, who herself was kept for some years by some distinguished men of the town.'

Polly went on to explain that apart from the women of the street, and those who worked in houses such as that run by Mrs Saunter, there were others – usually the more beautiful and intelligent – who became the kept mistresses of individual men – a nobleman, perhaps, an officer in the Guards, or someone of wealth in the City or on the Stock Exchange. These women had an income often of twenty or thirty pounds a week – some, much more – while their sisters who plied the Haymarket or appeared at the theatres and gin palaces rarely earned more than ten or twelve pounds in seven days.

Polly's sister Aspasia (not, it seems, her real name – which was Nan – but one she had adopted as soon as she went to work) had been from the age of seventeen under the protection of Mr Peregrine King, the well-known man of finance, who had become enamoured of her at first sight and proposed within a fortnight that she should keep company with him. She had accepted without hesitation, for he was then a man of distinguished appearance, though considerable age, and he had taken a house for her in one of the terraces overlooking the Regent's Park, allowed her two thousand pound a year, and came as frequently as he could to pass his time in her society.

'She brought me to London from Ipswich, where we both grew up, to be her maid,' said Polly, 'for she lived in great style, setting up a carriage, and taking a box at the opera on the pit tier. Her friend, far from finding her beauties cloying, grew the more addicted to her company as the months passed, and he was unhappy except when within her sight.

'Unfortunately,' she continued, 'Mr King's amorous performance was scarcely on a level with his generosity, and after eighteen months or so she found herself incapable of resisting the attempts upon her person of a young but impecunious Guards officer who, one evening, Mr King discovered in her box at Covent Garden. She introduced him as her cousin, but the incident aroused her protector's suspicions and he determined to watch her more closely. For a time, more by accident than anything else, she escaped discovery, but the betrayal of a footman, who we both treated too kindly, led to Mr King's appearing unexpectedly one evening to find her and the Guardsman in a state of nature enjoying each other and a bottle of champagne in the bed for which he was so generously paying. The next day, with a few sarcastic remarks, her protector gave her her *congé* and five hundred pounds.'

With this, however, Aspasia had set herself up in rooms in Curzon Street, and took her position among those who, in rank beneath the single kept woman, take several lovers who call upon them at different times. This life must be conducted with considerable skill and she was adept at it. She had no hesitation in admitting to her favours any man to whom she took a fancy, and when approached, perhaps at a fashionable ball, or at Vauxhall or some other public place, she would produce her diary and appoint a time when he could call at her rooms. She had led this life for the past five years, and was now in a comfortable way of life, with some half a dozen lovers who were happy to support her.

'She would certainly advise you,' said Polly, 'and might indeed consent, were the terms agreeable, to manage the whole affair.'

Much excited by this news, Frank asked whether we could not instantly call upon this paragon, and though it was now late, Polly happily consented, with the proviso that were she occupied, we must return on another occasion.

Hailing a coach, we were in Curzon Street within half an hour, and upon Polly's announcing herself and finding her sister at leisure, we were within a few moments ushered into a handsome sitting room.

Few men would, I imagine, be proof against such a beauty as Aspasia. Slimmer, though some years older, than Polly, her carriage was more graceful and her beauty altogether finer – though whether her passion matched that of her sister remained for us to discover. In addition she had – no doubt through her continually keeping company with the fashionable rich – an assurance of manner which was however matched by a lightness of wit, a humour and a delightful ease which at once commended her to me and, as I immediately saw, to Frank.

Having introduced us, Polly put, in a few words, the intention Frank had of opening – as she put it – 'the handsomest of private houses' in Brook Street.

'That,' her sister remarked, 'will be an expensive business.'

'Expense is not a bar,' Frank assured her – and indeed our visit to Coutts's bank a week before had assured us that the coffers were even fuller than we had had cause to hope.

'Then you cannot fail,' said Aspasia, and prompted by Frank went on to explain that although there were perhaps as many as twenty thousand prostitutes in London, most of these were what she called 'rank amateurs', mere harlots, and if one were to ignore those at both ends of the spectrum of love – those kept by the rich or living in private apartments and those frequented by the poor – only a minority lived together in houses, many in the neighbourhood of Langham Place but some as far afield as Pimlico or Brompton. These are what are known as 'board lodgers', for they give a portion of what they receive to the mistress of the brothel. Many are disreputable places, regularly raided by the police, the men who run them continually engaged in criminal proceedings – though these, it seems, are so tedious and expensive that the magistrates prefer that they are dealt with 'unofficially'. The few which are decently run are left alone, though with an occasional 'sweetener' to the local watch.

But was it not true, Frank asked, that only women who ran such houses were free of prosecution?

Indeed, said Aspasia, but if the house were properly run the law's eye winked upon it, provided some lady was at least prepared to lend her name to the house as its nominal president.

And were these houses popular, asked Frank.

Indeed, Aspasia replied. Men frequented them often because they were private – for many who were in a certain position desired secrecy above all things – and because they believed the women to be free from disease (which was often, though not always, the case). A house which was pleasant without being so luxurious as to be frightening, where the fees were substantial enough to command respect while not of a degree to be punishing, could not in her view but succeed, and the guarantee of a regular income of, say, fifteen guineas a week would enable us to engage girls of the first quality, and ensure their constancy.

And would Aspasia perhaps be interested in advising us?

'With pleasure, Sir Frank. I am at the moment somewhat at leisure, having only two gentlemen upon my books. Perhaps I could look over the house at some convenient time, and approve the plans?'

Indeed, said Frank, that would be of value, for he had no notion what was the done thing in the way of decoration.

Upon hearing this, Aspasia (as I intend to call her, for her surname was never used, even among friends, though 'twas

I believe known to tradespeople) kindly showed us the extent of her own rooms. That in which we had been sitting was delightfully set up, a double candelabrum shedding generous light upon handsome furniture, carpets and hangings. Next to it was a dressing room, divided into two. One part, which was Aspasia's own, contained all those articles which are most precious to the sex in the way of perfumes and pommades and a large closet in which her clothes were hung, while the second had only a mirror, chair and small hanging closet, together with razors and soap. And both had large tubs for bathing, though in light metal rather than wood, a new notion to us, but, Aspasia explained, easier for her maid to empty, for they could be tipped and the water thrown into pails, rather than disposed of by tedious baling.

'From what you have said,' she remarked, 'you will agree with me on the notions of cleanliness, and I find that even those gentlemen – usually the more elderly – who object to regular bathing can be persuaded to it if I offer my help, while the warm water often communicates to the most withdrawn or nervous of them an ease of intimacy conducive to amorous pleasure.'

Next, we were shown into her bedroom, which was simply furnished with a great bed capable of holding at least four persons, and surrounded by several adjustable mirrors.

'The tools of this trade are few, and the only prerequisites comfort and space,' Aspasia remarked. 'Cramped conditions, I do not enjoy, nor indeed do they permit of that freedom of movement which, if a mere immediate convulsion is not all that is required, is concomitant with real pleasure.'

As she bent to straighten a line of the bed's hanging, Frank caught my eye and with a nod and a wink indicated that Polly and I should withdraw. As we did so, I saw him lay his hand upon Aspasia's shoulder in a gesture the warmth of which was undoubted. Heated, no doubt, by the evening's research, and clearly admiring the person of our new friend, he was now ready for more corporeal congress.

I looked at Polly, who smiled back as we seated ourselves upon a comfortable sofa. I hoped, I said, that her sister would not regard an approach from Frank as impertinent.

That day, she replied, upon which her sister was not ready to entertain an amorous passage with a young man as personable as my friend would be one upon which pigs would fly. And by laying her hand upon my arm, seemed to say that where she too was concerned those animals need not expect too immediate a translation to the skies.

My difficulty was, of course, that I had not long since shot my bolt with my friend of the Haymarket, and as is often the case when a partner is new to me, my spirits had been considerably fanned, so that I was now exhausted to a degree which seemed unlikely to promise a quick recovery.

But I reckoned without Polly's determination, for she was not to be denied her pleasure, and leaning against me placed my arm about her neck so that my left hand was prettily close to those heaving breasts incompletely disguised by her dress. In a moment or two, indeed, almost of its own volition my palm found itself testing the softness of that globe nearest it, while she laid a hand upon that part of my person where normally a signal of approval of beauty might be expected to reveal itself. However, such was not the case, for I was still lobcocked, and it was impossible that she should not discover it.

Far from taking offence, however, she smiled and, placing a kiss upon my lips and fixing my eye with a kindly but mocking look, began at the greatest leisure to divest herself of her clothing – first bending to remove her shoes, then reaching up beneath her skirt to roll down her stockings, not neglecting to permit me such a bewitching glimpse of marble white thigh that 'twould have been a colder man than I who would not have felt a tremor at it. Finally, she bent and took hold of the hem of her dress, raising it as 'twere the curtain of a theatre to reveal the pleasures beneath – the line of her calves, then of her full thighs (a smudge of dark hair between them – for she was scornful of the filthy modern habit of wearing drawers), the deep dint of her navel, a narrow waist above the generous breadth of her hips, and finally, as she drew the dress over her head, those two splendid bubbies which were – or so it seemed to me – her most admirable part.

Slowly, she revolved before me, showing her figure to the finest effect, now her front, now her back, the full globes of her generous arse tempting my to run my hands over them. But on my starting forward she moved away, keeping me in my seat until I was once more entirely conscious that I was a man, my tool starting up from my lap until my breeches seemed ready to burst, so that when, drawing me to my feet, she divested me of my own clothing, I was proud to display an instrument whose vigour I do not hesitate to say she could scarcely have expected to encounter within the whole of Mayfair. Embracing me, she lowered herself, my standing the while, until her breasts, pressing like pliant cushions about my member, completely surrounded it with the most delicious tissue – whereupon she revolved them, as it were, in a movement conferring an astonishing pleasure, and despite my previous exhaustion I felt myself capable of anything, and bent to lift her with such vigour that, my arms under hers, and her legs now thrown about my waist, she was able to embrace my sturdy lower limb with her nether parts. Soon, however, the natural necessity for freer movement encouraged me to lower us both to the carpet, where I did justice to her beauty with the utmost pleasure, she being so ready for the combat that the smoothness and liquidity of the motion prolonged our ecstasy and it was only as we heard the door open, and our brother and sister appeared to smile down at us, that we finally reached a conclusion as charming as it was lethargic.

After a final embrace we climbed somewhat sheepishly to our feet, and were encouraged to follow the example of our peers and refresh our now satisfied parts in the dressing rooms before Frank and I took our leave and made our way back to Hanover Square – he having arranged for the fair Aspasia to view the house in Brook Street as soon as it was finished.

Chapter Four

Sophie's Story

The morning after my encounter with Viscount Chichley, Polly woke me at nine o'clock, bringing up a note which had been sent round by a one-horse chaise from Charles Street. 'My dear Mrs Nelham,' it ran, 'I trust you are in health, and that when I give myself the pleasure of calling upon you at noon, you will be ready to accompany me to see some of the sights of the town, and later to take supper at Ranelagh. Yrs affctly, Chichley.'

The reader will imagine with what alacrity I arose, what a fussing and fuming then took place as Polly was set to making neat my finest gown. I much regretted that I had not as yet had an opportunity to replenish my wardrobe, but I had with me a couple of gowns of the first quality which I had purchased at Cambridge at the end of the previous season. One of these I trusted would be sufficiently elegant; it was of gauze, in *eau-de-nil*, with long sleeves, and I prevailed upon Polly (who had great dexterity with her needle) to lower the bosom, especially at the corners, and to plait a dark blue ribbon round the top. Over it, I wore a dark blue velvet cloak and of course my pretty cap with a peak and a large full bow over the right temple. I believe that I presented myself in my full beauty, such as it was, and indeed when Chichley made his bow prompt at twelve I think I read in his visage an approbation as full as I could desire.

He escorted me immediately to a handsome private coach – which, I later learned, was leased to him at a guinea a week while he was in London – and proposed at first a drive, which indeed was what followed: to Piccadilly, down St James's Street and past the Palace and handsome park which mark the western extremity of the town; then to Whitehall Palace, which stretched along the northern bank

of the River Thames from Privy Gardens to Scotland Yard.
Here, next the Banqueting House, several of the nobility
have houses, among them the Earl of Fife and the Duke of
Buccleugh.

'I hope,' said Chichley, 'to have the honour of showing
you to them, at no distant date.'

I should have said that the noble boy – for I could think
of him only as that, his face being as open and ingenuous as
that of a virgin – presented himself as a figure of great
elegance which would have made my brother and his friend
(had they been present) seem shabby. His tight pantaloons
were of pale yellow, cut to show his narrow waist and
shapely rear parts to advantage. With them he wore a fine
pair of soft black boots which rose to a point, within a few
inches of the knee, from which a yellow tassel was hanging.
At the waist, the pantaloons were gathered into the waist-
band giving almost the impression of a petticoat under the
waistcoat, and a high-collared coat of a slightly darker
yellow set off his usual brilliant-white muslin neckcloth,
superlatively arranged in no less than five folds.

As we drove eastwards through the city it was my amusement to watch the street activities. The closer we got to
Saint Paul's church the less fashionable the crowd, and the
more merchants and men of business were to be seen. And
there were urchins of every age between five and ten, bowling
hoops among the people, dropping corks into the gutters to
race them in the rancid waters, vaulting over the wooden
posts, fighting with fists and stones – one of which striking
the glass of our coach and causing me to start, gave my friend
the excuse to grasp my hand and press it.

In due time we reached the Tower of London, that massy
dark structure to which some apprehension must always be
attached. I had not thought of it as a centre of amusement,
but to my happy surprise found there the most delightful
menagerie, to which for one shilling we were admitted,
seeing at close quarters lions, leopards, tigers, racoons, and
a curious mild beast known as an ant bear, from the country
of Canada. These, exhibited in dens behind bars, for the
perfect safety of the visitors, were of great interest and
considerable beauty.

By now it was almost three o'clock, and Chichley swept

me off to Tom's Coffee House in Cornhill, where many
Italian, French and other foreign merchants were already at
dinner. Our food was dressed and presented to us in a handsome mahogany chamber which Chichley had bespoken and
where a table was laid with good white linen and silver. But
behind it hung a curtain which failed to disguise a bed –
seeing my apprehension of which, Chichley stuttered a little
and murmured something about believing that I would not
wish to dine in the general press downstairs. I was in as little
doubt of the dessert I would be offered as of my readiness for
it, many of my night thoughts having revolved around the
previous afternoon's encounter. But my eagerness to match it
was balanced by my readiness for the viands brought to us,
which had been chosen with the care Chichley always showed
in each social department of life: a little steamed fish dressed
with some oyster sauce, a roast fowl accompanied by spinach
and potatoes, then a *ragoût à la Française*, macaroni and
pastry, and finally walnuts, raisins and almonds. The whole
was accompanied by champagne, of which we consumed two
pints.

While we ate I learned something about Chichley: that his
father had died a year ago and he had succeeded to the title and
estate in Buckinghamshire, a fine house set in a great number
of acres near Aylesbury, together with – it seemed – sufficient funds. His employment, he told me, consisted chiefly of
keeping a watch on his stewards. This, since he was an intelligent youth, was a source of disappointment to him, and he
had in mind a political career – 'For', he said, 'there is much
to be done to wipe away abuses and to confirm our freedoms.'
He was a splendid guide to London and its society, for his
youth encouraged him to explore it and his natural intelligence to examine its quiddities and to know its quirks.

When we had eaten all we could and drunk all we wished
there was a brief pause, which I did not allow to grow so long as
to be embarrassing for it was clear that it was for me to provide
a final *bonne-bouche*. So I rose to my feet and, to spare my
friend's blushes, affected to discover with great surprise that
a bed lay in the corner of the room.

'My lord –' I said.

'Mrs Nelham – Sophie –' he said, 'will you not call me
Robert?'

'With all the pleasure in life, Robert,' was my reply. Then I continued, 'I wonder if you will forgive my proposing a period of rest? The exertions of the morning have been happy and rewarding, but in order that I shall be fit to enjoy the time before us, which will no doubt be equally so, I would like to recline for a while.'

He bowed slightly, but looked, I thought, uncertain what his action should be – which I found enchanting, for after a passage such as ours of the afternoon before most men of experience would by now have thrown themselves upon me without ceremony.

'I beg,' I said, 'that you will not think of withdrawing.'

My hat and cloak already lying upon a chair, it was the work only of a few seconds to lift my sole remaining garment over my head and to lay myself upon the soft mattress. In his haste the previous day young Robert had perhaps not sufficiently regarded me, for now, not moving to undress himself, he simply advanced to the bed's side and looked down at me, his eyes full of tender feeling. At last, and looking a question to which I returned the warmest of approving glances, he divested himself of his clothing (folding each item, I was amused to see, with care before placing it upon another chair) and was about to lie by me, but thinking again turned and went to the door to lock it, affording me my first full view of his figure, which was that of a boy, certainly, but with all the appurtances too of manhood: a slight figure, but one the firm muscles of whose calves and buttocks advertised him to be a horseman. The narrow waist of a youth swelled to the broad shoulders of someone given to regular exercise – as I learned later, that of rowing upon the Cam during his period at Cambridge University. It intrigued me to think that I might have known him during my largely unhappy sojourn in that town only twenty months or so earlier.

As he turned, with some diffidence he held his hand to guard his manhood from my invading gaze, but when he reached the bed and laid himself beside me, I raised myself to enjoy the closer sight of a breast almost devoid of hair (the lightest shading only of it around his paps), and to see more clearly the springy, fair bush which lay about the base of an enquiring tool which was by now ready for another acquaintance with my person. As I laid my cheek against the springy brake, to nuzzle that most delicate of triggers, the flesh between the cods and the under parts, it seemed as though some great tower hung above me, where a parapet swelled at the top, surmounted by a handsome dome of deep red, even to purple.

By now he had turned so that he could direct his close gaze to my intimate parts – the first occasion, he later confessed, on which he had examined how a female was made, for apart from our single previous meeting his encounters had only been with women of the town whose persons had not been sufficiently attractive for more than a penny fuck (as it might be vulgarly be expressed). Now, the gentle probing of his fingers gave place to the delicious acquaintance of his tongue, grazing, as it were, upon my lower lips then stroking in so loving a manner that I could not prevent a violent tremor from exciting my limbs – at which he immediately raised his head to enquire whether he had hurt me! I gave no other answer than the most contented of sighs, and he returned to his ministrations.

He was ever quick of apprehension, and from our previous bout had learned that leisure was the best approach to final ecstasy. From time to time he would gently persuade my head from between his thighs, in order that too swift a culmination should not prematurely conclude our passions. When, in course of time, slow waves began to enfold my body as I rose towards the summit of the ecstasy, I ignored his signals and applied my lips more fully to his body, and as the wave broke within me felt that salty evidence of his delight at the back of my throat.

After only a moment, his concerned enquiry revealed that he believed I was offended by his spending in such a way, but placing a kiss upon his lips, I reassured him, pointing out that in a passage of genuine love nothing could be indecent nor improper – at which I felt his body relax, and within a short time we were asleep in each other's arms.

A rattling of the door and the voice of a serving-man awoke us some time later, whereat Robert gave out a roar louder than I would have thought him capable of uttering, commanding silence and departure with a picturesque eloquence. (What he actually cried was, 'Off, Jack Whore, or I'll cut off your whirlygigs with your own snaggs!')

His first action was to kiss me again and to ask if I was rested, and when I returned that I was, to enquire whether we might enjoy ourselves once more before continuing our more public explorations. My answer was to fall upon my back and pull him on top of me, where he soon found a more conventional home for his instrument than hitherto, and began with a slow and graceful motion to raise me once more towards the heights. His beauty was such, and his care and love so clearly honest, that I responded with an equal warmth, gently stroking the small of his back and the fine roundels of his arse as his bucking grew gradually the more urgent and I was unable to resist a smile as he let out a cry of satisfaction and pleasure and relaxed – only immediately to ask whether I had not reached his own degree of pleasure.

It was another lesson I was able to teach: that while most men need to achieve the expulsion of their pleasure in real form, with us the simple enjoyment of a caress may often satisfy.

'Then your natural enjoyment is at a lower level?' he asked.

No, I replied, and indeed at some times it was possible we could enjoy three or four eruptions of joy within as many minutes, something surely to be envied by men, who after their first enjoyment must wait some time before they can attain a second. But our satisfaction was perhaps more variously achieved, and more subtly, than that of men.

I could see he remained puzzled, but reflecting that he was as yet a child, I placed my hands beneath his hips and bodily lifted him from me – something he greeted with a surprised laugh, for he had not apprehended my strength. Kneeling beside me, he bent to kiss first my lips, then my breasts, and finally that part which had given him most recent pleasure, and we set to dress ourselves, a glance at his watch revealing that it was now no earlier than half past six o'clock.

As we drove westwards in his coach, Chichley told me about the two great pleasure gardens of the city – Vauxhall and Ranelagh. Vauxhall, he explained, was near Lambeth, to the south of London, and ten years ago had been simply a tea-garden enlivened with a little music, to which a shilling admittance was not too much. However, when other similar gardens opened in the neighbourhood, the proprietor engaged himself to make Vauxhall the best, and it now costs two shillings to enter – or more on occasions when there are particularly splendid illuminations among the variety of walks, where variegated coloured lamps and transparent paintings are disposed with the utmost taste.

An orchestra plays each evening under Mr Brookes, and Robert mentioned the names of several singers – Mrs Bland, Mrs Franklin, Miss Tyrrell, Miss Daniels, Mr Dignum, Mr Gibbon, and so on.

'Tonight is a quiet night there,' he said, 'and so I proposed Ranelagh, but I shall take you to Vauxhall on the night of a great display, for fireworks of the most ingenious kind have lately been introduced to heighten the attractions of that charming place, and can bring upon occasion as many as fifteen thousand people there, always well-dressed and politely behaved.'

The time passed in such description, together with an account of other distractions of London, including the British Museum, where there are now some wonderful marbles to be seen, recently fetched by Lord Elgin from Athens (that same Lord Elgin whose wife conducted so spirited an affair with Mr Ferguson, MP, that it resulted in the peer's divorce). Meanwhile we drove for some two miles to the village of Chelsea, notable only for the Ranelagh gardens and splendid rotunda. There, the place was just opening, and Robert having paid half-a-crown for our tickets we walked through some of the gardens to the rotunda, where a fine promenade accommodated the fashionable, and a neat orchestra played. We were shown to a small box where supper was laid, and though we seemed but recently to have eaten, we toyed with some more wine and with a chop or two, while a delightful concert took place, the most charming airs being performed. Then came a pleasant masquerade, and a mime during which a handsome young couple made polite but no less spirited love (though fully clothed) while Mrs Mackenzie performed Burns's ballad:

Come rede me, dame, come tell me dame,
    My dame come tell me truly,
What length of gear, when well drove home,
    Will serve a woman duly?'
The old dame scratched her wanton tail,
    Her wanton tail so ready –
'I learned a song in Annandale,
    Nine inch will please a lady.'

My friend became, as the evening proceeded, more and more affectionate and more and more thoughtful, and finally after some preliminary stammerings, enquired whether he might not install me in a small house he owned at Chiswick, allowing me a thousand pound a year to be his companion?

'I must marry,' he said quite frankly, 'it is expected of me, but the young woman my family has always destined for me is not someone to whom I have a great admiration, and to be frank with you I could only tolerate wedlock were it possible to have at the same time a friend like yourself who could solace me.'

It would no doubt have been possible for some women to take offence at the implication that I was good enough for his lordship's bed but not for his table. But while society demands such pretence, it is fruitless to pretend that one in Chichley's situation will not seek to solve the problem in the time-honoured way.

'My dear Robert,' I replied, 'I shall always be pleased to call you friend, and I hope that we shall have many more pleasant encounters, but I have never seen myself as one content to be devoted to a life of complete leisure, and have every intention of finding some useful employment, though to what I shall apply myself, I have not at this moment made decision. Please forgive me if I decline your handsome offer, and believe me when I say that if any man could persuade me to such a course it would be yourself.' Which speech I concluded with the warmest of kisses.

His disappointment was manifest, but he was too much a gentleman to press the point and once more, when he had poured me another glass of wine, we settled to enjoy the entertainment, after which he drove me to Frith Street and took his leave. Somewhat to my surprise Polly was absent, but I went to bed and settled to sleep.

Next morning I heard from Polly, with some amusement, of the activities of Frank and Andy on the previous evening. Her revelations about her sister were no great shock to me and, indeed, I longed to meet her.

As I had said to Chichley, it was my firm intention to turn my attention to some activity or other, for the wasting of time seemed to me to be a sin. But for at least a week or so, I would explore the town and come to know it as thoroughly as possible. At the time of which I speak this was not so great a task as it would be now, for it was then only some two miles in breadth (as it were), and while it extended for perhaps seven miles in length, the eastern extremities were given over to docklands, and much of the rest to that part of the city concerned with finance and business, which interested me little.

With no other object, I set out to walk to the British Museum, where one of the hours of admission, I learned, was twelve midday, and where I hoped to see the carvings of which Chichley had spoken, and which were everywhere described as extraordinary.

That great national depository of antiquities, books and natural curiosities I found in the noble house formerly belonging to the Duke of Montague, in Great Russell Street, Bloomsbury – a mere ten minutes' walk from Frith Street. I found it necessary from the manner in which the place was organised to pass through many other rooms before attaining those where the marbles are displayed, but such was my interest in what there was to see that this was no punishment. Two rooms, for instance, contained Egyptian monuments taken from the French at Alexandria during the last war; then came more Egyptian ornaments, including two great monuments of black marble from the mausoleum of Cleopatra, that most splendid of queens, and many things from Greece and Rome, one or two (because of their supposed indelicacy) awkwardly placed so that the erect members of fauns or – on one pot – of an athlete balancing a vase on the end of his tool, should not offend.

Finally I reached the room in which those marble relics

are which Lord Elgin has recovered from Greece. They are, it seems, fragments from the frieze of the Parthenon, designed by the great sculptor Phidias, and other buildings on the Athenian Acropolis, and are a marvel of the sculptor's art. Indeed I could not but take the opportunity, with some other ladies present, of passing my hand over the limbs of the warriors depicted there, for these are so true to life that it is impossible to praise the figures too highly, and it is a positive shock to feel cold marble beneath one's palm rather than warm flesh.

In a neighbouring room refreshment could be taken, and while I was sitting for a while to allow the impression of the carvings to form themselves in my mind, I was amused to hear two ladies at the next table discussing the figures as though they were alive, and how they would like to entertain them. This one would do for an afternoon, that for a season, the other, however, they would happily marry – except that as a husband he would immediately lose his attraction!

'Is it not strange, Maria,' said the younger of the two, 'that no sooner are we married than our husbands lose all their vigour, all their wish to persuade and to love, and thus all their fascination?'

'My dear,' said the second, ' 'tis a fact of nature. What is unfair is that they can enjoy their' – she lowered her voice – 'their whores and kept women, while we are left alone to whistle, or if we take a lover are held up to contempt. Why cannot there be convenient houses which we can visit in secret for our own satisfaction? 'Twould be an unparalleled convenience!'

The other agreed, and after a short regretful silence they turned once more to a discussion of the various points of the warriors they had seen figured in stone.

As I walked home, my mind began to revolve around what they had said.

Indeed, it was true that for a lady whose husband had lost his taste for her, unless she was unregenerate and out of society, there was no recourse other than complete retirement from the life of the senses. Certainly some notorious women, if they were rich enough, could have their lovers and keep their place in society – sometimes even with the connivance of their husbands – but for most no such relief was possible.

Back at home, I invited Polly to take chocolate with me and asked her after a while whether there had never been an attempt at keeping a brothel for ladies.

She had never heard of a successful one, she said, but then paused and left the room for a moment, returning with an old piece of newspaper.

'I took this from a paper called *The Voluptuarian Cabinet* three years ago,' she said, 'thinking it interesting,' and handed it to me. 'The Mrs Wilson who placed it was known to my sister as the madam of a well appointed brothel for gentlemen in Jermyn Street.'

It was a short advertisement for 'promoting Adultery on the part of Married Women and Fornication on the part of Single Women and Widows', merely announcing a plan to set up a house in which gentlemen of robust and handsome vigour would attend on ladies prepared to set down a few guineas in return.

'I never heard that the plan went into operation,' Polly said, 'and believe that for some reason it never did so. But Aspasia may know more.'

More than ever curious to meet that paragon, I asked whether Polly might introduce us, and nothing loath she escorted me at about seven o'clock to Curzon Street, where I found both the house and the lady fully as attractive as Frank had done (for Polly had recounted to me the speed with which he had been captivated).

Polly made her excuses and left, and Aspasia entertained me at first with perhaps somewhat less warmth than my brother and his friend – this I believe due to a simple preference for the male over the female sex. But she was pleasant enough, and on my opening the question on which I had come, confirmed that her acquaintance Mrs Wilson, though eager to experiment, had never indeed completed her plans to offer to the ladies of the town a convenience equal to that enjoyed by the men. She was quick to see what I was thinking of, and admitted that she had herself considered the idea.

'But,' she said, 'some considerable capital is required, for while most men will put up with a little dirt in this connection – and even prefer it – ladies will always require comfort and cleanliness, distinction and elegance, and such a house must involve the expenditure of several thousand pound! This was the reason Mrs Wilson finally abandoned the notion.'

'I think I can say . . .' I began, but the ringing of the bell interrupted me, and shortly afterwards the maid announced two gentlemen who immediately entered – Mr Winslow, a plump, hearty man of perhaps fifty, and his friend Mr Mulville, of much the same age, but thin and of a mournful mien.

Aspasia rose to greet them.

'You will forgive my bringing George,' said the first of the two, 'and I see now that indeed it is convenient, for your friend,' and he bowed in my direction, 'will no doubt be happy to entertain him.'

Aspasia bowed slightly, and seeing me about to speak, laid a finger to her lips behind their backs, then asked if they would excuse us for a moment.

In her dressing room she confessed that it was much in her interest to keep in with Mr Winslow, for he was a client whose payments were generous and regular.

'I have heard something from Polly of your life,' she said, 'and you will forgive me if I suggest that while of course never performing the rites of love for money, you are not averse to . . .'

I was about to dismiss the idea with contumely (in particular, since Mr Mulville's person almost repelled me) yet, considering the use Aspasia could be to me were I to go further with my idea, thought it best to concur.

'Excellent, my dear!' said Aspasia. 'Now do make use of my bed; I will accommodate Tom in the other room.' Whereupon she showed me into her bedroom and left me to undress, which I did without more ado, so that when Mr Mulville entered he found me sitting up in bed, a sheet clutched to my bosom – yet not altogether concealing my charms.

He strode at once to the bed and taking the sheet, tore it from me in silence. He seized me by both my arms, pulled me to my feet and into his rough embrace, the metal buttons of his jacket bruising my flesh as his teeth (which, surrounded by a rough beard and moustache, felt like some strange apparatus of torture) bruised my lips.

He did not even bother to remove his clothes, but merely unbuttoned the front of his breeches revealing a long, thin instrument – seemingly fleshless as his body must be, could one have seen it – which, throwing me onto the bed, he plunged into me without ceremony. I was greatly annoyed at this, yet was reluctant to deal as I would otherwise have done with the impertinent fellow – that is, in a manner which would in no short time have rendered him incapable of continuing the action in which he was now engaged. But as things stood I decided merely to remember the favour I required of my new friend, lie back, and contemplate Tom Thumb.

My difficulty was that the man seemed set to continue his performance for some hours. His action was strange – far from the generous, rocking motion of the best lovers, his was a short, sharp jig, almost a twanging, even a vibration, which became after some minutes distinctly arousing, despite my repulsion to his person and the discomfort of the roughness of his clothes. In short I found myself in a state of excitement which culminated in my reaching an apogee of pleasure as keen as it was unexpected. Ignoring my inadvertent cry, however, he grimly continued his action, until a second and even a third time my body responded with a climactic shudder. Over his shoulder I saw, after what seemed half an hour, the door open, and the curious face of Aspasia appear. I made a helpless and pleading face at her, but she vanished and I had to lie for some time yet, exhausted physically and emotionally, until without apparently having achieved satisfaction, the man simply and suddenly pulled himself from me and without comment or thanks merely stuffed his still rampant limb back into his breeches. He strode from the room and by the time I had recovered myself, both men had gone.

However, after Aspasia, not unashamed, had revived me with a cup of coffee, she said, 'My dear, I am sorry for that; I fear that neither gentleman is to be recommended as a lover, and I took Mr Winslow myself because his predilection is, from time to time, for the whip, and that is something many women are averse to. I feared that you would receive little politeness from his friend, but at least –' she raised an eyebrow.

'True,' I was forced to admit, 'there was a kind of satisfaction. But surely it must be unpleasant, in your line of employment, to have to face such importunity upon a regular basis?'

'Indeed,' replied my friend, 'but as with everything in life, 'tis a matter of checks and balances, and a comfortable living has much to commend it. Indeed, it is also true that from time to time business may be combined with pleasure . . .'

Thinking of Chichley, I could not but agree with her.

But to return to business: 'You think it possible,' I enquired, 'that such a house as I propose might be set up with success?'

'Certainly,' Aspasia replied, 'but with some care. For instance, it should be out of town – yet not so far out as to be inaccessible by, say, an hour's drive. Your brother's house, for instance, will be ideal for the gentlemen, for it is expected that they should visit such a house, and none of them would be shy of being seen to enter it. Ladies, however, demand a more modest facility: a place at Hammersmith, say, or Chiswick, would be better. It should be large enough to accommodate five or six rooms each with its own dressing room, and it should be comfortably furnished.

'Then there must be added facilities not necessary in a male house of assignation. You will have, I would say, no difficulty in recruiting a stable – there are many young men whose appetite for women is not to be confined to a single friend – though they will have to be most carefully chosen and tried, for of course none of them will be gentlemen. The ladies will talk among themselves – indeed, you can rely upon it to spread the news of your establishment – so however discreet, none of your stallions will remain unknown for long, and will be disallowed by polite society. However, this has the advantage that you may establish a legend for the best of them, who should become a positive hero, and an attraction on his own account.

'These men must also be well displayed, and discreetly. Once more, there is a difference – no man is shy of striding into a roomful of whores and chosing the one which he would most like to bed, but we women on the whole take a more modest view, and there is the necessity of a room where the men may be seen from behind a screen, or some such contrivance.

'All this will be expensive, as I have suggested, but if you have the means (and I do not wish to be impertinent) it seems to me that the investment would be a most satisfactory one – though we must always remember that investments can be ruinous as well as rewarding.'

I agreed with all she said, which indeed accorded strongly with my own feelings. I thanked her for her advice, and hoped that while she was working with my brother we would meet again, and that she would give me the benefit of further comment – adding that of course I would be happy to make a financial consideration in return, for clearly, Miss Aspasia was of the strong opinion that nothing should be given for nothing.

She made me a curtsy. 'Certainly, madam,' she said. 'I hope I may call you Sophie, for the future? Clearly you are a lady of business much as myself, and I shall look forward with pleasure to our future acquaintance.'

Once more she apologised for my experience with Mr Mulville whom, not entirely to my surprise, she revealed as a well-known preacher at an arcane but popular nonconformist church, which taught that illicit connections outside marriage could be sanctioned as long as there was no expulsion of the vital liquor – something which explained much. She then showed me to the door and I returned in a thoughtful mood to Frith Street, where in the evening I took Polly into my confidence; she greeted my plan with enthusiasm and with laughter.

'Why, what fun we shall have!' she exclaimed.

I had not thought of it. But of course, the wench was right.

Chapter Five

The Adventures of Andy

The next fortnight was concerned with alterations to the house in Brook Street. The cellars – or rather, the kitchen and single cellar – were to be made, as Frank intended, into a baths, and for that purpose a large charcoal-burning stove had been installed into the former, 'For,' said Frank, 'we can send out for what food we want, and there is room for wine to be stored elsewhere'. Meanwhile the latter was completely stripped of its storage compartments, its wine racks and its coal containers, and channels dug in the floor in which half-pipes were laid, then grills set atop them, so that hot water could circulate, its steam rising into the room above. Blatchford, it appeared, was to be engaged as stoker and general handyman, though he had not indeed been consulted in the matter, and I wondered what his reaction might be to a sudden transportation from the driving seat of a fine equipage to the fumes of a stoke-hole. However, that we should discover in time, and no doubt Frank would make it so considerably worth his while that any scruples he had would be balanced against the additional remuneration and would prove negligible.

At one end of the large cellar two sunken baths were dug, and excellent imported marble used to line them and to construct small steps at one end. These baths were large enough to take two persons, and deep enough for them to submerge themselves without difficulty – provided, I suppose, all our clients were not six-footers. A small room was constructed near the foot of the stairs, which was to be a warm room where rest could be taken before visitors repaired to the upper chambers. This was all on the Roman model, Frank explained, showing me drawings of men's baths uncovered in the town of Pompeii, near Naples. The steam room was known, in those ancient times, as the *sudatorium*, the warm room as the *tepidarium*. There should be, classically, a *friqidarium* or cold room, with a cold bath, but as Frank said, no one would come to Brook Street to be cooled down. There should also be a gymnasium for exercise, but this would be taken in sufficient vigour, we concluded, upstairs.

The ground floor was now one great sitting room in which the girls could take their ease, and where our visitors would be introduced to them. Frank had ordered the finest furniture from a Bond Street emporium, and had had the walls hung with a most delightful dark green silk to which were matched rich window-hangings. For lighting he had rejected the modern gas lights or 'mantles', as they were called, which an ambitious manufacturer had offered, for, Frank said, nothing could be more charming than the kindly light of candles. And so he had bought great candelabra from a house in Grosvenor Square which itself was being turned over to gas.

Upstairs – and the cold stone of the stairs had now been clad in fine, warm carpets of the deepest red – the single large room had been divided into four smaller compartments. To tell the truth, each was a handsome room of its own, for with Aspasia's advice Frank had scaled the contents to the space available, only the beds being of a full and generous size. The single chair and dressing table, which contained washing bowls and cloths, were the only furniture in the room and were of mahogany and rosewood with bronzed ornaments and inlay. All was handsomely done – but it was in the decoration of these rooms that Frank had excelled himself. He had noticed in *The New Monthly Magazine* an account by a Mr Francis Marsock, an artist, of some of the paintings recently discovered during excavations at Herculaneum, an ancient Roman town near Pompeii. Although the language of the account was somewhat veiled, Frank had concluded that the paintings were of an erotic nature, and indeed Mr Marsock, upon Frank's contacting him, confirmed that they had been discovered on the walls of a brothel. Frank immediately commissioned him to reproduce some of them in the form of frescoes on the walls at Brook Street – which he did, in splendid warm brown colours which recalled the hot southern sun. Here were

handsome women climbing upon the laps of readily aroused
Roman gentlemen, satyrs and nymphs in every attitude of
copulation, young men and young women disporting themselves in every ingenious way.

What all this cost him, I cannot imagine, nor did I ask.
But when I did show some surprise at the largeness of his
plans, he simply replied that if a thing was worth doing, it
was worth doing well.

A message came from Aspasia while he and I were discussing with the workmen the organisation of the space on
the second and third floors, where the bedrooms for our
girls would be. Frank was determined that they should live
in the house – though not as prisoners, for they would have
one day's leisure a week, and one half-day during which
they would also be at liberty. Meanwhile Aspasia invited us
to wait upon her the following morning with our carriage,
and to bring with us everything we required for a night away
from home – which indeed consisted merely of razor and a
change of shirt.

When we appeared in Curzon Street we found that interesting lady dressed for a journey and provided with a small
portmanteau, which Blatchford placed on the roof with
ours. She then climbed in, sitting opposite us.

'Where to, madam?' enquired the coachman.

'Brighthelmstone,' answered the lady, and we set off to
the south across Westminster Bridge, that most handsome
of edifices, in warm sunshine which quite soon made it
necessary to lower a window a little lest the interior of the
carriage should grow oppressive. Blatchford, being a fellow
of independent accomplishments, needed no instruction,
for he had been spending some time studying the city and
the land around it from various maps he had acquired at
Hatchard's in Piccadilly, and was equal to driving us anywhere between Cambridge on the north, Windsor on the
west, and any part of the coast between the mouth of the
Thames and the city of Portsmouth!

Aspasia meanwhile explained that through the agency of
a friend she had heard of a small house of some reputation
along the coast at Worthing, not far from Brighthelmstone,
which was closing due to the retirement of that friend,
its madam. The girls, who were of some refinement and

beauty, would now be available. This would be a considerable advantage to us, for not only would they be unknown in London, and thus a curiosity, but they would be familiar each to the others and problems of jealousy should therefore be avoided, for, she said, this was a great difficulty when setting up a house. If, for some reason or other, one girl was considerably more popular than the others, and in greater demand, an unpleasant atmosphere could result, fuelled on the one side by envy and on the other by pride.

'Besides which,' she said, 'I have enough confidence in my old friend to know that her girls will be in command of every refinement of polite society and every variety of comforting concupiscence.'

The warmth in the carriage was now considerable, and lowering the blinds we became somnambulent as we rattled south through the villages of Thornton Heath and Croydon, Sanderstead and Warlingham and Limpsfield. In a while, despite the atrocious state of the road, with potholes which every moment rattled every bone in my body (though the Brighthelmstone road was better than most, due to the royal paymaster who regularly used it to transport him from London to his mistress's arms) I fell into a doze, and was half-awakened some time later by what I fancied was a small cry from the lady opposite. Half-opening my eyes I saw a distinct tumble of movement in her lap, and realised in a moment that my friend had wriggled out of his shoe (which stood empty upon the floor) and had run his foot beneath her skirt to that point at which, no doubt, his enquiring toes could encounter a sensitive target the palpitation of which caused Aspasia some pleasure – for surely it had provoked the little cry which I had heard?

As for my friend, I could see from the corner of my eye that his breeches betrayed the presence of an unmistakable enthusiasm for the lady – an enthusiasm which soon became acute, for he made a pleading gesture to Aspasia, who looked to see if I was awake. But I continued to counterfeit a slumber, for who was I to interrupt their pleasure? Aspasia then leaned forward and opened the flap of his breeches, whereupon there was revealed something patently in need of diminution if it were ever again to be comfortable beneath a set of small-clothes. Taking it in her hand, she lowered her head, and my friend settled back in his seat with a sigh, inserting a hand beneath the front of her dress to take in its palm one of her generous breasts as she returned his compliment, bobbing her head as his breath came quicker, then was finally released in a gasp which advertised the culmination of his enjoyment.

It can be imagined to what a state the sight reduced me; I was determined to maintain my posture of sleep, and trusted that the bold evidence of my arousal, which an inspection of my lap would have revealed, would be put down to a dream – and indeed when I had allowed Frank and Aspasia time to recover and re-settle themselves I acted my awakening with a sigh and a stretch, to enquire where we were – at the very moment when Blatchford slowed the horses and asked whether we wished to stop for food.

We lunched simply but well at an inn at Horsham on shellfish and a dish of potatoes, with buttermilk and some ale, then made on for Brighthelmstone, where at the sea side we turned to the west and drove along the coast road, the ocean flat and calm and gleaming, to the town of Worthing – little more than a rural village only a decade ago but now, in addition to the miserable fishing huts which still stood upon the beach, it offered accommodation for the first families in the kingdom and began to vie with Brighthelmstone as the residence – in the season – of noble families and country gentlemen.

From the town itself we drove along the coastal road (on Aspasia's instructions) to where a fine pair of gates stood giving upon a drive; this in turn led to the front door of a remarkably handsome house of perhaps eighty years of age, and on knocking at the door we were shown by a rough but agreeable manservant into a parlour where we were greeted by a delightful old lady, I would guess only a few years younger than the house, who embraced Aspasia with great pleasure.

After we had been introduced and offered tea, which we declined, we were shown into a large sitting room at the back of the house where we found the girls we had travelled to see gathered demurely together and looking as though they were expecting a visit from the local Society for Giving Effect to His Majesty's Proclamation against Vice and Immorality.

'Shy' would not perhaps be the word to apply to them, for no doubt had we arrived in the evening as conventional customers they would have received us with enthusiasm. But they were now demure as tabby cats and, to be frank, I had doubts whether any of them had ever retired to bed even with a friend, let alone with some gentleman who had paid for the privilege – and wondered, even, whether Aspasia had not been the subject of some joke by her friend who, herself, seemed not the kind to run a house of pleasure.

Frank, however, had his own idea for getting to know the girls.

'Ladies,' he said, 'don your cloaks, for we are driving into Brighthelmstone for the evening!'

There was an immediate stir and flutter, and in no time we were all packed into carriages hurriedly summoned from a nearby stable, and in half an hour were set down in the neighbouring town, which as the world knows combines charm and elegance to a fine degree. Leaving the carriages, we walked by the Pavilion – upon which the Prince is said to have spent no less than fifty thousand pound – and then through some of the fine streets, which were lively with movement and cheerfulness even though the season was not yet started. Mrs Jopling Rowe, as I learned was the name of our elderly friend, informed me of the changes that had taken place in the town since the Heir Apparent had shown an interest in it:

'Every year 'tis more and more crowded,' she exclaimed, 'and where the people are to bestow themselves who are announced as coming here this summer, I cannot conceive, as the place was already so full last season that not a good house was unlet. The only ones that still waited for tenants were asking twelve and fourteen guineas a week, even until Christmas. But,' she continued as we strolled after Frank and the girls, who were now clustered around him delighting in his small talk, 'to my taste the society is not of the pleasantest. Of course there are exceptions: the most prominent among them being Lady Charlotte Howard, wife of the major general of that name now serving in the Peninsula and a daughter of Lord Rosebery. Another conspicuous character here is one of your Bath set – Lady Aldborough. She has one of the best houses in Brighton, and gives us, very often, little merry parties and dances where you can enjoy yourself immensely, and get a good supper.'

By now we were turned into a fine house of entertainment in sight of the sea, where we ate and drank well at Frank's expense, the ladies under the influence of wine becoming yet more friendly and free, though still extremely lady-like – something I expressed my pleasure in to Mrs Jopling Rowe, next to whom I found myself seated.

'My dear Mr Archer,' she said, 'I have always insisted on their behaviour being such as would attract only admiration even in the best society, telling them that their carriage when they are alone with, eh . . .' (she looked around to make sure that we could not be overheard) ' . . . with their gentlemen is a matter for them, but that in public they should be entire ladies. I trust I have succeeded.'

'You have indeed, madam. But where, if I may ask, did you acquire them?'

'In a variety of ways which would be tedious to recount,' was her reply, 'but I may say that had I not employed them they would all have vanished into domestic service, having to live on a few pence a week, and probably in the most fearful conditions. Perhaps Aspasia has told you that for some years I ran a very successful milliner's shop in Bond Street with a small room behind, and then two more above, where gentlemen could be accommodated, and I think I can claim to have entertained some of the cream of Europe as well as of our own aristocracy.

'But seeking a more healthy air, I came to Brighton some eight years ago, where in course of time I made the acquaintance of these delightful children. For five years I have educated them as best I might, with the help of local mistresses to teach them music, deportment, French and other niceties. I then explained to them that if they wished to leave me, they might do so, finding if they could positions as governesses in the neighbourhood. Or they could become part of the establishment which I meant to set up, upon which they would receive a proper proportion of the income from the business, together with their accommodation.

'I am glad to say that each, independently, decided to stay, and has remained with me ever since. But now I feel that the time has come to retire entirely, and when I heard from Aspasia of your friend's scheme – substantially similar to my own – which would also give the girls an opportunity to experience the pleasures of the city, I explained the position to them, with the result that you now see.'

Indeed, the girls were entranced by my friend and by Aspasia, who was describing the delights of London, and when we had returned to Worthing and Mrs Jopling Rowe's house they gathered around him to hear his proposal without a trace of shyness or distance. Indeed, by this time two of them had attached themselves to me, and seated one on each side of me upon a sofa were tenderly embracing and kissing me. But they ceased upon Frank demanding their attention.

'Ladies,' he said, 'allow me for a moment to address you seriously. You have heard I think from your delightful guardian that it is my intention to set up in London an establishment very like her own. You will be provided with accommodation and with necessary food. You will be protected from any unpleasantness by the presence, always, of Mr Archer, myself, or some other male guardian. You will have one and one-half days at leisure each week, and will receive one third of the sum derived from each visitor – and since I mean to charge the sum of five guineas for each encounter, you will receive the sum of one pound seven shillings and sixpence each. I would not expect each of you to entertain fewer than five gentlemen in a week, and indeed there may be considerably more.'

From their expressions, I could see they were working out the total, aware that this was a great deal more than they could ever have dreamed of!

'You need not answer me now,' said Frank, 'but I should wish you to come to Brook Street in two weeks' time – that is, on Monday May the fifth, for I wish to open my doors three days after that.'

The girls looked at each other, then one of them said, 'Sir Franklin, I speak for all when I say that we need not have time for consideration, but would be delighted to close with your kind offer this instant!' The rest nodded agreement, and all came to kiss him and then myself; and one thing leading to the next, we began to toy and play, and soon I noticed that Mrs Jopling Rowe and Aspasia had left the room – presumably to entertain themselves with talk and reminiscence – leaving us to ourselves. Frank was soon upon the floor, laughing with pleasure as two girls undressed him, while upon the sofa I had a girl upon each side undoing a button here or slipping a hand beneath my clothing elsewhere, while a third, standing behind me, had drawn my head back and, leaning forward, was allowing me to sip the honey of her tongue between parted lips.

There are moments when pleasure becomes so keen that it almost ceases to be pleasure, and to find myself part – as soon I was – of a band consisting of my friend and of six delightful girls, all of us as naked as the day we were born and each engaged in an attempt to convey the utmost zest to the other, was such delight that I almost found my senses slipping from me and was forced for a moment to withdraw from combat and observe.

The six girls were each entirely different in body and, as we were to discover, in temperament. Their persons were of delightful proportions, ranging from the extremely slim to the generously endowed, the long-legged to the almost plump.

The most slender, Xanthe, at this moment contenting herself with leaning over Frank to apply her kisses to his cheeks, was as one might expect from that name, a blonde. As I saw her, from behind, she might almost have been a boy, so narrow were her hips, so lean her thighs, except for that roundness of the haunches which can never be mistaken for those of a man. Those delightful thighs, with their velvet, white skin, were thrown apart to disclose a charming nest marked by tiny blonde locks which might have been curled by a hot iron, so tight and shapely were they. Her breasts were small, and as she bent over hung down like small lemons, and Frank was happy now and then to turn, gather one and convey it to his lips, as the strands of her long hair, now loosed, fell to brush his cheek.

Rose was almost a twin of Xanthe's, quite as slender, but very dark, with tumbles of hair which fell over her shoulders as she rose and fell upon Frank's lower parts, his tool (so large it might have appeared dangerous to insert it within so small a sheath) appearing and disappearing within her body, its length upon appearing to the view showing it to be bathed in a delightful dew, as much a sign of her ecstasy as his own. Upon the upper part of her right breast, a dark mole or beauty spot appeared, making its whiteness more apparent. Xanthe and Rose were inclined to solemnity, and so devoted to each other that each almost seemed to prefer the company of the other to that of a male companion.

Behind Rose knelt Constance, so dark as almost to be a Negress, her flesh in violent contrast to Rose's creamy skin as from time to time she laid it against her friend's back. The centres of her breasts were gathered to nipples which seemed almost the colour of chocolate, and erect with excitement as she reached around the body of Xanthe now to toy with a breast, now to lower her hand to explore the adamant hardness of my friend's busy vital part, and to discover the tightness of his cods beneath. Constance, I was to learn, was not only naturally dark-skinned but became more so by reason of her delighting to lie naked in the open air not only in summer but even in winter, were there the slightest trace of warmth in the sun. I was not surprised to learn that this display had attracted the attention of Will, the boy – or rather young man – who acted as general handyman about the house, and there was now what almost amounted to a marriage between them, except that he understood that she wished to continue to provide the service to male visitors which had been her common practice. She was saving her money in order to enlarge Will's savings so they could eventually purchase an inn when the time came for her retirement.

Two more of the girls, Sally and Cissie, could never have been mistaken for boys, for their figures were generously full, mirroring each other in the tremulous shivering of parts as they moved. Their temperaments were generous and happy; they were tomboys now very obviously delighted to be giving pleasure, which they did partly by caressing Frank's upper limbs, tweaking his paps and running their fingers over his chest and belly, and partly by encouraging him to apply his hands to their most delicate parts, even taking his fingers into their mouths and sucking them (something which, from the way in which he turned his head to left and to right, was entrancing to him).

There remained Ginevra, a brunette, and though with little trace of an accent, evidently of French extraction. She had been contenting herself by toying with the limbs of her friends – Frank's being unavailable to her – but now turned to me, remarking that I must not be left out of the feast and enquiring whether I was not inclined to be part of it? Her body was muscular and hard to the touch, for she was greatly given to exercise, and rode daily upon the downs behind the town. Like many European women (as I was to discover during those adventures on the continent which it is my intention to describe in a future narrative) she left her limbs untouched by the razor which British women now increasingly use as an essential part of their *toilette*, and beneath her arms sprouted little locks of hair, while her thighs too were covered not so much by that light down which most women's limbs bear, but almost by pelt.

My answer to her question was to draw her towards me, where I buried my face between two of the most delightful, flexible yet firm bubbies, licking from each a slight salt savour, and bringing their tips to small peaks of satisfaction. Delighted at this, she laid her hand between my legs and laughed aloud at what she found there – for, she said, she thought that I had come off early in the proceedings and was not yet recovered, yet here was a key ready for any lock!

I smiled, and explained that it was because I had not wished too speedy a consummation that I had retired from the play. 'But now,' I said, 'if you will allow . . .' – and pushing her gently back upon the couch, laid myself between her generous thighs and glided into a well-prepared refuge.

Not far away, Frank (whose stamina was ever greater than my own) was now upon his knees, with Xanthe on all fours receiving his still unsatisfied instrument. At her side stood Rose, one thigh thrown over Frank's shoulders so that his tongue could apply itself to satisfying her, while Sally and Cissie, one upon each side, encouraged his fingers to prompt them to the ultimate pleasure.

The sight of all this, together with the succulent, spongy embrace with which Ginevra was pleasuring me (in an embrace so typically female as to belie the slight moustache which I now saw decorated her lower lip) did my business, and with a delight which almost made me faint, I succumbed way to pleasure.

In a while, Frank having been made happy too, we sat and talked, the girls being curious about London, whence they had never ventured, and wishing to make comparison between it and Brighthelmstone. But the day had been a long one, and we soon retired to a room which had been made ready for us. The girls invited us to choose who should accompany us, or whether we would not prefer to share their company in the large room they all occupied, but I was entirely satisfied and ready for sleep – as indeed was Frank who, remember, had been pleasured twice that day!

Next morning, we awoke – rather as on our first morning in Brook Street – to find two ministering figures bending over us – but how great was the contrast! The curtains had been drawn, and the golden rays of the early morning sun struck through the window upon the spotless smocks of the girls – Xanthe and Rose – and set sparkling the white cups and saucers and the pot of chocolate which they had set upon the bedside table.

We sat ourselves up against the pillows which they pummelled and made comfortable for us, and they joined us in a breakfast of still warm, fresh bread and jam, prattling happily about their anticipated future – whether the clothes they had would be sufficient, whether the London men would require more heavily painted faces than their present sweet ones – just as though they were girls about to set out for a new school, and once more I marvelled at the education, both in deportment and pleasant manners, that they had been given by the remarkable lady under whose care they had been.

I enquired whether they had been completely happy in the employment she had offered them.

'Indeed so,' said Xanthe. 'Our practical instruction came from two gentlemen of our mistress's acquaintance to whom she brought us at the proper time, and whom she invited to demonstrate to us the duties which she hoped would be both enjoyable and profitable to us. Our masters were of middle age, kind and thoughtful, and with considerate caresses brought us to the full understanding of womanhood, and were so assiduous in proving to us the pleasure we could enjoy that from the first we were always looking forward to the next encounter.'

'But do you not sometimes have to entertain those who are less than courteous and considerate?' I asked.

Of course that was sometimes true, replied Rose, but most men, she found, were kind if properly wooed, and Mrs Jopling Rowe had employed Will, from the village, not only to act as groom, gardener, footman and general help but always to be present in the house when there were visitors, and to be ready at all times to protect them from any unpleasantness.

By this time we had finished breaking our fast and the two girls had slipped off their simple garments and were reclining for comfort upon the beds at our sides, not one whit discomfited by the informal nakedness of the group. And though I could not speak for my friend, my equanimity was beginning to be affected by the comfortable way in which Xanthe, at my side, was stroking my chest and belly with a delightfully soft hand. Then, as the bedclothes slipped to reveal another limb which seemed more in need of attention, she immediately transferred her courtesies, first wetting her finger and thumb at her lips and then turning them round and about the tip of that limb until my entire middle parts seemed to be one delicious knot of pleasure.

In the meantime, as I in turn caressed her neck, shoulders and back, I could see that Frank was exploring the rich contours of Rose's body, who herself was lying now upon her back with a welcoming and inviting flush enhancing every limb.

I leaned upon my elbow and attempted to persuade Xanthe, too, upon her back, but to my surprise she slid sideways to lie upon her belly, looking with keen invitation to me – and indeed her backside was a delicious sight, those narrow hips and that delightful bottom, in downiness and soft, full colour like a small peach ready for biting, needing no commendation. Without hesitation I placed my body on top of hers, nestling those delicious twin spheres against my belly, then reached beneath to raise her, when she herself took hold of me and guided me so that I slid into her, finding the aperture tighter than I expected. She showed such delight, however, moving with so free and enjoyable a

motion, the gasps of pleasure so freely expressed, that it
was with astonishment that I realised only after some
minutes – when she took my hand and brought it between
her thighs – that I had been persuaded to enter a foreign
port, and not that into whose harbour I had intended
passage.

Surprising though this was, it now seemed too late for
protest, and indeed a final wriggle of that entirely delightful
bottom brought me off, while she at almost the same time
sighed with pleasure and collapsed upon the pillows!

I glanced over at Frank: he and Rose had evidently been
regarding us with interest for some time, and he raised an
eyebrow with a quizzical look as he took my eye!

We rose, after a while, and took an early walk upon the
cliffs, where Frank expressed himself delighted with the
result of our expedition. And when we left, having bade
farewell to Mrs Jopling Rowe ('How large the house will
seem and how empty, when they have all gone!' she said,
sadly), the girls all waved to us with their handkerchiefs,
looking forward to a reunion in a short time. It did indeed
seem to have been a worthwhile endeavour.

Our talk on our return journey was all of the detail of our
plans, and I argued for the inclusion in our band – for it
had been Frank's notion that six girls should be the
complement – of Miss Riggs, whom I had met in the Haymarket. The other six, while delightful, and quite sufficiently riggish and high-spirited, were all of that polite and
genteel mould which might delight most men but could
deter others, and we needed one rough diamond among
them.

So that evening, when we had bade our farewells to
Aspasia and dined, we set out for Whitcombe Street, where
Sam Rummidge's coffee-house was as deserted as previously – it seemed he undertook precious little business
other than the provision of the upstairs rooms.

Moll, he said, had gone upstairs a few minutes before,
but would no doubt be down directly, if we would care to
take some coffee. Cups of somewhat unappetising liquid
having been set before us, we settled down to wait until
Moll and her friend had completed their arrangements. But
in ten minutes we were disturbed by the unmistakable

sounds of an argument upstairs, which in a moment or two were replaced by screams and the noise of what seemed a fight. We rose and made for the stairs, and without pausing to consider whether we might be breaking in upon some stranger (for we knew not whether Moll was the only woman in the place) we soon attained the room from which the noises were issuing, now more compelling than ever. Charging the door with his shoulder, Frank immediately broke the lock, revealing Moll lying unclothed in a corner of the room and, standing over her, a great ox of a man who, though naked, appeared to be clothed, so thick was the growth of black hair upon his enormous haunches and back, and in whose raised hand was what seemed the leg of a chair. He looked around at the noise of our entry, and in a moment was charging us like a bull. Our minds worked as one: at the last minute we stepped one to each side, then as he passed us took each a hold of a shoulder and administered a shove in the small of his back, whereat he vanished through the doorway and the entire house seemed to shake as he descended the staircase (without, I would guess, touching many of the stairs). Complete silence then fell.

Fearing that perhaps he had been killed, I went to the top of the stairs. Sam Rummidge was standing over the body, and looked up at me:

'Chuck 'is clothes down,' he said, ' 'e's only stunned. I know 'im – from Maiden Lane. Gets like this when 'e's 'ad a few.'

I gathered together an armful of evil-smelling clothes and threw them down the stairs, then shut the door behind me. Frank, meantime, was seeing to Moll, across whose back a darkening weal revealed that one blow at least had found its mark.

Through tears, she apologised for giving us trouble. 'I've just had a bad week, gentlemen,' she said, 'or I'd never have taken him – him always being bad luck. But . . .'

Frank laid a finger on her lips, and together we took her to the bed and wrapped her in the sheet and blanket there, when I went and fetched a dram of brandy, which soon encouraged her to realise that her ordeal was over.

After a while, Frank, with a look in my direction, explained that we had come to ask whether she would care to join a house of pleasure we were setting up in Brook Street, and described the same conditions as had been offered to the girls at Worthing.

She was immediately eager to acquiesce: 'If you two gents are running it,' she said, 'I shall be pleased.'

And could she, Frank asked, live for the next fortnight? But before giving her time to answer, he pressed ten guineas upon her in earnest of our intentions, which she viewed as though he was some prince from a fairy tale, and kissed him full upon the lips with the greatest enthusiasm.

We then left her, on our way out passing Mr Rummidge who was leaning over the great pile of our assailant, now groaning in a corner. He would not, we asked, return to an assault upon Moll, when we were gone?

'No, gen'lmen,' said Sam, 'he's for a drunkard's bed.'

Poor Moll had obviously caught him just at the wrong moment between rage and stupefaction.

Upon leaving Whitcombe Street we walked for a while and then, it coming to rain just as we were passing the Drury Lane Theatre, we slipped in and, finding a couple of seats, saw the final act of Edmund Kean's performance as Richard III. I had myself (as I have recounted elsewhere) some experience of the provincial stage, but never had I been in the presence of such transcendent genius: his vigour was astonishing, his appearance at once handsome, in his carriage, and malevolent, in his character, and the charge of his emotion could be clearly felt throughout that huge theatre, where the flushed faces of the women betrayed a keen interest, and the admiration of the men was not stinted.

After the performance was over and the plaudits had faded, I was hot to pay court to this amazing actor, and persuaded Frank to accompany me to the stage door, where upon slipping the door-keeper half a guinea we joined those who crowded at the door of his dressing room.

There sat that remarkable man, the upper part of his body bare, cleaning the make-up from his face, and attended by what I describe as a blowsy trollope whose person we would not for a moment think of engaging for our house. While she pretended to help him by disposing of the cloths with which he was cleaning his face, her hand could clearly be seen fondling his thigh and more, a fact

which roused all the keener spirits in the ladies who were
with us, and from whose bodies I could actually feel a glow
rising, as though they were animals in heat.

On my expressing astonishment to Frank at the actor's
freedom in allowing such attentions in a public place, a man
standing next to me remarked that 'twas common with
Kean, and that it was a known fact that he always consumed
a half-bottle of brandy and a whore, at the side of the stage,
between each act. I was inclined at the time to think this a
fiction, but have many times since heard it repeated as true.

Having joined with the people in shouting our plaudits –
which Mr Kean accepted as though they were his due (which
indeed was nothing but the truth) we made our way down
the stairs and passed across the stage, where a motley collection of actors and musicians were bidding each other
goodnight – the latter bringing me a little shiver of pleasure,
for I felt myself to be in a sense one of them, though I had
not touched my guitar for many weeks, and I determined to
do some practice, for who knew when my adeptness at it
might not prove useful?

Frank was all eyes for the actresses, and I had much ado
to persuade him against making an approach to one of them,
assuring him that for the most part they were respectable
girls – unlike those who appeared at some of the unlicensed
theatres in town, which he expressed a desire to visit. But
that must be for another time.

Chapter Six

Sophie's Story

My task now was first to find a house, and then to equip it to my purpose. I determined when I had discovered a property which suited to sell the house in Frith Street; I could then live in a part of the new property, the better to supervise it, while the funds I would raise from the sale – which should be considerable, the present house being in the heart of the town – added to those I already commanded would enable me to furnish with real luxury.

I was conscious of course of the gamble involved, but determined to try it, and as certain as might be of my success.

So I turned my attention to the newspapers, sending Polly out each morning for *The Daily Advertiser*, *The Times*, *The True Briton*, *The Morning Herald*, *The Morning Chronicle*, *The Morning Post* and *The Press*, and again in the evening for *The Star*, *The Sun*, *The Courier*, *The Traveller* and *The Globe*; then, at weekends, came in addition *The General Evening Post*, *The London Chronicle*, *The Observer* and *The Weekly Dispatch*. And with all these my time was fully occupied in the evenings, while the days were spent travelling around the outskirts of the city visiting some of the houses advertised for sale and – quite as important – examining each neighbourhood, for it was clear that this should be respectable if I was to attract to the house ladies of discernment, wealth and position – those, in short, not only willing to spend money but capable of finding it.

I had not till now apprehended the varying atmospheres of the suburbs of London, or villages as they still were in the time of which I speak. My first journey was to Hampstead, upon a hill to the north of London. Here, having first lunched at the Spaniard Inn near Caen Wood, the favourite retreat of the Lord Chief Justice Mansfield, Polly and I

strode among the delightful villas and elegant mansions
which comprise that pleasant district, the variety of whose
local situations recommends it to the inhabitants of
London as a place of retreat during the summer months and
of retirement at the close of life. A great number of houses
were to let here as temporary lodgings at prices varying
from twenty guineas to two or three a month, and charming
they were, often with a view to Windsor Castle, Leith Hill,
Boxhill and other places within twenty or thirty miles.

We looked, there, at one spacious villa next to Caen
Wood, but it was rather too large for my purposes, and I
apprehended at any event that Hampstead was too far from
the centre of town for ladies to travel for a few hours'
pleasure.

We walked in the sunshine, after our inspection, down to
a series of large ponds situated below Caen Wood, which
supply Kentish Town, Camden Town and the Tottenham
Court Road with water, and there we sat upon a seat for a
few moments' rest – when suddenly, out of a green thicket,
burst the unclothed bodies of perhaps a dozen youths. It
seems they are used to bathing here all year round, and were
now enjoying the uncommon warmth of this spring of 1818
and making the most of it. Upon seeing us they were not one
whit abashed, though they were of all ages from perhaps ten
to twenty, but hurled themselves straight into the water and
began to besport themselves. For perhaps five minutes we
watched, delighted, the play of golden sunlight upon their
young bodies, some swimming upon their faces, the water
eddying around their alluring haunches, others paddling
upon their backs, when it parted momentarily to show a
white, pliant something decorated with weed-like dark hair;
then while some continued to play, others climbed onto the
bank and lay upon the grass while the sun dried them.

The reader need not imagine that Polly and I turned
aside, but took our full opportunity to gaze – 'For', as
Polly said, 'a pastoral view is always pleasant to the female
eye.'

'What a place for our recruitment!' says Polly. And
indeed this was true – but how to approach these boys?
Looking down to where not six feet away an entrancing,
hard-muscled artisan was half-asleep, beads of moisture

sparkling on his broad chest and sturdy thighs (though the skin was made rough by goose pimples) it seemed an ideal opportunity to open with him the topic of his being employed to please ladies (and here were two ready to be pleased!). But at that moment we were startled by the light, warm voice in our ear of another young man who leaned over the back of the seat between us to wish us good day – not a whit embarrassed by the fact that while we were fully dressed, he was completely unclothed, though a bar of the seat did conceal that essential part to which a lady's eyes might otherwise fly.

'You will forgive me, ladies, for remarking that you have come upon an area of the heath normally reserved only for gentlemen,' he said – but with a smile which voided his words of even slight offence.

I opened my lips to apologise, but he raised a hand: 'Please, ma'am, think nothing of it; it is a pleasure to address you.'

I asked whether he and his fellows were usually to be found here.

'Yes, ma'am, some of us throughout the whole year, some only when the spring comes, and on through the summer. It is one of the most agreeable bathing places north of London.'

And what was the employment of the gentlemen, that they could afford to sport themselves during the afternoon?

Some, he said, were local workmen who happened for the moment to be out of employment; some few were gentlemen of no occupation; some youngsters not yet employed.

'But you will excuse me, ladies,' he said. 'I see that my friend has finished his swimming, and we must dress and be away. You will forgive me for not being able to raise my hat to you!'

And giving us a sort of salute by raising a hand to his damp locks, he straightened up and walked off, proudly displaying a body that I – and from her looks, Polly – would have been happy to pay amorous attention to. But he then greeted another young man, similarly in a state of nature, and they walked off towards the brake, arms about each other's waists, and with a lethargic affection in the resting of the fingers of each upon the flesh of the other

from which Polly and I assumed that he was not 'pricked
out for woman's pleasure', as Shakespeare puts it.

So we rose and made our way back into the city, but
determined to make a mental note that the Hampstead
Ponds might contain material worth engaging.

Two days later, we travelled similarly to the smaller village of Highgate, at about the same distance from London,
but that place does not possess the same variety of prospects, though its views are perhaps superior. A principal
road to the north passes through it, which would have been
perhaps to our advantage, but it is full of places of entertainment which lower its tone, and though the house we saw
there was convenient, we decided against it.

Kew, though enchanting, was too far to the west;
Richmond even further – eight miles from Hyde Park
Corner, and though the royal gardens attract many visitors,
the village itself seemed to be beyond the area we would
regard as satisfactory – though one villa there, on the north
bank of the Thames just by the elegant bridge, was most
attractive.

It was on our way back from Richmond that we paused at
Hammersmith to visit Brandenburgh House, once belonging to Prince Rupert and modernised with magnificent
additions before being purchased for no less than eighty-
five thousand pound by the Margrave of Anspach, who
married Lady Craven. On application, we obtained admission to view the house, whose state drawing-room, gallery,
hall and library all exhibit marks of princely taste and grandeur. On the west side, near the river, and connected to the
house by a conservatory of one hundred and thirty feet in
length, is an elegant little theatre where the Margravine
occasionally entertains the public with dramatic entertain-
ments, and sometimes gratifies them by exerting her talents
both as writer and performer.

It was from one of the windows of Brandenburgh House
that I saw a delightful little white villa standing in its own
grounds, the garden abutting the Thames, and asked the
housekeeper escorting us whose house it was.

The reply came that it had belonged to Sir Nicholas
Jocelind, an ancient city merchant long retired but who had
died six weeks ago, leaving a family so impoverished that

the villa was about to be placed upon the market.

It can be imagined with what speed Polly and I made our apologies to the kindly matron and found our way beyond the theatre to the small iron gates which opened onto a path winding through shrubbery to an enchanting small house, fronted by a handsome entrance flanked by pillars. We knocked at the door, but there was no reply, so we turned the corner of the house and, entering a door in the tall wall which lay on that side the garden, found ourselves in a smaller, private garden entirely sheltered from public view by tall walls, and evidently running down to the river. We knocked at another entrance to the house which advertised itself, but still no reply.

Then as we were turning away, a cry greeted us, from the lips of a sturdy youth across whose shoulder lay a shovel and whose whole body, almost bare, was covered in what seemed black mud. I prepared myself for a brush with a rustic, but when he spoke it was with a fine accent, and in a voice peculiarly vibrant and attractive.

'Ladies,' he said, 'I am sorry not to have been at the door to greet you. I apprehend that Mr Barlow sent you to see the house? I must apologise for my appearance, but I have been working down at the boathouse, which has become clogged with mud during the winter,' and he gestured towards the river. 'However, allow me to admit you, and if you care to explore the building while I make my toilet, I shall be ready to answer any questions.'

His sparkling brown eyes met mine for a moment, for by now he had determined that I was the mistress, Polly merely accompanying me. An open and catching smile flitted across his full lips. Reaching down to overturn a stone by the back door, he revealed a key and, opening the door, stood back to let us enter.

'Please allow yourselves the liberty to explore the house as you wish,' he said. 'I will see you in, let us say, half an hour?' And with this he ushered us through the door, motioning us into the kitchen, and then disappearing along a stone-flagged passage.

The entire house was beautifully furnished, though in a slightly old-fashioned style. In the kitchen pots and pans gleamed as though just now placed upon their shelves; a

pantry and capacious cellars were nearby. Along the passage
lay a door communicating with the main portion of the villa,
through a fine dining-room. From this we passed through a
second door which led to a retiring-room which I imagined
from the collection of pipes lying in a glass case upon the
table the late Sir Nicholas had used as a smoking-room.
Returning to the dining-room, we discovered that a third
door gave onto the hall just inside the front door – and a
similar door opposite led into a capacious sitting room
behind which was a music-room with a remarkably finely
decorated harpsichord – beautifully in tune, I found as
I ran my fingers over its keys – and cabinets of music.
Finally, at the back of the villa a library ran the whole width
of the building, disclosing a collection of books I longed to
examine.

Polly and I looked at each other and smiled.

Turning up the staircase, we examined the five bedrooms
which lay there, each happily appointed, with furniture
which would entirely fill our needs with the addition of
some more comfortable bed-furniture. One door only
remained to us, at the back of the house, and opening it we
were presented with a view of the young man who had let us
in standing in a tub of water, his body streaked like some
strange forest beast with black and white stripes and a fine
froth of white soap-suds covering his manhood. On seeing
us, he hastily turned to present to us a prospect of a back
scarcely less interesting, for while he had cleaned the lower
part of himself streaks of mud from the upper part had run
down covering his arse and the backs of his legs with stripes
of black!

'I beg your pardon, sir,' I said – at which he smiled over
his shoulder.

'Please,' he said, 'I did invite you to make a complete
exploration of the house. This, as you see, was my uncle's
bathing room.'

So, he was presumably the master of the house?

'Sir,' I said, 'you are very good. But perhaps I can be of
assistance?' – and, turning, I immediately closed the door
firmly in Polly's disappointed face. Well, there are certain
times when the mistress must take precedence over the
maid.

'I am afraid,' the young man said as I advanced, 'that your clothing will be in danger of fouling, for this river mud is very contagious . . .'

The answer to that was patent, and in a moment I had stepped out of my dress, at which he smiled and offered me the cloth with which he had been washing himself, and I took pleasure in passing it over his shoulders and back, then his lower back and legs. As it was removed the mud revealed a body perfectly white, not at all the leathery, brown body of someone used to working in the open air; he then turned, revealing an equally pearly breast, relieved only by twin pinkish nipples almost like those of a young girl – but below, a machine not at all resembling anything appropriate to the female sex, but being reared and ready was most fetching. And when I laid my hand upon it – merely to remove the soap which still surrounded it with a snowy cloud – it proved utterly rigid, like some warm marble – and yet, from the sigh which escaped his lips, still capable of transmitting sensation.

He reached to take me in his arms, but I dodged aside and, lifting the towel from a chair nearby, enveloped him in it and dried each part of him with a gentle but firm pressure which, as my hands passed to and fro over his body, clearly did nothing to assuage the fever which was increasingly gripping him. At last he took the towel from me and, hurling it across the room, enveloped me in a passionate embrace, his lips fixed upon mine and his tongue exploring my mouth as his handsome equipage below found its way between my thighs, where I could feel it a-twitching, eager to explore my lower lips.

In a moment, he picked me up in his arms with a strength his slender frame might not have been thought capable of and, releasing the door, strode into the passage and straight across it into a bedroom – where, we had noticed, a bed lay partially made. Clearly this was his own room, and now he made it mine, showing to its ceiling the most intimate parts of my anatomy as, like a monkey with a nut, he turned me to view every aspect, then to test it with lips and fingers in such a tender display of love-making that it was clear he was no novice. In the end he knelt upon the bed and I sat astride his thighs, my arms about his neck while, with his hands clasping my arse, he raised and lowered me upon his still impervious tool, and we reached a mutual apprehension of pleasure before collapsing exhausted to lie with our heads together on the pillow.

After a while he raised his head and kissed me tenderly upon the lips.

'I need not express in words the pleasure you have afforded me,' he said, and by my smile I let it be known that an equal delight had been mine.

'Perhaps I could ask your name?'

I gave it, then demanded his.

'Philip Jocelind,' he said. 'In fact, Sir Philip, for upon my uncle's recent death I have succeeded both to the title and alas to his debts, for as I think you know – the family fortune, or lack of it, compels me to sell this villa.'

In a few words he gave me his history. Orphaned at an early age he had been brought up by his uncle, his only blood relative; had left university, travelled to Italy, and returned to England only in time to be present at his uncle's death-bed, and to learn that the old man had died leaving no funds whatsoever, but only the family's house, which now he was forced to place upon the market.

'I am reluctant to do so,' he said, 'but I have no money, and while I discover how to earn some, must live!'

'Perhaps,' I said, 'we could come to some arrangement, for this house would be ideal for a business purpose I have . . .'

'Which was why you obtained an order to view from Barlow?' he asked.

I explained that I knew nothing of the agent, but had simply happened upon the villa, and asked whether he would consider a scheme whereby I would either rent or buy the house, but perhaps – if he approved my scheme – he could remain in it in some capacity.

He was of course agog, and taking perhaps some slight risk of his disapproval – but doing so in the confidence that the events of the past hour had denoted him a young man of spirit – I explained my plan.

As I had hoped, he was interested, amused and finally enthusiastic, and offered that we might dine together to discuss the matter further – whereupon we recovered our

clothes and found Polly amusing herself in the library with
a number of books on marriage customs among the Indian
tribes of North America. She raised an eyebrow as we
entered, and was clearly understanding of the situation, but
when I explained that Sir Philip might be of help to us was
all too happy. And after I had introduced her and she had
been greeted by the young man (I was glad to see) with a
warmth completely free of condescension, we made off for
town and the Royal Hotel and Tavern in Pall Mall, which
Sir Philip said the nobility and gentry found the finest of its
kind, with the choicest viands and every luxury in season.
There we bespoke a table and settled down to discussion.

Our new friend proved entirely sympathetic to our
scheme and intensely interested in the practicalities of it; he
had no doubt, he said, of its success, and would be
delighted to engage himself to help us. When I expressed
some surprise that a gentleman of title should be prepared
to turn his talents in such a direction, he laughed and said
that he saw no difference between Sir Franklin Franklyn
running a brothel in Brook Street for the entertainment of
men (for I had told him of Frank's enterprise) and Sir Philip
Jocelind running one in Hammersmith for that of women –
with which we were forced to concur.

Seizing a napkin and producing a pencil, he immediately
began sketching a number of possible alterations to Riverside Lodge (as his villa was called): his uncle's retiring-
room, he said, could be made into a sitting room for the
lads, and between it and the dining-room might be broken a
sort of window in which a screen could be inserted – 'Not
unlike,' he said, 'those screens which the Moors have in
their palaces to protect their women from the view'. It
would be of pierced wood, so that with one room kept dark,
anyone standing in it could look into the other and contemplate those inhabiting it without themselves being seen!

I had obviously found someone with much my own
notions and very much my own enthusiasm. But what
about our stable of stallions, as I put it to him, which much
amused him.

'Well,' he said, 'of course it would be possible to find
temporary staff of that kind; there are young men in uniform
who will be pleased to take an evening in Hammersmith once

or twice a week, when their duties allow, and who at the moment are reduced to working the Parks . . .'

And what, I asked, did that mean?

He explained that St James's Park in particular was a known place where any Miss Molly could pick up a lad who would permit him a fondle, or even for a sufficiently large consideration, offer the double jugg . . .

At this I had to invite a translation, to Polly's amusement, and she explained in a low voice that Sir Philip was talking of those men who enjoyed carnal amusement with their own sex, and whose particular pleasure was intercourse with the only male aperture capable of receiving them – something I had heard of and, had I been quicker, might have apprehended. However:

'Most of these boys simply lie down for the money,' said Sir Philip, 'playing a part while thinking of their female friends; they would, I am certain, be happier in your establishment.'

'But,' I said, 'would it not be better to build a more regular stable, so that ladies who wished to return could be sure of finding their favourites?'

He took my point, but wondered how it could be achieved, though he was sure some way could be found if only (he suggested) by my own and Polly's efforts at exploration, something to which he guessed we would not be entirely averse.

At this point we were interrupted by a voice at my shoulder – it was that of Chichley, who had just entered with an extremely beautiful, dark young lady, splendidly dressed, on his arm.

'My dear,' he said to her, 'may I present Mrs Sophia Nelham and Mrs Playwright – Mrs Nelham, this is Lady Frances Brivet.'

We rose, and I introduced Sir Philip.

'Lady Frances and I have just announced our engagement in marriage,' Chichley said, with a look whose meaning I alone could apprehend – a mixture of public pride and silent rebuke. I wished them joy, not perhaps without some hint of melancholy, and they were conducted to a table not far from us.

Sir Philip was curious; he had heard something of Chichley at Cambridge, who it seems had a reputation as something of a mother's boy, and had never joined in that exploration of the connections between the sexes which has ever been an essential part of a university education. I refrained from informing him that the young man's education was now in a fair way to being completed, and both Polly and I listened with amusement to the sympathies Sir Philip expressed towards Lady Frances in her engagement to a eunuch. Only an exchange of glances between us conveyed our mutual suspicion that if that lady was marrying Chichley in the belief that she would be spared the task of sharing his bed, she would be disappointed – though her appearance being decidedly cool and haughty, I wondered to what extent he would be satisfied.

But we returned then to our plans, and continued our discussion of the best way to use the space which would be available to us at Riverside Lodge. Sir Philip was of the opinion that some of the upstairs rooms should be made into luxurious accommodation for those ladies who might wish a prolonged stay, while the library might be divided into four or five small closets to accommodate those who merely wished an evening's entertainment.

'I do not see,' he said, 'why you should not offer weekend parties, in the summer. The gardens are most attractive, there is a corner of the river which runs through the private grounds and where bathing can take place, and it may be that some ladies whose husbands are perhaps a-travelling or otherwise engaged, would be pleased to spend two or three days from home in the company of agreeable men.'

This seemed to me to be an excellent idea, though it introduced some new notions – as of providing meals, and so on – which I had not previously considered.

Sir Philip declined to discuss the terms on which I might purchase or hire his villa. That, he said, was a matter for his agent, for his uncle had died leaving many debts which he was under some obligation to pay – 'otherwise I would of course be happy should you wish it to come in with you upon equal terms'.

Then what part did he think of playing in our affair? I asked.

'That is largely a matter for yourself,' he said. 'My own

susceptibility to the ladies is well-known to my familiars, yet I am not sure I would wish to sell my charms, such as they are, upon the open market.'

'It seems to me that we will need no protector,' said Polly, 'as a female house might do – at least, not in the usual sense. Yet it might be that we will need a peacemaker among the young men themselves, for it is not always the case that the male sex, any more than the female, is able to resist argument and even quarrelling when in a close confinement.'

'Then may I not be your major-domo, so to speak?' asked Sir Philip. 'To see to the general running of the house, as well as supervising the young men? If it were convenient, I could continue to occupy my room and another could be reserved for yourself. This would still leave three for the use of long-stayers, while in the attic (which I believe you did not see) the former servants' quarters are remarkably comfortable and capacious, and I am sure that Mrs Playwright would be happy there. It is even the case that, were the demand great, you and I could occupy other rooms there – it might at all events be well to have them made ready.'

Our conversation was broken off from time to time as the waiters appeared with dish after dish, for Sir Philip was clearly determined that he should show us the greatest hospitality: cod's head and shoulders was followed by boiled turkey and celery sauce, then by roast woodcock, and finally by a large selection of fruit, while he plied us first with champagne and then with Constantia, and now with Sauterne and port. As the cloth was withdrawn, he asked for paper to be brought.

'And now,' he said, 'we must plan our advertisement.'

Polly and I glanced at each other: he now clearly saw himself as part of our company, but we said nothing – we would discuss it later.

He sat writing silently for some time, which I spent watching the ladies and gentlemen around us – including Chichley and Lady Frances, who seemed completely preoccupied with each other. Yet from time to time her eyes fell elsewhere and I caught a glance or two from him which spoke still of some regret . . .

Finally, Sir Philip threw down his pencil and handed me the paper; in fine, clear handwriting I read the following:

AN ANNOUNCEMENT TO ALL LADIES FATIGUED BY THE INDOLENCE OF THEIR HUSBANDS

I have purchased extensive and luxurious premises situate within a few miles of the centre of town, entered discreetly by a private way near a place often frequented by ladies of complete respectability.

Within a handsome villa has been contrived a large saloon contiguous with boudoirs most elegantly and commodiously fitted up. In this saloon are to be seen the finest men of their species I can procure, occupied in whatever amusements are adapted to their taste, and all kept in a high state of excitement by good living and idleness. Some fine, elegantly dressed young men play at cards, music, &c, while others, more athletic, wrestle or otherwise sport themselves, in a state of perfect nudity. In short, there is such a variety of the animal that no lady can fall short of suiting her inclinations.

A lady need never enter the saloon, but views the inmates from behind a darkened screen. Having fixed on the man she would like to enjoy, she has only to ring for the chambermaid, call her to the screened window, point out the object, and he is immediately brought to the boudoir in which she is installed. She can enjoy him in the dark, or have a light; masks are provided for those who wish to preserve a complete anonymity.

A lady may stay for an hour or a night, and have one or a dozen men as she pleases, without being known to any of them. A lady of seventy or eighty years of age can enjoy at pleasure a fine, robust youth of twenty, and to elevate the mind to the sublimest raptures of love, every boudoir is surrounded with the most superb paintings of Aretino's Postures after Julio Romano and Ludovico Carracci, interspersed with large mirrors; also a sideboard covered with the most delicious viands and richest wines.

The greatest possible pains have been taken to preserve order and regularity, and it is impossible that any discovery can take place by the intrusion of the watch or enraged cuckolds. No male creature other than those occupied in the business is admitted into any part of the temple (other than the trusted, tried and appointed functionaries who are well paid for their services, and not let in to gratify curiosity).

The expense of this Institution, which has been notable, is defrayed by a subscription from each lady of one hundred guineas per annum, with the exception of refreshments, which are to be paid for at the time.

Having thus made it my study to serve my own sex in a most essential point, I trust to their liberality for encouragement in my arduous undertaking and am, Ladies, your most obedient servant.

Sophia Nelham

It must be admitted that I was most impressed by this document – though upon reading it my first thought was that the preparation of the place would strain my finances to the utmost. Sir Philip clearly saw this, for he hastened to point out that the terms of no advertisement coincided entirely with the thing advertised, and that there were ways of making the most luxurious impression without too great a cost with low lighting and other similar devices.

And the sum asked as a subscription? Would this not be too great? Here, I found Polly and our friend at one: the former confirmed that, on the evidence of her sister, there were many ladies to whom a hundred guineas was a slender sum, and the latter insisted that the charge suggested was moderate, and the lowest possible upon which the place could be properly run.

Clearly, Polly and I should now discuss the matter of Sir Philip's involvement in our project; that he was a prime gallant, a considerate and inspiriting lover, and a knowledgeable gentleman, were not in question, but did we wish to employ him? Clearly, someone whom we had first seen grubbing out a river was not a man to stand on ceremony, nor to be afraid of work, and provided he showed no inclination to take over the entire organisation of Riverside Lodge, all would be well.

I nodded to Polly, and rose to my feet. But she was blushing, and was slow in following my example – from which I believed that my foot was not the only one to have felt the pressure of his, beneath the covers.

A man came hastening with the bill for the evening's entertainment which he offered to Sir Philip, who took it with some embarrassment, and I realised that he was incapable of paying it – as indeed I might have realised had I given the matter any thought. The freedom with which he had pressed us to eat, and with which he himself had enjoyed food and wine, now took on a slightly different complexion. But I was not angry and, having settled up, we found ourselves in the street and I bade him farewell with a good spirit.

He shifted uneasily upon his feet, however. 'It is somewhat late to make my way back to Hammersmith,' he said softly, 'and to a cold and lonely house . . .'

I was still comfortably reminiscent of the entertainment he had offered only a few hours ago, but could see that Polly would be gratified by any offer he might make, and so said that if he wished to walk with us to Frith Street he could perhaps find a chair in which to spend the night.

And so we walked back in the evening air, one of us on each side of him, and our arms through his. And when we had reached the house and he had admired it sufficiently, a silence fell, which I broke: 'I am now for my bed, sir, if you will excuse me. Polly, perhaps I may leave you to find Sir Philip a corner in which to sleep?' – and took my leave.

As I settled into my bed, I heard not one but two sets of footsteps making a quiet way up to Polly's room, above my own, and as I sank into an undisturbed slumber, could not but hear, though quietly expressed, those sounds which escape from a man and woman engaged in that comfortable activity to which we are all delighted to address ourselves with an agreeable companion.

Chapter Seven

The Adventures of Andy

Over the next few weeks, Frank was much engaged at the house supervising the workmen in interpreting his plans and revealing, I must confess, an application and talent for detail which I had not suspected in him. Meanwhile, Aspasia had obtained from Mrs Jopling Rowe the measurements of the five young ladies of her Worthing establishment, and had commissioned a number of dresses for them (at Frank's expense) which were intended for a surprise which would both gratify them and please their eventual partners.

I was invited to obtain the measurements of Moll Riggs, and went off to Sam Rummidge's to find that she had not been seen since our last encounter, and indeed had announced her retirement from business on account of coming into a large fortune (by which I assumed she referred to the present we had made her). After some persuasion, and since I was her particular friend, he directed me to her address, which was in the neighbourhood of St Giles, close by Seven Dials, of which I had no previous knowledge.

I reached it from the Strand by walking up the narrow street of St Martin's Lane – and there to my surprise encountered none other than Blatchford, our coachman, in company with another young fellow whose face was not known to me, and who was introduced as Bob Tippett, a Cockney who worked (as I gathered) on the edges of criminality, never quite descending to rob, but not shy of a little sharp practice, and whose acquaintance Blatchford had cultivated for the sake of getting to know London and its ways better. They were spending the morning, he said, in just this way of exploration, for Tippett was pointing out to him some of the notorious sharks and thieves of the area.

Asked if I would care to join them for an hour, I acquiesced, for my own education in the ways of the city was sadly lacking. First, we were taken into a beer shop, and there over a pot of ale several gentry were pointed out to us, among them a quiet, intelligent looking man who was a distinguished coiner just released from ten years' penal servitude for coining and passing base coin. With him was his friend and assistant, who watched out that no officers of justice were near while the coining was performed, and carried the bag of base money when they went out to sell it at low prices – five shillings worth being usually sold for tenpence.

Tippett explained that apart from selling base coin, it was easily 'passed' by one man offering a shopkeeper a good sovereign to be changed, which would be 'rung' upon the counter and found true. The coiner would then discover he had change after all and did not need it, pocketing the true coin. But then, he would find that in fact he had not sufficient small coins, and would produce a false sovereign which the shopkeeper would generally change without testing it.

Leaving the beer shop, we walked to Bow Street, where Tippett pointed out three young pickpockets, who looked like well-dressed costermongers, in dark cloth frock coats and caps. Then we saw a fashionably-dressed man arm-in-arm with a companion, dressed out with watch-chains and rings; they seemed pleasant and friendly, and as I caught the eye of one of them he paused to ask if we would accompany them to a gin-palace nearby. But Tippett shook his head, and we passed along – he then explained that they were well-known card-sharpers looking out for rooks. A young man of the most engaging appearance and tasteful in dress, he pointed out as a burglar; then came two more pickpockets dressed in suits of superfine black cloth cut in fashionable style, who were entering an elegant dining-room. And nearby, another expert burglar of about twenty-four years of age, standing at the corner of the street – his friend, Tippett explained, had been taken from his side about a fortnight ago on a charge of burglary.

Moll's address was at a house in Church Lane, a narrow street which at first seemed decked out for carnival. But we

soon saw that the wooden rods suspended across the street
from windows on the second and third floors bore nothing
more festive than clothes set out to dry – cotton gowns,
sheets, trousers, drawers and vests, some ragged and
patched, others old and faded. The street itself was
crowded, groups of the lower orders sometimes drinking
and laughing, sometimes merely standing and watching
each other with what seemed an air of suspicion – though
all seemed reasonably clean and orderly.

Here were several lodging-houses – out of some of
which landlords made an unconscionable profit. Tippett
pointed out one house, number twenty, which had been let
for twenty-one pound a year, then re-let in separate rooms
for ninety, and finally again let by parties who made a total
of over one hundred and fifty pound – the demand for
rooms was such that this could easily be done despite the
general poverty of the area, which forced many young
women into prostitution of the most desperate kind.

The house at which I was told Moll had her rooms was
evidently a lodging-house, and, having bade farewell with
thanks to my friends, I entered through a basement kitchen
(for the front door had evidently been unused for many
years, and looked as though no force could open it) where
several people were gathered around a group of tables, so
that it resembled almost an eating house; some were reading, others pipe-smoking, yet others supping on potatoes,
bread and fish. Others lay asleep, perhaps drunken.

Upon asking for Miss Riggs, I was directed to the second
floor, and climbed three sets of narrow stairs, finding
myself on a dark landing with a choice of three doors. I
tapped upon one, which was opened by a young woman at
whose breast a large child was assiduously sucking; she
pointed to one of the other doors, at which I knocked, and
hearing what I took for an invitation to enter I walked into
a small room crowded with furniture, but mainly occupied
by a large bed upon the pillows of which two heads lay, one
of them Moll's.

Muttering an apology, I made to leave, but Moll, sitting
up with a fine disregard for decency (she being unclothed),
welcomed me by name, then dealt her companion a dig in

the ribs with an elbow, whereupon a surprised youth of perhaps sixteen sat up beside her.

'Why Mr Archer,' says Moll, 'what a pleasure to see you! May I present –' then she giggled, aware no doubt that neither the time nor the place required formality, and went on – ' 'Tis my brother George, sir. George, get along out of it!' Whereon the youth threw back the covers, jumped from bed, thrust a tattered pair of trousers over his nakedness and, taking up a shirt, pushed past me to the door, muttering something under his breath which I did not catch.

'George works nights, sir,' said Moll. I thought it best not to enquire what at. 'Well, now, am I to rise, or will you join me?' she asked – a question which I answered by sitting upon the bed and informing her that I had come merely to ask her for her measurements – a request which seemed to nonplus her, and indeed which seemed at first incapable of answering, since she had no idea of a tape measure, nor any notion of her girth or height.

We solved the problem by my discovering a number of pieces of string lying upon the floor. Throwing back the covers, she passed one first around her waist, knotting it to indicate length; then another about her breasts; a third from shoulder to ankle; a fourth from shoulder to wrist. Upon her asking whether any other dimension was required, I was unable to answer, but in play she then undertook to examine my dimensions, which required the removal of my clothing and culminated in the measurement of my proper male parts, which I demur from recording for fear of being accused of pride – and which she then requested should be put to a proper use. I had some reservations about her cleanliness, and half thought I should wait until I could ensure it, but at that moment a tremendous noise arose in the street and, curious, Moll rose from her bed and went to the window, throwing it up and leaning out, displaying as she did so that entrancing open triangle between thighs and cunny which so distinguishes the fair sex – and which was so inviting that I could not resist coming behind her to close the void, an action which from the delicious wriggling of her body, she did not at all resent.

So busy did I become at pleasuring us both, that I failed

to recollect that we were displaying ourselves quite clearly
to anyone who wished to see, and was reminded only by a
cheer from below, whereupon I saw that the crowd which
had previously been giving its attention to a street brawl
had had its notice directed to us by one sharp-eyed boy, and
was now entirely aware of what was going on, encouraging
us by ribaldries the nature of which I would not wish to
offend any lady readers by recording. Moll was nothing
loath, not even troubling to conceal her breasts with her
hands, but waved to her friends, then lowered her head so
that my own action could be the more readily observed,
which attracted a renewed cheer.

This, alas, had the opposite effect upon me than Moll
might have expected, for instantly my courage and my
prick failed, the one leading me to withdraw to the interior
of the room, and the latter reducing itself to the proportions of a peascod. Moll, I regret to say, was ill-tempered at
this, though no less ill-tempered than I, who blamed her for
the disruption of our passion. She tried to make amends by
falling to her knees and attempting to rouse me again to
enthusiasm, but failed, whereupon I gathered up my pieces
of string and bade her a cool farewell – sent on my way by
waggish remarks from some still gathered in the street as I
left the house, which put me in no more pleasant a temper.
Ere I reached Hanover Square, I regretted the frigidity of
my farewell, and could not resist chuckling at the memory
of the situation in which I had, after all, placed myself;
finding Blatchford in the street outside our rooms, I sent
him back to Moll with half a guinea and a cheering word. I
learned much later that she had taken the money for his
own, and encouraged him to finish the job I had started.
But his honesty in the end led him to admit my message,
which comforted her considerably, for she had feared that
my ill-temper signalled perhaps the intention not to employ
her in Brook Street. It occurred also to me that Bob Tippett
might make an admirable addition to our household, for it
would be too much to expect Blatchford to be the only man
concerned with the work of stoking the stove, keeping an
eye on any visitors who might be difficult, and having also
to continue his duties as coachman and general factotum to
Frank and myself.

In time the day came when our young ladies were to join us. Frank and I made our way around to Brook Street after breakfast, to find Blatchford in the hallway. He had already admitted Moll, who had arrived, he said, at nine o'clock by hackney coach, with nothing but what seemed like an old tablecloth stuffed with soft goods. Upon Frank's enquiry, it proved to contain what clothes the girl possessed, and he persuaded her to place them in the corner of an upstairs room, to be inspected by Aspasia when she arrived, for he suspected that the new wardrobe to be provided would supply her entire needs.

Bob Tippett, who had also arrived, had been entertaining Moll with some ribaldry in the hall. But now she was much overcome by the splendour of the sitting room in its full glory, and even in the cold morning light (for the windows were now curtained and admitted the sun, the candles only to be lit when darkness fell) it looked sufficiently imposing. Frank and I were in the hallway, where he was showing me the small but comfortable cubicle constructed there for Aspasia's use, when an incoherent cry from the sitting room brought us back, and we found Moll looking with a mixture of respect, fear and admiration from the window. When we joined her, we saw Aspasia climbing from the chair she had hired, for she enjoyed that rather old-fashioned mode of transport during the daytime, it being capable through using the pavements of avoiding the press of traffic in the public street.

Having admitted our friend, we introduced Moll with feelings perhaps as tentative as her own, for although Aspasia had agreed with us that in theory at least one girl of rather rougher origins would be an excellent addition to the house, we wondered whether she and Moll would hit it off. But had reckoned without the fact that Aspasia, while a made rather than a born lady, entirely lacked those false airs and attitudes which the imitation aristocrat too often assumes, and soon they were chattering away comfortably, and on Moll's part with an enthusiasm she had not revealed even to us.

It was in late afternoon that at the Swan, Charing Cross, we greeted the stage from Brighthelmstone. Our party of young ladies comprised most of the passengers, some inside, some out. The girls outside were accompanied by Will Pounce, their servant and chaperone (and Constance's favourite) who, quite frankly, I had completely forgot. One bemused merchant who had spent the ride inside crushed between Rose and Cissie emerged with the look upon his face of one who has seen visions. The girls' excitement was such that it was almost impossible to control them, and it was all Blatchford and I could do to keep them from rushing off instantly into the streets. Finally, however, we persuaded them into three hackneys, together with their luggage, and conveyed them (hanging half out of the windows in order to see as much of the city as possible) to Brook Street, where the house silenced them immediately with its grandeur – not, indeed, that their home in Worthing had not been sufficiently capacious, but Mrs Jopling Rowe's taste had been that of a previous era, and the furnishings here almost appalled her pupils by their sophistication.

Frank and I stepped aside to discuss Will Pounce, whom he too had forgot. We could scarcely turn him away, we agreed, for not only had we in a sense promised employment, but there would be difficulties with Constance, his friend, and probably with the other girls, for they were used to his company and protection. And after all Bob Tippett was still rather an unknown quantity to us. So we instructed Blatchford to obtain accommodation for him in the house where he himself lodged, and decided to use him as a general handyman.

Leaving the girls in Aspasia's care, Frank and I made off for dinner at Dolly's Beef-Steak House in King's Head Court, and then spent the evening walking around to some other eating places frequented by gentlemen of a certain tone – the Marlborough Head at Bishopsgate (where the gentlemen of South Sea House are accustomed to dine), Guidon's French eating house in Poland Street, the Constitution in Bedford Street, et cetera. And by dint of dropping half a guinea here and there we were able to persuade the waiters to take a supply of the cards which Frank had had printed, and which simply gave the Brook Street address, the words 'Sympathetic female company assured', and, in one corner, 'Under the supervision of Madam Aspasia', which we were decided would be advertisement enough. Across several of these had been stamped the words 'Premier opening', followed by the date and the promise of free wine and eatables.

A few days later – twenty-four hours before the official opening of the doors – I dined at the Royal Hotel and Tavern with Sir Philip Jocelind, a young acquaintance of Sophia's; we were to act the parts of visitors to Brook Street, to be received as strangers (which indeed he was) in order to test the girls' behaviour no less than the conveniences of the stablishment.

After two bottles of claret and a few glasses of port – for strangely enough, I found myself a little nervous at the coming experience – we arrived at the house at nine o'clock and knocked upon the door, which was opened to us by Pounce, looking somewhat uncomfortable in a handsome footman's dress, though with hair unpowdered in order to establish a certain informality. Bidden to enter, we were received by Aspasia, handsomely dressed completely in black, relieved only by the glitter of her personal jewellery.

'Welcome, gentlemen,' she said. 'May I outline to you the rules of the house? A fee of five guineas will introduce you to the lady of your choice, comprehend accommodation for no more than three hours, and include also the use of our heated rooms, unique to this city, and as introduced by the establishment in imitation of the hot baths of Turkey, much admired by visitors to that place.'

Having counterfeited to hand over our guineas, we were shown by Aspasia to the sitting room, lit now by candles, in which seven of the most charming ladies imaginable sat. I scarcely recognised my former friends, so altered were they; the simple clothes they had worn before had been put aside in favour of charmingly modern dress, enhancing their beauty so that one could not but admire Aspasia's taste, who had chosen it.

None was altered so much, it may be imagined, as Moll, whose fresh, forthright charms were now emphasised by the low neck of a rich crimson gown which cleverly lay between the reserved and the forward, close-cut to emphasise the charms of her body while at the same time artfully concealing what it most seemed to promise.

Ginevra's rosy, delicate skin was set off to great advantage by a pale pink *crêpe* dress, her dimpled arms quite uncovered and encircled with elegant but simple bracelets composed of plaited hair. There was a voluptuous and purely effeminate languor about her character which made her infinitely graceful – as indeed was Rose, darker than Ginevra, whose skin was of quite as delicate a texture, but without its vermilion tinge, and the blue veins less defined; she wore a dress of white silvered *lamé*, on gauze, with a Turkish turban of bright blue, fringed with gold. The large, straight, gauze sleeve did not at all conceal the symmetry of her graceful arms. Xanthe wore a yellow satin dress, fastened round the waist with a gold band. Her profuse yellow locks were entirely unadorned, and her neck, arms and fingers were devoid of decoration, relying entirely on the loveliness of their shape to impress. Constance's dress was of figured white French gauze over white satin, making her dark skin seem even more voluptuously strange and attractive, and she wore a delightful pair of earrings which emphasised the perfect oval of her face.

But I cannot give over more space to description of the appearance of our nymphs; without having met any of the young women, Aspasia had cleverly provided a dress for each which not only suited her character but was a comment upon it. And I could imagine no spirited young man who would not stand – as Sir Philip and I did – undecided who he would be most delighted to entertain, for it was a constituent of the ladies' elegant appearance that one felt instantly that we were to distinguish them by our favours, rather than the other way about.

After a moment or two, Aspasia took us by the arms and withdrew us into the hall.

'Gentleman, have you made your choice?' she asked.

Sir Philip announced for Sally while I chose Xanthe. Aspasia nodded.

'Pounce will show you downstairs, and they will join you,' she said.

Downstairs, we were invited to divest ourselves of our clothing, Pounce showing himself sufficiently polite and helpful, though indifferently perfect in folding our clothes, which he threw over his arm and disappeared with as, wrapped in two large sheets of towel, we were directed to the hot room. Blatchford had evidently been at work all day, for the place was full of steam and of a pleasant, determined heat, so that in a moment we had thrown our towels aside, made our way over the floor to the baths, and lowered ourselves into them – one to each.

'I did not know that your friend had travelled in the east,' said Sir Philip.

He had not, I explained, but had constructed the baths in counterfeit of those he had seen illustrated from Pompeii. My new friend offered his congratulations, and lay back with a sigh of pleasure – for which he had additional cause in a moment, when the two girls stepped into the room, themselves also divested of their clothing and wrapped in towelling, which fell gracefully to the floor as they joined us in the baths.

The heat had already created a certain lethargy, and the sight of the two beauties in rosy nakedness added to the delight of our pleased senses, so that our immediate desire was to rise and take them to the place where we might embrace them. This they were not averse to and, indeed, we were to learn that one of the advantages of the hot room was that even gentlemen chilled from the night air, or who for some other reason were not in an amorous mood, were speedily raised to a state of passion requiring immediate slaking, which resulted in a speedier turnover of custom than might otherwise have been the case.

So, we rose to our feet and I saw that Sir Philip was as disposed to *amour* as myself, and were led to the warm room, and to benches covered in more loose towelling and forms of cushions. Here, we were invited to lie while Xanthe and Sally took bowls of warm water and soap, and with them washed our lower parts, not without certain gestures and caresses which raised our expectations of delight even further – so much so in my case, I must admit, that I was forced to dissuade Xanthe from her work and complete my toilet with my own hands, lest I should in a moment betray her and myself. Sir Philip, I saw from the corner of my eye, had no such inhibitions, and lying upon Sally's bosom was massaging her body with his own, his prick pleasuring itself upon her belly while he nibbled the lower parts of her ears so that she already gasped with pleasure.

Now, wiped dry with more towels, for a while we lay with our ladies while still the heat was upon us, our skins slippery with perspiration which had almost the effect of oil, and offered a delightful pinguidity to the palms of the hands.

After a while, they rose to their feet, wrapped their towels about them, and led us upstairs, where now hangings tactfully hid us from the gaze of anyone entering from the street, to the suite of retiring-rooms upstairs, where we parted, Sir Philip and Sally going into one, myself and Xanthe into another. Here was a fine painting upon one wall of a handsome girl lying upon her back, her legs thrown over the shoulders of a bearded warrior who was about to penetrate her with a vigorous instrument to which she showed no aversion.

Handing me to the bed and taking my towel from me, Xanthe enquired whether I found the room cold. On the contrary, heated as I was, the cold air playing upon my body was charming, and I felt a new vigour upon me as she removed her own towel and asked me, now, whether there was any particular game I wished to play? None, I replied, but that which would give her equal pleasure with myself – upon which she lay down at my side and began to stroke my body with her pliant hands, gradually moving closer and closer to the centre of my being, until, reaching it at last, she joined lips to fingers in raising my emotions once more to a pitch.

After a while, wishing to delight her – for it has ever been part of my pleasure in making love that the object of my desire should also experience some luxury – I raised myself, turned until my head was towards her feet and, kneeling with my knees each side of her body, bent so that my tongue could play about her belly and thighs before making its way to that delightful aperture where sensuality is concentrated. Meanwhile, she was able by raising her head only slightly to take me into her mouth, while her hands remained free to rove over my body, stimulating my breast and sides, then sliding over my back and reaching my loins, to play within the crack of my arse, producing a sensation which made me stretch my thighs wide to welcome her exploring fingers.

By now, she was panting delightedly, and finally almost threw me off before placing herself in a position mimicking that of the woman in the fresco, whereat it was the work of a moment for me to raise myself and become part of her body. And so happy were we both at the union that it was after only three or four motions of my loins that we collapsed upon the bed with a mutual expression of bliss.

We lay for a while in a state of pleasant lethargy, when I became consumed with curiosity to see what was happening elsewhere in the house and looked about for my clothes. Xanthe explained that I could ring for them, but produced from a small cupboard two charming robes of silk which, she said, were provided for those who wished merely to lie for a while and relax, perhaps with some food and drink, which also a ring of the bell would bring. But that evening, it being a purely private one, there would be food downstairs – upon which she led me down to the sitting room, where Frank and Aspasia had joined the girls, and the company greeted us with a cheer, at which I fear a blush rose to my cheeks.

A table had now been set up on which was a selection of cold dishes, together with red, white and rosy wine, glasses of which were pressed upon us. After a while, Constance approached Frank, and asked whether her friend Will might not be sent a glass.

'I had quite forgot!' said Frank. 'Please fetch him, and Blatchford and Tippett. They can let the fire out, and may certainly join us.'

While we ate and drank, he and Aspasia questioned me closely upon my experience of the house, the appointments of which I had no criticism to offer. Certainly Pounce's manner had been a little rough, but time and experience would cure that, and the hot rooms had been a notable success.

'Yes, I count on them to become a talking point,' said Frank. And when Sir Philip and Rose joined us, clad also in silk gowns, he, similarly, had nothing but praise to offer, of the appointments and conduct of the house.

Pounce, Blatchford and Tippett now joined us – a curious looking trio, for Pounce was in full footman's uniform, Tippett in ordinary day dress, and Blatchford was merely clad in a shirt undone to the waist and thin pantaloons (for he had been attending the fire all evening).

We attacked the food with enthusiasm, washing it down with generous draughts, and then Frank invited me to provide a little music. I slipped out and fetched in my guitar, which I had not played for some weeks, but I was soon able to produce a tune or two, to the delight of the ladies.

By this time Tippett had removed his coat and Pounce, his footman's jacket discarded and his wig hung upon the corner of a chair, had Constance upon his knee, his hand in her bosom.

'Pounce,' said Frank with imitated severity, 'your friend's gown was extremely expensive, and I shall be severely displeased if it is made dirty.'

Pounce looked suitably discouraged.

'Yes, sir,' he said, removing his hand, at which Constance pouted.

'Would it not be best if Miss Constance removed it?'

Both parties brightened at this, and standing for a moment, Constance stepped out of her gown before replacing herself upon Pounce's knee, but soon began to wriggle upon it in a strange manner, as though something was making her uncomfortable – or perhaps was instilling some pleasure . . .

Frank had clearly determined that everyone in the house should feel at ease, for he now, without false modesty, simply removed his own clothing and, inviting Aspasia to do the same, took her in his arms and began a waltz. Within a very short time a ballum-rancum had begun – as Tippett called it – the Cockney name for a dance at which the dancers were altogether unclothed. Frank danced with Aspasia, Pounce with Constance, Tippett had taken Sally in his arms while Sir Philip was embracing Cissie; Xanthe and Rose were in each other's embrace, breast to breast, while Moll and Ginevra were seated one on each side of me, Ginevra admiring my fingering while her arm was about my neck and her lips fumbling my ear, and Moll showing her own adept fingering at quite another instrument.

In due course the lascivious movement of the waltz had brought Tippett and Sally to a point at which they simply sank to the floor in each other's arms, whereupon Frank announced that for this occasion everyone was free to make use of the rooms provided – and though Tippett and his friend were now in too close an embrace to be capable of rising without discomfort, the party broke up. Despite the ministrations of my two angels I was not yet myself ready for a second bout, so excusing myself I simply wandered from basement to attics, bringing the sound of my guitar within earshot of the lubricious couples, who in their eagerness to embrace had neglected to close their doors. Within the finest of the upstairs rooms, Frank was deeply engaged with Aspasia – the older woman's embraces proving, it seemed, ever more attractive to him despite the younger flesh which had been all about him. Indeed, as she half-lay, half-sat upon the bed, his head between her thighs, her wonderfully prominent breasts rising and falling in her passion, she was a noble sight. Passing on to the next chamber, I saw – nay, heard – Cissie at the height of pleasure, yelping as Sir Philip, once more in full vigour, which I envied him, bucked between her legs like a young and untamed colt.

Pounce and Constance lay in a quieter embrace in the third chamber, his body almost as brown as hers – though a white band appeared about his loins, for unlike her he, working in the open rather than merely lying in the sun, had been used to be covered in case of prying eyes. Aroused by these country sights, I beckoned with my head to Ginevra, who was with me, to come to the fourth room – which I had occupied with Xanthe – only to find on reaching the door that it was already taken by Xanthe who, still warm from my embrace, was now locked in delighted combat with her friend Rose, lying head to toe, each with her free-flowing hair enveloping the loins of the other, their hands tightly clasped about each other's buttocks, which themselves were moving in unmistakable rhythm.

Reaching around me, Ginevra pulled the door quietly shut, and without a word she and Moll took me each by an arm and led me downstairs, past the sitting room – where

Tippett and Sally were still in vigorous play – to the warm room, where I lay between them upon piled towels, my hindquarters pressed into the belly of Moll, whose hands lay upon my hips governing the movements with which I was now able to satisfy Ginevra, who lay facing me, one thigh thrown over my hip to lie across both our bodies.

We woke next morning, all three of us, chilled by the cool air which had replaced that of the night before, and to the sound of Blatchford raking out the ashes of the fire to replace them with fresh charcoal for the evening, for this was to be our official opening.

The day was spent first in repairing the ravages of the previous evening – cleaning, removing the soiled linen and replacing it (Frank had obtained what seemed a bottomless store of sheets and towels – 'For,' he said, 'I am determined that everything about the place shall be fresh as paint') and in making sure that every smallest detail was in place.

Sophie and Polly appeared at the middle of the day, and without describing with exactitude the events of the night before – for my regard for Sophie is such that I am shy to reveal any commerce I may have with any other woman, though I am sure sure she must realise that I do not live as a eunuch – I was able to assure her that our 'rehearsal' had come off smoothly. Walking around the house, she expressed herself pleased. Her own plans, it seems, go forward smoothly, with the help of Sir Philip. I have not yet myself established what might be termed a friendship with that gentleman, who must himself feel on less than intimate terms with myself, but it appears that he is making himself useful to Sophie, and perhaps in more than one sense, for when they met (he having spent the night here) I felt that she hung upon his hand with rather more warmth than she might have been expected to betray to an employee – for such I am to believe he is or is to be. I must confess that I gave myself the pleasure of enquiring pointedly after Cissie's well-being, but my thrust did not land, for he merely announced that he believed he had given her every satisfaction, at which Sophia laughed, bade me farewell, and left.

I need not perhaps describe the success of our first night. Though the earliest guest did not arrive until seven o'clock, and in the meantime we had wondered whether anyone would appear at all, a steady trickle of gentlemen then knocked at the door, so that all our four rooms were continuously occupied, the girls once out of their dresses never having the opportunity to replace them, and Frank forced to tell them to do their best to satisfy their partners in the lower parts of the house. This they had no difficulty in doing, the warm room becoming an additional bedroom as it had for Ginevra, Moll and myself, and one gentleman being satisfied in the hot bath itself, which Moll described later as having the property of complete freedom from weight, 'a floating fuck,' as she described it, being for her a most pleasurable sensation she commended to us all.

The last visitor did not leave the house until three in the morning, by which time we were all tired, the girls through an obvious cause, Blatchford through his attendance to the stove, Frank and Aspasia through attendance upon the clients, Pounce through looking after the carriages to and fro, and myself with fingers aching from playing the guitar. The girls, delighted by the sound on the previous night, had decided that it added to the pleasure of the atmosphere – something which may be so, but it is too much like hard work for me to wish to make it a common pleasure!

Before we retired to bed, Frank called the girls together and announced that the house had taken exactly a hundred guineas.

'I have given some thought to this,' he said, 'and have decided that rather than each of you receiving a proportion of the fee a gentleman might pay for being entertained by her, it is fairer that you should each receive a proportion of the complete profit. I therefore intend to pay each of you a seventh share of one-third of the takings for each evening. You will receive this invariably – that is to say, should one of you be ill, or on a regular leave of absence, she will still receive her share. Should one of you be remarkably more or less popular with our visitors, then some adjustment may in future have to be made, but I do not at present envisage it.'

He then handed each girl six guineas – considerably

more than a proper share for the first night, but a generous gesture at which their faces lit up. I wondered whether he might be being a little over-generous, for he had also to pay salaries to the three young men, and then had the expenses of the house and its renovation to recoup, but I must trust his instincts and superior sense of business to my own, and wait to see what the future holds.

Chapter Eight

Sophie's Story

The eagerness with which Frank and Andy set about their plans resulted in the opening of their establishment in so short a time that it was impossible for me to believe that all could run smoothly. Yet I must confess that the furnishing of the house at Brook Street exceeded in comfort and beauty anything I had imagined possible. Polly and I looked over it on the day before its opening, and were as pleased as my brother with its effect. And from what I subsequently heard from Philip – for we now, as partners, refer to each other simply by our forenames – the house is as well-managed as it has been well-designed.

About the ladies Frank has employed, I am not sure; briefly introduced to them, I was pleased with the modesty of their demeanour – apart from one Cockney woman who is clearly from the streets and betrays it in every word she utters and many of the actions she performs. Yet she too seems well-intentioned and cheerful, and is a great favourite with Andy (he betraying in this a taste for coarseness perhaps originating with his own birth, which was not gentle).

But to return to my own plans, I had soon made arrangements through my late husband's solicitor, an honest man who has continued to serve me as he did that miser Mr Nelham (and I believe with considerably more pleasure) to buy the Lodge from my friend's estate, and without difficulty sold the house in Frith Street to a merchant from York who is setting up in business in the city, and at an excellent price, so that it was my pleasure to sign a draft to Sir Philip Jocelind for a sum considerable enough to keep him out of financial difficulty for some time to come.

He had the best of all worlds, indeed, for he continued to live at what had been his home since childhood, and had the

additional pleasure of improving it in line with plans he had
had for some time for its modernisation: the piping in of
water, at no small expense, from the source which also
supplied Brandenburgh House next door, and the renewal
of certain furnishings – though many we retained, as we
wished to preserve the atmosphere of a pleasant, private
house at which our guests were to be guests, no matter how
much they paid for the privilege.

For two or three weeks we worked at this – or rather
Polly and I worked, while Philip appeared, disappeared,
and reappeared, for I had handed over to him responsibility
for stocking our stable with young men. Though I was to
make an inspection of them before they were finally
engaged here, it was not proper for me to roam about
London on such a mission, however much the task might
appeal in my more riggish moods. I did, however, suggest
to Philip that he might make an excursion to the pools at
Hampstead, for the scene we had witnessed there frequently returned to my mind.

One afternoon, Polly and I were taking tea when Philip
appeared to announce that preparations were complete, and
that six young men to whom he had spoken would appear
before us on the following day! Since we had just been con-
gratulating ourselves that our task was completed, we could
now fix the date for the opening of our establishment –
which we did for a week's time, Philip promising that the
bills (on the lines he had sketched some time ago) should be
distributed to a number of shops in town whose owners
would, for a small consideration, ensure that they came
into the hands of a likely clientele.

'And this evening,' he said, 'we should enjoy some entertainment; I have taken the liberty of obtaining tickets for
the Contrary Ball.'

This I had never heard of, but Polly assured me that while
it was not precisely fashionable, it was attended by many
ladies and gentlemen of note. 'Besides', she said, 'it is
invariably the source of great amusement.' She would not
reveal more, but busied herself readying clothes for us to
wear, and in the early evening had me in a chair while she
arranged my hair with a care and wit that I had not suspected in her.

The ball was held in a large house somewhere south of the river – where, precisely, I do not know to this day, for it was after dark when we set out. Our carriage set us down at a fine entrance where we were received by a footman who directed us to rooms where we left our cloaks, and then up a grand staircase at the head of which stood a fine, tall woman who (Philip told me in a low voice) organised the Ball each year. I curtsied to her, and was raised to my feet by a steady hand, and greeted most kindly in an enchantingly husky voice.

The sound of the German waltz greeted us, and a picture of great gaiety, colour and movement, a swirl of masked dancers – for each wore a mask, some of plain black, others in beautifully embroidered silks of various colours, some of painted canvas.

We stood for a moment and watched, and gradually the meaning of the occasion came upon me, for while many of the guests were entirely conventional, a number were far from what they seemed. The first I saw who was an obvious pretence, was a large, fat woman who stood nearby, drinking wine at such a rate that she could surely not for long remain upright? There was something too square, too solid about the great haunches which could be seen under the silk of her gown, while the skin of her shoulders – though pale and hairless – seemed somehow over-coarse, as did her face, in profile, the heavily rouged lips and cheeks underhung by enormous jowls. But then she dropped her reticule in reaching out to take yet another glass of wine from the tray of a passing footman, and as the front of her dress fell away from her large and pendulous breasts, I saw not flesh but what seemed to be padded bags within the bodice.

I looked with amazement to Polly, who grinned.

'Bean-bags, madam!' she said. And immediately, upon looking about me, I saw that many of the ladies in the room were in fact gentlemen in masquerade – some acting the part with such enthusiasm that they were caricatures, others so neat and graceful in their behaviour that only the large size of their hands and ankles betrayed them.

I had never been before in the presence of so many gentlemen whose preference was to imitate those of the opposite sex, nor did I feel that they especially held any interest to me, and was surprised to see Philip, from time to time, dancing with one of them, talking and joking in an animated manner, and later, when he asked me to join him, asked him what satisfaction such a proximity could give him. To which he replied that he found it 'amusing', and had nothing more to say on the subject.

Happily, there was a sufficient number of ladies and gentlemen present in their own character, though most of them seemed to be in attendance to laugh at the others, which I found to be disconcerting. I saw Polly from time to time in conversation with other ladies present – I mean, real ladies – and myself spent my time observing the scene from a corner of a room, uneasily occupying myself with inspecting the furniture if anyone came too close to me.

But in time, I found myself addressed, happily by a young man in the clothes of a gentleman and with a polite demeanour.

'Ma'am, I find you alone. May I hand you a glass of wine?' – and with a bow, offered me a libation, which I was pleased to accept.

'You seem somewhat uncomfortable, if I may remark,' he observed.

I admitted that that was the case.

'It is your first attendance at the Contrary Ball?'

It was, I said, nor had I any notion of how it was composed until an hour ago.

'It was somewhat unkind of your escort not to have informed you,' said the young man, in a grave tone, and with a head sympathetically inclined.

I made no reply, simply inclining my head in turn.

'You are new to town?' he asked, and after my reply, went on to speak of other similar occasions, which had begun – he said – as a meeting for those gentlemen who found a satisfaction in dressing in women's clothing, and even pretending to be women – though it was by no means the case that all such were eunuchs, either in fact or in imagination, for many found great satisfaction in making love to the opposite sex, and simply took pleasure in silks and satins, cottons and gauzes.

'However, there are some who are interested to regard such people as one might look at the animals at the Tower,'

he said. 'And others who – to put it plainly – are only stirred
by the embrace of their own sex, and hope to find such
partners here. So, the ball has become a popular affair. You
will forgive my speaking of such things, ma'am,' he said,
'but it is as well to be informed.'

'I am grateful to you, sir,' I said; and indeed was, not
only for his exposition of the situation but for his company.
He was of slight build, and I supposed very young, for his
voice still seemed to have the tone of a boy's. His manners
were gentle, and his address impeccable.

'Perhaps,' he said after a while, 'you would like to retire
from the noise for a few minutes? There are some retiring
rooms where we could sit for a while, and I could inform
you further.' At which he laid his hand upon my bare arm,
with a tender and melting touch, and I felt a slight pressure
of his fingers which was a patent invitation to dalliance.

And why not, I thought to myself, looking around?
Everyone was enjoying himself; Polly I could see talking
animatedly to an elderly gentleman whose whiskers seemed
unequivocally to confirm his sex, while Philip was for the
time nowhere to be seen. I looked at my companion, and
thought I glimpsed, behind the mask, a pair of invitingly
sparkling, dark eyes. I inclined my head again, at which he
took my arm and walked me from the room and along a
corridor, then another, with many doors, behind some of
which I seemed to hear sounds of pleasure. Finally, we
came to a door which stood ajar and, first knocking gently
to ensure that the room was empty, my companion stood
aside and allowed me to enter.

I found myself in a small withdrawing- or perhaps
dressing-room, simply furnished with a couple of chairs
and a *chaise longue*. But before I had time to see more, I felt
myself clasped in my new friend's arms, and his lips upon
my own, a tender tongue playing about my mouth and
finding my own tongue, while his hands fumbled at my
back attempting to discover the laces which held my dress in
place. His attentions were sudden but, after all, neither
unexpected nor repugnant to me, whose preoccupation
with business had now for some time restrained me from
amorous activity.

He released the bands of my dress, loosed it gently from

my shoulders, and for a moment withdrew so that it fell to my waist, freeing my breasts – which have ever been, though I myself say it, a major adornment of my person. I heard him catch his breath, and he bent his head to kiss for a moment each peak, while I in turn slipped his coat from his shoulders, and began to unbutton his ruffled shirt. He stood, smiling, while I did so – a smile which broadened at the sight of the expression upon my face when I discovered beneath that shirt not the broad, manly platform I expected, but a pair of small, perfectly formed, inexpressibly feminine breasts. Despite myself, I drew back. The smile vanished instantly from his – her – face.

'Why ma'am,' she said, 'surely I cannot be mistaken? Surely you were aware . . .?'

But it was clear from my face that I was not, and instantly, though with a certain coldness, the girl turned and drew her shirt about her, beginning once more to button it.

'I apologise, ma'am,' she said. 'Had I realised . . .'

But almost despite myself, I stepped forward, placed my hands upon her shoulders, and planted a kiss upon the back of her neck, beneath the short, curly black hair. She turned at this, and clasped me in her arms, our bosoms meeting, then in a moment leading me to the *chaise longue*, upon which we collapsed, still embracing.

The truth was that I had certainly expected the embrace of a gentleman, and that a certain disappointment was unavoidable. Yet I was also too warm for my fire to be extinguished instantly, and my past experience had taught me that the embraces of my own sex were by no means invariably repugnant.

My new friend's body was soon fully revealed by my first removing her boots, then pulling the breeches from her, and it was slim and muscular as a boy's. Indeed, but for her breasts (which, when she was lying upon her back almost ceased to have any prominence) and the silky shrub between her legs from which no attentive engine arose, it could have been that of a young man of fifteen or sixteen. My own figure is much fuller, but evidently offered the greatest gratification to my partner who, having already paid tribute to my upper body, now watched me step out of my skirt and paid my hips and thighs the compliment of admiring them, turning me so that she could possess every plane with her eyes. And finally she lay me upon my back and knelt between my legs (one of her knees pressed tightly against my sex) to cover my face, neck, bosom and arms with kisses so vehement and rejoicing that even were I not already committed to enjoying her attentions I would surely have been persuaded – for what is more aphrodisiac than admiration, which here was to the point of adoration?

No one has a keener apprehension than myself of the hard, firm body of a man, even of the discomfort of his rough face pressed against the softness of an intimate part. But it must be confessed that even this firm and somewhat unwomanly body possessed a smooth and supple sympathy which was as inspiriting, in its own way, as the male embrace. One thing, of course, was lacking, but as the most sympathetic of men understand, the male part is not always that which provides ecstasy, and the attentions first of the girl's tender fingers, then of her sinuous tongue, brought me over the cliff of my desire once, then again. More than once I attempted to persuade her to turn her body so that I could similarly compliment her, but she firmly declined, remaining half-kneeling before me, her head buried in my lap, her slim backside in the air, far from my reach so that all I could do was to grasp her shoulders and perhaps reach round to her small breasts – now almost rigid with pleasure – before delight swallowed me again, so acutely that I almost fainted.

When I recovered, I found her turned and lying so that her head was upon my belly. I half sat, and again attempted to take her in my arms, but she rose, and slim as a wand stood for a moment, then said: 'Please ma'am, do not put yourself out. I am entirely satisfied by having given you pleasure, and would not wish to incommode you.'

By this time I was in fact desperate to show her my admiration of her own delightful form, but before I could find words in which to express this, she had drawn the male breeches once more over her loins, and was buttoning her shirt, and it was once more the young man who stood before me.

Making her bow, she withdrew immediately, leaving me

curiously unsatisfied, and also wondering who she might
be. I dressed myself in thoughtful mood, and found my way
eventually back to the ballroom, where the scene was now
one of strange lassitude, for many people had withdrawn,
either to other rooms in the house, or altogether, while over
those that remained a sort of weariness had descended.
Philip was still nowhere to be seen, but Polly made her way
to me across the floor. She told me in a low voice, and with
obvious irritation, that she had been courted by an
extremely good-looking young man who, the moment they
were alone, had plunged his hand into her bosom, and
discovering that it consisted of flesh rather than padding,
had in a moment angrily withdrawn. 'To have been mistaken for a Miss Molly,' said she, 'is a compliment I could
well do without!' – but upon my laughing, could not but
herself smile, and we took ourselves off home, leaving
Philip to return as best he might. I could not but feel
(though not opening the matter to Polly) that it was a curious
event to which to have brought us. And then, where was he?
I had last seen him dancing with a young person who might
have been female, but could equally have been male. The
impression I had received on the first occasion we had met –
indeed, his behaviour when I had approached him – was
not that of someone whose devotion was directed at
members of his own sex; moreover, Andy had informed me
that he had much enjoyed himself at their establishment.

But I was now too tired to speculate further, and retired
to bed, falling asleep long before any sound could have
announced his return to his room, next door to my own, if,
indeed, he did return before morning.

At what time Philip did return I know not, but he certainly appeared at midday the next day – the time at which
we usually met to survey the work which was being done
about the house, and to discuss what was to be done, over a
glass of wine. Today, it seemed that there was nothing left
to do except approve the young gentlemen he had engaged,
which was planned for the afternoon. In the meantime, we
walked back to what had been his uncle's library, and was
now divided into a series of small but comfortable retiring-
rooms, each decorated in a different colour but with the
same furnishings. Fine, full curtains hung at the windows

and, where there were no windows, covered a space where such might have been – in the former case to ensure privacy and in the latter to avoid a feeling of closeness or stuffiness in the atmosphere. Then there was a low couch in each room, expressly made for the house by a furniture-maker at Chiswick Philip had recommended, sufficiently wide to allow space for two, or even three, bodies and carefully sprung so as to be comfortable without being too soft, for nothing is so inimical to love-making as an over-soft bed, on the surface of which no purchase is to be had.

Apart from this and a small closet, together with a table with bowl and jug, to be kept continually supplied with warm water and fresh, clean cloths, that was all. I was well pleased, as indeed was Philip, who insisted on bouncing in turn upon each couch, to ensure its pliability and resistance to his form. I had half a feeling he wished me to join him in the test, but for several reasons I refrained.

At three o'clock in the afternoon, Polly and I were joined by Aspasia, who had been invited to inspect the premises and to look over the livestock. The three of us went into what had been the dining-room, but was now a pleasant sitting room. A screen stood in front of the window which had been broken into the next-door room, hiding it from view, while a table and chair stood by the outside window, where business could be done, and a contract drawn up between the visitor and the house, to ensure the payment of the annual subscription. This could be paid at once, or in the sum of twenty pound a month – an additional forty pound per annum being in recognition of the delay in receipt of the total sum.

Drawing the curtains and plunging the room into darkness, I led the way behind the screen, where three chairs had been set before the pierced wooden barrier laid across the window. I explained to Aspasia that of course there would normally be only one chair, though if two or three friends wished to share the pleasure of choosing their partners together, there would be no objection.

So finely cut was the barrier – again, Philip had discovered a craftsman who had counterfeited a genuine Moorish screen in the collection at the British Museum – that it afforded me a clear view of the room beyond. I had that morning tried it from the other side, and found that though Philip called to me that he could see every detail of my dress, I was entirely unable to discern that anyone was watching me.

The room which was to be devoted to the young men, for their recreation and also their display, had again been comfortably and elegantly furnished. About the walls were several couches on which they could sit or recline; by the window (hung only by the lightest curtains, for it gave onto the private garden, and there was little if any chance of anyone looking in at it) was a table and chairs at which card games could be played. Another table was to bear daily and weekly newspapers; just within the window was a small billiard table, ready for play.

I had scarcely looked about and made myself comfortable when the door opened and Philip showed the first of the young men in.

'This is the room where you will spend your time when unoccupied by guests,' I heard him say – for there was no barrier to sound passing from one room to the other.

'Please divest yourself of your clothing, which can be placed in the closet next the door. Your colleagues will be joining you shortly.'

This first young man was of perhaps twenty years of age. He was dark, and well-built – indeed, as he removed his clothing he revealed a body not only extremely muscular but, even so early in the year, dark with exposure to the sun. I guessed – rightly as it turned out – that he was one of the bathers from the Hampstead ponds. The breadth and strength of his shoulders seemed to confirm this, for they were well-developed, as were his thighs, seeming to speak of the exercise of swimming as well as of whatever occupation he had formerly been engaged in.

'Excellent,' whispered Aspasia. 'Such an animal is essential – one with which almost every female would enjoy a ride.'

But our eyes had not long enjoyed the pleasure of examining a body which embodied every elegance concomitant with strength and virility, when Philip ushered in a second – as dark, but slimmer than the first – with the same words.

'This is a rum go,' said the first.

'It is,' said the second. 'I'm William. And you?'

'Harry,' said the first, holding out his hand, which the second gripped briefly. Then he began to undress himself, while Harry threw himself upon a *banquette*, his hands behind his head.

William was, by appearance as well as by his speech (which was softer and more educated than that of Harry) evidently more of a gentleman. His limbs were less developed and whiter, his body almost completely hairless, and more slender but as shapely, if in a less athletic mould. His arms were almost like those of a girl, his breast less muscular, but his belly flat and without a trace of fat. He folded his clothes very carefully as he took them off, and placed them neatly upon a shelf, then sat upon a chair, somewhat uneasily, at a distance from his new friend.

'What d'you make of this?' said the latter.

'No more or less than you, I suppose,' replied William. 'I am told that we are expected to – er – minister to a number of ladies.'

'Fucking's the name of the game,' said Harry, 'and I've waited all my life to be paid for it!'

'Not to my taste,' said Aspasia in a low voice, 'but there are those who look for a young man of somewhat delicate nature, in order to offer a more motherly affection.'

But the conversation was broken off by the unexpected appearance of the third stallion of our stable – who to my surprise as well as that of the two others, was a black man, whose brilliant white teeth flashed as he threw the two others a broad smile.

'This,' said Philip, 'is George – I'll leave you to instruct him.'

Harry looked at George with what seemed to me to be a great deal of suspicion, but to my surprise William, who had seemed to be the more withdrawn, was quick to rise, step forward and greet him, giving their names. George's voice, when he spoke, though it was low and as dark as his face, proved mellifluous and cultivated, and he was clearly of a pleasant disposition. I watched with curiosity as he divested himself of his clothing – which was of a decent quality, though not fashionable – for I had scarcely seen a man of colour before, and never undressed. The colour of the skin of his shoulders, back and buttocks (for he had his back to me) was the same as that of his face – deep and rich, and with a bloom almost of purple. His backside was delightfully firm and well-shaped, positively demanding a caress, and his body beautifully proportioned and shaped, so that I believed him likely to be one of Philip's most successful discoveries. As he removed his trousers, I thought I saw a shock pass over the faces of both other men. Was he in some way deformed, I wondered? That would be sad indeed. But as he turned to put away his clothes, I saw what had caught their eye – a member so large that I was forced to rub my eyes and lean forward for a clearer view, not believing it possible. Though clearly unaroused, it was as formidable as most male instruments when they stood ready for the fray. Of what monstrous dimensions, I thought, could it be when persuaded to stand? Would not the thought of being split by it frighten most ladies? It certainly frightened me yet my curiosity was such that I could wish it possible to see such a display. As he sat, it lay across one thigh, seeming as thick as his wrist, for his limbs, apart from this essential one, were rather delicate and small.

In her excitement Polly had gripped my arm with her fingers, and was clutching it so that I felt sure my flesh would be bruised – yet in my surprise I had scarcely at the time noticed her grip.

'Well,' said Aspasia drily, 'you certainly have an original member of the household there! I have never myself seen a black man unclothed, but I have been told of their inordinate size, and now see the rumours confirmed. You either have a great success, or –'

She was clearly much of my own opinion.

The three men sat in silence until, in a moment, Philip appeared again with two others.

'Ben and Tom,' he said, 'here are Harry, William and George. They will show you where to put your things.'

Like Harry and William, the newcomers were transfixed by the sight of George's remarkable weapon, turned to each other, and giggled.

'What chance have we got against that?' asked Tom,

whereupon all the boys broke into laughter, including George, who had begun by looking embarrassed, never perhaps having occasion to be seen unclothed by other men.

Ben and Tom turned out to be brothers. Both fair, their bodies rather short and squat, everything about them seemed to have much the same plumpness – buttocks, muscles of the calves and thighs, little pot-bellies (though not what one could call fat), and chests upon which there seemed under-developed breasts. Yet there was nothing in the least feminine about them, though their chief male attributes seemed so small as to be almost altogether absent.

'Well,' said Harry, who seemed to be the one among them least given to equivocation, 'there's a contrast. That's the biggest one I ever set eyes on. All you darkies that size?'

'I believe I am particularly blessed,' said George, modestly.

'I should think so,' said Harry, 'but' – turning to Ben and Tom – 'if George has too much, you've scarcely enough, between you.'

'Never had any complaints,' remarked Ben.

'Get along!' said Harry.

'No, really,' said Tom seriously – and both he and his brother had a rather endearing, somewhat childish, solemnity about them – 'you've no idea how we grow . . .'

But now the door opened once more, and Philip introduced the last member of the party, who turned out to be by far the elder – a man of perhaps forty years of age, with tinges of grey hair at his temples. He carried himself well, and when introduced – as Spencer – nodded his head in an almost military manner and, turning his back, unclothed himself deliberately and without either ostentation or undue modesty. He had kept in good shape, for though the hair upon his chest was similarly greying, there was only a slight thickening about the waist to show him any less fit than the others.

'Now that is an excellent notion,' said Aspasia. 'Time and again you will find that a lady desires a man older than herself, and though the world knows that they are easy enough to find, they are usually either ugly or faithful to their wives!'

Spencer's arrival, and his faintly military bearing,

seemed to have dampened the spirits of the others, and they sat in silence for a while.

'Congratulations,' said Aspasia quietly. 'You are more adept than I took you for – where did you find these gentlemen?'

I had to admit that they had all been found by Philip, who of course Aspasia had met for a short time in Brook Street.

'Ah,' she said, 'Sir Philip has hidden depths. It is not every man who has such a fine eye for what will please a lady.'

But now the door opened once more, and Philip reappeared and, taking up a position with his back to us, addressed the company.

'Gentlemen,' he said, 'I have put the same proposition to all of you, and you have all agreed to its terms – that is, that you shall be paid the sum of five pound a week each as a retainer, and that upon each occasion when you lie with a guest, you shall receive an additional three pound. Food and wine will be provided, but accommodation only if you are required to stay overnight with a lady. That is understood?'

They all nodded.

'Now just a word as to procedure. You will be here each day at eleven o'clock in the morning, unless you have stayed overnight or have been specially summoned at an earlier time. As soon as you arrive, you will bathe yourselves and then make your way to this room. You will be expected to remain within call until midnight, or later if required. If the weather is fine you may of course walk in the grounds, but must always be within hearing of the bell which will be rung when a visitor is due, or arrives. We expect as time goes on that more and more ladies will come by appointment, which may allow some slight relaxation of the rules, but this will depend on circumstances.

'As to dress, in order that the ladies may make their choice, we would prefer that you remain unclothed while you are in this room, though if you wish to devise some covering which seems to you likely to attract the opposite sex, we have no objection – except that clearly should it have the result that you are not in fact chosen fairly regularly, it will be to your advantage to reconsider.

'As you see, a billiard table is provided; also cards, for play, and newspapers. If you wish to bring anything else with you to occupy the time, please do not hesitate to consult me.'

He glanced at some notes he had in his hand.

'When you hear the bell ring, you will know that a lady or ladies have arrived, and from that time on you must behave in the supposition that you are being observed. Behind this screen' – and he seemed to point straight at us – 'is a room from which the ladies will be able to see you without being seen. Someone there will point you out by your Christian names, and the ladies will make their choice and be escorted to a room; you will then be informed who is to attend her. Allowing perhaps five minutes in order that she may prepare herself, you will then put on one of the gowns which you will find hanging in the cupboard there' (he pointed to a corner) 'and will go to her. You will be expected to behave satisfactorily in her presence. That is to say,' he went on sternly, silently rebuking a laugh from Harry, 'you will endeavour to satisfy her physically but you will also behave as a gentleman is expected to behave. The manner in which you make love is entirely a matter for you, but you are expected to match it with what the lady requests or seems to expect, and not to force upon her any attentions she does not request, remembering always that here the more normal state of things is reversed – the lady does not exist to slake your passion, you exist in order to make her happy. Is that understood?'

Again there was silent approbation.

'Very well. Only two more points. Firstly, remember that the ladies behind the screen can clearly hear what is said in this room, for there is no glass behind the screen, so be careful in your language. Secondly, you are not to make appointments to meet any lady away from this house, and anyone discovered doing so will be instantly dismissed.'

He paused.

'Are there any questions? No?

'Well, you may have wondered why I asked you to divest yourself of your clothing on this occasion. In fact, three ladies are at this moment behind the screen and have been observing you.' At this there was a general stirring, each man reacting in a different way – Ben crossed his legs, while Harry threw one leg from the *banquette* to the ground, displaying his male parts with ostentation. Spencer drew himself up even more erectly in his chair, while George lay his hand along the length of his instrument, attempting – but failing – to conceal it.

'They will now make their choice, and three of you will be asked to go to them. Of course this will not suggest that those of you who are not chosen are in any sense inferior, and indeed, you must not feel this upon any occasion.'

Whereupon he left the room, and the boys looked extremely uneasy, glancing out of the corner of their eyes. Only Harry, with what seemed perfect equanimity, smiled towards the screen with a sort of easy insolence, at the same time reaching down between his thighs to lift the trappings there as though for our inspection, at which I felt Polly positively shiver at my side.

We rose to our feet and made our way back to the other side of the room, where by now Philip was waiting, and had pulled the curtains. Blinking in the light, Aspasia said: 'Sir Philip, I congratulate you.'

'They'll do?'

'Admirably.'

He looked at me, and I nodded my approbation.

'You have done splendidly,' I said.

'And you wish now to try the goods?'

I looked at Aspasia.

'I have the first choice? Then I choose the older man – what was his name? – Spencer,' she said.

I was slightly surprised; I would have thought that most of her gentlemen friends were of a certain age, but it was not for me to criticise or show any emotion. I turned to Polly.

'Well, if it's all the same to you,' she said, 'I'd like the first one, with the wicked eye.'

'Harry,' said Philip. 'And Sophia?'

'George,' I said.

Polly giggled.

'And the best of luck,' she said. 'Shall we send for the surgeon now, or later?'

'Mmm,' I said with mock solemnity, 'I feel merely that I have a duty to the cause of research!'

We made our way each to one of the small rooms, where for myself I was not long in attaining a state of nature. A soft knock at the door was followed by its opening, and the appearance of the splendid figure of the young negro, clad in a brilliantly white gown, which no doubt seemed more pristine than upon the bodies of any other of the young men.

From my position upon the couch, I smiled, and beckoned.

He was – as I suppose was to be expected – somewhat nervous, but walked over and stood uncertainly at the couch's side. Again I smiled, and this time had a glimpse of those white teeth as his lips also parted. I reached up to the single tie which caught the robe together at the waist, and pulling, undid it. The edges parted, and at first it looked as if there was no body beneath, so dark was it, but then he shrugged it from his shoulders, and stood before me in all his beauty. My eyes fixed, whether I would or no, on that one feature which must startle any beholder. And seeing my gaze, he could not but smile again, and stepped forward so that reaching upward I could hold in my hand that amazing limb – it was as though I caught at a forearm, except that it was utterly pliant.

I drew him down to me, and he laid his body along mine, warm and smooth, the skin feeling almost oily, and that remarkable limb lying up the whole length of my belly, the tight, hard, wiry hairs below tickling as he pressed against me. Throwing at once my arms about his shoulders and my legs about his waist, I felt a certain stirring, and stroking the length of his back, lightly tickling the curve of his buttocks, all the time taking between my lips his own thicker lips, I endeavoured to rouse him, and then rolled over and raised myself to inspect the effects of my labours.

What was my surprise to see no change at all – or, rather, a change only in angle, for his tool remained of the same size, though it was now utterly firm. Seeing the expression on my face, he said softly: 'I hope I don't disappoint you?'

In answer, I bent and kissed the now unyielding flesh.

'We are different from your men,' he said. 'We do not grow – we are already big!'

I did not care; the unusual sight of that shining, blue-black skin had captivated me, and placing the tip of his prick within me, I slowly pressed down until it disappeared within my fluid lips, then gently moving, while he lifted his head. With an expression that suggested that the experience was somewhat new to him, he paid my breasts the compliment of kneading them with his marvellously soft, thick lips, at the same time gripping my waist to encourage my movements.

If he was young, he was – unlike, for instance, Chichley – either practised in love-making, or somewhat insensitive, for I twice rose to ecstasy, and still he lay, his instrument perfectly firm. Finally, worn out, I was forced to lift myself from him and lie at his side, panting.

'I am sorry,' I said, 'you do not find me sufficiently attractive?' – for I hate to leave a man unsatisfied.

'Not at all, ma'am,' he said, 'it is simply . . .' and he looked embarrassed.

'If there is any way in which I can help?'

In answer, he raised himself, and throwing one leg over my body, sat astride me, and while his left hand played about my body, with his right he rubbed his instrument with a positively angry vigour, while to make the sensation perhaps more effective I caressed his cods at the root. Within a minute, his action being so violent that I feared he would do himself a damage, he gave a sigh and one or two drops of white liquid fell upon my belly.

'You see, ma'am,' he said, 'I must employ such vigour that I might injure a lady . . .'

I was sure that some ladies would welcome so remarkable a motion, though given the size of the instrument I doubted whether my body could have sustained it. But he was looking embarrassed and guilty, so I reached up and kissed him upon the cheek.

'That is of no concern, George. Thank you.'

We lay for a moment in comfort before he rose, and taking a cloth wiped my body and then handed me my clothes before bidding me farewell and leaving me to complete my *toilette*.

Polly and Aspasia were curious, when we met a little later, as to my experience, but I told them they would have to try for themselves, thinking it would do no harm that they should think me capable of accommodating a thing so large as they thought George's tool to be, *in extenso*! They themselves had been well pleased; Spencer was, Aspasia assured me, a gentleman of experience and sympathy, while Polly's choice, the athletic Harry, proved sufficiently active and courteous, though 'a rough stone' as she said, comparing him to the girl Moll, at Brook Street – as indeed in my mind I had done.

Leaving them to take tea, I made my way to the boys' room, where I found them all dressed, and announced myself as the mistress of the establishment (which George took with some surprise, and the rest, I thought, with some envy of him). We would open the business, I said, in five days' time, with an evening party by invitation only. They seemed entirely satisfied – especially when I handed them a guinea each for their trouble in coming this day – and so they made off, already it seemed on friendly terms each with each.

Chapter Nine

The Adventures of Andy

Affairs in Brook Street went on with remarkable quietness, the girls settling to their work with all the professional zeal for which one might have wished, and with what seemed an almost remarkable degree of mutual friendliness. This merely underlined the wisdom of Frank's decision to employ them as a group rather than hunting the streets of London for a random collection of women, most of whose time might well have been occupied in distressful rivalry and internecine jostling. Even Moll, previously unknown to the others, was popular, enjoying the opportunity of 'setting the girls right' about London low life – as she put it – while she in turn was ready to learn from them that degree of discreet but affable behaviour which she was all too ready to agree she lacked.

Business was brisk from the first, then as time went on and the reputation of the house was noised abroad it became almost too much for our seven ladies to cope with, so that from time to time Aspasia herself was forced to attend to the requirements of superfluous guests – though 'forced' is probably the wrong word, since she was in general more than happy to celebrate the rites of love with any personable visitor who showed her polite attention.

There came a day, however, on which we found ourselves in the early part of the afternoon, almost for the first time, without a clientele – a result, we supposed, of its being blustery and unpleasant weather, for normally there was a knocking at the door not much after one o'clock, the earliest time at which we admitted friends. We sat for a while in idleness, then Frank took himself off with Aspasia to Bond Street, where he was to search for some cloth with which to furbish a fine summer room which he was building into the garden at the back of the house, to give us some additional capacity. The girls and I, in relaxed mood, began to talk. First I told them of my capture by the press gang (which I have recounted in an earlier volume) which they heard with some excitement though without surprise, for living for the past few years near the coast they were not unfamiliar with those villains who plunder the streets of our towns to conscript our able men for the naval service.

Having exhausted my tale, I asked whether one of them would not in turn regale me with the story of her life, and after some hesitation, Xanthe agreed.

'I was born,' she said, 'the daughter of a county family near Brighthelmstone, my father a merchant in a good way of business, and my mother with a charm which made her the belle of the neighbourhood. However, when I was no more than seven years of age my father's business suffered a blow so serious – through the late wars – that in no short a time he was declared bankrupt, and we found ourselves thrown upon the streets. Even those who had seemed our greatest friends – for such is man's inhumanity – now deserted us. My father survived only a few nights of inability to afford my mother the comfort to which she had been used all her life and, though the poor woman made no moan, in a fit of awful remorse he strangled her and then threw himself from the cliffs, leaving me to wander in the cold night until found by a neighbour, who for a while gave me shelter, then sent me to the care of my paternal aunt in a small village not a hundred miles from the town.

'My aunt's husband was a mere journeyman, making his living by whatever came to hand – throwing up a partition at a small charge, mending a roof here, laying a floor there. He was not an unpleasant man, and though he seemed to me to be old, had in fact perhaps about forty years. His wife, my aunt, was friendly enough to me, but immensely scornful of him, perhaps due to the financial expectations raised upon her marriage, which had never been fulfilled. One of the results of this was her refusal of all those rights a man might properly expect of a wife, as I now realise, though at the time, without the slightest knowledge of commerce between the sexes, I was not aware of this. I knew not the reason for his fidgets, nor for his fondness to have me play upon his lap when his wife was without doors in various games, which I now suppose were all designed so that my body should come as closely as possible into contact with that part of his own most sensitive of his lady's neglect. He was, however, careful not to display his naked self to me – perhaps more for fear that I should in childish prattle tell of him than because he did not wish to do so – and I reached the age of thirteen years without knowing more of man than was apparent from his street-appearance. Nor, though my own body was beginning to take on the appurtenances of womanhood, did I know anything more of that than I could discover by the examination of it in a mirror, or through the enquiry of my own fingers.

'When I was sixteen, another person had joined the household, a pleasant young boy named Robin who had come to help my uncle in general by carrying his tools and making himself useful about the house. He was older than myself by two years or so, and considerably more knowing, so that he was continually looking for excuses to come upon me unclothed or to brush against me in the passages of the house or make jokes which I did not understand. This was far from disconcerting to me, for starved of the company of young people of my own age I welcomed his presence, and we got on well enough, though without my understanding why he should find my company preferable to that of boys of his own age.

'However, I soon discovered the reason, for on a day when he had been given the afternoon off, my aunt was visiting her cousin four miles away and my uncle had driven into Brighthelmstone on some errand or another, I took myself into the garden at the back of the house and in the balmy summer's air stripped off my clothes and bathed in the sun – something to which I was then much given.

'I must have dozed in the warmth, for the next thing I knew I suddenly awaked (perhaps through the sound of a breaking twig) to see Robin standing over me, his eyes wide and his mouth thrown open, obviously enjoying a sight such as in eighteen years he had never been offered before. I too found a sight to interest me, for Robin's breeches, at second hand, were not only worn but positively in holes, revealing firm flesh, and at the front a strange bulge where the cloth was lifted away from his body in an odd fashion; perhaps by a stick which he had in his pocket? Yet some instinct – together with his thrusting his hands into his pockets in an attempt to conceal it – told me that was not the explanation.

'I had no idea of covering myself – and indeed in raising myself had even thrown my legs somewhat apart, which peculiarly captured Robin's attention and seemed to move him curiously, for a groan escaped his lips, and in a moment he dropped to his knees before me and appeared to be pleading for something, but in words so incoherent that I could not understand him. However, clearly I could not have seemed unsympathetic, for in a moment he reached out his hand and I felt it very gently but firmly placed next to my body in a place to which no human hand but my own had ever adventured.

'It will come as no surprise that after a first pleasant shock from the unfamiliarity and unexpectedness of the movement, I was not inclined to consider his attentions impertinent. I wondered whether perhaps he wished me to reciprocate the motion, so placed my own hand as high up upon his thigh as I could reach from my recumbent position, whereupon he fell to his knees the better to enable me to explore the strange elongated shape I discerned there. It was more pliant than I had expected, and at the end nearest the body seemed to be decorated with two ball-shaped appendages whose purpose I could not guess at, but which were certainly attached to his body, and seemed by nature to be somewhat tender, though upon my weighing and trying them, pleasure seemed to be conveyed.

'My curiosity was at once enlarged and, reaching for his hand, which was still familiarising itself with my body, I prevented it from further progress and informed Master Robin that should he wish to continue his explorations, he should strip as bare as myself. This was not a notion repugnant to him, for almost before I had concluded, his shirt and trousers were thrown to the ground, and I saw before me my first manly machine, no less intimidating than beautiful, no less frightening than exciting, for even in one so young it was of considerable proportions, not only in length but girth, and in its proud standing assertion of boyish masculinity displayed an admirable elegance and firmness.

'For some time we were content simply to explore each other's persons, but then became more adventurous. With that instinct with which the Creator has endowed humanity, we were soon attempting to place ourselves in such a position that those parts of our bodies in which we already felt uncommon pleasure should be more delightfully engaged, rather than provoked merely through the agency of our digits. It can be imagined that we had no idea of applying our lips to such a task, they being as yet untutored even in kissing let alone any more adventurous activities.

'Such is the ingeniousness of youth that we soon discovered how it is that a key unlocks a door, and within a few minutes had made each other happy. After a short pause, we were once more at the game, and so occupied in it that we did not hear my uncle return, so that coming into the garden he saw two bare young animals cavorting freely upon the grass, limb entwined in limb with a fine lascivious freedom, enjoying an activity which he himself had been denied for some years – for I suppose he was of far too nervous a disposition to engage with any other woman than his wife.

'To cut a long story short – for I fear I grow tedious – Robin found himself, from lying between my thighs, flying through the air, while his master, pausing only to open his clothes, took his place with such an enthusiasm that he came off even more quickly than the boy had done, and was as quick to recover and offer another bout. Despite the fact that, plundered so thoroughly upon a first engagement, I was more than a little sore, I cannot deny that I thoroughly enjoyed the occasion and continued to relish a two-fold engagement – for though my uncle now crept to my bed at every chance that offered, and was madly jealous of the boy, he could not turn Robin away for fear the lad would inform my aunt. So almost every night for sixteen months I was enjoyed by one or the other, and between them learned as much as any girl of my age needed to know about the pleasure that can be obtained from congress. One contrast between them was that my uncle (for the reason of preventing my being with child, though I knew it not) introduced me to congress from behind, which far from abominating I actually came to enjoy, especially when it was accompanied by other manual dexterities, and I still occasionally persuade my gentlemen to take me so, sometimes to their displeasure but often to their surprised delight.

'Our eventual discovery by my aunt – which was of course inevitable when we were all living in the same house – put a stop to our enjoyment with an argument loud enough to apprise the whole of the village of the circumstances. Indeed it made an end of my living with my relatives, for unable to countenance life without even the few comforts my uncle's house provided her, and so unwilling to leave him, my aunt turned me away. Driven to Brighthelmstone and left there to sink or swim, I found myself upon the streets, and but for the happy circumstance of my encountering that very evening our dear friend Mrs Jopling Rowe, must have come to a far worse pass than that in which I now find myself.'

Applause greeted Xanthe as she finished her narrative, and – not, I thought, without a sly glance which promised some secret about to be revealed – she persuaded her friend Rose tell her own story.

'Mine,' Rose said, 'is a simpler tale, and one known to everyone present except you, sir. But it might, perhaps, amuse you in its somewhat unexpected conclusion.

'An orphan, I was chosen by Mrs Jopling Rowe from a house on the outskirts of Brighthelmstone, and taken straight to the place where you found me. I discovered more friendship there than I had encountered during the relatively short course of my previous life, and was so grateful to Mrs Jopling Rowe that I would have been happy to reward her by my aquiescence in a fate far more unpleasant than that for which she designed me. Though to tell the truth I was far less pleased than my friends by the attentions both of the kindly gentlemen who made me a woman, and those others who later were eager enough to pay me the compliment of making me their bedfellow.

'I felt myself, indeed, to be entirely unsuited for the profession for which I was chosen. And not only that, but inferred that something was missing from my life, for my

friends were always recapitulating, almost boastfully, the
pleasure they took in the embraces of certain of their gentlemen friends, while in the arms of the most handsome of
those who courted me I felt nothing but impatience that
the affair should be over. Their beards chafed my skin, the
hairiness of their bodies was unpleasant to me, and the
forceful bucking of their ridiculous bums encouraged me
rather to laughter than to passion.

'So dispirited was I – considering it a sad lack in my
nature – that after a while I found it impossible not to dissolve into tears after each such encounter, until one day
Xanthe, coming into our room, found me in such a state
and enquired if someone had insulted me or been more than
usually rough, reminding me that Will was always within
call should I require assistance. But continuing to sob, I was
able after a while to confess what I was bitterly ashamed of
– that I was completely lacking in that proper feeling which
the others possessed, that clearly I was unnatural, and that
I was bitterly jealous of the pleasure that was felt by the
others in an occupation which at best bored and at worst
nauseated me.

'But had I never felt such pleasure? Xanthe enquired.
Even (and she excused herself for asking an indelicate question) when I had employed my own fingers, as all girls did in
their youth? Yes, I admitted, there had been such pleasure,
but a lonely pleasure of that kind was not what I sought,
and was I never to experience it in the arms of another?

'Her reply was to lift her dress over her head and to take
me in her arms, naked as I was from my recent encounter
with Mr Miners, a Brighthelmstone fishmonger. I had of
course many times seen my friend unclothed, for no modesty
of that sort existed between us. We had even embraced each
other innocently, but I had never so eagerly clasped anyone
as I now clasped my dear friend, and with a passion new to
me, which she clearly reciprocated, for as my breasts pressed
against hers, and her thighs parted so that mine could
insinuate between them, our bodies shook with an emotion
we scarcely knew how to contain. So complete was my
surrender to that embrace that it was without the least surprise that I found myself lowering my head to take between
my lips those delightful buds that broke from my friend's

charming breasts. Nor, on feeling her body respond to my embraces, was I amazed to find my own way to that grove where sweetness resides and there graze upon those soft brakes, so much silkier and kinder than the rough pasture (if you will forgive me, sir) that surrounds the base of that great oak with which men love to batter us.

'The pleasure of that afternoon taught me how to love and continues to comfort me to this day, for though I have learned, I trust, to comport myself so that the gentlemen I entertain believe me to enjoy their embraces, yet I must still counterfeit the ecstasy that I genuinely find in the arms of my dearest friend' – with which she leaned forward to plant a kiss upon Xanthe's cheek, who received it blushingly and looked about to protest. Rose put a finger to her lips, and went on: 'I must tell you, lest you reach a wrong conclusion, that my friend's pleasure in her engagements with men is unfeigned; but she is kind enough also to delight in my company, and you will I think in neither case find us wanting in our duties to this house. But you wished to hear our stories, and there is little point in telling them unless honesty is a requisite.'

There was, I thought, a slightly uneasy silence as Rose's story ended, and I soon realised that the ladies waited with interest my reaction – upon which I took Rose's hand and kissed it, saying that I was honoured by her confidence and would respect it, and that I had every faith in her loyalty and professional deportment. Whereat the atmosphere immediately lightened, and we all laughed.

'And who will be next?' I enquired. 'Constance, will you not give us your narrative?'

'I too,' said Constance, 'was an orphan, and at an early age was taken in by a tailor and his wife of Brighthelmstone, less as a daughter than as a maid of all work, for from my earliest years I remember nothing other than what was virtual slavery. Up at five o'clock in the morning cleaning out the grates, and to bed at ten at night after waiting upon my master and mistress, who liked to feel they had a much larger establishment than was indeed the case, for they were

of no class or consideration in the town, and their neighbours laughed at their pretensions.

'Unlike Xanthe, I did not even have the pleasure of being
introduced to love by some vigorous lad, and at the age
of sixteen had known nothing more gratifying than
housework – for even in summer I was kept indoors, with
no time of my own in which to take the air and no garden to
the house in which I could snatch so much as five minutes'
breathing.

'Where I found the courage to run away even from so
unpleasant a life, I know not, but finally I did so, leaving
one afternoon when my master and mistress were both
from home, and happily was discovered by our friend Mrs
Jopling Rowe as I wandered along the edge of the sea positively intoxicated by the fresh air, the sunshine, and the
bright blue of sky and water. Had it not been for that
beneficent lady, Lord knows where I would have found
rest. But discovered I was, and she took me in, looked after
and educated me with the same assiduous care she devoted
to my friends.

'There was some difficulty when I discovered for what
occupation she intended me, for my former master had
been notoriously religious, given to reading the Bible at all
hours, and had convinced me that to have any commerce
with men (not that I understood his words) was to be for-
ever damned. Mrs Jopling Rowe was not of that opinion,
and persuaded me to accede to her wish that one of her two
friends should introduce me to the pleasures of the bed. I
did not find these as lacking in interest as did Rose, yet was
far from welcoming them as did Xanthe, and determined
merely to put up with them in deference to my good mistress,
and to make the best of things.

'I was by no means discontented with my fate – indeed
happy that provided I was prepared to tolerate the
fumblings of those gentlemen who from time to time visited
me, I was to enjoy a life of comparative leisure and considerable comfort. No woman could fail, after a time, to be
cognisant of those little attentions which best please a man,
and I found that a little pretence at enjoyment – for the
gentlemen like to be flattered that their bodies are irresistibly
attractive to the female sex' – and here she glanced at me –

'resulted in my being popular enough to pay my way.

'My other great pleasure was the open air, for after so many years of being starved of it, it was delightful to me to bathe and run upon the beach in a state of nature, for, except at the height of the season, the beaches near to us are devoid of people, and what people use them for bathing will have no truck with the modern conceit of bathing clothes. And I loved to take my ease in our secluded garden. By this, my body became after a while completely brown, which I found an advantage, many gentlemen deeming it an interesting contrast to the milk-white flesh of ladies of fashion.

'It so happened that on one occasion a visitor, a former seaman in a somewhat drunken condition, attempted to force Cissie to a kind of commerce she was averse to, and it had taken three of us all our strength to subdue him – indeed, it was only the shrewd employment of a full bottle of wine applied to the back of the head, by Xanthe, that finally concluded the altercation.

'Mrs Jopling Rowe decided that it was time that there was a man about the house, and going off to Brighthelmstone returned not with a man, but with a youth of some twenty years, strong and intelligent, whom she employed as a general handyman, and who should give her ladies any help they required.

'I dare say that Will (which was his name) thought that he had died, proceeding straight to the Elysian fields. And upon seeing him, for he was comely enough, one or two of my companions may have felt that some entertainment was at hand rather more attractive than that offered by the somewhat elderly gentlemen who usually came to the house for the purposes you know of.

'However, as it happened, I did not hear of Will's engagement,' nor did I know upon what day he was to come,' here there was general laughter and expressions of disbelief, upon which she insisted, 'Nay, but 'tis true! So it was that in the heat of an afternoon I was asleep in the costume of Eve upon a grassy hillock in a corner of the garden – that very corner to which Mrs Jopling Rowe dispatched Will in order that he should tidy up a brake of bushes.

'It was there I first saw him. He had taken off his shirt

against the heat of the sun, and was wearing only an old pair
of pantaloons rather too big for him, so that the piece of
string with which they were secured having loosened, they
hung about his hips, revealing a slim waist and an
entrancing swelling towards the twin spheres of his back
side, which was towards me. Indeed, in the very failure of
his clothes completely to conceal the figure they veiled, he
was unconsciously accomplishing what we women pur-
posely design – the advertising of our charms by a discreet
and apparently negligent revelation.

'Will was of course unaware of the picture he presented
as he stood at work, the muscles beneath the light brown
skin of shoulder and back reacting to the pressure upon the
handle of the rake he wielded, a fur of brown hair running
across those shoulders, then down his spine to that very
point where I clearly saw the beginning of that cleft dividing
a posterior which promised to be so charmingly round, so
enchantingly limber, that my eyes almost pierced the cloth
in their attempts to uncover it. How I wished that that string
would break, and the covering slip from those lower limbs!
Or that some circumstance should permit me to loosen it!

'But now I speedily closed my eyes, for turning to spy out
more ground for raking, he suddenly saw me – lying, as I
have said, clothed as Eve was when Adam first saw her in
that other Eden. I almost felt his eyes devour me, afraid to
re-open my own for fear that he should take fright, for I
may admit that for the first time I was conscious of a positive desire to be clasped by a pair of male arms!

'Happily, I need have had no fears, for Will, unlike
myself, had been raised in a large family in which the
presence of four sisters and four elder brothers had resulted
in that easy familiarity which had made him aware at a very
early age of what woman expects from man. My eyes still
closed, I heard soft footsteps approach, and then a rustling
of clothing, at which I could no longer pretend but opened
my eyes to that view which can never fail to impress a
woman – that of a splendidly formed cock in full anticipation of pleasure, springing from a dark cloud to stand
against the furry background of a firm, small belly. Seeing
me open my eyes, Will stood for a moment, hands upon his
hips, his trousers kicked from his legs, and far from

attempting to conceal his eagerness for congress, he positively advertised it. He was waiting, as now I suppose, for a word of protest from me, or some sign that I found the prospect unattractive. No such hint escaped me, which he properly took for acquiescence, and kneeling between my legs bent to press a tender kiss upon my willing lips while his hands, rough with work but tender with an eager mildness, clasped my bosom, then moved down to my waist, and finally drew my thighs even more widely apart while he lowered himself. As I looked wonderingly down, struck dumb with surprise that the approach of a male appendage so obviously ravenous should fill me rather with delight than with apprehension, he placed its pouting point at the entrance to my cunny, already swamped with the eager juices which stood ready to render its passage the more easy. Slowly, its long length slid within me – so slowly, so gently, yet with such determination that the sensation of that gliding motion made me almost faint with pleasure – until our fleeces met, and with gradually increased pace he began to swive, my hands the while embracing what felt to me like the soft pelt of a satyr, so completely were his limbs covered with enchanting and velvet fur.

'Need I express the pleasure our encounter brought? The sun shone down charmingly upon his body and mine as they acted and reacted in delightful unison, and I cried out again and again with pleasure – until fetched by the sounds Xanthe and Rose came running to see whether I had injured myself! Then, seeing the quality of the injury and the instrument which was inflicting it, they paused to applaud, whereupon a shudder ran through Will's body as joy erupted from him, before lifting himself from me he reached for his small-clothes and attempted to cover himself.

'Myself, I was much beyond shame, and simply lay upon the warm ground, legs apart, the dew still falling from my most satisfied part. And in a fit of laughter my friends tussled with my lover, trying to drag his breeks from him, and eventually forcing him upon his back where, in no ill humour, he suffered them to examine his fallen staff, and – such was their expertness – revive it to a full stand, whereupon Xanthe in no time had removed her meagre clothing and was ready for him.

'But with a blush, he protested, "Lady, forgive me, but I have ever been of opinion that man should cleave to one woman at a time – and this is she!" – pointing at me.

'If I was astonished, it was no more than they, for in the nature of things we had grown to regard men as always craving some other creature than the one with which they were yoked. Well, I thought, that time might come, but until then . . . And reaching up, I captured my friend again, so that in a moment we were once more enjoying each other, while my two friends consoled themselves as best they might.

'From that time to this, Will has remained my lover; I cannot say my only lover, perhaps, since my profession precludes that declaration, but he is the man to whom my love, rather than simply my body, is given, and I have grown adept at pretence where other men are concerned. Will, I think, will be happy enough when we have saved sufficient money for me to retire from my present occupation, but until then, he tolerates my way of life.' At which Constance looked for a moment I thought sadly, but then smiled again: 'And that is my story,' she said.

Now Sally and Cissie looked at each other, and encouraged by Xanthe offered their narrative – first one then the other contributing a word or two, for they were so inseparable and so alike that it had often occurred to me to wonder whether they were not sisters. But no, they said, they were merely cousins, and the latest to attend Mrs Jopling Rowe's academy, having come there only at the beginning of the previous season from the city of Bristol.

There, they had grown up in two houses, side by side, belonging to their fathers – brothers who were successful merchants in the town. They had been raised to the age of fifteen with every advantage of polite society – for which, Sally asserted, they were not especially grateful, for the activities of society were ineffably boring to them, they having no enthusiasm to learn music, or set dances, or the art of conversation. Indeed, most of their time had been spent playing in and around the docks, and wishing that they had been born boys so that they could sail upon the tide for the Indies or for China.

'However,' said Cissie, 'we were soon to discover another occupation to please us even more than playing shadows to the cabin-boys upon the Bristol quays.'

In answer to their incessant pleas – they had been continually in each other's company from the very time they could stand and walk – their fathers had broken down the wall between the attics of the two houses and there had constructed one room which the cousins shared. It contained their beds, their clothes and all they had, and was sufficiently large (running as it did over the tops of both houses) to provide a quarterdeck for any nautical games of exploration they devised.

One warm day in summer, not long after their fifteenth birthdays (both celebrated in the early weeks of August) two young men appeared. They had been engaged by the brothers as apprentices to learn the trade of chandling, and were given a room upon the second floor of one of the houses, lying immediately below the girls' room.

'These were the first young men with whom we came into daily contact,' said Sally, 'for Cissie and I could not be familiar with ship-boys, and our families kept us apart from other young men expressly because they had it in mind to marry us to two particular gentlemen, with an eye to empire-building on their own account. And so, meeting Mr Gossage and Mr Mordan – if only at breakfast (at which we now became more punctual than before) and supper – we discussed them thoroughly between ourselves when we had retired to bed. They were reasonably handsome specimens of young manhood, being perhaps seventeen years old, upright in carriage, well-built, and with that happy elasticity of limbs which in youth gives each movement such interest and charm.'

It was Cissie who suggested a means of studying these two young animals more intimately, and borrowing a carpenter's auger from a quayside store, bored two holes with it in the floor of their room, above that of the two young men.

That evening, retiring early upon the excuse of a headache, they waited until they heard the shutting of the door of the room beneath their own, and then applied an eye to their peep-holes – to find themselves immediately rewarded with the sight of Mr Gossage and Mr Mordan entirely unclothed, lying face downwards upon their beds in the heat of the evening, each studying a book of mathematic problems upon which they were to be examined upon the morrow.

'Our pleasure was only equalled by our inquisitiveness,' said Sally, 'for it was the first time our eyes had fallen upon any naked creature other than the small boys who daily bathed from the quaysides, and whose childish bodies had quite failed to raise in us the emotion we felt upon studying the long backs of the two young men below us, so pleasantly relaxed, the swelling of their backsides so differently shaped to our own.'

'And here,' said Cissie, 'we stripped ourselves, the better to examine the difference in contours between our own arses and those of the gentlemen which consisted in theirs being rounder and higher, as it were, while ours were fuller and more oval. We could not but agree that their bodies were far more interesting than our own and longed for a further exposure, for between the legs of Mr Gossage, which were thrown open, a shadow seemed to conceal something which might we believed be of unusual interest.

'After a while we thought of withdrawing, for though we lay upon pillows, the posture of applying an eye to a hole in a floorboard is without charm. Then Mr Mordan threw down his book, and said (for with the keen ear of youth we could hear, though dimly, their conversation), ''There's enough of study, Bob. A little exercise before we sleep?'' To which his friend in reply placed his own book more carefully upon the floor, and to our surprise rose, walked over to his friend's bed, and sat down, resting one hand upon the other's bum and sliding it between the cheeks until it rested upon that something which lay there, and which now seemed to stir.'

Thereupon, Mr Gossage turned over and rose to sit at his friend's side, enquiring what was the record, whereupon his friend replied that it stood at three foot ten. And without further exchange they reached into each other's laps and began to make there with their fingers motions which clearly gave each other pleasure, and which soon offered their onlookers equal joy in presenting to them their first view not of one but of two male instruments in their full glory. When these erections had been achieved, each took hold of his own tool and manipulated it with increasing enthusiasm until from the end of each sprang a positive jet of liquid, which flew through the air to some distance before falling upon the bare boards of the room. Thereupon Mr Mordan produced from his wallet a tape, and measured the distance between the bed and the point at which the furthest jet had fallen, then announcing that his friend had 'broke the record', which now stood at three foot ten and a half. At this they laughed and, having wiped the floor – and themselves – with their handkerchieves, fell into bed, leaving the girls to withdraw from their spyholes and retire together to satisfy their own excitement with manual dexterity, after which they discussed for no short time what they had seen.

They continued to repair, each evening, to their spyholes, despite the redness of their eyes due to a draught, which caused some concern to their mothers, and were regularly regaled with the sight of those two handsome young men in a state of nature, who seemed almost to pose for them, so completely did they exhibit their every limb to such advantage. The cousins were regularly reduced to near an hysteria of desire to come at them – until, one evening, they overheard Mr Mordan and Mr Gossage, lying together upon one bed and toying with each other in an idle manner, discussing *themselves*. How Mr Gossage would like to teach Miss Cissie 'what it was for' (whereupon he caressed his tool in strangely meaningful manner), while Mr Mordan longed, he said, to set eyes upon Miss Sally's Thing. At this Sally rose from the spy-hole and, beckoning to her friend, left the room quietly and repaired down the staircase, opening the door of the young gentlemen's room without knocking. To the girls' pleasure the admired ones showed no sign of reticence, but rose to welcome them as though they were expected guests, striding towards them preceded by that limb in which the cousins were most keenly interested.

Motioning to her cousin to shut the door behind them, Sally at once lifted her smock over her head, providing Mr Mordan with a clear view of what he had so eagerly wished to see, and which, falling upon his knees, he saluted with a kiss.

To the girls' surprise, Mr Gossage burst out laughing, joined by his friend, and the two young men embraced them closely. 'We thought that would bring you!' they exclaimed, and confessed that from two small piles of sawdust upon the floor of their room they had discovered the holes in the ceiling at the first, and from that time onward had been putting on a display each night for the girls – even speaking somewhat above their normal tone of voice in order to enchant them further.

The boys and girls then took immediately to bed, where Cissie and Sally learned at first hand the game of love. But alas, after two weeks of such pleasure their parents became suspicious. One evening, engaged in a game at fours in which no part of a single body was sacred to any participant, they heard loud cries from the girls' room above, where, finding their children absent and noticing the holes in the floor, their mothers had applied their eyes. They had been rewarded by the sight of Sally drawing the cheeks of Mr Gossage's fundament apart in order more closely to caress with her tongue what lay between, while the latter's face was buried between her thighs. And Cissie stood leaning, her hands upon the bed, while Mr Mordan caressed her ready bubbies, enjoying her from behind with a fine bucking motion like nothing so much as the ready randiness of an enthusiastic ram.

The long and short of the discovery was that the two mothers had the vapours, breaking off to fetch the fathers. The fathers dismissed the apprentices and, seeing in the local newspaper an advertisement by a Mrs Jopling Rowe for young ladies prepared to offer themselves to a life of sacrificial devotion to the care of the elderly and lonely, dispatched Sally and Cissie immediately to her care with the desire not to see them again until they had repented – which, their being inclined rather to enjoyment than repentance, had not yet occurred.

The story was told with such enjoyment and zest that I could not but relish it, and indeed we all broke into applause. Shortly afterwards, two guests made their appearance, and the business of the day began. I took myself thoughtfully from the room, and spent some time conversing with Aspasia, now returned. I had always inferred that for young ladies of our sort the ordinary commerce of love must be undertaken as a duty, but that it should be so often so little pleasurable dismayed me somewhat; when performing the act, was their smiling, were their cries, always a matter of deceit?

Yes, said Aspasia, that was more often than not the case, for they felt not infrequently that the men who used them were not doing so in real admiration – 'but to be plain, Mr Archer,' said Aspasia, 'as a mere substitute for their own palms, rather than in genuine compliment to their beauty.' Often, having made love to them, their partners would be contemptuous, even rebuking them for their way of life; complimenting them on their beauty before the act, they would go out of their way to criticise, after it.

'Leaping between our thighs,' she said, 'men feel they have won, and that letting them win we have in some way insulted them. The performance over, they feel sullied and disgusted, and they show that disgust to us. It is, of course, themselves that should examine their own actions. All we wish, in the situation in which we find ourselves, is that the gentlemen who visit us should be reasonably friendly and pleasant – which many of them are, and in my position I can afford to turn the others away. It is more difficult in a house, but I shall attempt to build here a clientele of agreeable visitors, for women need affection more than men, and I see no reason why our girls should be altogether deprived of it.'

I returned to my room in a thoughtful mood, for everything that Aspasia said was true, and though the girls were charming, there had been in the career of each more than a touch of neglect. I determined to do my part to see that their lives with us were as pleasant as possible given the circumstances of their occupation – to which, I must say in our defence, none had voiced objection.

Chapter Ten

Sophie's Story

What an agreeable time we had of it during the first months or our experiment! I would not have desired things to fall out better. The boys all got on well together, there was no sign of jealousy or envy, no quarrelling. Our custom built from the first moment to a regular trickle, then to a stream of visitors – not so broad nor so fast that we could not cope with it, but not in any way diminishing, so that we were all kept busy and in profit.

Polly, Philip and I also lived in perfect amity. Though Philip spent perhaps more time abroad than I had anticipated, he carried out his duties to perfection, watching the boys with particular care, correcting any faults, making a suggestion here or a comment there which might result in an easier or more pleasant running of things. Polly continued to please me with a perfect combination of service and friendship. The only thing that cast a slight shadow upon the weeks was my being deprived of male companionship.

How, you may ask, could this be, when I was surrounded by the male animal, whose sole employment was to please ladies? But the truth is I felt disinclined to lie with my boys (as Andy and my half-brother did, I believed, with the girls in their establishment at Brook Street). While as for Philip – the truth is that the original interest he had shown in me seemed now to have declined until our association had become purely a matter of business.

I realised this on the very occasion of our first opening our doors, when I had spent the evening showing off our lads to some fourteen ladies. The conceit of escorting them to the window where they could see, while remaining unseen, was a perfect success. All the boys had determined – the room being quite sufficiently warm for it – to appear entirely unclothed, and the contrast between them, and their carefully contrived 'careless' poses invited admiration. Harry, as usual, seemed to flaunt his maleness, William generally lay face downwards upon a *chaise longue* so that his neat buttocks positively invited a caress, Spencer's lean and hard body was displayed to advantage as he played billiards with Tom and Ben, while George – why, the mere appearance of his splendid instrument attracted attention in whatever attitude he stood, sat or lay!

Our choice – or rather Philip's choice – was proved immediately to be an excellent one, for the ladies who visited us by no means showed any disposition particularly to favour one boy above another, though a certain type could not resist George for his uncommon and individual appearance, black men being very rare in London at this time. And it was interesting that William was similarly always attractive – ladies showing, as I have noticed, a peculiar delight in the rear *façade* of a gentleman's body, even those who would have preferred a more muscular figure often finding the prospect of connexion with William an irresistible temptation.

At the end of our first evening, then, I was in a state much enlivened from the continual spectacle which I could observe but not taste (and you will remember that at this time the bodies of the boys were still unfamiliar, and thus the more attractive to me) and the general excitement of the evening – not least the satisfaction of our guests, each of whom was enthusiastic in praise of the entire operation.

It was past midnight when all were gone; some few of the boys had accepted our invitation to sleep in the house, and Polly had taken herself to bed in exhaustion, while Philip and I sat over a bottle of wine discussing the arrangements, and any changes which might profitably be made – which were few. He had thrown off his coat and sat in his shirt, while I had still the low-cut single muslin dress I had worn all evening, and – as was the fashion – nothing beneath it. I could not but believe he was entirely conscious that my body invited his attention, yet he sat at my side without offering any caress, nor even responding to my placing my hand upon his thigh as I leaned to refill his glass with claret.

At last, my need being considerable, I bent to offer him a

kiss, lifting his hand at the same time in my own and placing it upon my breast, but to my surprise he returned my kiss in what can only be described as a fraternal manner, looking extremely uneasy, and after a while was forced to admit that he was not ready to embrace me. My look must have spoken volumes, for he immediately laid a hand upon my shoulder and assured me that he had the utmost regard for me, 'but,' said he hesitantly, 'sadly 'tis the case with me that after one passage of love with a lady I am usually unable to repeat that pleasure . . .'

Why should this be, I enquired? To which he said he did not know, but volunteered the following story of his life, which went some way to suggesting an answer.

'I was brought up, as you know,' he said, 'by my uncle, in this very house from the age of three years, at first with a nursemaid, but then from my sixth year by a series of male servants who all treated me extremely well and kindly, so that I have no complaints upon that score. My uncle was something of a recluse, but having had the responsibility of caring for me placed upon his shoulders had determined to do the best he could for me, and gave me a great deal of his company during those hours when I was not engaged upon lessons given me by a series of excellent tutors.

'This did not mean, however, that I swiftly became educated in the ways of the world, for my uncle's main interest was in literature, and he spent almost his entire time with his books, so that my experience of a social life was to sit at the other end of a long table, opposite him, giving my attention to some volume of prints while he merely looked up from his work from time to time long enough to throw me a word. After a while I begged to be excused such daily attendance, but was still confined to the house and, in summer, the gardens.

'I thus reached the age of puberty without any sensible knowledge of the corporeal world, and it was something of a surprise to me when my uncle – certain stains upon the bedclothes having I suppose been reported to him as evidence of my young manhood – summoned me one day to the library.

' "My dear Philip," he said, "you are now, I understand,

a man. That is to say, hmmm, you are ready to perform that manly act which our creator devised for the propagation of the species. You will be aware that humanity consists of two sexes, the male and the female.''

'Here I interposed to say that while I was indeed cognisant of that fact, it was a theory short of demonstration, for the entire household was male – even to the cook, a Frenchman, and those who cleaned the place. I might have gathered from this my uncle's taste in the matter, had it been a subject I ever considered, but as it was, since the world outside these walls was unknown to me, I had no means of knowing what was normal and what unusual. However, to return to my narrative, my uncle continued thus –

' ''I have always found the female sex to afford me little pleasure – neither that of conversation, nor that of companionship – though I believe that I am perhaps relatively unusual in this. I have no wish of course to dictate to you, my dear boy, the slightest course of action, but I have suggested to Robert that he may place himself at your disposal, and that if you find yourself unsatisfied he should enable you to continue your education – um – elsewhere.''

'At which he dismissed me to leave the room knowing little more, I must confess, than when I had entered it. I was entirely unaware of the kind of pleasure to be offered me by women, whose pictures in the prints, even naked, had stirred nothing in me. Nor did I take in the fact that my uncle was, as I now realise, confessing to me his inveterate addiction to his own sex (if only infrequently) as bedfellows, and suggesting that I should follow his example. This, however, was soon to be made clear, for outside the door of the library I found Robert waiting for me – a charming young footman whom I had of course seen about the house, and who had always been affable. I had understood his main employment to be as body-servant to my uncle, but without fully understanding that the term, in this case, meant more than it might have done in another establishment.

'Robert greeted me kindly – he was perhaps five years older than myself – and said, ''Now, young Philip, I believe I have something to teach you?''

' "I believe so," I said, not knowing how else to respond. To my surprise he placed an arm about my shoulders, and walked me upstairs to the guest bedroom next my uncle's (only used, to my knowledge, once or twice in the past five or six years, when he had legal or literary advisers to stay in the house). Entering the room, Robert turned and locked the door, and then to my surprise clasped me in his arms and planted a smacking kiss upon my lips.

'I did not, I confess, find this unpleasant, nor did I demur when, first removing his own clothing, he stripped me bare, admiring my person as he did so – for my young prick automatically rose at the caresses he conferred upon it, not in the least to my amazement as those four or five months past I had been delighting myself by manually persuading it to such a stand.

'The pleasures we then enjoyed, however, were surprising, for it had not occurred to me that what I had assumed to be a private matter could be so charmingly enhanced by sharing, nor that it would give me pleasure (as, after a while, it did) to imitate the actions of my lover.

'Not to prolong a description which must surely be somewhat uncomfortable to your ears' – which was far from the truth, for indeed his account fascinated me – 'I took much pleasure from Robert's attentions, and Robert, I believe, found his additional duties not at all unpleasant, for my uncle was an old man and though generous and undemanding, was no great ornament to a counterpane.

'One afternoon as Robert and I lay bathed in a delicious perspiration after a passage of love, he asked whether I never felt it a lack that I had never lain with a woman.

'No, I did not, I said, for what could they offer that someone of my own sex could not?

'Well, said Robert, there were attractions, as he himself knew who was as attached to them as to any other, though at present circumstances confined him to the embraces of myself or my uncle. It seemed a shame that I should not be permitted familiarity with a female, for, he said, why should I live my entire life with one hand tied behind my back? And apart from enjoyment, what if I wished to procreate? This was something no male lover could aid in. And in short, he persuaded me to try, and to that end introduced me to his sister, who lived with her mother not far from our gates. She was a fine young woman of some twenty years or so, sufficiently spirited to welcome the opportunity of congress with a handsome young boy (as I confess I was) some years her junior – any more than she had been, it seemed, to reject the embraces of her natural brother, for they had grown up in a small Kentish village far from the city, and in those days incest flourished where the roads were bad.

'I had not been prepared for my first passage with Robert himself, my uncle having given me no hint of what was to come. However, I set about preparing myself to meet Mary (for such was her name) much in the manner of a schoolboy preparing to meet his master at examination time. I pored over those books of prints in my uncle's library which depicted unclothed young women – and such there were, for my uncle was a genuine student of art, and if his preference was for such prints as those of the paintings of Master Caravaggio, or the sculptures of Michelangelo or Donatello (and he had a fine miniature copy of the latter's charming portrait of David upon his desk) he also had portfolios of other great paintings. Among these I paid especial attention to Mabuse's *Hercules and Deianeira,* where the entanglement of the couple's lower limbs speak an enchantment not to be contradicted by the intent gaze with which they fix each other, to Corregio's *Io*, in which a young woman positively swoons in the embrace of a cloudy monster, and to the numerous paintings of mythical scenes in which gods and goddesses pay less attention to ruling the mortals in their care than to affording each other carnal pleasure.

'I also asked Robert his advice on my approach to his sister, upon which he asserted that the things I did with him, with the addition of one other which he explained as best he could, and which sounded no less exciting than curious, would equally delight her. But would she permit the liberty? I asked. He responded that he was in no doubt of it, insisting that nothing we had done together would render his sister uncomfortable.

'We met one late afternoon in the boathouse which still stands upon the bank of the river. The sun was low and

striking warmly across the lawns. My new friend, Mary,
was awaiting me when Robert ushered me through the door
and stood guard outside – for my uncle might not, he said,
be happy at my choosing to sample the company of a young
woman. My first sight of his sister struck me instantly as
the counterpart of a scene from a painted Elysium, for she
lay quite naked and face downward upon a rug on the
floor, her legs slightly parted, and a cushion beneath her
throwing her fine posteriors into a prominence highlighted
by the golden rays of the sun striking upon them.

'Divesting myself of my clothes, I advanced at her beckoning gesture, and sat at her side, laying a hand upon the
warmth of her back, and without considering it, I found
myself stroking the length of it in a languorous gesture
which clearly did not displease her.

'Somewhat to my shame, I was not at first able to display
any enthusiasm for the congress to come, for my nervousness took from me the power of standing. However after
a moment or two the purring of contentment which greeted
my caresses conveyed to me a warmth which soon resulted
in a display of vigour. This led Mary to place her hand
admiringly upon my firing-piece, then to bend her head to
examine it more closely, and finally to take it between her
lips with a liquid embrace which sent a shiver of pleasure
through my limbs. In a moment, I persuaded her to turn,
and saw before me the first vision it had been my privilege
to encounter of an unclothed female.

'My delight at the sight of her ravishing breasts (and
indeed at their tender weight as I hesitantly put my hand to
them) was unfeigned. But I could not restrain a start of
astonishment as my eyes passed from them down over a
gently undulating belly, carrying in its centre the deep dent
of a bewitching navel, to her most secret place – for there,
in violent contrast to the smooth surface I had observed in
paintings or sculptures, I saw a nest as plentifully endowed
with hair as that which lay between my own thighs!

'Mary could not but observe my amazement and, opening
her legs, took my hand and placed it between them, where I
found a resilience and softness far from repulsive. You
can imagine that soon I knelt to examine the phenomenon
more closely – and what was my surprise, as I watched,

caressed and kissed, to see certain changes there which seemed to mirror those others I had observed in my own and Robert's bodies: the swelling and opening of the lips even as I touched them, the alteration in the colour from pale pink to a deeper, purplish-red, and the appearance of what seemed a miniature replica of my own swiving instrument which, when I touched it with the tip of my tongue, I conceived from her movements and pantings gave Mary not inconsiderable pleasure. Indeed, as I continued to apply my tongue and lips to the purpose, fascinated by the effect I was producing, her response became more hectic until at the last her body bent like a bow and a thin wail escaped her lips.

'As I lifted my head, I saw Robert as he still stood in the doorway give me an unmistakable signal of approval, then by moving his forefinger within a circle made by the finger and thumb of his other hand, he indicated that I should mount his sister in the manner which, in a drawing remarkable more for its explicatory than its artistic effect, he had demonstrated to me.

'Rising, then, from my position at her side, I knelt between Mary's still open legs, and lowered myself so that my prick was at the entrance to the portals and paused, afraid that the action would prove painful – for without boasting I must repeat that my instrument was of uncommon size for a boy of my age. But she impatiently raised herself so that already its tip slipped between her lower lips, lubricated to a fine mucosity by a combination of my own saliva and those natural juices which we extrude in moments of passion, so that it was almost without effort that I found its entire length sheathed in that welcoming scabbard, while sinking upon her body, breast to breast, I felt her hands upon my shoulders and back, stroking and caressing, then slipping between us, toying with my cods in much the same way as her brother was used to do.

'It would take a more adept tongue than mine to define the difference between lying with her and lying with her brother. He and I had never played the beast with two backs in the manner of the sodomites, for though he had offered, I had a natural objection which he could not overrule. But in lying together face to face, the natural friction afforded by a rapid motion of our bodies naturally brought about the completion of our pleasure in much the same manner as it did, now, with his sister – except, of course, that in the latter case the culmination was reached in a manner rehearsed by man and woman for a thousand years. The smoothness of Robert's body counterfeited that of his sister; the roughness of a hairy man is of course most different – but I need not say this to you, my dear Sophie, who must be sensitive of it.'

Philip paused for a while, and looked at me as if to discover whether I was offended. But I was indeed more interested than affronted, and begged him to continue.

'My story is nearly over,' he said, 'but now comes the sad part, for though I was delighted by my experience, and grateful both to Robert and his sister, I found that the next time I met with the latter, my piece remained unfired, and despite her most ardent caresses, failed to stand. And indeed I found I could not be enthusiastic to repeat our mutual pleasure, though she much wished it, and was I fear offended. And ever afterwards, though I delight in the company of women, I find that once I have been granted familiarity, I am unable to repeat my tribute to their beauty – which explains my failure to pay you the compliment you richly deserve, and will no doubt receive again and again from happier men.'

I could find no reply, except to wonder at it.

'I wonder, myself,' said Philip, 'and sometimes believe myself cured, for I have no difficulty in accommodating ladies who are strange to me – as your brother will testify, my visit to Brook Street being a test of my manhood which I did not fail. However, though that young lady was the most energetic and handsome of partners, I fear that were we to meet again I would disappoint her.'

It would be fruitless to pretend that I was not myself disappointed, and though I attempted to smile sympathetically, and kissed him upon the lips as I left, I was not comforted. If I had been warm before, Philip's description of his passage with Miss Mary had heated my blood yet further, and I went into the hallway intending at the very least to make for my room and find what comfort I could in solitary caresses. But who should be standing ready to leave the house, but Harry. He looked at me and smiled, and almost before I was conscious that my good resolutions had crumbled, I found myself looking deep into his eyes with what meaning I could convey – and that, I fear, as open an invitation as any of the ladies in Brook Street could offer.

He was not slow to react, for in a moment he had lifted me in his arms and turned back into the room, now deserted, where my boys were usually seen at home. Placing me upon the couch, he took my dress at the throat and with one movement tore the slender material from me, almost in the same moment releasing his trousers and falling upon me. Dewed as I was by the liquor which had fallen in my excited state, his sturdy prick, strong as an iron bar, seemed to mount to the top of my stomach, and beneath my hands his brown body seemed carved from wood, so firm and hard was it. In my pleasure, I tore the shirt from his shoulders and sank my teeth into his flesh, which persuaded him to a violence of motion which sprung both from that and, I would guess, from a kind of desperation, he having already given service to three women during the course of the evening, a scant hour separating the last from the present time.

Concomitant with his ardour was the slowness of his body to respond – a delight to me, for no less than three times was I roused to the utmost rapture, draining my body of its gathered tensions, before with a shudder he ceased, and lay upon me as if dead, his body and mine in a lather of perspiration which as we drew apart smothered our lower parts in a foam.

I wriggled from beneath his weight and, reaching for a towel, wiped his limbs, then with a push turned him onto his belly and dried his back and buttocks – noticing as I did so a strange, triangular mark upon one, a birthmark almost hidden by dark hair.

He should sleep there, I told him, for I was sure he was now too exhausted to leave, and should he do so, so heated that the night air even of a mild evening might do him harm. Covering him with another towel, and bending to kiss his cheek, I left him already asleep and went to my own bed, conscious that I might have been foolish in favouring

one of my boys rather than another, yet also that the
occasion was a remarkable one.

As I walked to the door, I am almost sure that I heard a
rustling movement behind the screen below which we had
been exerting ourselves. The only person who could have
been there, watching us, was Philip. Should I have been
angry, or pitiful, or scornful? I could not, at the time,
decide, but I did not allow the episode to create difficulties
between Philip and myself – we were too much friends,
and indeed were making too much money, to permit anything to place a barrier between us. I felt more sorry for
him than anything else and, conscious of his comings and
goings, wondered how he satisfied those itches which must
surely be in the blood of so young and virile a man. Was he
a secret but confirmed twiddlepoop? But this was clearly
not my concern.

Two weeks or so after the episode I have just related, I
received an invitation to the marriage of Viscount Chichley
with the Lady Frances Brivet, which was to take place at St
George's Church in Hanover Square (where I recalled Sir
William Hamilton married that lady who subsequently
became the mistress of the Lord Nelson). Then to supper at
a house in the Portland Place, Mary-le-Bone, which
Chichley had built upon the edge of the great field where a
thousand cows grazed, providing much of the town with
milk. It was the only house north of Devonshire Place,
between which and Hampstead no other dwelling was to be
seen.

It can be supposed that much time and some expense was
spent upon my preparing a costume for the occasion which
would distinguish me among the horde, yet would not be so
distinctive as to mark me out as more a cynosure than the
bride, who wore a magnificent white gown from France.
Chichley was splendid in a simple and plain cut-away coat
in dark blue with a crimson waistcoat – not a wrinkle to be
seen either in these or in the breeches which clad his fine
lower limbs.

The ceremony was conducted with great solemnity by a
bishop carried from the provinces for the occasion, who
seemed amiable enough but was clearly unused to such a

great occasion, and whose voice in consequence was
scarcely heard beyond the immediate vicinity of the altar.
Afterwards, we were taken by a fleet of coaches to
Chichley's mansion, which proved as handsome and sufficient as one might have imagined, furnished according to
the latest taste.

There, a splendid feast was set out to which the large
company gave full attention. This banquet quite exceeded
in profusion anything I had previously seen: a first course
of oyster sauce, fowls, fish, soup, roasted and boiled beef,
boiled turkeys and celery sauce, pigs' feet and ears, tongue,
fricandeau, saddle of mutton, roast woodcocks, wildfowl,
spinach, bacon and vegetables, followed by creams, pastry,
cauliflowers, *ragoût à la Française*, cream, game, celery,
macaroni and pastry, and finally by walnuts, raisins and
almonds, apple cakes, pears and oranges. The wines comprised champagne (white and rosy), burgundy, claret,
sherry, Hermitage (red and white), Constantia, Sauterne,
Madeira and port, with small-beer for those who wished it.
Toasts were made, first to the bride and groom, then
between guests, until for the most part those at table were
virtually incapable of remaining upright or making themselves understood. Coarse jests and erotic undertones
became common and, by nine o'clock, half the company
did not know whether they were on their heads or their
heels. The reverend and learned orientalist of the British
Museum (having taken glasses of brandy at intervals
between his port wine) at length fell helpless and insensible
beneath the table, from which position he was lifted by the
servants, at Chichley's direction, and placed in a hackney
coach to be driven to his lodgings.

My friend had remained, I noted, remarkably sober, as
did his bride. The latter had received me coolly, her husband with a warm pressure of the hand, yet no other sign of
familiarity, which indeed I would not have expected of
him. And I could not but recognise, regarding them as they
sat at the head of the table, that they did not behave as
a newly married couple might have been expected to behave
– there was no exchange of smiles, no catching of hand in
hand, let alone the placing of lips to palm or cheek to cheek,

but a solemn politeness as formal to each other as to the least known of their guests.

Finally, though neither of them seemed eager for it, the moment came when the bride must prepare for bed. Her bridesmaids rose and, taking her by the arms, wafted her from the room. Chichley immediately caught my eye, and with an appealing look excused himself from the table (no difficult task, since those around him were to a large extent insensible) and went from the room – again looking at me as though to invite me to follow him, which after a moment's pause, and looking about me to make sure I was not particularly observed, I did. I found myself in a small ante-chamber where my young friend stood moodily, one arm stretched along the mantelshelf, staring in melancholy fashion into the dying embers of a fire.

'Well, my lord,' said I, 'this is no mood for a groom upon his wedding night!' – whereupon he took me by the elbows, and tears started to his eyes.

' 'Tis like marrying a sister,' he said. 'She is no warmer now than when we were eight; she is insensible to all approaches, cold and distant, with no notion of what could please a man – and here am I shackled to her for life!'

I did not enquire what had led him to this pass; it must, I supposed, have been a family requirement. Nor, I confess, did I resist when he clasped me to his bosom and pressed kisses upon my lips, for he was clearly in search more of sentiment than of carnal comfort, contenting himself with my lips and making no motion to improve the occasion.

I said nothing, and he said no more, but in a while and with a deep sigh released me – just as a group of his drunken friends broke through the door with incoherent cries. Taking him by the shoulders they bustled him off, myself following, into the hall, up the stairs, and through a door into what must surely be the bridal chamber. So indeed it proved, for once through the door I saw the bride, sitting upright in the large four-posted bed, now clad in a simple shift cut sufficiently low to show a breast which no man would be ashamed to covet, but which she was protecting by a modest inflexion of her hand, her looks betraying neither fear nor lust, but simple indifference and a desire that the charade should be immediately terminated.

Meanwhile, not content with snatches of bawdy song which they were in no position to render either melodiously or even coherently, Chichley's friends had undone him at the waist, encouraged by the women who now resembled harridans rather than wedding guests, and were engaged in stripping him bare. Off came his coat, his shirt, finally his breeches and stockings, and naked as he was born he displayed (as they mockingly drew attention to) a manly part shrunken to the size of a hazelnut. One of the brides-maids (though 'maid' was indeed no word for her) sank to her knees before him and, encouraged by his friends, tried to rouse him to a show of enthusiasm, but signally failed, at which there was more ribaldry which I knew to be falsely founded, having the keenest recollection of the sensitivity and feeling of which his male instrument was capable when aroused by the propinquity of a woman to whom he was genuinely attracted. Finally, tiring of their sport – with a 'one, two and three!' – his friends simply threw Chichley upon the bed, drawing the curtains about it (how grateful he must have been for the relief) and with a final fusillade of bawdy cries, swept from the room.

I paused for a moment. From the bed came only a faint rustling; no other sound, either of pleasure or resistance, and I could not but conclude that it would be a cold night of it – and very possibly, a cold life – for the newly-wedded couple. It was not a fate I would have wished upon Chichley, a boy capable, as I knew, of as much ardour as humour, as much tenderness as high spirits. Damnation, say I, to all made marriages.

Determining to leave the house immediately, I made my way from the room and prepared to descend the staircase – but passing an open door, my eye could not escape falling upon the orgy taking place within the room upon which it gave. On the bed, but also on the rugs of the floor, lay in a variety of lascivious attitudes perhaps eight or twelve persons of both sexes engaged in the performance of every variation of the act of love – not only man and woman in natural congress, but man with man and woman with woman. It was a scene which, painted for the pleasure of exciting lust, or even presenting itself to the senses under different circumstances, would no doubt have excited my susceptibilities. But in this case the persons engaging were so voided, by liquor, of sensibility that their actions were those of animals rather than of men and women – a fact reflected in a certain vicious carnality which divested their actions of consideration, taste or subtlety. This circumstance was underlined when two of the ruffian men, looking up from the women they were swiving and seeing my passing glance, leapt to their feet naked as they were and reeking from their congress, and came towards me with a cry of 'Here's a fine bushel bubby! Come and blow the grounsils, wench!' – which I understood only by their obvious intention, which was to force me to their pleasure.

Inclined though I usually am for pleasure, there were several reasons for my disinclination at that time: the first being my melancholy from observing Chichley's unhappiness; the second my reluctance to throw myself into such a tangle of strangers' bodies as lay before me; the third that the two men who now stood before me were to the last degree unattractive. One was vastly plump, his great belly hanging so low it seemed to be supported only by his pouting instrument (though that, indeed, was not of such dimensions as to bear even a lesser weight), while the second, though hung to a punishing degree, and evidently of such corporeal power as under other circumstances might be promising, was so drunk as scarcely to be able to stand. Even did I not suspect that this would damage the prospects of his continued phallic erection, I was not ready to bear closer acquaintance with that stinking breath which assaulted my nostrils even as I stood some feet away.

However, there was a difference between my reluctance and their insistence, and before I could move, they were upon me, and one, taking my delicate and costly dress at the throat had with one lunge split it to the waist, releasing my breasts, upon which he placed his horny hands. The second got himself somehow behind me and pushed me into the room, where in a moment I stumbled and fell to the floor among the mess of unclad bodies – each of which was too engaged in incoherent pleasure to take notice of my sudden appearance. I steeled myself for the assault to come.

Happily, however, my two assailants now fell out, one

with the other, about which should take me first, and soon
came to drunken brawling, the one planting a fist in the
pendulous belly of the other, who immediately vomited
copiously over several of the lovers nearest to him. This
caused a considerable confusion, during which I was able
to make my escape, flee down the stairs and, clutching the
remnants of my clothing about me, summon my carriage
and return home. Too shaken by the experience even to
speak to Polly, I took myself to a bed more solitary than
Chichley's and, I suspect, as quiet if more content.

Chapter Eleven

The Adventures of Andy

It is a strange fact that even the most unusual circumstances, if prolonged, become common, and that the most remarkable incidents, if repeated, appear unremarkable. If only a few months before coming to London I had been told that I should be occupied in the administration of a house of pleasure, and that during the course of each day I should be continually in the presence of a number of delightful women in all forms of dress and undress, I should have considered myself fortunate. And that such a situation should be anything less than exciting would have seemed strange.

However, as the weeks became months, both Frank and I had to confess to a certain tedium; each day was like the last, and the hours became – to tell the truth – more than a little long, for as was not the case with Sophie, we felt that we should attend at the house while any guests were on the premises, in order to guard the women from possible unpleasantness. Blatchford, Will Pounce and Bob Tippett were of course men enough to outface any physical force with which they were likely to be confronted, but being of no education were easily confounded by a display of superior carriage, whereas I, though humbly born, had by now had considerable experience of putting the unruly of whatever rank in their place, while Frank had a natural haughtiness which gave him authority.

In time, however, we worked out an arrangement whereby one or other of us absented himself and found what entertainment he could about the town, though generally making sure that the other knew where to contact him in case of emergency. I took to practising my guitar once more, which pleased the ladies and gave me also some pleasure, while Frank began to establish himself at a political club nearby, for he had an eye to enter politics perhaps as a member for the constituency in which Alcovary was situate.

I continued to learn a little more about the characters and histories of our friends, though indeed once the bare bones of their stories had been told there was little to add. Moll was the last to tell me her secret, and that in private conversation, for with her somewhat rougher manners she felt partly ill at ease with her companions, friendly and kind though she agreed they were, for indeed never an unpleasant word was exchanged between them.

A knock upon the door one evening was answered by Will and, hearing raised voices and believing that there might be trouble, I went to his aid. I found him denying entrance to a youngster who seemed a little familiar, and who indeed revealed himself as Moll's brother, whom I had seen fleetingly as he left her bed upon my visit to her room in Church Lane. I immediately afforded him entrance and summoned Moll, and having thrown her arms about him they went to a private room, whence eventually he departed and I found Moll in tears. Pouring her some wine and putting my arm about her, I did my best to comfort her and asked what was amiss.

It was nothing, she said, but simply a disappointment. John had come to tell her (and here she whimpered a little) that some hope he had had of finding their lost brother had failed.

Had she two brothers, I asked, and one lost?

Ay, she answered. It was her elder brother, with whom she had grown up. He was some five years older than she, and her companion from as distant a time as she could remember, for they had shared a bed from her being five or six years old. This, she said, had made her familiar with the sight of the male body before she had seen that of any stranger – though it was all in innocence, 'for Harry never touched me in the way of carnality, and whenever I in teasing mood attempted play – as when in the morning I discovered his prick at stand, and came to toy with it as with a doll or other plaything – he would dissuade me. And he only once hit me, which was when I took hold of it while he was asleep, and toyed until, as he awoke, it involuntarily gave forth its juices, whereupon he said 'twas wicked for brother and sister to play so.'

Later she was to follow this rule with John, the young one, and though they were often naked a-bed together there was no familiarity except that of sisterly and brotherly comfort, and though they lived in the closest propinquity they were as moral as any preacher's family.

'But when my mother died,' she proceeded, 'my father having long since left us and she raising us by simple work, the landlord of our small room threatened to throw us out upon the street – whereupon Harry, then only fifteen, assured me that he would support us. But his work as a labourer in a brickyard fell away, and we came into debt. He would go further and further abroad to find employment and so was out when the landlord came and claimed our room, throwing me and John, then only five, into the street.

'I asked to remain at least until Harry returned, but was driven away, so that when he came we missed each other, and despite all my efforts I have not seen him since for eight clear years; though returning again and again to the street in which we once lived, in the hopes of seeing him.

'It was to support myself and my brother, who without me would be forced into chimney-sweeping or some other dreadful trade, that after some precarious years begging for crusts in the streets, and surviving only by the kindness of a few friends, I turned to the work of which you know, though my mother had always spoken much against it. And once I had taken the first step, I found myself quickly too used to the comforts I could purchase by only a moderate effort to forgo them either for me or for John.

'But,' she said, 'I have never lost hope of once more finding Harry, and John had recently heard that someone like him had been seen at work ditch-digging in Southwark. But now he tells me enquiries have led nowhere.'

But how could she describe her brother, I asked, one young man being much like another, and it being so long since she had seen him – for a young man of fifteen may be much changed in ten years.

Indeed Harry had been unremarkable, she said, and it would be difficult to give a description which would not apply to any young man of his age, save that he had a small three-sided red birthmark upon the right cheek of his buttocks – a thing which would come to the notice of others only in intimate circumstances, and which would be difficult to noise abroad without indelicacy.

The wine, of which we had now drunk an entire bottle, had considerably enlivened Moll, and expressing her gratitude to me for having lent her my ears, she began those familiarities which through long acquaintance she had learned provide pleasure to the male sex. And since I was, as ever, susceptible we soon arrived at a mutual warmth, and with my breeches loosened she sat astride my lap with my prick happily housed in that warm and moist habiliment where it was most at home. So, comfortably embraced, we began a second bottle, but before we could turn our attention fully to carnal pleasures, Will Pounce broke into the room without knocking – something which had never happened before.

'Master Archer! Master Archer!' he cried. 'The watch is below and demanding to see the mistress of the house.'

Here was a pretty pass, for Aspasia, pleading a proposed visit by an old friend, had begged absence and been accorded it. And now the very purpose of her presence here was foiled, for she had told us it was entirely illegal for a man to run such an establishment as we had at Brook Street, and there was no woman here capable of impersonating an experienced madam.

In my consternation I had leaped to my feet, tipping Moll inconsequentially to the floor, and now stood there anxiously, my essential part shrunken already to a poor thing.

But Moll leaped to her feet and cried, ' 'Tis no use, Andy, 'twill have to be you!'

While I stared uncomprehending, she sent Will below to equivocate until his mistress came.

'How many is it?' she asked.

'But one,' Will replied.

'Bring him upstairs and give him a glass with the girls, and tell them to make themselves pleasant.'

Will looked at me, but all I could do was nod. As he left the room, Moll already had me by the arm and was leading

me – hanging on to my drooping breeches with one hand –
into the room across the passage where was a cupboard in
which Aspasia kept some of her clothing. Opening it, Moll
seized a gown of purple velvet.

'Throw this on!' she said, and when I hesitated, almost
tore the shirt from my back, so that willy nilly I stripped and
obeyed her. She looked at me critically, and bundling up
two dusters thrust them into my bosom to fill the empty
space beneath the bodice.

'I have always envied you your complexion,' she said,
'and now, with a little help . . .' And taking a dish of powder
which lay nearby she began to redden my cheeks and,
spitting upon a finger, to apply some colour to my lips.

'A bonnet next –' and she reached down one which,
being of an antique style, had side-pieces and when fastened
disguised my head completely. 'Speak in a low voice,' Moll
said, 'do not attempt to raise it. You will know the answers
to the questions he will ask. He may simply be after a bribe.'

This was true, for the constables and watchmen of
London at that time depended for their wages mainly on fees
and perquisites, and were almost invariably extortioners,
connivers at every form of wrong doing, pensioners of
tavern and brothel keepers (frequently of the lowest order)
and receivers of stolen property. It should not indeed be too
difficult to deal with one of them. But still I hesitated.

' 'Tis no crime you commit,' Moll said, 'and if you do
not make a try, the entire venture must fall!'

Perhaps happily there was no glass in which I could see
myself, so I simply obeyed, making my way – almost
tripping over my unaccustomed skirts – downstairs and to
the door of the sitting room, in which I could hear a male
voice among those in conversation. Drawing a deep breath,
I entered to be faced by the girls, whose countenances were
blank with surprise at they saw me, and the back of a man in
dark clothes who, turning, disclosed a face covered with a
bristling beard.

I strode in, trying to restrict my pace to a womanly
tripping.

'Who have I the honour of meeting, sir?' I asked in what
I hoped was a matronly voice (though a hysterical titter
from Cissie suggested I was not entirely successful).

'Watchman Muffin,' said a thick voice. 'You are the mistress of this establishment?'

'I am.'

'May I congratulate you upon these admirable young ladies?' said the watch. 'They show a spirit only equalled by the delightful aspect of their persons.'

'To what, sir, do we owe the honour of this visit?'

'It is a happy part of my duties to visit all similar establishments in order to ensure that they are properly organised. You are . . .'

'Mrs Aspasia Woodvine,' I said (another titter from Cissie).

'May I ask where you attained the experience to govern such an establishment?'

I coughed.

'Ah – in the university of life, watchman,' I finally replied, provoking a laugh this time from Xanthe. 'You wish to inspect the house?'

'No, no, madam, I am quite sure simply from a view of this room that the appointments are excellent, while I need make no comment on the admirable qualities of the young ladies I have already had the pleasure of meeting. Perhaps, however, it might be possible . . .' and he raised his eyebrow in a gesture I thought I understood.

'Perhaps, sergeant, we might offer you the hospitality of the house?'

'My dear madam, it would give me the greatest pleasure.'

Mightily relieved, I asked whether he would care to indicate which of our ladies he would like to show him the hot baths which were the signal distinguishing attribute of the house? But he demurred.

'I had hoped, madam . . .' he said, and stepping forward stretched out a hand as though to place it on my bosom. I felt the blood drain from my face as I apprehended his meaning. But what was this? To my horror, Moll, who had been standing beside me, stepped forward and plunged her hand into the sergeant's beard. I opened my mouth to remonstrate, when with a tug – and to my amazement – the beard came away in her hand, revealing the face of none other than Frank, who a moment later sank almost helpless with laughter into a chair!

I was too relieved to be either angry or amused.

'Forgive me, my dear old fellow!' said Frank, when he had recovered himself, 'but boredom got the better of me, and besides, I was curious to see what solution you would offer were a watchman actually to call. I must congratulate myself on my disguise, which so thoroughly deceived all save one!'

I turned to look at Moll – had she been a part of this plot? But she assured me she had not, and indeed it turned out that Frank had conceived it entirely of himself, and had gone unrecognised both by Will and by the girls.

'I think a revenge should be taken!' cried Xanthe. 'Seize him, girls!' – which they did, and in no small time had stripped him and laying him upon a couch bound his hands and legs to the arms so that he could not move. With the utmost deliberation they then slowly removed their clothing and stood before him in their naked beauty – and though, as I have already said, I was accustomed to seeing each of them in every stage of undress, I must admit that it made a delightful picutre. Xanthe, her fair hair about her shoulders, her arm about her friend Rose's shoulders, their slim bodies, small breasts and slender thighs one a counterpart of the other; then Constance, her skin almost as nut-brown as it had been in the country (for she slipped into the garden at every possibility to lie in the sun, to the pleasure of Will, who would sit admiringly at her side); Sally and Cissie, as like as Xanthe and Rose, but rounder-limbed, their breasts plumper and their hips broader; and finally Ginevra and Moll, each with her peculiarly entrancing points of admiration. I felt my own manhood stir, despite my ridiculous attire, and Frank, bound as he was, had no way of disguising the interest that this display of beauty had for him – a fact to which Xanthe drew attention, saying, 'Look, friends, scarcely yet a display to frighten a lady. But we must see what we can do.' And she immediately took Rose in her arms and, the latter nothing loath, led her to the very foot of Frank's couch and began to kiss and clip her, passing her hands over her person to display its every delight, and compliment it by a touch of finger or tongue. The sight was delightful enough to raise the dead, and Frank's tool soon swelled to its full proportion and, empurpled, stood in approbation of the view offered him. His smile had by now faded, and he was gripping his lower lip with his teeth, determined to be silent.

But how long could he do so? Determined to have my part in the revenge, I threw off Aspasia's dress and, myself prepared for pleasure, took my place between Sally and Cissie, throwing an arm around each pair of shoulders and bending to kiss their pouting titties while their hands found their way, as water does to a vacant channel, over my belly and thighs to stroke and make much of that part of me which longed to compliment them upon their beauty.

By now Frank could not resist imploring his release, but no one took more notice of him than to concentrate even more upon their own pleasure, Xanthe and Rose falling to the floor at one side of his couch, and my kneeling at the other so that Sally could straddle my knees and, as I entered her, I could pleasure her cousin with my lips, while Cissie's hands employed themselves where they might about our occupied bodies.

'But do not forget our master!' cried Xanthe at last, raising her head from her friend's breast; 'Constance, Ginevra, Moll!'

And to Frank's delight, the three girls came towards him – but rather than releasing him, merely sat upon the edge of the couch and made much of him, one kissing his mouth, then flicking his nipples with her tongue, kissing his breast, his neck, his shoulders, catching with her lips at the hair which sprouted from his armpits, his hands the while desperately attempting to catch at the breasts which brushed his lower arms, but always failing to reach them. Meanwhile her friend was running her tongue between his toes, then sucking each in turn as she stroked his calves and thighs. And the third – Ginevra, whose lips were peculiarly adept at it – was bringing his now throbbing tool time and time again to the point of eruption by the most gentle, feathery touch, now upon the tip, now at the base, first running full, liquid lips over its whole length, then merely covering the tip like a cap. When he could release his lips he cried for relief, but Ginevra, whenever she felt by the tautness of his instrument that release was near, would fall to nibbling his cods, or that muscle which runs beneath their base like a second, concealed cock.

Finally, Frank found release, imagination no less than caresses overrunning his body. With a great shout he bent himself into a bow, and like a fountain erupted to a height I would have thought impossible – whereat I, too, for some time in the same critical state, also voided myself into Sally's friendly embrace.

Frank, when he was recovered and had been released, explained that while the whole exercise of his disguise had been, certainly, amusing, it had also been something of an experiment for, he said, the possibility of a real visit from the watch was not something we should entirely discount, and must indeed be prepared for. And though my impersonation of Aspasia had been a brave attempt, he was not entirely sure that it would have deceived the dullest officer for long (nor was I!) and we must persuade Aspasia to train one of the girls to take her place should she be away, though she should always be referred to as the proprietor of the place, while myself or Frank should pretend to be clients rather than having anything to do with the running of the house.

'Will, Blatchford and Tippett we can leave alone,' he said, 'for the place must have its men about both for service and protection. But it would be a pity if the operation should come to a premature end' – as indeed it would, for we, and the girls, were making more money from it than we had ever imagined possible. The girls were indeed delighted, for our visitors, having paid their fees, were only too pleased to leave them more money in recognition of their kindness. We at no time enquired about this, but there was no pretence that it did not take place, and everyone was content that it should.

It was shortly after this that Frank received a letter bearing news that Mrs Jopling Rowe had suddenly died, just after placing the house in which we had visited her upon the market, and that her man of business wished to see him upon an urgent matter. Since it had been some time since we had been out of town, it was decided that we should both travel down to the coast, the weather being now extremely warm, and spend a night or so there not only to deal with whatever business was in hand, but also recreate ourselves. Blatchford was left in charge of the house, though we gave

Tippett and Will to understand that the three were to work together – for indeed we trusted all of them equally – while we hired two good mounts and set out on horseback for Brighthelmstone, which we reached after two days' pleasant riding, sleeping one night at an inn on the way.

We rode out to Worthing, and past Mrs Jopling Rowe's house, the windows of which were all shuttered, on our way to the office of her man of business, a plump and agreeable person who greeted us pleasantly, and immediately asked after all the girls, but particularly Constance (who, it seemed, had been his special favourite). In short, he revealed that just before preparing to sell up the house Mrs Jopling Rowe had made a will leaving all she had to the girls, in equal portions, which would amount to a sum enabling them to retire immediately from business should they wish to. 'But,' said the lawyer, 'they all seem to me to find their life so enjoyable that they will not desire it.' I was not quite so sanguine but of course we delighted in their good fortune and agreed to convey the news to them, while Mr Forfeit (as was his name) would complete the formalities.

'I hope,' he said, 'I have not dragged you this distance without cause, but I felt the matter to be of sufficient import to deliver the news personally, and I travel, these days, as little as possible.'

Not at all, returned Frank, we were glad of the excursion, for we had been busy of late . . .

Mr Forfeit had heard from Mrs Jopling Rowe of our venture, and was now full of questions on the subject, which we answered as completely as we could. Then we asked of him the address of an inn in the neighbourhood where we could stay.

'I can do better than that!' he cried. 'I have a small cottage which is let by the week, in the season, and which happens just now to be vacant; you are welcome to it. I shall send straight away for the girl to go in and open it up for you, and by the time we have enjoyed a glass of claret and a chop – for I hope you will join me? – it will be ready to receive you.'

The message having been sent, we indeed sat down with him, and he entertained us with highly indiscreet anecdotes about the people of the town while we ate and drank. Then he sent us off with his man to the cottage, with the invitation that we should make use of it for as long as we wished.

This little house lay at the top of a small cliff or incline a few feet above a beach. The windows opened to the view of a sparkling ocean, and we were greeted by a buxom young maid who dropped us a curtsy and showed us the place – which did not take long, since it comprised simply one small sitting room with a bedroom over (Worthing becoming so popular that even the smallest cupboard could command a considerable rent in the season).

The girl then departed, with the indication that there were cold meats in the tiny kitchen, together with milk, but that the centre of the town lay only five minutes' walk to the east should we wish to take a meal there later.

It was now one o'clock in the afternoon, and the sun beating down out of a cloudless sky, and sitting in the small garden, separated only by a low hedge from a path which descended to the sea side, we soon became drowsy and, stripping to our trousers, fell asleep in the sun, lying upon the grass.

I woke, some time later, to the sound of whispering and giggling, and half opening my eyes saw against the sky the outline of a row of heads looking over the hedge. It was half a dozen girls, of what age I could not guess, but I supposed not of many years. And glancing to my side I could understand their interest, for before falling asleep Frank, thinking us safe from prying eyes, had thrown off the rest of his clothes, and now lay quite naked to the view, a handsome enough figure to engage the interest of any female.

The girls had seen my movement, however, and now withdrew, so I nudged Frank and, when he woke, informed him of the entertainment he had afforded, whereupon he did not demur, but asked why I did not invite the young persons in!

Soon, cries and the sounds of splashing were heard from below, and looking cautiously over the hedge we saw that the girls had thrown off their clothing and were bathing in the sea – a delightful sight for, as in those days was the custom, they had not crammed their limbs into swimming dresses but were as free as fish, and their flesh so shining in the sun that indeed they resembled strange aqueous creatures, and had they proved tailed we would not have been surprised!

'What do you say,' Frank enquired, 'to our allowing ourselves the pleasure I gave them?' And he began to stride from the garden and when I followed, persuaded me to remove my clothing altogther for, he said, it was our beach, and our right to descend to it and use it in what manner we might. It was they were the trespassers and must bear the consequences.

It can be believed that a considerable furore was consequent upon our appearance on the sands; Frank was utterly assured, and walked down to the water's edge without the slightest diffidence, the sun flooding every inch of his body with light. I was less inclined to display, and hung back, but turning, he beckoned me forward – and after all, why should I be less proud than he? – for I did not suppose myself to be less well built.

The girls for a while pretended not to see us, giggling, screaming and playing in the water, though we could see them casting their eyes towards us as we strode to and fro, when they thought we were not looking.

'Shall we join them?' I asked, but Frank said no, the moment we were in the water they would make good their escape, and he was not inclined to let them off so easily. Whereupon he lay down at ease in the very centre of the small beach, and I lowered myself to his side, the sand warm to my flesh. There, we enjoyed the sight of the girls, now clustered together and wondering what to do, for the sides of the beach gave onto steeper cliffs which were unscalable.

After a short period, they reached a decision, and simply turned and walked towards us, emerging slowly from the sea as Aphrodite did at Petra tou Romiou, the water falling first below their shoulders, then revealing twelve handsome breasts (a feast so ample my eyes did not know which way to glance), and finally hips, thighs and what lay between – only two of them being sufficiently shy to attempt to shield their most intimate parts with their hands.

Their leader was a fine young creature with red-brown hair, who coolly strode up and stood over us, so that water drops fell from her body upon our legs, and the tiny bumps upon her skin brought out by the cold were clear to view.

'Perhaps, gentlemen,' she said, 'you would not object to sharing the sunlight with us? Unless, of course, this part of the coast is your private property?'

Frank smiled, and patted the sand at his side – where without mock modesty the girl lowered herself and sat, and after a pause the others too lay near us, looking like nothing so much as a group of mermaids suddenly endowed with human limbs, and none the less handsome for that.

'I had heard,' said Frank, 'of the beauties of Worthing, but had not thought to encounter so many of them so readily.'

'And we have heard of sea-monsters,' the girl replied, 'and had not thought to encounter *them*, for we come here regularly by permission of Mr Forfeit, and have always previously been private.'

Inclining his head, Frank admitted that he had believed them to be making use of the beach without leave, but now (he said) it was his duty to apologise – though, he reminded her, it was their looking over the hedge that had led to the degree of openness which we were now enjoying.

'Not at all,' said the red-headed one, and reaching out drew her finger down the side of Frank's shoulder, along the lower side of his breast to his hip, and along the line where the leg joined the trunk to the very point at which, in a cluster of hair, lay a limb now betraying some enthusiasm for the propinquity of so many delightful creatures. And, indeed, I felt a similar stir of interest, and was conscious that the ladies were also cognisant of this.

'You will forgive me for suggesting,' said Frank, 'that young as you undoubtedly are, none of you seem to be entirely unfamiliar with the male form?'

'Not,' said the young lady, 'so familiar that we decline any opportunity enabling us to examine it further – which I trust explains our perhaps overweening curiosity of half an hour ago, and may even excuse a further familiarity which the present situation suggests.' And she placed two fingers upon that part of my friend's anatomy which (I guessed) was all too happy to welcome their caress. At the same time there fell upon my own shoulders a pair of hands which then slipped down until they embraced my breast, while against my back I felt the gentle pressure of two cool breasts, the nipples of which – whether by cold or desire I could not say – were hard as pebbles.

In a moment we were submerged by a tide of flesh, at first cool from the recent embrace of the sea, but soon, from the warmth of increasing lust no less than of the sun, torrid as in any bed-couplings.

To what extent those embraces were the product of genuine curiosity it was impossible to discover, but certainly the nymphs seemed intent upon exploring every secret we had to offer, their fingers prying into each corner, their eyes devouring each surface. I was too much the object of the attentions of three of them, myself, to observe the activities of the others, but could imagine that these were the counterfeit of those I was welcoming. One was intent upon kissing every part of my face, her tongue probing the whorls of my ears, the corners of my eyes, my nostrils, passing under the corners of my chin, inserting itself between my lips. At the same time I could feel another turning my hands, sucking each finger in turn, exploring the dint of my elbow and the pit of my arm, tiny nips – delicious as 'twas painful – of the flesh announcing her progress from shoulder down across the platform of my breast. And the third – ah, most adventurous! – was examining my middle parts, exploring the dint of my navel and pulling with gentle lips the hairs of my belly before proceeding to the tops of my thighs, biting the skin there with appreciative pleasure before thrusting my knees apart with her hands so that she could feast her eyes upon those parts normally more modestly possessed. I felt, after a while, her fingers weighing my cods, then the soft gesture of lips enclosing each in turn before proceeding to that instrument which (I need hardly say) was by now almost aburst with appreciation of such tender attentions, measuring its length, and with gentle fingers pulling the skin away so that its lambent tip could be annointed with tender kisses.

But now, the other two, bored with the more frequently displayed parts of my body, joined with the third, and I had the unaccustomed view of three female heads – two blonde, one black – pressed close together as their owners concentrated attention upon my essential maleness; a sight balanced by that a few feet away, where Frank was in the same circumstance. We caught each other's eyes, but our situation was so grave that we could not even raise a smile, simply observing each other's state, now approaching a remarkable fulfilment. I began to draw short breaths as my pleasure rose, placed my hands upon the nearest shoulders I could reach, felt the lips move softly, gently. . . . Then, I apprehended a shadow fall across my face. With a rude shock, just as the curve of pleasure was about to reach its height, all sensation had ceased, and opening my eyes I saw my three tormenters standing looking down at me – as the other three stood regarding Frank, who half sat with the same dumbfounded expression as myself, and the same distended and unsatisfied limb between his thighs.

'Gentlemen,' said the leader of the band, 'we now bid you good afternoon.'

And without looking back, they strode to the spot a few yards away where their clothes lay, and in a moment – women's dress still being scant – had drawn them on, and were climbing the path away from the beach.

Uncomfortable though we were, we could not but laugh at their revenge and rising, thrust ourselves immediately into the sea to cool our ardour – looking up as we did so to see several arms raised in farewell from the line of girls walking back around the cliff towards the town.

We enquired of good Forfeit who the young ladies might be, and were informed – to our amusement, for we had thought they were perhaps the denizens of a girls' school in the area – that they were in fact employed at a place of entertainment in Brighthelmstone which was the equivalent there of our house in Brook Street. 'I frequented it when younger,' said the lawyer, 'but I find the exertion now too much for me, and give myself only the pleasure of allowing them to use my beach for their summer entertainment, when they drive over. For them to bathe at Brighthelmstone would be impossible, since they are so well known about the town.'

We did not tell him of our adventure, but could not but be amused at our being so taken in. We shared a lonely bed that night, but the next afternoon repaired to Brighthelmstone, and for a modest fee – considerably less than that we charged in Brook Street – gave ourselves the pleasure of a renewed acquaintance with our tormenters, enjoying the joke at our expense, but this time reaching a conclusion which left us – and at least two of the girls – replete. We then returned to London to give our girls the happy news of their enrichment – which however would not be real for some weeks, until the estate had been gathered, the house sold, and an official determination made of the property. Whether they would then wish to remain in our employment was a question with which we would have to deal when the time came.

Chapter Twelve

Sophie's Story

I heard with some amusement of the prank brother Frank had played upon Andy and the girls in Brook Street, but was warned by Philip that nevertheless I might expect a visit from the local watch – partly because my uncommon arrangements would arouse their curiosity – 'but also,' he said, 'because I am in no doubt they will wish to take a proportion of the profits which they will have heard accrue to us here.'

When I asked about the degree of payment I would have to make, he could not say, for it would depend, he said, upon the cupidity of the officer concerned.

I had not long to wait for this information, however, for one evening Polly answered the door to a ring and found not a lady eager to inspect our wares but a man from the local watch-box, who demanded to speak either to Philip or myself – asking for us by name, so that it was clear he had some knowledge of our proceedings.

As luck would have it, Philip was out on one of his private excursions. I received the man in the front room, which he entered unceremoniously and without more of a greeting than a simple nod in my direction. He was a large, sturdy man, with close-cropped hair and a bullying manner, carrying his enormous rattle as if it were a lethal weapon. He minced no words.

'You will have expected a call, no doubt, ma'am,' he said. 'Such a house as this may be tolerated – if only for its originality – but since we are not paid by the public to protect organisations of this nature, you will agree that it is proper you should make a contribution to our expenses.'

I did not ask what expenses could have been incurred when he had to the best of my knowledge never set foot within a half-mile of the house, but merely enquired how much he wanted. To my amazement, he answered that ten pound a week would suffice – which indeed was a ridiculous sum, as I told him.

'Whether you pay it or not is a matter for you,' he said absently, 'but your friend will be aware that his own association with the place will be enough for us, should we wish it, to close the house down – much though we would regret the inconvenience to the wives of West London.'

All this time he had been wandering about the room, casting an eye on the decorations; then he came to the screen and went behind it.

'Ah,' he said, 'I have heard of this convenience, and indeed 'tis a remarkable one.'

It was a quiet evening, and all but William were occupied; he, as was his wont, and no doubt hearing voices and believing that a visitor was approaching, was lying face downwards upon the *chaise longue*.

'Very handsome,' said the sergeant. 'You will not object if I sample your wares?'

I must have looked uncomprehending, for 'Come, come, madam!' he said. 'It is a pity for such a delicate rump to be unoccupied.'

'This house is not for such purposes, sir,' I said. 'Moreover, William would not permit it, and at all events I have no room – they are all occupied!'

'I doubt that, ma'am, but in any case the boy need not move from his present position, which is admirable for my purpose! Nor will he, my strength being superior. His consent is not necessary – indeed, resistance adds a spice. You will prepare my little – *pourboire*? I shall be only a few moments; this display has quite engaged my fancy!' With which he strode from the room.

Amazed, I called to William through the screen. He rose and came towards me, but in a moment, the door opened and the sergeant burst into the room, unclasping his belt as he came.

'Come, ma'am, watch if you please, but do not intervene!' he cried in my direction, seizing the astonished William and throwing him once more upon the couch, then without pause lowering his breeches to reveal an enormous instrument – one which might have been welcome to some ladies, but from which a male person could only have shrunk, as William did, who alas was far too light of build to think of opposition!

Pausing only to spit on his hand and anoint his instrument, the watchman leapt upon William and thrust at him, whereupon the unfortunate young man gave out a howl of pain which might have been heard clear across the house – and indeed was, for in a short period the door opened and in strode Spencer, who had just said farewell to the lady he had been entertaining, and crossing the hall had heard the disturbance. In a moment he apprehended the situation, strode to the couch and, seizing the watchman by the arm with surprising strength, hurled him off William's body and clear across the room.

'Out!' he said to William, indicating the door. The latter rose and without argument left the room while the watchman, with a roar of anger, climbed to his feet. But in the face of this man, much larger and more powerful than himself, Spencer maintained a silent dignity which halted him in his tracks – and then, the watchman seemed to recognise him, for he looked curiously at his face.

'Why, Sergeant Gross,' said Spencer.

Despite himself, it seemed, the watchman came to a sort of attention – ludicrously so, with one leg still entangled in his breeches, and his shirt tails barely concealing his now much diminished person.

'How interesting that we should meet again.'

The man was silent.

'I had heard that you were attached to the watch hereabout,' said Spencer. 'It is fortunate that you have called upon us, for I am sure you will wish to use your influence to ensure that we are not troubled by the attentions of your colleagues?'

To my astonishment, the man – though looking unhappy – nodded.

'Sir!' he said.

'I trust not to see you here again,' said Spencer, 'and you will kindly refrain from paying your attentions to any of my colleagues. No doubt many unfortunate lads in the neighbourhood will be as used to your depravities as some were in the field – here, we enjoy more conventional pleasures. In short, should we see you here again I may be forced to mention the circumstances of La Haye Sainte, and even perhaps to communicate to the Duke himself some facts about that unfortunate affair.'

The watchman seemed to shiver. 'No, sir, of course, sir, I shall – we will – you shall not be troubled.'

'Well, sergeant, I suggest you cover yourself and leave,' said Spencer, seating himself negligently on the corner of the billiard table. Scrambling into his trousers, while still somehow comically giving the impression of remaining at attention, the sergeant saluted and left the room almost at a run – so speedily indeed that by the time I reached the hall, the front door had already closed behind him.

I entered the back room, where Spencer was now reading a newspaper.

'Ah, good evening, Mrs Nelham,' he said as though nothing had happened.

'My dear Mr Middlemas,' I said, feeling that a little formality was the least I could afford him, 'how on earth did you do it?'

He raised an eyebrow.

'Ah, ma'am,' he said, 'I had not realised you were an observer. Oh, 'twas nothing – I happened to have met the man before.'

'Evidently,' I said. 'But how did you subdue him? What is La Haye Sainte?'

He showed a marked disinclination to explain – but on my pressing him, admitted that he had served as an officer under the Duke of Wellington at the late great battle of Waterloo, and had been with the King's German Legion at La Haye Sainte, just towards the centre of the Duke's main force. The French forces had mounted a severe attack on this stronghold, and one English sergeant's nerve breaking, he had cried defeat. Whereupon the Dutch-Belgian brigade which was assisting had broken and run, and the position had only with the greatest difficulty been held, only a last-minute charge of the cavalry – Royals, Scots Greys and Inniskillings – saving the situation.

'I see,' said I, 'and the cowardly sergeant . . .'

'Exactly, ma'am,' said Spencer. 'I happened to know the man, and recognised him. I said nothing at the time; we

were all frightened enough, and no man can be fully respon-
sible for his actions under such pressure. The Duke himself
made attempts to find the culprit, but none but I could
identify him, and I refrained – and for that reason sadly
was forced to leave the service. But I see nothing wrong in
using such knowledge to protect this enterprise.'

'Indeed, I am most grateful – we all must be.'

'I pray, ma'am, that you will not inform the others,' said
Spencer. And indeed was determined that I should not do
so – nor, especially, make known the fact that (as was
clearly the case) he had held an officer's rank upon the
occasion of the battle. It seemed sad that circumstances
should have rendered it necessary for him to seek his present appointment. At all events, the particulars of his rescue
of William were never known – though the latter told his
story, and the others ever afterwards regarded Spencer with
additional reverence – though, indeed, he had always been
regarded as a sort of father to them, being older by some
years than they.

I reported this incident to brother Frank only in case the
same man should trouble him, though the distance between
us made it unlikely, and thereafter life resumed its even
tenor, disturbed only by an unexpected message from
Brandenburgh House, summoning me to call upon a
Madame Fouquet, who was at present renting it from its
owner. I found her a spirited lady of perhaps forty years.

'Mrs Nelham,' she said, 'we have not met, but I have
heard of course of your establishment, as who has not?'

I inclined my head, wondering whether perhaps she was
about to rebuke me for conducting my business under the
shadow of her walls. But not at all.

'I have three daughters,' she said, 'twin girls of eighteen,
and another of sixteen, who have been raised (because of
their father's feelings upon the matter) only with the barest
notion of the connection between the sexes. There are also
staying here two English girl cousins equally innocent. It
has now come time however when they should be educated,
for I am cognisant as you are, ma'am, of the troubles which
may arise later in life as the result of ignorance in that
important area.'

She paused. Was I to be asked to propose some of my

stable to entertain the girls? There would be no difficulty in that. But no.

Indeed it was the case; but more – in order that such intimate business, suddenly proposed, should not be too shocking, 'What I wish to do,' she said, 'is to demonstrate, as it were, the mechanics of the business, and to that end engage your help. We have in France a book written a century and a half ago by a M. Michel Millot and a M. Jean L'Ange.'

'You mean *L'École des Filles*, or as we know it here, *The School of Venus*?' I asked.

The lady bowed.

'I beg your pardon, ma'am,' she said, 'I had not realised you were a scholar.'

'To no great degree,' I said, 'but that book I have been familiar with since the subject has been a preoccupation with me.'

'Sadly,' she said, 'none of my girls is of a scholarly disposition, and I could not hope to persuade them to read it, despite the warmth of its contents. So I wish to present it in dramatic form, with your help.'

The little theatre attached to the house sat only a dozen people, she explained; she hoped that I could persuade one of my gentlemen to appear upon its small stage with some lady, and there to act out some readings which she had prepared from the book.

In short, I saw the benefit of the plan – not only to the young ladies, but to the actors, to whom she was prepared to pay fifteen guineas each. I was sure that there would be no difficulty, and took away with me a copy of the readings my lady had extracted, and the following day went to Brook Street and engaged the services of Xanthe, whom my brother kindly released for the purpose, and introduced her to Harry. Both were delighted at the prospect before them, and though they had never before met, instantly showed a keen pleasure in each other's company. Within the week we repaired to one of the larger cubicles of my house, where we examined the text we were to illustrate.

My lady had chosen the second dialogue from that excellent book, in which Fanchon explains to Susanne how her lover, Robinet, first deflowered her. Harry, of course, was

to play the part of Robinet, and Xanthe that of Fanchon,
while I was to sit at the side of the stage, playing the part of
Susanne but at the same time reading the words of Fanchon
(which indeed appeared to me to be dramatically something
strange, but was convenient).

I explained the situation to my friends: that Susanne had
asked Fanchon what had happened between her and her
lover, and that the scene began with the latter coming to the
former's chamber while she was busy with her needlework,
and after some polite conversation agreeing to a kiss –
which soon became sufficiently passionate to enable the
actors to discover to their young audience the part played
by a tongue in the excitement of passion. Though they found
this difficult (for it entailed always keeping their faces at
one particular angle) Harry and Xanthe clearly did not find
the contact unpleasant, nor was it difficult to persuade
them to counterfeit Fanchon's discovery of a large bulge in
Robinet's trousers and their continuing exploration of each
other's persons, with Robinet's pleas to Fanchon to stroke
his member, and his eventual removing of his trousers in
order that she should see his instrument.

We worked to place Harry so that he faced the audience,
his thighs parted so that the young ladies should share
Fanchon's education in the matter by having the clearest
possible view of his body, placing Xanthe behind him so
that by reaching back he could raise her skirts and seem to
be exploring her body. The young ladies being, I supposed,
familiar with their own and each other's person, they would
clearly be more interested in Harry's appurtenances than
Xanthe's.

However, as the narrative became warmer and, the couple
being unclothed, Robinet approached his body between
Fanchon's limbs, it became more difficult to place the
actors revealingly. Some time was spent in arranging their
limbs – so long indeed that Harry, whose prick had raised
itself in appreciation of Xanthe's beauty, was quite undone,
and there had to be a pause while Xanthe returned him to
full vigour with her hands, before he could enter her. I was
then to recount the various positions the lovers adopted
before Robinet finally deprived his mistress of her maidenhead, and then go on to the authors' descriptions of the

complex amours which could give pleasure to a couple once that state had been achieved.

As we had completed the final pose, in which Xanthe lay with her legs thrown back and her calves lying over Harry's shoulders as he lay at an angle upon her, I noticed that Philip (aware, of course, of our scheme) had quietly entered the room and was admiring the tableau as I was – for I must confess to being somewhat heated by our rehearsal, as our two actors were. I must have looked longingly at him, for he smiled and, laying a hand upon my shoulder said, 'I am sorry, my dear Sophie, but you remember my difficulty. However, this young lady I have not tried, and if you both consent – and you, young Harry –' and with the words lifted Harry from Xanthe's body and turned him towards me. He was only too ready to step in my direction, and I welcomed him by thrusting up my skirts and falling readily upon my back, while Philip removed his breeches and took his place between Xanthe's welcoming thighs. So excited were we by our rehearsal that both Harry and I came within a moment, while Xanthe too was raised almost instantly to pleasure, and judging by her cries was again raised so by Philip's energy in but a short time. Watching his lean body at work, I could not but again regret the unfortunate state of affairs which seemed to deprive me for ever of the hope of a renewal of the exercise with him.

The performance took place two nights later. The little theatre was enchantingly lit by candles, and there was a nervousness in the air as we took the stage, the five girls and my lady at first silent in their chairs, but later giggling and paying a sighing tribute to Harry's body – the first unclothed male they had seen. Their interest was all-absorbing, and upon his entering Xanthe they with one accord left their seats and came down to the stage the more closely to observe how the act was done, one of them going so far as to stretch out her hand and pull at Harry's knee, to reveal more clearly how his instrument stood in relation to Xanthe's body. They all showed astonishment that so considerable a prick could enter a woman's body without causing her pain, and even wished to question Xanthe about it – but in the character of Fanchon she naturally could not answer. When – as we had designed – upon

approaching the culmination, he pulled away from his
mistress's body so that the juices spurted upon her belly,
there was a unanimous cry of amazement, followed by an
impressed silence, and then by applause, which our actors
happily acknowledged.

The girls were now more than somewhat red about the
face, and speechless with the strangeness of what they had
seen. But then an elder one, one of the sisters, said: 'Mama,
you cannot intend that all shall end here? Surely we must discover for ourselves the pleasures we have seen represented?'

Whereupon my lady revealed what she had secretly
planned with me – that indeed five of my gentlemen had
been reserved for their entertainment and further
education. And in no time we had walked the hundred
yards through the warm summer evening to the house,
where I took each girl to a room where one of the boys
waited – for they would not have had the experience to
choose for themselves, nor would it have been convenient.

I had taken the liberty of not including George, his
person being of such a size that it might positively injure a
young girl at her first game, whatever her enthusiasm. This
made for a little difficulty, but knowing his capacity for a
speedy recovery of vigour, I had appealed to Harry, who
had said that where a sparkling virgin of eighteen was in
prospect, he would 'get it up again' before I could recite the
Collect for St Felicitas' day. And the pleasure with which
one of the elder sisters greeted him promised that neither
would be disappointed.

In order to ensure that no distress would be caused, the
girls' mother and guardian had insisted that I should maintain a watch, and I had arranged with the boys that each
door be left ajar in order that I could glimpse the situation,
or hear any cries which betokened more pain than would be
properly concomitant with the situation, for I cannot disguise the fact that I feared my boys, enjoying the unusual
pleasure of being invited to deflower five virgins, might be
so inspirited by the occasion as to be too enthusiastic for the
girls' true pleasure.

I need not have concerned myself: each scene was one of
delight. Happily, I seemed to have struck on the right
pairing for each young person, though none had been

known to me before that week; indeed luck must have played its part.

In the first room I beheld one of the English cousins astride Spencer's knees, riding with such tender pleasure, and with such a look of engrossed adoration in her eyes, that no picture of father and daughter could have been more delightful. In the next two rooms, Ben and Tom were entertaining their young ladies – their plumpness encouraging both to tempt their charges to crouch above them, which also enabled the girls themselves to control the manner in which their unaccustomed bodies received the male instrument. Not that they showed very considerable hesitation, and indeed their pleasure clearly much outdid their pain.

William, however, his body being lithe and light, entertained one of the French girls in the traditional way, so that all I saw when I peeped through the aperture of the door was the bottom so admired by our watchman, embraced by a pair of slim but muscular legs, that charming posterior (showing no sign of damage from those recent rough attentions) moving more slowly than might usually be the case, but – from the panting words of encouragement – giving no less pleasure.

Finally, Harry was proving himself yet again in the final room – his companion, the younger of the French daughters (it amazed me to see) with her legs thrown over his shoulders just as Fanchon had welcomed Robinet and his lower body moving with such vigour that I feared for the well-being of the girl. However, her energy was equal to his own – to such an extent indeed that I could not believe that she had not enjoyed such pleasure before, in one way or another. It may have been possible, as I have since observed on my most recent adventures that in her native country an early education in erotic acrobatics is common, often without the knowledge of parents or guardians.

The reader may assume that my overlooking of such pleasure did not leave me unmoved. And when upon returning to my room I observed George, hopefully naked but as yet unoccupied, lying alone upon the couch, I once more broke the rule which was now becoming 'more honoured in the breach than the observance', and summoned him to my bedroom.

There I was able once more to admire that fine and sturdy tool which, by a not prolonged persuasion, changed its limp length for the consistency almost of marble, the veins standing proudly out upon it. George himself was now so used to exclamations of amazement, and admonitions to allow himself to be inspected like some prize animal, that he behaved similarly with me – merely sitting, legs apart, with the standing instrument up against his belly as he stroked it to persuade it (if such persuasion was needed) not to bow its head.

Even I, who was entirely used to the sight, having introduced it to so many surprised visitors, could not resist paying it the tribute of a kiss, once again delighted and astonished at the effort needed to part my lips sufficiently to take even the tip between them. I then beckoned him to approach, applying to his body that ointment I insisted he should carry to facilitate the act, and feeling that satisfying fullness with which he was able to gorge even the most capacious part.

As I received the sum assured by the evening's activities, regarded the happy and fulfilled faces of our young guests, distributed the proportion of the fee to the boys, and retired to bed with the twin comforts of gold in my hand and the comfortable warmth of recent pleasure below, I once more felt a pleasant satisfaction of the manner in which providence permitted me to earn my living.

Several days after these events, a closed carriage arrived at the house not long after six o'clock, and from it descended a figure completely covered by a light silken cloak. The lady, when admitted, proved masked.

She was clearly a person of quality, for her gown was of the latest fashion, splendidly cut, and though without the decoration of jewels, marked by a distinguished elegance. She herself was not old, judging by the clarity of her skin and the firmness of her flesh, and her voice was low and musical. Polly, who admitted her, came to fetch me, saying that she had asked for the governess of the house. When I descended to the reception room, she was glancing at a portfolio of etchings of the male figure by Michelangelo, which I had placed there for the amusement of visitors.

'Mrs Nelham?' she asked, with a slight hesitation.

I inclined my head.

'I come recommended by an acquaintance.'

There was a silence, which after a while I broke with the suggestion that she made herself easy. 'We find here,' I said, 'that any slight diffidence which ladies may have upon broaching the reason for their visit is speedily dissipated by the friendliness of everyone in the house. It is, incidentally,' I continued, 'unnecessary for you to continue masked, for everyone here has the utmost discretion – we could not function were it otherwise – and there can never be the slightest chance of your being recognised in public by any of our people.'

She raised her hand to her mask, which was an elaborate affair of black and silver, clearly the relic of a fashionable masquerade.

'If you will forgive me,' she said, 'I will continue with it. I fear I am unused to . . .'

'As are all our ladies,' I said. 'This is the first establishment of its kind I know of in the town, for no one has previously thought to afford our sex the privileges freely enjoyed by the gentlemen, and it is not amazing that upon a first visit you feel somewhat insecure – but I am sure that will change. In the meantime, please of course retain your mask. And now perhaps you would like me to show you our men?'

She nodded and, first ringing the small glass bell which I had had placed for the purpose, to warn of our approach, I escorted her behind the screen, where a view of the room beyond revealed all six already prepared for the evening's entertainment. For a moment, my new friend seemed almost to stagger, placing her hand upon the back of the chair set before her to steady herself. Clearly the prospect was one which moved her. She slipped into the chair and sat for a moment, silent.

'I know not . . .' she said hesitantly. 'Which gentleman would you recommend?'

'It is difficult to say, ma'am,' I said, 'for it depends on individual inclination, and my choice might not be yours. The young man upon the chair by the window is Harry' – who was, as was his wont, carefully exhibiting himself by the simple means of sitting facing the window with his thighs wide apart examining his prick with an interest that suggested he had never previously seen it. 'He is of a vigorous nature, and should you desire a passage to exhaust, will more than satisfy. Next to him are Ben and Tom, whose persons are more – you might think – domestic and comfortable, but who are both adept in the science of lovemaking. It is possible, incidentally, for a small charge, to engage both at a single moment – or indeed, to couple any of our gentlemen together for your pleasure.

'The boy you see reclining upon the *chaise longue* is William, of a light and almost feminine sensibility, yet perfectly virile, and with a member stronger and more substantial than might appear from a rear view; he has, I am told, a particular charm and grace which can raise the most lethargic spirit. The older of our friends, now practising billiards, is much admired by those of our ladies whose tastes turn towards maturity. Finally, as you will not have failed to observe, there is our friend George.'

George was now sufficiently confident of his body's attractions to make little effort to capture attention other than ensuring that his chief and most unusual characteristic was open to the view – as now, while he read a newspaper, it simply lay across his thigh, astonishing even to me, who had so recently experienced the pleasure of accommodating it. I was ready for our visitor's amazement, and sensible of it.

'Can it be . . . *safe*?' she asked in a whisper.

'Quite,' I reassured her, 'and the experience is a memorable one, though I must confess that our friend is not much adept in the art of love-making, so that the instrument in question is in fact his sole attribute – though a considerable one, and should be experienced at least once.'

'I think, perhaps, Mr Harry?' she suggested. 'My husband,' she continued in a whisper, 'is uninterested in the act, and having introduced me to it upon our marriage – when I was a virgin – had no sooner given me a taste for that most delicious of sports, than he abandoned me and comes no more to bed . . .'

I felt a little shudder run through her body as I put my hand upon her shoulder, and am sure that a tear started to her eye, behind that elegant mask.

'My dear,' said I, 'if you wish a bout which will entirely satisfy your longings, I cannot too strongly recommend Harry.'

'He will not wish to remove my mask?' she asked.

'I am sure he would wish to see your beauty in its entirety,' said I, 'but all our people have instructions that the guests' wishes must at all times be respected. Indeed, if you would care to remain here, you shall hear me give instructions . . .'

Leaving her in the position from which she could hear as well as see, I made my way around to the boys' room, and entering it informed Harry that a friend awaited his services.

'The lady,' I said, in a slightly louder voice than usual, 'is masked, and wishes to remain so; she counts upon your discretion.'

Harry rose to his feet, and realising that we could be overheard, remarked in a similarly raised voice that of course he would respect her anonymity. Then he reached for the robe hanging nearby and wrapped himself in it, accompanying me from the room.

'The fourth chamber, I think, Harry,' I said.

'Aha!' he replied. 'You wish to observe . . .?'

Indeed, the lady's identity interested me, for I felt almost sure that I knew her, and had the uneasy feeling that perhaps she was in some sense a spy.

'But,' I said, 'of course you must on no account remove the mask, for should she be a genuine visitor the news would quickly get about, and discretion must ever be our hallmark.'

I should explain the significance of the fourth chamber: when planning and executing the alterations, Philip had insisted that we should have one room onto which a spy-hole should give, for, he said, sometimes there were ladies whose pleasure included the observation of others at play. But also we might at times wish to observe, ourselves, for reasons of security.

I was not happy with this idea, for spying is something which has never commended itself to me; moreover, even at an early stage in our relationship I suspected that perhaps Philip wished such a facility for his own amusement, and I was later convinced that it was so used. But I had agreed at the time to its provision, which entailed the construction of a small room, scarcely bigger than a cupboard, which was entered from a concealed door behind a hanging at the end of the corridor, and from which a small hole communicated with the chamber beyond, in its turn concealed by the shadow of a large picture of Venus and Adonis.

Returning to our visitor, I found her much comforted, and she accompanied me without demur to the chamber where Harry awaited her, whereupon I repaired to the hiding-place whence I could see everything that occurred.

Our guest was standing just inside the door, having closed it behind her, and was apparently transfixed by what was certainly a pleasant sight – of Harry, naked as the day he was born, lying upon the bed, his manly part relaxed but, from its half-raised size, clearly persuaded of pleasure to come. She stood so long, simply looking at him, that after a while he raised himself and asked whether she would not join him.

'Forgive me, sir,' she said, 'but the sight is not one to which I am accustomed; pray maintain your position while I disrobe' – which she did in a trice. She then walked to kneel at the side of the bed, where – I can find no other term to describe it – she knelt to worship Harry's body, first observing it with her eyes alone, from every angle, then reaching out a gentle hand to stroke its length from shoulder to ankle, running her fingers through the hair of his head, articulating each finger, testing the muscles which activated knees and elbows, tracing the line of the chin and testing the contrasting textures of the flesh at the inside of the arm and the breast, the chin and the belly.

That Harry found this unaccustomed attention entrancing was testified by the raising of his tool to its full and impressive size, and the appearance at its tip of several drops of liquid, which overspilled and ran down its length to lubricate it with a slippery humidity.

Our friend's body was no less delightful than his; indeed, together they made a picture Rubens or Titian would have been delighted to paint. Her back was to me – a long back, divided by the dint of a spine in which each articulated bone was marked, falling to full globes scored by two deep dimples and underpinned by thighs sturdy but slim. And when she turned, I caught a tantalising glimpse of breasts shaped like the spheres of wine glasses, and tipped with pink buds now reared with pleasure.

But each time he raised his hand to touch one delightful curve or another, she took it gently and returned it to his side, intent upon devouring each plane of the surface of his body with eye and palm, so that I could see from the darkening of his eyes that his passion was becoming unbearably roused.

At length, her eye and hand had encompassed every part of Harry's body but that last essential, whereupon she reached out with a tender shyness, and placed a single finger at its tip, running it down the underside to where his cods were raised by the tightness of the skin. Then, bending forward, she placed the most tender kiss upon its very peak, and turning to Harry said some words which I could not hear, but which were clearly – and at last – an invitation to action.

I could not but admire the restraint with which he rose to his feet, and clasped her with what was almost reserve, placing his arms about her shoulders and (unable to kiss her lips because of the mask, which she was still most careful to retain) contented himself with running his hands down the length of her body until they embraced her lovely posterior. Then he pulled her towards him so that she could not but be aware of that instrument which was now placed in pleasant juxtaposition with that part of her most anxious to receive it.

She appeared almost to swoon at the sensation, whereupon he laid her upon the bed and in his turn paid homage to her body which, now that it was laid open to my view, was indeed of a most particular elegant and form, the breasts as fine as my former glimpse had suggested, now with their pouting nipples pointing each slightly outwards from her body, clearly tenderly excited by his lips as he sucked and kissed them. Between those slim thighs could now be seen a small but springy nest of fair hairs which, as he drew her legs apart the better to facilitate his love-making, revealed to Harry (as to me) a pair of rosy lips distended with anticipation.

But now she reached down and, taking him by the hips, guided Harry into her body, his prick, fully basted by

mucous juices, slipping resistlessly into its proper domicile
– which it immediately sought to leave, only to be drawn
back, expelled, and once more welcomed with an ever-
increasing motion. A small bead of blood appeared upon
Harry's lower lip, a mark of the difficulty with which he
restrained himself from spending before time, for by the
manner in which her head was thrown back, lips parted,
breasts heaving and legs thrown around the hips of her
lover, his partner was in an ecstasy which it was his duty no
less than his pleasure to prolong.

At last, with a spasm which almost seemed to shake the
room, the two gave up the ghost simultaneously, she lifting
the body of the man clean from the bed with the final thrust
of her slim hips, while he drove it to the sheets again with
the force of his own coming. As they lay panting and
exhausted, beads of perspiration running down his sides, I
left my vantage-point – not, I must confess, proud at
having witnessed the scene, but at the same time much
inspirited by it – without, however, having a single clue as
to the lady's identity. Yet I was still sure I knew her.

I waited in the hall until Harry, once more decently
covered, escorted the lady from the chamber. He made his
bow, and she handed me a purse containing our fee.

'I hope you will visit us again, ma'am,' I said, leaning
across her to open the door. As I did so she stepped back,
and came for a moment into collision with one of the sup-
ports of a large china vase which stood by the door. Putting
up her hand to steady it, her sleeve caught the corner of her
mask, and it fell to the floor – revealing the pale face of
none other than Lady Frances Chichley, the bride of only a
few weeks!

Her countenance was uncertain whether to pale or blush.

'Mrs Nelham,' she said, 'I trust . . .'

'My lady,' I said, 'your secret is safe with me.'

Without another word, she left. But how sad that my
friend should, it seems, be unaware of the richness of his
bride's passions. And that she should be a stranger to those
qualities which he so amply demonstrated to me!

Chapter Thirteen

The Adventures of Andy

For some time Frank had been attempting to persuade me to introduce him to the backstage life of the theatres, under the impression that since I had spent some time touring the western parts of the country with a theatrical company led by a Mr Samuel Prout Higgens, I must know all about the subject.

That this was far from the truth, Heaven is my witness! However, I was sufficiently used to the practices of the theatre to know that my experience would open certain doors to me, and upon presenting myself at the stage door of the Royalty Theatre in Wellclose Square, soon acquainted myself with the keeper, Mr Tony Rudge. Upon my explaining my theatrical connections and offering certain emoluments he readily agreed to admit me and my friend to the back of the stage during rehearsals, an honour then more easily come by than in later years.

The Royalty Theatre (which, it must be admitted, is not of the first degree of fashion) was built about thirty years ago, but failed to obtain a licence because of the nature of certain of its performances, and for some years was shut – or 'dark', as theatre people term it. It was then however opened by the late Mr Astley, junior, for pantomimes, and more lately has held exhibitions of dancing which have attracted wide audiences whose interests have been, however, more in the persons of the dancers exhibiting there than in the performances themselves – a fact which it seemed would all the more make a visit interesting to brother Frank, whose attention to artistic matters has never been more than scanty.

He was indeed delighted to accompany me one morning to the Royalty, which we reached after traversing some narrow and dirty streets in the eastern part of the town.

Mr Rudge welcomed us with a broad grin and a wink and passed us through the stage door, where a noticeboard bore a wafer informing that there was to be a rehearsal that day of the Female Warriors' Dance in *The Battle of Eurypylus*, to the music of Mr Digby Trantrum (an opera soon and best forgot), and 'Ladies and Gents of the Ballet are to attend at ten o'clock.'

Frank was astonished at the dirt and muddle attendant upon the back of the stage, his previous slender experience of the theatre having encompassed only the apparently fresh and bright aspect of spectacles as viewed by the audience. A little grubby daylight slanted down from a skylight to fall upon the bare boards, palely illuminating a confusion of ropes and pulleys and bridges by which the scenery is organised. The curtain was raised, and the auditorium itself seemed no less dingy, being lit now only by the same daylight coming through windows at the back of the sixpenny gallery, where a number of brooms seemed to be making their way to and fro uncontrolled by the agency of human hands and stirring a considerable dust into the already foggy atmosphere. The dim light of a candle occasionally glimmered for a moment in one of the boxes, and at a rickety table towards the front of the pit a long-wicked flaring candle lit a pile of paper holding, I assumed, the description of the ballet to be performed.

There was a cough at my elbow.

'I believe, sir, you would like to see the dressing rooms?'

'Ah, Mr Rudge, if we may,' I replied, knowing very well that the expenditure of half a guinea had ensured that that pleasure would be afforded us.

'This way, gentlemen,' he said, and led his way to the side of the stage, then up an almost vertical ladder to a gap in the wall – a narrow corridor which led to an open attic where was stored a vast pile of scenery: the sides of Chinese houses, an Italian bridge, an ornamental balcony, a boat on wheels . . .

Rudge led us to the end of this attic, where beneath our feet a glimmer of light in the dimness showed that the floorboards failed completely to meet.

'Take your ease, gentlemen,' he said, 'the *corps de ballet* here, the *coryphées* five paces to your left.' And he was gone.

Upon our knees, we did not even have to approach our eyes to the gap in the boards to see that we were immediately above the dressing rooms where the dancers were changing. But unfortunately the ladies of the *corps de ballet* had almost completed their dressing, for their street skirts were upon the backs of chairs, and they had already donned the short substitutes in which they were to rehearse, while their upper limbs were still clad in outside dress, as was their habit in rehearsal.

'Better luck with the what-you-call-'ems, eh, Andy?' said Frank, and moved along the attic.

The *coryphées* were what in the theatre were termed the two or three leading dancers, and here indeed we were more fortunate, for they enjoyed a little more freedom than their lesser sisters and had only just arrived. We were able to enjoy the sight of their stripping off their clothing and for a while walking about their room in the full freedom of unclothed beauty, conversing before putting on their costumes, which they finally accomplished, though the word 'costume' did not comprehend much. Their clothing consisted of golden boots, a short golden skirt hanging in strips with the merest suggestion of a covering to their essential nakedness, and a cuirass of gold which barely concealed their breasts.

'Well,' said Frank, 'it will be interesting to see the sort of ballet which is exhibited in such dishabille.'

There being no promise of further disclosures, we made our way back along the corridor and down to the side of the stage, where by this time the ballet-master was drilling the *corps de ballet* with the help of a tambourine, tapping out the measure of their dances – which without the accompaniment of an orchestra, seemed dull indeed.

'Miss Pollock, where's your sword?' he asks one girl.

'It's not ready yet,' she replies.

'Then take this stick . . .' – concerned to manage which she contrives to get out of step.

'Stop! Stop!! Stop!!!' cries the ballet-master, and by stamping and thumping the tambourine manages to persuade her at last to keep time. But now some of the other girls have stopped dancing and are standing idly by: 'Now then,' shouts the ballet-master, 'what are you gaping for?

Why don't you move? *Why the devil don't you move?*'

I was most interested in all this, but could feel that Frank began to find it boring, not himself being inclined to matters theatrical, but interested chiefly in the personalities of the girls. However, as I concerned myself with watching, he soon found a more fascinating occupation, for just in front of us stood one of the *coryphées* awaiting her summons to the stage, and her delightfully round haunches, decorated only by the strips of gold cloth which hung from her waist, being at hand, he could not resist to place one palm upon the inside of an ample thigh, raising it until his little finger could make its way within the thin piece of cloth which alone guarded her virtue.

After a moment or two, and without moving, she simply said over her shoulder: 'Well, my ducks, if you want to be about it, you had better move, for my cue comes in two minutes' – whereupon Frank was not a moment in releasing from his trousers his ready appliance and, tearing the flimsy cloth aside, passing it into the body of the dancer, who reacted only by bending slightly forward to enable its easier passage.

While Frank began to pump away, she showed not the slightest evidence of interest, tapping her fingers upon a piece of scenery not in time with his vigorous thrusts but to the banging of the ballet-master's tambourine. It was remarkable also that no one else took any notice, her colleagues simply averting their eyes while men passing by with pieces of scenery gave not so much as a cursory glance at the two persons so intimately engaged.

At last the girl recognised her cue, and without preparation or comment leapt upon the stage while Frank, stimulated no less by her sudden movement than by his enthusiastic engagement, was left to bedew the boards with the proof of his passion – upon which he looked slightly shamefaced, and packed his machinery away to the accompaniment of giggles from two other *coryphées* who had observed the matter from a few feet away.

'Hah! I shall go and eat,' he said. 'Will see you outside before the performance.' And left.

I remained, interested by the rehearsal, until at half-past three it was concluded, whereupon the girls quitted the stage to obtain refreshment before returning at a little after six for the performance.

I too determined to find some refreshment, and turned to make for the door when there was a shout from above, and down a rope like some monkey came a small figure, hand over hand, who then slapped me upon the shoulder with great familiarity.

'Why, Andy, don't tell me you've forgotten? David? David Ham?'

I clasped the fellow immediately to my bosom with surprise and delight. He had shared his bed with me over some months of travelling with the theatrical company of which he was a humble member, and while his amorous attentions had at first been embarrassing and always undesired by me (though upon one occasion had been fulfilled, as readers of my former chronicles will recall) we had parted excellent friends, and now went off together to the Orange Coffee House where I treated us to chops and small beer while he told me news of my old friends.

Mr Prout Higgens and his good wife, Mrs Plunkett Cope, were at present at the Theatre Royal in Richmond appearing as Othello and Desdemona (which I well remembered as two of their favourite parts, rousing as considerable a passion of laughter in their audiences as any comedian might wish), while their daughter, Miss Cynthia Cope, was recently retired from the stage and married to a wealthy merchant of Shoreditch. Here, he said, she has made herself known to every apprentice and ship-boy, every clerk and manager – in short, every likely lad in the neighbourhood. For, he said, her appetite in the fucking line was as voracious as ever, and she touted her crinkum crankum about the drawing-rooms of London with such vigour that scarce a gay stopper in the city could keep up with her – at which I laughed heartily, having forgotten David's command of the common language of the streets.

'And you, David?' I asked.

'Well, I'm no doodle,' he said. 'I work here at the Royalty for a penny or two and the company of friends, but I have acquired a protector' (and here he gave me a shrewd wink) 'who is desperate in love with my double jug, and I can edge him on to the extent of a guinea or two at will, and am getting together a good hoard against my old age' – which, since he had no more than my own share of years, must be some time a-coming.

'Well, I am glad to hear it,' I said.

'Good for you!' he said. 'And yourself?'

At which I told him of all that had happened since I had left his company, of my meeting again with Frank and Sophie (whom he remembered my talking of, from past days) and of the house in Brook Street which, I said, he must come and see, though he would find little there to engross him in the way of madge culls (his term for those gentlemen who enjoy the carnal company of their own sex).

'I shall, I shall,' he said, 'and you must meet my friend. He lives at Chiswick, though I have never been to his house, he being surrounded (I believe) by his family, who would not be as sympathetic to his inclinations as I – or indeed you.' And here he placed his hand upon my thigh and gave it a gentle squeeze which, knowing his good will and that it was in fun, I accepted as it was offered.

We talked for a great while, and then it was time to make our way back to the theatre, where I was to meet Frank. I mentioned to David the latter's hope of some closer contact with the ladies of the ballet, whereupon he suggested that we should accompany two of them to a *soirée dansante* after the performance, at a house he knew of in the area.

'I will arrange two likely ladybirds,' he said, 'and meet you at the stage door after the show' – and with that vanished towards the back of the stage, while I soon found Frank, having acquired a box at three shillings, to which we made our way. He was more than a little glum, Mr Rudge having denied him entrance to the dressing rooms on the ground that the manager had strictly forbid it – and having accepted half-a-guinea for the favour, still refused to grant it. I told him of my meeting David, which at first failed to cheer him, for 'I want no bony boy,' he said, 'but a good fleshy lass', whereupon I told him of David's suggestion, which cheered him much, so that he spent the evening contemplating the ladies of the *corps* and attempting to decide which, had he the choice, he would wish to have presented to him after the performance.

Of that performance there is little to say: the fairy dancers flew on their wires, the military dancers stamped their feet and smacked their thighs with will, the *coryphée* who had so cheerfully accommodated Frank during the morning caught his eye and continually made gestures with her sword which only the blind could have failed to interpret, whereat the pit cheered and shouted. And all in all, with the help of two bottles of wine, we were in high spirits by the end of the evening, when we poured out with the rest of the audience into the narrow, crowded street, and made our way around the corner where a number of other gallants waited in the knowledge or the hope that willing female company would soon be forthcoming.

Eventually, David appeared among the press, with a young woman on each arm – somewhat chicken-breasted, as is the case with most ballet girls who do not, as a matter of course, make enough money to eat so well as to fill out their limbs to the extent of, for instance, the girls at Brook Street, but nevertheless vivacious and willing.

'I suggest, gents, that we make for Parker's Supper Room,' said David, 'where there is food in plenty and dancing afterwards of whatever kind' (and here he nudged Frank familiarly) 'you may desire.'

We crammed into a carriage, and after a short ride were decanted at a dark doorway through which there burst upon us a brilliance of light and movement, with a forest of tables, waiters tumbling over one another in their frantic hurry to take devilled kidneys to a man who has only ordered beer, or a dozen oysters to another who is asleep after a large meal. David was well known here, as were the girls, Miss Portland and Miss Markham, for we were not only seated immediately but a waiter instantly appeared with a tray heavy with food, which our friends consumed with the appetite of those who had worked all evening. While they were going at their boiled mutton, David made his excuses: 'I join my friend across the road at Almack's,' he said, 'but we shall meet again, make no doubt!'

'A lively spark,' said Frank, 'as lively as you tell me.'

'Oh, that David,' said Miss Portland between mouthfuls of steak pie, 'he's a bright puppy – and with a fine leg, too, if he turned to dancing.'

'Much use his leg'd be to you,' returned Miss Markham, digging her friend in the ribs, at which the two went into a paroxysm of laughter. They were indeed mightily dissimilar to the young ladies we had left in Brook Street, even Moll being a paragon to them where polite behaviour was concerned. But they were none the less good company, being continually high-spirited and merry, and once they had satisfied one carnal appetite were clearly ready to set their sights at another, for no sooner had they finished the food and drink set before them than they leapt to their feet and led us into the next room, where dancing was in progress.

It was a long, narrow hall with a row of seats down each side and a gallery in which musicians sat – playing, as we entered, a polka to which a dense crowd was dancing, men and women turning and chasing and banging against each other in all directions. Many of the young women present were clearly recognisable as *coryphées* escaping the strict discipline of the stage to engage in a looser kind of dancing altogether, leaping with great enthusiasm but also with a kind of elegance which set them apart from the other women present. These were bakers' daughters or whatnot, clumsily flinging their legs about and getting in everybody's way, turning their heads wildly and plunging and diving and leaping indiscriminately, while our friends danced gracefully with their heads over their right shoulders, arms extended, carefully avoiding all collisions. The men were of all kinds, but notably of the world, some in uniform, some in suits of mufti, all set on enjoyment.

We happily joined in the dancing with our friends, I being partnered by Miss Portland, whose forename was Jenny, while Frank happily took Miss Markham in his arms, who rejoiced in no other name than Pussy, from, she alleged, her tendency to make tart comments upon her friends. But, Jenny confided, in fact for her freedom with a part of her body sometimes denoted by the name of puss. The dancing was warm work, and our partners' happy pleasure in pressing their bodies close to ours brought on a further enjoyable heat which we looked forward, later, to cooling. Just as we were preparing to propose a departure for some quieter place, a young woman with a flushed face came up to Pussy and whispered in her ear, whereupon she wishpered in turn to Jenny, and the two looked at us in the most serious manner.

'Your admiration for the arts suggests that you would enjoy a performance which is in preparation, upstairs,' said Pussy.

Frank expressed himself as having seen as much theatrical performance that evening as would last him for the rest of the year.

'But I think,' said Pussy, 'that this performance would prove most inspiriting to you, for you are not, I believe, totally without an admiration for the female form?'

At these words Frank began to look more interested, while Jenny tipped me a wink suggesting some pleasure to come. To cut the story short, we followed them up a staircase which led to an upper room, at the door of which no less than five guineas was extracted from Frank's purse for each of us. 'I trust the offering will be worth it,' he muttered as he handed over the gold.

Inside the room we found a small but delightful theatre prepared, with banquettes each seating two persons upon which we placed ourselves, only a few rows from a stage hung with red velvet curtains, before which a menial was lighting a row of footlights. Now came a fellow with a violin, who as the main chandeliers were snuffed struck up a charming tune which proved to be (as Pussy whispered to me) from the new opera *La Muette de Portici* from which we were, she said, to see an interlude danced by the famous Louisa Veron with her partner Jean Fiorentino. My heart sank at this, for though I delighted in dancing, it was not for such polite entertainment I had been preparing myself, and I was sure that Frank would be more impatient with such frippery (as he called it).

But I need have had no fear, for when the curtain was swept aside revealing a stage merely hung with black, it revealed also the two dancers in a complete state of nature, finely lit by the warm glow of candles, which gave to their flesh a rosy hue like that upon the limbs in a painting by some old master in love with his subject.

Mademoiselle Veron had been much spoken of, with admiration, by society, and it was clear that no compliment paid her could have been too great, even were her audiences

deprived of the unhindered view of her limbs which we
enjoyed. Her poses were now chaste and meditative, now
voluptuous and enticing; her movements first swift and
inspiriting, now languorous and melting. She twisted and
turned like a snake around her partner – who himself,
while slim and boyish, was clearly of great strength, for he
lifted her as though she were a mere wraith. She whirled
with him like a leaf carried away by a gale then, a moment
later, walked with a superb, nonchalant step, happy to
show us her beautiful arms and shoulders, her marble-like
bust, her supple shapely figure.

Then she darted anew into space and fell dropping,
quivering, writhing in one supreme convulsion, her head
touching the ground, her eyes bathed in light – and in all
her attitudes, especially those in which she was supported
by Monsieur Fiorentino (with whom she appeared to be
much in love), there was always that same grace, that same
harmony, that same charm, that same unexpectedness, that
something which can be learnt from no teacher and in no
school.

The performance was by no means an indecent show, and
were it not for the complete lack of costume, could have
been given upon the stage before an audience of the most
conventional sort. Yet it was this very fact that made it
among the most rousing that I had ever seen, for the expectation of passion was continually aroused without being
satisfied. When Monsieur Fiorentino's hand slipped upon
the inside of his partner's thigh as he lifted her above his
waist, one expected the gesture to lead to the result such a
passage would have in the bed-chamber; instead of which,
he merely set her again upon the stage, and the ballet continued. Similarly, she would perhaps adopt a pose in which
she reclined upon the stage, her cheek leaning against her
partner's thigh, almost brushing his vital parts, yet he
remained unmoved – as indeed he must, for it would have
been impossible for the dance to continue should he be
aroused.

Strangely, these circumstances, as I have said, were particularly attractive to the audience; as the performance continued, I could almost feel a warmth emanating from my
companion's body, through the thin muslin of her dress.

And I could not but be conscious that in the neighbouring seat Frank, always quicker than myself to give way to his passions, had passed his hand within his friend's clothing and was caressing her breast, while her own hands were occupied in his lap. Soon it was clear that the activities upon the stage were now uninteresting to them; I preferred, however, still to give them my attention, though Pussy's hands were by now busy about my person too, provoking a desire which was almost too acute to contain.

As the dance ended, and the couple took their bow, the applause was inconsiderable, the hands of most members of the audience by that time otherwise occupied. I, however, rose to my feet to offer my applause unconscious until a moment later of the fact that Pussy had succeeded in loosening the laces of my breeches so that my person was exposed in a manner which offered to Mademoiselle Veron a compliment such as she would normally have accepted only in the privacy of her private apartments.

As the curtains fell, Pussy leaned forward and placed her lips over my tool, clutching at me with an urgency which suggested that she, too, had been sufficiently enlivened by the performance to desire comfort. However, I had been too captivated by Mademoiselle Veron to content myself with even so willing a companion, and gently but firmly withdrew myself. Whereupon, with an ill-tempered look, Pussy turned to my friend and his companion, and kneeling at the side of their bench began to offer assistance in their love-making, which by this time was as open as that which went on around them.

I had already noted that there was a door at the side of the stage, and it was thence I directed my steps – but upon opening it was stopped by a large fellow evidently placed there with the single intent of stopping importunate visitors. The production of my purse loosed his hold upon my shoulder, and the extraction from it of a couple of guineas, pressed upon him with a whispered word, resulted in his stepping aside, and indicating another door at the end of a corridor.

Knocking at this, I was greeted with an invitation, in a lady's voice, to enter.

Inside, at a dressing table, sat Mademoiselle Veron,

wrapped in a silken gown. At the sight of an unknown man, she rose to her feet, alarmed. But I hastily reassured her: 'Madam, be not alarmed. I do not come to offer an assault, but merely the admiring tribute of someone captivated by the beauty of your person and your movements. I offer no compliment other than words, and my admiration, and will now withdraw.'

With a bow, I made to go – at which she smiled, and beckoned.

'Please, sir, be seated if you can spare a few moments of conversation.'

I sat upon the chair she indicated.

'You will forgive, sir, my mistrust,' she said, 'but I will not disguise from you the fact that too many rude fellows have in the past made their way to this room, and the sight of a stranger is one in general I cannot welcome. But' (and she smiled again) 'your words reassure me, as your person indicates your gentility.'

I could not resist, at this, falling to my knees before her and pressing my lips to her hand, whereat she was evidently moved, for leaning forward she placed her hand upon my head and planted a kiss upon my forehead. I cannot but confess that proximity to those delicious globes upon whose beauty my eyes had so recently been fixed, and the lady's kindness, sharpened my desire, and almost before I had formed the thought, my lips were pressed to her neck and my hands, upon her shoulders, made ready to slip from them the silk which clung to the delicious flesh beneath.

She rose at this, I feared to rebuke me. But no – 'Sir,' she said, 'your compliments are those of a gentleman, your carriage that of a tender lover – and this place is not marked for either.'

Then, allowing the silk to slip from her shoulders, she stood before me in that naked beauty with which I was familiar, but upon which I had not hoped to graze. With a speed Monsieur Fiorentino could not but have envied, I freed myself of my clothes, and in a moment we were stretched upon a nearby couch, and enjoying a dance more commonly performed than those of the ballet, but susceptible of equal skill and vigour. No less than three times Mademoiselle Veron cried out in extremity before my own performance ended and the curtain fell upon our endeavours. Finally, on my raising myself from her body (now bedewed with a happy amorous perspiration), she smiled and thanked me, gesturing towards her gown, with which I covered her before saluting a most gracious and beautiful lady, and leaving her room.

Downstairs, in a refreshment room, I found Frank, with Jenny and Pussy, he having satisfied both of them in one way or another before they left the performance hall. He neglected to ask where I had been, and I had no intention of volunteering the information, for that could only be construed upon the one side as boasting and upon the other as telling tales outside the bedroom, to neither of which (as the reader knows) am I subject.

Slipping a coin or two into their hands, we left the girls, and made our way from the hall to hail a carriage for Brook Street, where by this time of evening the house would be quiet.

Letting ourselves in with our key, the first sign we had of any impropriety was the sight of Blatchford lying upon the floor, his hands and feet bound and a gag across his mouth, bleeding from a blow upon the forehead. Frank quickly knelt to release him, and upon his taking off the gag he began to whisper a message. But before he could get more than a single word out, the door of the reception room was suddenly flung open by an unknown man, and we saw the girls and Aspasia sitting at one end of the room, while at the other two men held Rose, one with a knife at her throat.

'Gentlemen, come in,' said the man at the door, 'but quietly, if you please. I would advise no sudden motion, or this young lady will suffer for it.'

We walked in, and sat upon two chairs indicated to us, whereupon the first man, producing cord, tied our hands behind us.

'Now, which of you is Sir Franklin Franklyn?'

Frank gave a curt nod.

'Ah, Sir Franklin, it is a pleasure to meet you. I come with a message from a number of gentlemen occupied in the provision of similar entertainment to that which you purvey here. That message is that they are not inclined to sit by while you take all the profit in the town, for we cannot

disguise the fact that through an unreasonable expenditure
of money in this place you have attracted custom which is
naturally ours. Yet you are largely unknown to the town,
and have no friends here. We are largely known, and have
friends of influence. We feel that you have now taken
enough profit and should retire to some part of the country
where you may continue to ply your trade without depriving
us of ours. If you do not . . .' He made a gesture to the two
men holding Rose, and in a flash following a quick movement of the knife, a thin line of blood appeared beneath her
jaw.

'We are careful, as you see, not to disturb the young
lady's beauty. Upon another occasion, however, should
another occasion sadly present itself, our actions will be
considerably less accommodating. Gentlemen, ladies, our
apologies for disturbing you. Good evening.'

And the two men, dropping Rose – who fell to the
ground – quickly crossed the room to their colleague, and
the three left together, the front door slamming behind
them.

The chaos of the next half hour can be supposed. We
were released, Rose was put to bed, her wound proving to
be entirely superficial, and her state brought on by alarm
rather than pain, Blatchford was set free and, apart from a
fearful headache proved more angry than hurt. And in the
basement we found Tippett and Pounce, similarly bound
and gagged, and released them. Only then were we able to
discover precisely what had happened.

It appeared that the three men, two of them somewhat
rough but all decently dressed and in funds, had appeared
at about nine o'clock, and admitted by Aspasia had retired
to the hot rooms before going upstairs with Rose, Constance
and Ginevra. There, they had behaved entirely as might have
been expected, though they were perhaps more leisurely in
their love-making than others – by intent, clearly, for after
all other visitors had left the house they dressed and all
descended together, Rose already threatened by the knife
which her partner had recovered from his clothing. By threat
of harm to her, the men had had no difficulty in persuading
Pounce and Tippett to be bound, while Blatchford, making
a rash attempt to intervene, had been silenced by a blow to

the head from a truncheon one fellow had produced. Despite all attempts, it had proved impossible to persuade them to converse, and it was not until we had appeared that it became clear what the motive of the unpleasantness was.

We were, of course, equally amazed and outraged; Aspasia less so, however, for, she had been previously aware of threats of a similar nature made against those who had started houses without first arranging to pay a financial tribute to those who ruled the game in the city, of which, she said, a certain Charles or Carlo Gaskill was the head. If we cared to seek him out and offer a considerable share of the business, it might still be possible to recover the situation, though from the tone adopted by our visitors it might be that Mr Gaskill's intention was indeed to throw us out of business, as an example to others.

Frank enquired whether, since the girls were shortly to inherit a considerable sum from the estate of Mrs Jopling Rowe, they would not prefer it if we closed the establishment immediately? For they would not be in need, while he and myself did not want funds, and it was no part of his desire that his friends should be placed in danger.

The unanimous response was, however, that we should remain in business rather than giving way to such threats, and upon that note we sent the girls to bed – Aspasia only remaining to warn Frank that the ready determination of her charges not to be bullied rested rather upon ignorance than upon courage for, she said, Mr Gaskill was a man of great ferocity and cruelty, and a dangerous enemy.

We decided to consult with Sir Philip Jocelind, who might have among his friends those who would best know how to deal with Mr Gaskill. And in no happy mood we retired to bed, any residual longings which remained after our evening's experience thoroughly cooled by the new and unpleasant situation now pressing upon us.

Chapter Fourteen

Sophie's Story

My recognition of Lady Chichley upon her visit to our house did not prevent her from regularly returning, usually conferring her favours upon Harry, for whom she clearly formed a genuine admiration not wholly physical in its nature.

She confided in me that Chichley, on their wedding night, having paid her the compliment of rendering her no longer a maid, had then returned to that formal manner and address with which he had always treated her. They had been designed for each other, she explained, almost from birth, their parents being neighbours in the country. But they had met rarely, and then under the careful eye of their elders, so that they scarcely knew each other until a week or two before their marriage.

'Not only,' she said, 'does Chichley feel unready to be tied to one woman – and I believe that that would be his view even were she a wife of his own choosing – but it seems the case that he is uninterested in the sex, for his attentions to me were cool in the extreme, or rather warm only to the extent that allowed him to function as a man should. When I attempted to renew the familiarity on subsequent evenings, he simply declined, despite my pleadings. Some women – nay, many, perhaps – would have been pleased at this lack of interest, especially should they have been wed for their estate to men older and less attractive than they would have wished. But Chichley is a fine figure of a man, and one whose body I craved the more upon my brief close acquaintance with it. But alas, he does not find the sex attractive, and I might as well be a widow. Are you surprised, then, Mrs Nelham, that I should visit your establishment so regularly? Harry is, of course, scarcely my match in social standing, let alone in estate, but to be frank I find his attentions comforting in the extreme. But I run on – please forgive me for boring you with detail!'

I was astonished to hear of Chichley's attitude to his bride, for as I had plainly seen during my somewhat untoward observations, she was a young woman of great physical attractions, whose firm and pliant body would surely be coveted by any man. I determined to renew my acquaintance with her husband and attempt to discover what had possessed him since he had proved to me his capacity for energetic masculine action.

In the meantime, spring had turned to summer and the days had grown longer and hotter, and one weekend I decreed a day of leisure. We had always, of course, been closed upon the Lord's Day, when the boys remained at home and no doubt occupied themselves in those tasks they were largely forced to neglect during the rest of the week. But now I summoned them, one Sunday, to be entertained by me to a day's leisure, during which we could take our ease, eat, drink, and recreate ourselves.

The day dawned clear and bright, and as I looked from the window down over the gardens I reflected that even Alcovary could not surpass in beauty my present surroundings. My room looked over the high-walled private part of the grounds which stretched down to the river, where the boathouse gleamed white in the as yet low-slanting rays of the sun beyond lawns as close-clipped and even as a green tablecloth.

We were all up early, the boys having slept, some of them in slight discomfort, at the house, and enjoyed a fine breakfast. Then by ten o'clock, when the air was already warm, we took ourselves into the gardens by the riverside where the light breezes over the water would cool our bodies from the extreme heat of the sun.

Nevertheless, by midday we were all stripped bare, William, George and I careful to lie in the shadow of the trees, for they, like me, wished to shade their bodies from the effects of the sun. But the rest lay in the open, the buttocks of Ben and Tom already beginning to turn pink, while Harry's skin, already brown, seemed likely to turn mahogany. Spencer, proving a fine swimmer, was more often in the river than out of it.

Luncheon came to us in baskets, accompanied by claret in quantity. And afterwards, as we lay in a delightful langour, I recalled Andy telling me how his girls had regaled him with their former adventures, and suggested that we should play at a similar game. To start the proceedings, I told the story of my own adventures at Miss Jessie Trent's boarding school (which readers of my former chronicles will doubtless recall). This amused them considerably, especially when I described with some vigour the fate that unpleasant woman met at the hands of her rebellious pupils.

'But now,' I said, 'who will be next?' – and looked meaningfully at Harry, for I must admit that of all the boys he was the one who interested me most, and I longed to hear his history.

'I was born,' he said, 'in London, to a mother who, though poor, cared for me and my younger sister and brother with all the devotion a diminutive purse permitted. My father deserted us soon after my brother was born, and my mother got what money she could by washing and cleaning and other means, but never from any activity which the most puritanical critic might condemn. We lived in a single room and seldom enjoyed more food than would merely keep us alive, yet we were not unhappy, until that sad day came when my mother, worn out, I do believe, by her efforts, died. I was then fifteen years old, and had already for some time been bringing home what money I could earn by running errands, holding horses, and lately by labouring.

'My sister Moll was five years younger than I, devoted to me and our younger brother. We had grown up within arm's length of each other, and had shared a bed for as long as I could remember. This might be condemned by moralists, for it certainly led to a familiarity more than common between brother and sister, yet experienced, I believe, by many of the poor. You will understand, then, that we soon knew perfectly well how a man and woman – or rather a boy and girl – differed in bodily shape from each other, which led to no embarrassment nor even any curiosity. For what was well known to us bred no questions until the time came when that part of my anatomy which is most valuable in my present occupation showed signs of raising its head. This phenomenon was discovered by Moll even before I myself noticed it, for I awoke one morning to a delightful and comfortable glow centring on my lower parts, and upon achieving full consciousness discovered Moll stroking and cosseting a strange growth which had started from between my thighs, and which upon closer inspection proved to be the thing I had formerly considered only an instrument for pissing with.

'It is a strange mark of natural modesty that I somehow knew that it would not be proper to encourage Moll to continue to occupy herself with her new plaything, reluctant though she was to desist. However, I persuaded her to relinquish her hold, though I was most reluctant to forgo that most pleasant sensation which her handling of me had produced. So much so indeed that privately, when I had turned her out of bed and sent her on some errand – perhaps the comforting of our younger brother, then only four or five – I seized the opportunity to see whether I could not myself provide some shadow of that pleasure by handling myself, with a result that you will no doubt believe.

'Moll was not easily persuaded to leave that newly developed part of my anatomy alone, and for a while I would wake in the night to find her hand exploring it. But after some time, my continuing to counterfeit disinterest (for anger would have set her on rather than dissuading her) together with her having thoroughly satisfied her curiosity, she discontinued her provocations, and by the time she herself became a woman, I was perhaps fortunately though sadly removed from the scene. For when, as I have explained, my mother died, I was left sole provider, and was forced to travel further and further afield in search of work.

'For me to raise sufficient money to pay the rent of our single room was not easy, and we fell behind with our payments – the result of which was my returning one day to find the room occupied by someone else, and my sister and brother gone, no one could tell me whither. I returned time and again, in case they were to be found, but was forced in the end to conclude that they had either been stolen away by some persons and forced into a form of slavery, or had been murdered, or simply had decided to try their luck alone.

'My sorrow at my loss, and disappointment that Moll should have thought so little of me, came just when my manhood demanded expression, and at the same time I obtained work at Hampstead with a small group of workmen engaged in demolishing a building which stood on the brow of the hill. The fellow who employed us – myself and five other men – instructed us that upon no account were we to attempt to explore the building next door, which was surrounded by a high wall. His instructions, from his own employer, had at first been that all his workmen should be blindfold – at which he had, of course, laughed. But his paymaster, who was a clergyman of some years' experience but entire lack of sense, finally explained that the two houses were the property of the church. The one which we were knocking down had been a seminary for young clergymen, while its fellow was still occupied by twenty-five young ladies sent by their parents to be educated by nuns, and destined eventually for the convent.

'Our master, who looked to fresh employment by the church, warned us that to be seen looking at, much less attempting to converse with, the young ladies would result in immediate dismissal together with other penalties so dire that he dared not express them in words. The result of which was, in my case at least, to provoke extreme curiosity, though all but one of my fellows were so concerned to keep their employment that it became quite a joke with us to call out that a young lady was to be seen, whereupon they would scurry away to some corner, out of view.

'It was of course the case that while we were working upon the upper floors of the house, we had an entire view of the gardens of the school, and indeed could not help, from time to time, seeing the flash of a dress upon the other side of the wall. I must confess that, feeling as I did the itch of manhood, my curiosity was no greater than my lust, and I inferred that any young lady shut away within such walls, and with such a fate ahead of her, might be likely game if only I could come at her. I was happily aided in my ambition by the weather, which that summer was as hot as it is now, and so we worked stripped to the waist. And it was not long before my friend Bill and I were conscious that some of the young ladies – how many, we could not tell – were regularly congregating in a small thicket of bushes near the wall, where their eyes were, we suspected, upon us.

'We ignored them until one afternoon, when the other men were resting at lunch time, and Bill and I were lazing upon a scaffold watching the garden out of the corners of our eyes, when two girls actually walked into the open patch of grass by the bushes, and there lifted their hands and signalled to us. What they meant by their signals we did not at first know, but since their movement was so obvious, had no hesitation in waving back. Upon seeing this, they positively skipped with excitement, and made gestures with their hands upon their breasts which seemed to indicate that they admired what they could see of our bodies – whereupon we turned about and about, exhibiting ourselves to their view. And to our delight, one of them actually loosed her clothing, despite the other's attempt to prevent her, and with a promising lasciviousness displayed a pair of breasts which would have slain us outright had we been near enough to see them in any detail. As it was, Bill almost met his death from leaning over the scaffold in an attempt to do so! In the meantime the young lady who had so delighted us was again making motions, which this time seemed to invite a reciprocal gesture – whereupon I, with a forwardness which I can only set down to youth, loosed my trousers and let them fall to my knees, displaying a person roused to some enthusiasm by both sight and imagination.

'The effect upon the young ladies was all I could have hoped, for one appeared to faint away – though from the fact that she also shaded her eyes in an attempt to see more clearly, I believed her faintness to be temporary. And the other jumped up and down in a display of delighted pleasure, but this was cut short when they suddenly vanished into the bushes, and immediately thereafter, as I hurriedly pulled my clothes together, the sight of an elderly woman in a dark habit reminded us that our admirers were not altogether at liberty.

'It cannot be supposed that two hot-blooded youths were to be persuaded not to take up what appeared to be a warm invitation, and upon the nun's vanishing and all once more becoming quiet, we descended to where, upon a level with the top of the wall, a plank could be set so that we could make the leap – which we did immediately, falling rather than jumping to the ground inside the garden. We were immediately greeted by our delighted admirers and drawn within a clearing in a small thicket, only just sufficiently broad to take our four reclining bodies but offering grass sufficiently thick to make a bed as comfortable as any I have since occupied. And here the delightful enthusiasm of the two young ladies met our own hopes in as happy a consummation as any virgins (for so we were, all of us) could hope for.

'Our two friends had, I now guess, comforted each other in mutual play, for there was none of the pain of maidenheads broken, only a breathless pleasure which rose quickly to a pitch which was almost frightening to two lads whose experience of the sex had previously been confined to admiration at a distance. The space being so narrow, we could not but be conscious of each other's joys, and our eyes continually met in wondering and rejoicing astonishment at our luck, as once and again our companions milked us, or so it seemed, of the very marrow of our bones.

'So confined was the space, and so eager our new friends lest their pleasure should be cut short, that we had little time to admire them, our sight being confined to a close view of an eyebrow or an ear or, when we insisted, to the admiration of a smooth and firm breast. Though having for the second time lain down my life, I insisted upon a view of the place of battle – I had of course seen my sister unclothed, but that was when she was a child and bald as an egg in that essential place. But now the silky nest which had welcomed me seemed so entrancingly dressed and coiffeured as positively to invite a renewal of the fight which, my being so new and fresh to such combats, I was able to achieve.

'In half an hour we had tried, or so we thought, every form of pleasure our bodies had to offer – though indeed that was not truly the case, for youth and inexperience precluded the more unusual of exquisite pleasures. We lay, however, damp with perspiration and the exhalation of the grasses, and for a moment, I believe we slept. Not for long, however, for we woke to the rustling of the bushes and to a shriek of feminine anger, to see two elderly but muscular men and the woman we had previously seen looking down at us. Though the men were distracted by their view of the two naked girls, and the nun by (as I believe) her first view of two naked men, their preoccupation did not prevent them from arresting us. We were hauled unceremoniously from the thicket without pause even to clothe ourselves, and led across the lawn to the house, stopping halfway to allow us to pull our trousers on, for the nun noticed the windows crowded with young ladies all with a clear view of our relaxed but perhaps still disconcerting masculinity.

'To cut the story short, we were thrown out of the school and out of our jobs, and presumably our companions also were forced to leave. However, neither of us I suspect repined, and certainly once having had a taste of the pleasure to be obtained from the intimate company of ladies, I was not disinclined to continue to seek such pleasure. I now consider myself fortunate, after some years of random employment, to have been seen one day at bathing by Mrs Nelham, and subsequently invited by Sir Philip to join an establishment the purpose of which might be solely the pleasure it affords me!'

Harry's tale having been received with laughter and applause, he leapt to his feet and, running across the grass, cleaved the air with a bound to vanish into the water of the river. I asked George, then, whether he would not favour us with the story of his life, certain, surely, to be unusual and interesting.'

'Some twenty-five years ago,' our black friend said, 'my father was captured upon the African coast by Portuguese slave-traders and set aboard a ship for the New World. He would doubtless have died there in irons – for he was a proud man who would never have bowed to the regulations of a master – had he not contrived to escape from the ship when it put in for supplies in the Canaries, and begged succour of the captain of a British trader then moored nearby. The captain would have turned him away, but by good fortune the owner was aboard – a merchant of Christian virtue and natural grace, who brought my father back

to England and took him into his family. Here he worked
as a general servant and in time met and married my mother,
a woman from the West Indies who had been brought back
by that same merchant a year previously, and educated as a
Christian.

'My parents were happily employed and when I was born
their contentment was complete, their master taking a similar interest in me, and upon my reaching ten years of age
and having outgrown such lessons as his housekeeper could
devise, sending me to school in the country. However, I was
unhappy there, for I was made fun of on account of the
colour of my skin, and hated for being different from the
others. So much so indeed that finally I could bear it no
longer, and ran away.

'My future was uncertain, for I knew that if I sought out
my parents they would be distraught at my ingratitude to
their master and insist on my returning to school, which I
could not bear. And so I slept under hedges for several
days, and eventually, finding myself at a lodge gate, was
begging a crust of bread when I was noticed by the lady of
the house, passing in her carriage. She stopped, picked me
up and enquired who and what I was. I spun her, I am sorry
to say, a tale of escaping from a cruel master who intended
me for the slave trade – I had heard my father's story often
enough to be able to lend such an invention credibility. And
I so impressed her with my forthright bearing (which I had
learned in order to withstand unkindness from my fellows)
and by my excellent command of the English language (for
which I must thank my master) that she invited me to enter
her service – which I did.

'My duties were not onerous; clad in silk and velvet and
provided with a white wig, I was simply to dress the rooms
of the mansion in which Mrs Damerel dwelt, to fetch and
carry, and to impress her friends and acquaintances with
my presence, which took little enough of intelligence. My
fellow-servants were, happily, pleasant enough to me, and I
felt that domestic service must be my natural calling.

'My downfall began some four years later, when my
employer played hostess to Lady Curd, a dowager. She
seemed to me to be sufficiently ancient – though indeed
may not have been much over forty – and was of a lusty

and coming-on disposition. Her husband, being older than she, was not inclined to serve her, and not being rich enough to purchase lovers she was in considerable desperation for want of one.

'Before she had been in the house five minutes, she had set her eyes upon me, and I believe had inferred that beneath my breeches was something to interest her. I should say that my physical development had not been invisible to my lady, who only a few days earlier had commented that I seemed no longer to fit my breeches, and that some new clothing must be obtained for me. The truth is that my developing person was already more considerable in size than anything a white page might have had to conceal, and I was forced to the expedience of cramming it down between my legs and attempting to disguise it by a slightly stooping gait, which of course only drew attention to the unseemly bulge which there was no real way of concealing.

'The dowager requested that my lady lend her my services, and the latter – who was a great innocent – did not demur, but instructed me to wait upon her friend, whom I then accompanied to her rooms. My first task was to fetch warm towels for her bath – which I did from the kitchen, where a cupboard of them was always kept next the fire. Upon my return to the bedroom I found my new mistress seated in the hip-bath, and for the first time was confronted by the view of the female body. Never having seen it even depicted, much less in the warmth of flesh, I was not offended by the wrinkles of the neck, the slackness of the breasts nor the spreading of the hips, but found my breeches straining to confine a display of interest which made my posture even more ungainly than usual.

' "George, the towels," cried Lady Curd. "But no! Wait, your beautiful livery will be soiled! You had better remove it first!"

'The eccentricity of this order did not altogether dismay me, for I was used to unquestioning obedience. I obeyed, and clad only in my shirt – too short, even though I bent almost double, to conceal me – carried the towels to the bath, when standing up she commanded me to dry her body, which I did without difficulty, being already almost of my complete adult height.

'I could not but notice the pleasure she took in my attentions but was nevertheless surprised when, having rested her hand upon my shoulder as she stepped from the bath, dropping the towels she pressed her body against my own, and gasped with astonishment as she laid her hand between my legs.

'I could not guess the reason for her surprise but infer, through subsequent experience, that it was the astonishment of a white woman at the size of my member, which I need not hesitate to claim is larger than is the average with lighter-skinned men. The touch of it enlivened her, and ripping my shirt from me, she held tightly to my arms and dragged me to the bed, where throwing me upon my back she mounted me, and to my astonishment took my prick in her hand and introduced it into what appeared to be an aperture in her own body!

'My ignorance of the female frame being complete, I had had no notion of how the act of love was performed – nor indeed that such an act was possible between a man and a woman, though I had heard hints from my fellow servants, and had felt that natural pull which attracts the young male to his female opposite.

'To anyone who believes that a boy of fifteen must be revolted by the person of a woman perhaps thirty years his senior, I must offer a contradiction. No doubt if a girl of my own age had introduced me to the pleasures of the bed, my view might have been a different one. But as things were, I was only too delighted at the course things had taken, and my new mistress's voracity at the game introduced me, within a few days, to almost every variation of carnal pleasure – for she quickly recognised an apt pupil, and in quest of her own satisfaction was delighted to show me how hands, lips and tongue could prepare, enhance and complete the pleasure a sturdy prick suggested.

'Upon Lady Curd's leaving, she presented me with a purse of five guineas and the invitation to enter her service any time I wished – which, since she lived in cold Northumberland, was an idea that did not commend itself to me. However, I was sorry to see her go and to return to my usual duties, for my mistress, the innocent, had no idea of the reason why her friend took such pleasure in my company and seemed so enthusiastic in my praise.

'Within a week I was desperate having now been used to two or three sessions at love in each day, and disinclined to search for satisfaction in the servants' hall, having become used to perfumed cleanliness rather than the stink of sweat, and worse, which the kitchen maids gave forth.

'Finally, I was at my wits' end, and took the desperate measure of employing a knife to loosen the seams of my breeches before, first thing in the morning, going to attend my mistress as she prepared for the day. I had awoken, as usual, with my fellow's head raised, bursting for employment, and had trouble enough persuading him into a sufficiently relaxed state to occupy his place without bursting forth. My mistress then only twenty-seven years of age or less, dressed in her dishabille and seated at her dressing table, was a picture so delicious that by allowing my imagination to play upon what we might do together, I had no difficulty in rousing my prick again to such enthusiasm that just as she reached out her hand for the scent-bottle I held for her, he burst his bounds and his head struck forth between the seams of my breeches!

'The scent bottle fell to the floor unnoticed, my mistress transfixed by the sight she now saw before her. There was no question what it was: she was not so ignorant! But once more the size was a surprise to her, though not an unpleasant one.

'The effect was all that I hoped for. My mistress's husband, I should say, was a politician of great influence, but much preoccupied with affairs of state and though young, handsome and vigorous, often from home – as he was upon this occasion, so that my lady was as ready as I for an encounter.

' "Why, George," she said, "is this the explanation of Lady Curd's interest in you?"

' "I believe so, ma'am," I said. "You will pardon me, but I have been in and out of my breeches so often in this past week that they have grown weak . . ."

'She laughed at this, and rising to her feet opined that since they were now of little use to me, we must find me other clothes; and in the meantime perhaps I should remove the offending garment.

'My lady's body, being younger and more perfect, extended and sharpened my taste for beauty, and she was amazed at my knowledge of what best pleased a lady. Though as with others, it was my size which provoked most astonishment and delight, a fact which, if I may say so, becomes a little fatiguing, for those ladies kind enough to invite me to their beds seem to do so on that basis alone, while there are other tricks at which I am adept. Nevertheless, I do not grumble, and nor did Mrs Damerel, who from that time on dismissed her maid and commanded that I should bring her her morning chocolate – which frequently grew cold upon the bedside table while we were warming between the sheets.

'A short while ago, however, my lady's husband was appointed Governor General of one of our colonies abroad and my situation was terminated. At one of the dinners he gave during which he and my lady made their *adieux* to their friends, Sir Philip Jocelind and his late uncle were guests. How Sir Philip came to be cognisant of the position I held in my lady's esteem, you must invite him to convey, but he approached me with news of your present enterprise and I was all too glad to join it – for to be honest, the ambition to spend my life making money by performing an act which offers me at least as much enjoyment as it does to any other male creature, is something of which I never dreamed.'

It was now, by consent, the turn of William to let us know his story for, as Harry said (now once more lying close by, a mist of steam rising from his body as the sun dried it after his swimming) he had always been somewhat secret, and no one knew his antecedents.

'This,' he explained, 'is because my family is one whose reputation would be known to you all. You know that I call myself Langrish, but that is not my true name – which I shall still keep from you, if you will forgive me, for reasons which will be obvious to you as my story progresses. Or, indeed, at its very beginning, for I must tell you that I grew up not only in a house in one of the most distinguished cathedral closes in this country, but as the son of a dean of one of its best known cathedrals.

'My father,' he continued, 'was a man of considerable reputation in the church, and married to a lady whose beauty and intelligence were ornaments to their drawing-room. I was the youngest of seven children but there had been a gap of seven years between myself and my elder brother Ned, so that by the time I was fifteen years old all my siblings had for one reason or another left home: two brothers for the Navy and one for the life of a curate in a distant parish, while my three sisters were all married. My mother was now over forty years of age, and my father almost fifty, so that while I was deeply beloved of them, they seemed to me to be ancient, and it was the younger members of their household – the maids and kitchen-boys – who were my friends. And my father being a man who considers all to be his equal, I was always allowed great freedom among them, and considered them as brothers and sisters.

'My every whim being indulged, I was allowed too to meet and mix with all kinds of boys and girls of my own age, and consequently grew up in the greatest freedom. But yet, through good example and teaching, I learned to regard kindliness and good nature, together with a gentlemanly deportment, as the natural concomitant of an agreeable and proper life. I was (though I say it) a good-looking lad, and my pretty appearance together with a friendly and open character made me a favourite with all – especially perhaps when I appeared as a member of the cathedral choir, when my appearance was positively angelic, I am informed. I found it difficult not to respond to the whispers and glances of the female members of the congregation; at first, to those elderly ladies who were happy, after service, to offer me sweetmeats and even money, but, as I grew older, to those young ladies nearer my own age to whom I felt an inexplicable attraction.

'Neither my father nor, of course, my mother gave me instruction as to my conduct with the opposite sex, leaving that task to my tutors, one of whom, being younger than the others, did offer me the most explicit description of the action a young man can perform with a young woman. However, one of my father's trusted elder servants happened to enter the schoolroom just as, having lowered his small-clothes to indicate the dimensions which I could expect my private parts to reach upon my attaining puberty, my tutor was attempting to persuade me to do the same by way of comparison – something which, for no reason I could have readily given, I found antipathetic. The tutor left the following morning, to be replaced by an older man.

'My realisation that I had attained the age of maturity came upon me one summer's afternoon when, in a wood not far from home, I had decided to cool myself by bathing in the river, to which end I removed my clothing and plunged in. Having enjoyed ten minutes of swimming and diving, I climbed out and after a while fell asleep lying in a pool of sunlight falling between the trees – to waken, some time later, to the realisation that I was not alone.

'My companions were two young sisters of my own age, whom I had often seen at the cathedral. Though forced by the presence of their mama to be discreet in their actions, I had seen them direct many a twinkling glance in my direction and after service, while their mama and my own were exchanging compliments, I would make them my bow, and never hesitated to direct them a smile or two.

'Now, however, they were most serious – as well they might be, for the young man whom they found lying at their feet as they strode through the wood made a very different figure than when he was dressed from head to foot in a black cassock, or in his Sunday best. I had neglected to cover myself, and in sleep my essential part had swelled to an extent which can only have been surprising to young ladies who had not even a brother whose body might have taught them what to expect.

'Through my lowered eyelashes I could see them, dark against the light, their arms about each other as they strained to see more closely that startling sight, and then they began to tiptoe towards me, the more closely to examine the phenomenon. By lying still, not so much as moving a muscle, I tempted them yet closer, so that in the end they knelt at my side, confident that I was in the deepest of sleeps, and bent so that the yellow locks of one of them actually brushed my belly – when involuntarily my muscles tightened and my prick quivered in a manner which made them at once start and giggle.

'By this time, eager to note their reactions and seeing them preoccupied, I had opened my eyes, and at their movement our gazes met, and they started to their feet.

' "Nay, Miss Priscilla, Miss Louise," I cried, "pray do not disturb yourselves!"

'They were silent, but at least did not fly, and I raised myself on an elbow, and to give them confidence turned so that I could shade my lower part with my hand – or at least make a gesture at doing so, which reassured them.

' "Master William," said Miss Priscilla, and they made a little curtsy, seeming at once to wish to go, and longing to stay.

' "Will you not sit in the sun for a while?" I suggested, and after a moment, indeed they sat, some way off.

' "It is remarkably warm for the time of the year," said Miss Louise, perhaps the more forward of the two. "I am quite bothered by the heat!" And she began to fan herself with her hand.

' "Indeed," agreed her sister, " 'tis quite overcoming!"

' " 'Twas why I bathed myself in the river," I said, "which has cooled me remarkably. I would suggest that you did the same . . ."

' "But we cannot swim," said the elder, "though Mama allowed us to disport ourselves in the sea at Margate last summer."

' "No matter," I argued, "the water is shallow near the bank, and I would be there to ensure that no harm would come to you."

'In short, they agreed, and having seen at the seaside the habit of ladies and gentlemen of bathing quite naked within sight of each other – though certainly at a greater distance than separated us – retired behind a bush, where in a moment I saw their dresses laid upon a branch, and then two white figures lowered themselves, with faint screams, into the water. I felt, of course, that I should be as good as my word in protecting them from possible danger, and after a moment joined them, the interval together with the coolness of the water reducing my lower limb to a size which could no longer frighten even the most nervous of ladies.

'While I swam around them, the girls were content to submerge themselves, only their shoulders above the water – though occasionally, from their happy jumpings, I caught a glimpse of a rosy-tipped breast, which interested me much.

' "Master William," Priscilla eventually said, "could you not show us how to swim? I see the motion of your arms, but when I attempt it –" And trying to support herself, her head disappeared under the water, to reappear with a splutter.

' "Certainly, Miss Priscilla," I said. "If I come behind you and support you." And stationing myself behind her, I placed my arms beneath hers, so that she lay back and in a moment was floating, and when I lifted my own legs from the ground and swam backwards reclined deliciously against my naked body, my hands over her breasts (for it were impossible to place them otherwise). Which gave her the most pleasure, the sensation of floating or that of feeling for the first time the embrace of a male, I would not say.

'By now, Miss Louise was clamouring for her turn, and nothing loath I made my excuses to her sister and supported her, now so in command of the situation that I could look over her shoulder at the length of her body, scarcely veiled by the flowing water which parted about her breasts and hips, and revealed where it flowed between her legs strands of what might (had we been at the seaside) have been the lightest seaweed. Miss Priscilla was so interested by the sight that, forgetting herself, she was standing up in the water, only covered to the waist, drops trickling from her body and her delightful bubbies for the first time fair to my view. The sight, and the sensation of her sister's body in my arms had the effect of recovering me to full vigour – which Louise could not but feel, as it pressed against the small of her back. And in a moment, she reached about to confirm with her hand the presence of something whose size and shape would have more confused her had she not set eyes on it while I was asleep.

' "I grow somewhat chilly," she said, "shall we not lie in the sun once more?" And taking me by the hands, walked me to the shore, where we all climbed out – myself, I must confess, with a certain sense of shame attempting to hide from them my once more rampant part. But 'twas vain, for each was determined to further their acquaintance with it, and pinned me to the ground, a willing victim, while they bent over to inspect the phenomenon at close range.

' "Does it not hurt you to enclose it in trousers?" they asked. And when I explained that 'twas not always of such a size, wondered at this, and asked why then it was now of such dimensions.

' " 'Tis in tribute to your beauty," was my reply, which occasioned much laughter, and the question whether it was always so in the presence of ladies, to which I replied only when they were so pretty, which brought a blush to their cheeks. Meanwhile, it can be imagined that I was not averse to catching what glimpses I could of their own anatomy, confirming the statement of my former tutor as to the formation of the landscape.

' "Oh, look," cried Miss Priscilla, whose cool fingers I felt about me, "he weeps! Why does he weep?"

'With a presence of mind unusual, I fancy, for my years, I replied that he wished to make a closer acquaintance with them. And when they asked how that could be, when we were already as close together as was necessary for polite conversation, explained that the purpose why we were made so different could only be demonstrated by our embracing, which they were clearly curious to try, while at the same time wishing to appear reluctant. And now there came the cry of "You first!" and "No, you are the elder!" and so on, until – confident of my powers – I suggested that I could show them both, and that Miss Priscilla, as the elder, might perhaps properly be the first object of my attentions.

'The drawing with which my tutor had illustrated his lesson in love had shown merely the most basic of all positions in amorous congress, and so I invited Miss Priscilla to lie upon her back – whereupon she rolled over – and to open her legs, which she did with the utmost freedom, never, I suppose, having heard it suggested that 'twas improper (for I am sure the subject had never been broached to the sisters either by their mama or their governesses). I then knelt between her thighs and, lowering myself, placed the tip of my prick against her lower lips, which from her drawing of breath was, I think, no less delicious to herself than to me, for throwing her arms about me she drew me so closely to her that without further effort I slipped into harbour, and with that instinct common to us all, bucked once, and again. And then, so extensive was the emotion I felt, I gave up my soul, to Priscilla's intense disappointment, who thrusting with her hips in imitation of myself found only a diminishing firmness in my person.

' "I do not consider that much to my advantage," she remarked somewhat sourly as I lifted myself from her. "If I was you, Louise, I should not trouble myself!" However, her sister was determined upon the same experience, and with the natural resilience of youth I found her excited fumbling in an attempt to recover me had its effect in a very short time. And on the second occasion was able to contain myself until, with a cry sufficiently loud to startle the birds from the trees, Louise dug her nails into my bum and threw her body into such a paroxysm that I rolled away, fearing that I had hurt her.

' "How can you say 'twas nothing?" she asked her sister. "Why, 'tis the most delicious, the most wonderful, the most . . ." But words failed her – not before encouraging Priscilla to wish for a renewed passage. This time, both she and her sister had to spend some time recovering my sensibilities, but their efforts only further sharpened their desire, so that by the time I was again able to mount the elder, the younger had also to seize my hand and thrust it between her thighs. And in this way I satisfied them both – which was as well, for I doubt even at that age that I could have performed a fourth time within so short a period.

'It need not be said that we met again many times that summer, nor that in natural play we discovered many tricks and pleasantries which I hope were of as much advantage, later, to their husbands (though perhaps surprising to them) as they were to me in those other amorous adventures I have since had. And just at a time when I was beginning to believe that I would have at last to acquiesce in my father's long-expressed desire that I should follow him into the church, Sir Philip made my acquaintance upon his revisiting the University of Cambridge, and introduced me to yourself, Mrs Nelham, and to this present life.'

*　　*　　*

By this time the sun was beginning to lower, and it was time to dress and remove ourselves to the house, where again we ate and drank. And it was a pleasure to us, for once, to relax in each other's company without the knowledge that at any moment the ringing of the bell might summon one or other of us to an arduous, if no doubt pleasurable, demonstration of his masculine powers.

Chapter Fifteen

The Adventures of Andy

Though two weeks passed without our hearing any more from the gentlemen who had so seriously threatened us, the event was never far from our minds. We discussed our problem with Sir Philip Jocelind, upon one of his visits to us, for he came from time to time. Though he had employed each of our girls at one time or another, he now for some private reason seemed not to wish to use the house for the purpose for which it had been established, but was happy to sit of an evening and take a glass or two with Frank and me.

Hearing of our visitation, he grew grave, agreeing with Aspasia that it was most likely that Carlo Gaskill was at the back of it. 'A man of no little influence in the dark corners of London life,' he said, 'but I have someone I might consult on the matter; leave it with me' – and went on to talk of other things, notably of the strange incident of his meeting in the hall one evening none other than Viscount Chichley, who had been for a time a confidante of sister Sophie's.

'It is a strange thing to meet him here,' he said, 'for he was recently wed to a lady of complete beauty and accomplishment, who I would have thought to be an ornament to any marriage. Yet within weeks comes here to escort Xanthe or Rose to bed – not that every one of your ladies is not a complete compendium of delights, as I have had the pleasure of proving. But were I to wed, I would hope that it would be a month or two at least before I made any excursion to another bed, and Chichley is after all still a young man, his appetite not jaded by familiarity with vice. 'Tis odd indeed – but men are indeed strange animals where love is concerned' – a statement Frank greeted with a heartfelt 'Amen', for where would we be, he enquired, were lovers not to be faithless and married men to stray?

It was nevertheless a pleasure to me to have the occasional

opportunity to talk with Chichley, and one night, upon our discussing the vast difference between London society and that of even the most advanced of our provincial cities, he most generously procured me an invitation to dine with the Lord Mayor, who regularly holds levees for the more prominent merchants and business men of the city. 'Amongst whom you must be counted, Mr Archer,' he said, 'though perhaps not in a business whose purpose you need noise abroad at that particular assembly.'

The Mansion House, sometimes called the City Palace, certainly resembles a royal domicile in size, but is badly situated close by the Bank and Royal Exchange. The streets are so narrow that it is impossible to see the building properly, and it is difficult for carriages to approach it at all. However, inside all is extensively handsome, and I found the company amazingly various – from merchants whose only ornament was their banking account, to the royal dukes and some of the nobility. Chichley and his wife, at his side but yet treated with a noticeable coolness, were among them. These, with the diplomatic corps, occupied seats on a platform at one end of the Egyptian Hall, a large room brilliantly lit, in which a band played. The tables below the platform were filled with citizens, and the Lord Mayor and Lady Mayoress presided side by side, the latter in full court dress.

After the courses were over, toasts were given, music kept up, and everything was of a becoming festivity – although I must confess that my enjoyment was somewhat dampened by the fact that my neighbours were stiff and uncommunicative, disposed to converse only with each other rather than offering any friendly gesture to me, despite my best endeavours to be companionable.

Then came a ball in another part of the building, and if the scene in the Egyptian Hall had been picturesque, that upstairs transcended it. The doors of the rooms were all open, and through them one saw a thousand ladies richly dressed, all the colours of nature displayed together like the bursting out of spring. No lady was without her plume; the whole was a waving field of feathers, some blue, some tinged with red, here violet and yellow, there shades of green; most, the purest white. The diamonds surrounding them caught the light and sparkled brilliantly, throwing out sharp beams of light. It was now that I saw for the first time so many hooped dresses, each lady seeming to rise out of a gilt or silver barricade; it was a feast of feminine grace and grandeur.

It would have been improper for me to have approached Chichley, nor did I feel able to introduce myself, where I was not known, to any of those present, especially since they showed a supreme lack of interest in me. After a while I became somewhat melancholy at the thought that I was to spend the evening alone, and decided to leave. But as I made my way towards the door, it was my good luck that a lady coming in the opposite direction stumbled, and would have fallen had I not caught her in my arms. Under other circumstances I might have taken advantage of the fact, for though my thighs were positively bruised by the hoops of her dress, her upper part was not similarly barricaded, and the softness of her breasts, largely uncovered and of an enticing creaminess, much raised my lowered spirits.

I set her upon her feet, wereupon she curtsied in thanks, and I made my bow. Standing near the door for a while and looking after her as she entered the room, I saw that like myself, she was alone, and though she was clearly in search of someone, she returned to the door unaccompanied, whereupon I ventured to bow again.

'You will excuse me, madam, if I venture to observe that you are unaccompanied, and to offer my services if –?'

I broke off, fearing to offend, but she smiled most graciously.

'You are very good, sir. I have missed my aunt, who was with me; if you are going in the direction of the refreshment hall, a cold drink is what I most desire.'

I offered my arm, she laid her hand upon it, and we walked to the room where long tables bore great tureens of claret cup.

My companion was of such beauty that I could not but be conscious of admiring looks from those about me. Of almost equal height to myself, she was of perhaps nineteen or twenty years, slim, excessively elegant, with a carriage of the head inexpressively haughty – yet at the same time her expression was friendly and her comportment condescending. Her hair

was of a becoming brown, and all her own, I dare swear –
no wig. Her forehead was broad and open, her lips full, and
her eyes a clear and bright, unusual blue. As for her person,
sated though I was by feminine company I could not but be
conscious of the inviting beauty of that part of her body not
constricted by the hoops of her fashionable gown. And I
may say, in parenthesis, that the sudden disappearance of
revealing muslin in favour of barricadoes, which made the
lower limbs of womankind as difficult to breach as the walls
of a fortress, was viewed by me with abhorrence! However,
happily the fashion did not conceal the swell of breasts, the
beauty of which would alone have marked her out for
admiration.

I ventured to introduce myself, but she did not respond
by venturing her own name. However, we talked friendly
enough, until after a while an elderly lady made her appearance to claim her niece, and with another curtsy she bade
me farewell. After a while I followed her, but on the way
found my arm taken by Chichley, who called me an adventurous young dog and congratulated me upon having
attached myself to one of the most considerable heiresses
in London that season – a Miss Mary Yately, the only
daughter of a private gentleman who owned, he said, most
of Shropshire, and was unattached.

I was entirely convinced that Chichley was joking in his
implication that I had known who my young friend was –
or indeed that I had 'attached myself' to her. However, the
fact that her beauty and charm were additionally burnished
by a large fortune made me all the more interested in Miss
Yately, and I devoted the next day or so to a little research
into her circumstances. This revealed that she had taken for
the season a large house off Piccadilly, where she lived with
her aunt. And according to Blatchford, who spent the
morning in conversation with a footman of hers he made
acquaintance with in a tavern, she was without an admirer,
though there were certain comings and goings, presumably
of those who wished to become so. But, the man had said,
she was cognisant that her fortune would attract those more
interested in it than in her, and was determined to avoid
capture.

Having worked out a plan, I took myself to St James's,

and from a jeweller's there bought at considerable expense
a small silver reticule in which (having enquired of our
ladies, without explaining my purpose, what they would
expect to find in the purse of a lady of fashion) I placed one
or two niceties – viz., handkerchief, perfume, *et cetera*.
Then, at about three in the afternoon, I took myself off to
Piccadilly and rang at my lady's bell.

I gave my name to the footman who answered it, and
enquired for the aunt, the Honourable Mrs Mathilda
Yately, whom I had seen ten minutes before drive off
towards the city. He replied that Mrs Yately was not at
home, but that he would announce me to Miss Yately. He
then vanished, to return and usher me up a splendid staircase to an elegant drawing-room where my friend sat at her
embroidery stand.

I was full of apologies: I would not have ventured to
announce myself to her but that her aunt was out, and yet it
was, I thought, on her business that I was here. And I
produced from my pocket the reticule.

'Just after we parted,' I said, 'I found this upon the floor
where you had been standing, and believing it yours, have
come to return it.'

She took it, curiously, but to my astonishment, having
examined it, recognised it as her own, with expressions of
gratitude! I fancy my jaw may have dropped, but simply
bowed and said that I was delighted to have been the agent
of the reticule's return. What could this mean? Was my
little scheme discovered, and I therefore discounted as a
fortune hunter? But she continued affable.

'You will take tea?'

I demurred; I had taken too much of her time.

'Not at all, it will be a pleasure to renew acquaintance.'

So tea was brought, and meanwhile we talked. I dropped
no hint that I knew anything of her circumstances, but
admitted that I had gone out of my way to discover her
name – which, I said, had not been difficult, since she was
uncommonly beautiful, and therefore the cynosure of all
eyes and the focus of all talk. I was 'in business' I said, and
hinted that I was in a fair way of wealth.

All this time I was becoming more and more enamoured
of her. She was dressed now for the boudoir rather than the

ballroom in a loose gown which revealed more of the beauty of her charming frame than could have been guessed at from her body's former fashionable imprisonment. And what I saw was of even greater charm than I could have suspected – to such an extent indeed that I felt the stirring of a passion which, I knew, I could not allow myself to show.

But things were to take a sharp turn, and soon. I do believe that her senses in some way apprehended my feelings almost before I knew them myself, for she suddenly remarked that surely I had spent much of my life in the country? And upon my asking how she came to understand this, she said simply that she could recognise a town gull as soon as sniff at him, whereas I had that natural vivacity of manner and – if she might say so – naturalness of bearing which marked me out a countryman.

'I grew up in Shropshire,' she said, 'and though in a great estate was entirely conscious of country matters. Here, there is a circling and circling before one can come at a matter, while there a stone is called a stone and a spade a spade.'

I was silent for a moment. Then, 'I cannot believe, ma'am, that any gentleman in town would not be as quick in apprehension of your beauty and parts as myself,' I said.

'Ah, that may be,' she said, 'but would they show it?'

A wink being as good as a nod to the blindest of horses, I took this for the invitation it was, and rising to my feet fastened upon her hand and pressed it to my lips – whereupon she too rose, and in a moment had fixed her own lips to mine, while pressing the length of her body against me in a manner unmistakable in its implication. As we were still embraced, I passed my hands beneath the muslin of her dress and felt, beneath their palms, flesh as soft as it was creamy.

Finally, she withdrew from my arms and somewhat to my dismay went to a bell pull at the wall and tugged at it. But then she immediately loosed her dress and began to climb out of it, so that when the door opened and the footman appeared, he saw a mistress clad only in her shift, while a young man only too obviously amazed – myself – stood at the other side of the room, his eyes goggling.

'Albert,' she said, 'I shall be occupied for the next half of an hour. Should my aunt return, kindly inform her that I am not to be disturbed.'

The fellow bowed, and without the merest suggestion of a smirk withdrew, while even before he had closed the door behind him Miss Yately had shed her sole remaining garment, and turning to me had enquired whether I was to disappoint her by proving as slow as a townee?

Not wishing to be accused so, I was soon as bare of covering as she, who had by this time laid herself at my feet upon the thick carpet, one leg drawn up, one arm behind her head, and a look of anticipation which was emphasised by the rising and falling of those breasts whose full disclosure was no disappointment.

I was under orders to be swift in action, but my mind was even swifter: the situation was not one which I had anticipated, nor had I come with the intention of seducing Miss Yately. Indeed my body was no more ready for such a scene than my mind, for the previous evening – the house being quiet – I had spent a happy hour with Xanthe and Rose which had left us all exhausted, and despite my youth I would not normally have expected to renew a carnal interest for at least twenty-four hours.

This was no an obstacle to fornication, mark you, for what youth of under twenty could not fuck three or four times a day were the opportunity to arise and were the lady to be of a coming-on disposition? And Miss Yately certainly was, but then my intention had been to ingratiate myself with her rather than to offer love-making, and the way to an heiress's pocket was not necessarily through her . . .

Well, now that I was in this position, the only thing to do was to be as pleasing as possible. Fortunately during the past four or five years I had had considerable training in the pleasuring of ladies, and in particular the past three or four months had taught me much, the ladies at Brook Street being quick to inform me what did and what did not contribute to their pleasure. Having to devote much of their time to satisfying the male appetite without necessarily experiencing a reciprocal delight, they were all the more eager to be satisfied when bedding Frank or myself. Though we were their employers, we were clearly also their friends, and should be counted upon to provide some gratification rather than merely accepting their favours in the way of trade.

So I set to with the intention of positively slaying my new friend with delight – which I think I may say I accomplished. No two ladies being utterly alike in what pleasures them, I spent some little time in experimenting whether the lobes of the ears or the tips of the breasts, the sucking of the lower lip or the nipping of the tongue, the stroking of the arse or of the thighs, gave most delight. I then offered consideration to that organ which lies just within the threshold of woman's portals, a prick in miniature, and caressed it with my tongue, first softly, delicately, regularly, then gradually more and more speedily and vigorously, even pausing to nibble and nuzzle. At the same time my fingers played about the rest of her body, particularly rubbing the tight nipples of the breasts, while I distinctly felt the muscles of her thighs tightening as though she longed to close them upon my neck to strangle me in her pleasure! It was indeed with some relief that, as her cries mounted, I sensed that the time had come for full congress. Should it be from the front or the back, should she lie beneath or mount above? Should my riding be swift or slow?

These questions were all tried, and in turn were plainly answered by Miss Yately with a fierce cry or a grip unmistakable in denoting satisfaction. She failed to respond to the long and regular thrusting which pleased most women, but rather encouraged me to place the tip of my prick just within her nether lips, drawing it entirely from her body at the end of each short stroke so that those lips were continually stirred and stretched – which she controlled by the pressing of her thighs together, thus not permitting me a full entry. This was not to my complete satisfaction. Nor was she, I must say, a very active participant, preferring to allow me to exhaust myself in her service rather than to pay any other tribute to my attentions than to suffer them, which was of no help when, after a while, already sapped on the previous night, my energies began to ebb. However, this had the merit that I was able to contain myself to her contentment, and fortunately her fourth paroxysm of enjoyment resulted in her almost losing consciousness. And so, kissing her, I withdrew myself, and she, seeming content, invited me to ring the bell – which I did, and Albert once more entered and ignoring our nakedness brought fresh tea, during the sipping of which we resumed our clothes.

'Mr Archer,' she said, finally, 'it has been a pleasure to make the acquaintance of one whose energy and aptness matches his personal elegance. I trust we shall meet again.'

I trusted so, too, for I must admit that while her love-making was of a certain selfishness, I found her extraordinarily attractive – while her fortune was not in itself a discouragement from my making myself agreeable to her. The attitude of the footman, Albert, caused me some disquiet. Indeed, as he showed me out there was no sign of impertinence nor of complicity. Did this simply betoken his excellence as a servant, carefully taught not to betray the slightest surprise or interest in his mistress's doings? Or could it be an indication that Miss Yately was not the innocent I imagined, and that the sight of a lover was not as unusual as I had thought? That she was not a virgin was certain, and indeed her references to country matters suggested that – as with many maids growing up among farmyards and fields where animal couplings are readily to be seen – her maidenhead had probably fallen to some lusty lout or other beneath a hedge, or more likely in some corner of her own garden. But even if this was the case, her scornful attitude to city suitors nevertheless promised well, and her positive enjoyment of the game of love – on her own account, at least – seemed to indicate that she would welcome a lover whose interest was entirely in her personal qualities rather than her fortune.

I returned to Brook Street and retired almost immediately to bed, being more than a little exhausted. But I was shook awake in the middle of the evening by Frank, who said that there was to be a conference below with regard to the demands of Mr Gaskill, and that Philip had brought a friend to advise us – and a friend I would be surprised to meet.

What indeed was my amazement upon joining them, to

find none other than David Ham, engaged deep in conversation with Jocelind, Blatchford, Will Pounce and Bob Tippett. He grinned at my surprise.

'I told you of my friend, Andy?' he said. ' 'Tis Sir Philip, here!'

Philip had the grace almost to blush, and indeed I was somewhat surprised to find that he had been keeping David as a bum-boy while at the same time enjoying not only our ladies but my Sophie! However, my surprise was not so great as it would have been had not Sophie hinted to me of certain problems he experienced with the ladies. And at any event 'twas not my habit to raise an eyebrow at any trick performed in bed, for they are too various not to provide, from time to time, an occasional wonder.

'I was not aware . . .' said Philip.

'Ah, yes,' said I, not averse to turning the screw, 'David and I are old friends, and indeed bedfellows' – at which his eyebrows rose. But I was not about to explain the circumstances of our familiarity, which had arisen on account of an interesting accident not unconnected with a theatrical performance, and not out of my own pleasure in being sodomised, which indeed had been entirely negligible, and had certainly not persuaded me to progress any further down that particular path.

'Well,' said David, 'you have yourselves in a pickle, but fortunately not too sharp a one, for I happen to know that your friend Carlo is no longer as popular as he might be, due to his inordinate lust for money. 'Tis time he was seen off, which as it happens I believe I can accomplish on your behalf with the aid of these good fellows here, especially Mr Tippett, who is a lad of my own heart. Now, Frank – if you will allow the familiarity?' – at which Frank smiled – 'the first thing is to appoint a meeting with Mr Gaskill, which can be done by a message sent to the address I know of. The second is to ensure the ladies are out of sight when he arrives. The third is – well, you can leave the third to us.' And he winked.

I believe that Frank was little inclined to trust the business to so young and apparently inexperienced a youth, but I was able to inform him privately that David was by no means the innocent he might appear. Indeed, an unpleasant

night in Bristol gaol had been my own experience of a result
of his occasional indulgence in crime, which had not as far
as I knew yet embraced murder, but which had at least displayed a certain competence where matters of illegality
were concerned. So an invitation was sent to Gaskill for the
night following, he to be accompanied only by two fellows,
and an agreement would be reached, to be confirmed by the
payment of a certain sum in gold.

The following night, the Brook Street establishment was
quiet, and the occasional visitor knocking was disappointed
to hear that due to sickness the house was closed that night.
At ten, however, a more determined knock revealed Carlo
Gaskill – a tall, middle-aged man of saturnine appearance,
accompanied by two of the fellows we had encountered
before.

Frank and I met them in the hall, wrapped only in towels,
which occasioned him some surprise.

'I think, sir,' said Frank, 'that our business should be
private. You will consider it, I believe, such that your escort
need not be concerned to hear the details' – and turning
aside he tipped a wink, which the man clearly believed
referred to the financial accommodation, and promised
him a share larger than would be the case should his accom-
plices know the details.

'As you are no doubt aware, we have hot baths here for
the convenience of our clientele. My friend and I are
unclothed' – and here both Frank and I unwrapped our
towels to show indeed that we concealed no weapons about
us – 'and we invite you to clothe yourself similarly, and to
accompany us downstairs, where we can discuss the matter
at leisure over a bottle.'

Gaskill thought for a moment, and then decided that he
would have no difficulty in defending himself against two
relative weaklings like Frank and myself. So in the neighbouring room he divested himself of his clothing and, wrap-
ping a towel about himself, accompanied us below while his
two friends remained in our receiving-room.

'Your facilities are as generous and luxurious as was
reported to me,' said Gaskill as he entered the warm room.
'I am delighted that we are to reach an agreement, for if
the ladies are as handsome and accommodating as report

suggests, there is no reason why your business should not continue to flourish and expand!' He then seated himself near the warm bath, and while the steam rose about us from the channels in the floor, Frank poured us all wine.

'This is indeed an exceptional arrangement,' Gaskill said, 'and one which must become more general; I doubt not that it attracts almost as many gentlemen as your stable of fillies. It may be that we should work more closely together. But first, what is your proposal for solving our current little difficulty?'

Frank began a long preamble concerning the income we commanded, the proportion given to the girls, the proportion which might be spared in tribute. Gaskill became notably more impatient, but sufficiently interested to keep his eyes fixed on us, sitting opposite him – which was as well, for on bare feet, David Ham accompanied by Blatchford, Tippett and Will Pounce, crept out of the doorway leading to the boiler room, and approached behind him. At the last moment, some instinct warned the villain, for he started and looked about. But too late – a piece of sacking was thrown over his head by David, and Blatchford and Pounce, each taking an arm, tipped him backwards into the water of the bath. Then Tippett mounted his struggling body and weighed it down.

I had never seen a man killed before, nor do I wish to again – yet if it must be done, drowning is relatively swift, relatively silent, and without the necessity to spill blood. In two minutes or less, all was over, and the sacking removed. The staring eyes of Gaskill were seen to be as empty of life as his lungs were of air.

I cannot say that I was sanguine in the affair; murder seemed to me to be too radical a solution to any problem, yet what we had heard of Gaskill had clearly indicated that he would have had no compunction about wounding and scarring our ladies, nor indeed about murder should we have stood out against him.

'Well done,' said Frank, grimly.

David, on the other hand, grinned broadly. 'A good night's work, as most of London will agree!' he said. 'Now for the rest of the plan.'

Retiring upstairs, we dressed and armed ourselves with

pistols before opening the door upon the corpse's two attendants, who looked vastly uncomfortable that their master was not among the six men who stood before them.

'Now, thumpers,' said David, 'Carlos has met with a sad accident downstairs, and you must find a new master – or make yourselves masters!' The bullies looked at one another. 'Yes, Johnson,' continued David, 'you've had your eye on the throne for some time now. Well, 'tis yours if you want it, for if you depart and no word spoke we'll keep you out of this; otherwise there might be a word to the watch – and 'tis common knowledge you'd have done the deed yourselves long since had you the wit and the courage.'

The men were silent; one fingered his pocket, but seeing our weapons kept their own out of sight, thinking better of action.

'Very well, young Ham,' said the elder.

'But mind you,' said David, 'no thurrocking from this house; all's to rest quiet here – as quiet as old Gaskill, below. Now, off with you.'

The men whispered together for a moment then, surly but quiet, left the house.

'You'll have no trouble,' said David. 'Johnson'll slit the throat of the other before they reach Blackfriars, then he'll have the whole gang where he wants it, and he won't want the trouble of worrying you – he'll be too busy establishing his monarchy. So to the rest of the plan.'

Within ten minutes the girls were downstairs dressed as for usual business; Philip and Pounce stripped and accompanied Cissie and Constance upstairs to amuse themselves in whatever way occurred to them – in case the watch should wish to examine the house – while Aspasia was established in her usual glory in the hall, and I went forth to find authority.

Returning in ten minutes with a sturdy fellow from Grosvenor Square, I let myself into the hall, where Aspasia greeted us with, 'Ah, officer, I trust this may be kept quiet. 'Tis an accident would do us no good in our business . . .'

'Well, ma'am,' said the watch, still clutching in his pocket the three guineas I had handed him, 'it indeed sounds an unfortunate matter. Where is the poor gentlemen?'

'Down here,' I replied, and escorted him to the hot room,

where a towel decently covered the remains of Gaskill. Having inspected the corpse, the watchman enquired for 'the young lady concerned' and I sent for Rose – who, her slight injury completely recovered, had begged for the satisfaction, and indeed gave a splendid performance.

The gentleman, she said, had been happily toying with her – 'for, you know, sir, that the heat oft sets 'em on' – when he had suddenly grasped at his chest and collapsed into the pool, from which he had been too heavy for her to remove. And by the time she had fetched Blatchford his heart had stopped, whether from its own inaction or from the inhalation of the water could not be known.

'He looks a sturdy enough fellow,' said the watch.

'But exertion of this kind can bring on a stoppage of the heart in many an unsuspecting chap,' said Rose. 'I have known it before.'

'And who might he be?' enquired the man.

'That, I cannot tell,' she said, and I pointed out that in the nature of our business most of the gentlemen attending the house either used false names or gave no name at all.

'Well, now,' said the watch, ' 'tis clear the whole thing was an accident, and the least said the better. The coroner must know, in course, but my report will be that, summoned instantly, I found all to be as explained, and there will be no trouble.'

'Infinitely obliged to you,' said Frank and, as he prepared to leave, and was exchanging eyes with Moll, added, 'perhaps one evening you would care to be our guest here, and try our company?'

The fellow was clearly delighted, and went on his way. Indeed there was no trouble; we heard no more of the gang, the body was removed, and the coroner merely said a few words about the inadvisability of gentlemen of a certain age indulging in too much excitation of the flesh. The whole matter died as swiftly and quietly as our enemy himself.

I found it impossible, during the following days, to shake my mind free of Miss Mary Yately. It is true that I did not make an unusual effort to do so, for not only was she exceptionally beautiful, but exceedingly rich. She clearly found me not disagreeable, and though during the short

course of my adult life marriage had always been far from
my thoughts, I could not escape the conception of what a
fine thing such a match would be for me. Born the son of a
labourer, I had risen through my own efforts from general
servant to footman, then through my fortunate friendship
with Frank and Sophie to almost the condition of a gentleman – for so they at least treated me, and my familiarity
with them and the circles in which they moved had given my
manner a patina of respectable civility.

I began to court the lady in earnest, carefully keeping
from her my occupation in Brook Street, and in answer to
the questions she put to me maintaining a mysterious
reticence which I fancied was an additional attraction.

I returned to see her only a day or two after our first
acquaintance, and upon sending my name in was immediately bidden to the drawing-room, where I was introduced
to the lady's aunt, the Honourable Mrs Mathilda Yately,
who greeted me with excessive condescension and – while
her niece was commanding tea from the egregious Albert –
was pleased to whisper that she had heard much of me from
her, and to my advantage. After tasting a single cup she
then took her leave, whereupon it was not three minutes
before Miss Yately's delicate fingers were occupying themselves with the buttons of my shirt, and she escorted me to
her bedroom, where a fine and energetic fuck passed an
hour before we noticed it; after which, as we lay in a state of
nature, she confided that she found me mighty attractive.

'You need not conceal from me,' she said, 'that you are
not nobly born, for not only does your speech betray you –
though only to the nicest ear – but your love-making is more
delicate and considerate than is the habit among the gentry,
whose concern is only for their own quick gratification.'

'Then you have experience of it?' I asked, impertinently.

'I have not grown to twenty-five,' she said – so that was
her age! – 'without acquainting myself with a prick or two,
and there has been no scarcity of gentlemen willing to
demonstrate what they can do, my fortune – as you will no
doubt have heard – being considerable.'

I looked, I fancy, a trifle shocked, but she went on: 'Do
not colour so – you will have been told that I am heir to an
estate, and I doubt not that the news has played a part in

your so soon returning for Act Two of our little play. However, you will have remarked that I have not yet sent you packing, and I assure you that I do not suffer fools gladly, nor fortune-hunters.'

My blushes redoubled, for I could not disguise from myself that thoughts of her fortune played some part in my courting her – though her body was a fortune of a different sort, which I was pleased already to be able to command. And I proved the fact to her a second time before we parted, to which she was far from averse.

It now became my habit to wait upon Miss Yately almost every other day – even to the extent that Frank suspected that I was wooing someone, but did not expect it could be anyone of consequence. The girls, too, noted that I neglected them, and were coarse upon the subject, my having been (I must confess) a continual companion of theirs when business did not call them – as sometimes it did, warm from my arms, so that more of our customers than might have thought it were served a buttered bun!

Miss Yately herself made no bones about her enjoyment of the main purpose of my visits, frequently having me shown directly to her bedroom, where she would be lying unclothed upon the bed and, once more, in full view of Albert. But I have had cause to note here before the habit of the upper classes of regarding servants as having no more apprehension than a piece of furniture, and came to believe it was so with her.

Mrs Yately was evidently privy to our encounters, for once as I encountered her in the hallway, she stopped, dug me in the ribs, winked lewdly, and enquired whether my spirits were up, for her niece had been 'skitting about' all morning, and was clearly in need of 'a good poke' – which I took to be a saying of yesterday, for I had not heard it before.

At last, after perhaps two months, just as summer was beginning to fade towards autumn and the trees beginning to drop their leaves, I decided to make my move towards regularising our situation – choosing a moment when I had, I believed, raised my lady's spirits to the point at which she could have refused me nothing. Pausing for a moment in my labours I enquired whether 'twas not time we reached an understanding, so that we could 'do this' (and here I resumed my movements, at the same time seizing her buttocks to draw her more closely towards me) all day and every day?

'Oh, yes! Yes!! Yes!!!' she cried, which I took to be assent and, delighted, brought us to a mutually satisfactory conclusion. After a suitable pause, I kissed her upon the lips and asked when she might make me the happiest man in London – at which a twinkle came to her eyes, and she equivocated. Despite my persuasion she declined to reply, but with a kindly energy and teasing roused me to another bout, and so we concluded the afternoon, parting with an understanding, if not with a positive date for our marriage.

Chapter Sixteen

Sophie's Story

I could not banish from my mind the unhappy nature of my friend Chichley's marriage, for though I had not conversed with him for some time, I had the most cordial recollection of him – and not only, as the uninformed reader may imagine, because he had been the first person in the capital to entertain me to the pleasures of love, but also for his gentle and agreeable humour.

I was at first perplexed by my brother's report of his so regularly deserting his wife's bed to attend the house in Brook Street, but then learned from Andy, who had become a confidant, that he found his bride cold and unresponsive – something I could put down only to nervousness, for certainly she showed herself, in her dealings with us, warm and ready for amorous combat. She was also an extremely amiable creature whose manners toward me and the boys were of the utmost delicacy. There were some ladies who used the boys to satisfy a carnal itch, without the slightest sign that they might be capable of human feelings, but Lady Chichley was always informed by courtesy, and never left Harry without giving him some small present (unnecessary in view of the large fee she had already paid the house). He, on the other hand, clearly enjoyed her company uninspired by the fact that she was paying for his attentions, and welcomed her more as a lover than a client. Indeed, unquestioned, he assured me that she came to him as a beloved mistress or even a wife might, and that as much time was spent in happy talk and sentimental caress as in the excitation of copulation. When introduced to Philip, though initially shy, she was now so confident of our entire tact that she was happy to take tea with him and to converse in the most intimate manner – though never prepared to hear a word against her husband uttered by any lips other then her own.

And she herself took great care never to denigrate him after her first confidence to me.

The situation was the more sad and confusing because I learned from Frank and Andy that the ladies in Brook Street had confided that Chichley's vigour in the act of love was unmatched even in their extensive acquaintance with the sex. While he still lacked that nicety of action which comes with experience, he was keenly appreciative of every lesson he received, and contributed to it more than the usual pupil's apprehension of what is owed by a man to the sensibility of any lady who agrees to match with him.

When I expressed my melancholy at the situation, Frank entirely concurred, for he found Chichley as pleasant a companion as I, and though he had never seen Lady Chichley, was content to accept my assurances as to her beauty and zest. At this point Andy, who had been quiet, asked whether we would be prepared for a little deception if it had the result of bringing man and wife together. When we assented, he put forward a plan which, while it entailed the risk that should things go wrong we would incur the displeasure of both Viscount and Lady Chichley, might certainly have the desired result. So I agreed to it, and after we had worked out the details made my way back to Chiswick. There to my astonishment, for I believed the place to be empty (it being scarcely midday and none of my men yet arrived) I heard a considerable hoo-ha from the back of the house – shouts, and a female voice crying out in protest. I swiftly made my way thither and, throwing open the door of one of the cabinets, saw to my astonishment three figures engaged in a fierce struggle: the first my eyes fell upon was Polly, stripped half-naked, her breasts bare and her skirt almost torn from her. She was held, her arms behind her back, by a man who lay half-beneath her upon the couch, while another, clad only in his shirt, was crouching between her thighs and had either succeeded in forcing her or was about to do so. The latter, his back to the door, and intent upon his purpose, was ignorant of my entry. Seizing the only weapon to hand, my parasol, I automatically thrust with it in the first direction a passion of anger suggested, and scored a hit on that portion of the assailant's anatomy which most readily offered itself.

His shriek of pain was louder than any other noise in the room, even Polly's not inconsiderable cries, and he fell to the floor writhing in agony, my parasol (now, alas, seriously bent) carried with him. Polly in her turn now thrust backwards with her bum, winding the other fellow, and we made good our escape, quickly extricating the key normally used to lock the door on the inside, and making the room secure.

Administering brandy to Polly, I quickly heard her story: she had come downstairs in answer to a ring upon the door to find the two men enquiring whether there was work they might do in the garden or about the house. As they were lusty fellows she had engaged them to chop some wood from a recently fallen tree, for we were beginning to lay in fuel against the coming autumn.

After an hour, it being hot, she had invited them into the kitchen for a tankard of small beer, and there they had sat and conversed for a while, eventually admitting that they lived nearby and had heard rumours of what went on in the house, and asking whether there might not be employment for them of a more agreeable nature than chopping wood.

Polly had replied that the stable was at the moment full.

'In any case, ma'am,' she said, 'they were rough trade, and not in the manner which might attract ladies – as, say, with Harry it does – but dirty and sweaty, unshaven and unmannerly.'

They seemed not to take her refusal amiss, and she (unwisely as it turned out) left them to finish their beer while she went back to tidy the cabinets, replace used towels, and make the rooms ready for the day's work. To her anger and dismay the two men suddenly appeared and demanded she lie down to them, and upon her refusing, both seized her, in a state of excitement tearing her clothes from her, which made them the more frenzied. One held her fast while the other ripped open his trousers revealing an empurpled instrument of admirable dimensions (had it been a welcome sight) and had actually entered her when the door opened to admit me and the instrument which pierced the assaulter to rather more painful effect than Polly had already suffered from him.

Pausing only to take a loaded pistol from the desk where I always kept it in case of such emergencies, we made our way back to the room in which we had left the ruffians, and called to them whether they would come out peacefully, for we were armed.

'A likely story, ladies with pistols!' jeered a voice, whereupon I fired my weapon through the door, happy to sacrifice the woodwork to instil a proper sense of fear into the attackers, who indeed were now reduced for a moment to silence. But in a moment we heard a private muttering, and finally, in very compliant tones, they fell to begging our pardon and pleading for release.

In fact, it was best we sent them upon their way rather than complain to the watch, for the less attention we drew to the house the quieter and less disturbed our lives would be. So Polly unlocked the door and threw it open, while I levelled my pistol and covered the two men, who came out, one hobbling severely and clutching his shirt to his rear, where I could see it was stained with blood.

'I hope you have not damaged my parasol, for 'twas a present from a dear friend,' I said. 'Kindly hand it to Miss Polly –' and insisted that the victim of my accuracy with the instrument should fetch and hand it over, which he did obviously in discomfort and with little grace.

'And you, sir,' I said, 'may be thankful that you were protected by the body of my friend from a similar assault. You have got off very easily –' which, had he not greeted the words with a sneer, might have been the truth. But Polly, seeing his lack of gratitude for his escape, took the opportunity of his passing in front of her to direct a kick which, her feet being clad with sharp-pointed shoes and her aim being as accurate as her leg was strong, connected with his cods and, from his cry, caused him considerable discomfort. In the face of my pistol, the pair dared do nothing, and we saw them from the house, carefully locking the door afterwards.

We had not intended to alarm anyone with a repetition of the events, but when the boys arrived the state of the cabinet door could not of course be disguised from them, and since it was clearly the result of the percussion of a firearm I had no recourse but to explain the occurrence. This caused considerable surprise and distress, most particularly to William, who immediately embraced Polly with the fondest solicitation, to which she was clearly not averse, and indeed relapsed into tears, which was of some surprise to me since she had been careful to assure me that she was not hurt nor had seemed more disturbed than the unpleasant circumstance had warranted. However, since she was clearly now disturbed by unhappy recollections I assented to her lying down for a while, and William supported her from the room.

Spencer, meanwhile, was grave upon the event, for, he said, such ruffians were often not without friends, and an attack upon the house could not be ruled out. He suggested that more firearms should be brought in and those boys unfamiliar with them be taught to handle them. I dissented, for it was ever my view that violence should be avoided whenever possible, and that the more guns available to be used the more likely they would be set off, with results that might be as damaging to us as to any enemies we might wish to assault.

In a short while came the first ring upon the bell, and Polly not being visible I answered it to the earliest of our visitors, who was amused upon being conducted to the window to find the boys hastily removing the last of their clothing – which scene she watched with such considerable enjoyment that it occurred to me (not for the first time) that to see a man disrobing might be of a nature to stimulate the most jaded of palates, and worth contriving as a part of our service.

Having seen her happily ensconced with Tom, whose plumpness often commended itself to our more motherly patrons, I went in search of Polly – and indeed of William, who had not returned. Going to her room, I entered it as usual without knocking to see the boy's shapely and smooth buttocks framing the top of my friend's dark head as she sucked happily upon his cock, while his own head, plunged between her thighs, was clearly giving her similar pleasure.

He looked around in some embarrassment, and seemed ready to offer some excuse or even apology, but Polly, confident of our friendship and my fondness for her (as she might well be) merely relinquished her titbit to intimate that she had found she needed a more corporeal comfort than words could alone convey.

' 'Tis not only that, ma'am,' said William, swinging his leg away and coming to sit upon the edge of the bed, 'I have long admired Mrs Playwright to distraction, and mean to ask you whether you would object to my offering her marriage. I have heard within the past week that my father has sadly passed away leaving me, even as the younger son, a considerable competence, and my feelings for Mrs Playwright are such that I must make the attempt at carrying her off, whether or not I can hope for success.'

I could not help smiling at Polly's face, which was a picture, she clearly not having had the faintest idea of the offer being made. Indeed for a moment she seemed positively angry that William had not spoken to her of the matter before, as it were, asking my consent – and I was not in a position to object, even had I wished to do so. But I had noticed her fondness for William over the past several weeks, not only in their slipping away together (when opportunity allowed) but in her observing with an envious jealousy those ladies who, having chosen him from among our other stallions, he escorted to a closed cabinet, after which, she would markedly flirt with Harry or George until his pleading looks reached a sufficient intensity for her to forgive him.

So, it may be imagined that in this case she swiftly overcame her scruples and, rising on one elbow, offered her lips, which he saluted with his own, the kiss growing to an embrace, so that drawing him down they once more fell into a languorous love-making which promised the fulfilment of unfinished business, his manly instrument, which had somewhat lost its proudness during the brief interval of my interruption, again stirring into life.

It was clearly unnecessary for me to intervene, but crossing to the bed, I bent to kiss them upon the shoulders – those being the only innocent areas now exposed to me – and left the room. They remained together for the rest of the evening, my making excuses for William to the two ladies who enquired for his services. And late that night we all drank to their engagement in rosy champagne, though plans for their marriage were not yet made, Polly insisting that they both owed me the consideration of remaining at Chiswick until substitutes could be found for them.

Two evenings later, as I had expected (for her visits were regular) Lady Chichley came again to the house, and retired with Harry. An hour later, handsome in his silk gown, he brought her to my room after their encounter so that (as was her wont) she could take a glass of wine before her departure. With her usual courtesy she handed him a gold coin and kissed his cheek before sitting to lift her glass. For a while we talked of nothing, but I offered the impression that there was something more serious to say, and in due course I said, 'Lady Chichley, I have a request which may strike you as impertinent and if so, you will please discount it. It has come to my notice through the agency of my brother – of whom you have heard me speak – that you have an admirer.'

Few women can hear those words with complete indifference, and though she made a certain pretence at disinterest, she invited me to continue.

'We were conversing the other day about the beauties of the town, and your name was raised – not by myself, I hasten to say, for I am careful to keep confidence, but by my brother, who said that a certain nobleman of his acquaintance was mad in love with you. "It is a shame," he said, "that my lady is of such virtue and so in love with her husband that she should not encounter him, for he is of the utmost discretion, of fine family, wonderfully handsome, of all young men in town the most adept at making love, and all in all the perfect lover. He has had adventures – two ladies to my knowledge have been forced to retire to their rooms for some days with exhaustion after a bout with him – but has so far lacked the perfect companion to make him happy. And now nothing will do for him but to languish after my lady Chichley, who as we all must know is a lost cause." '

Lady Chichley's cheeks had coloured.

'I can confirm that the reputation of this gentleman is no mere tale,' I continued, 'for a lady who will be well known to you – but whose name I must naturally conceal – has sworn to me that her own single brief pass with him has made her completely discontented with any other lover, and the latest I hear is that she considers entering a convent. Were it not that your ladyship has done me the honour to confide in me I would not be so impertinent as to repeat this anecdote to you, but it occurred to me that you might not be averse to taking a lover from your own class. 'Tis something not unheard of, and would be a more lasting answer to your problem than these encounters, which while they are a reasonable solution in the short term, cannot by their nature last. Were you inclined to grant this gentleman's wish . . .'

I paused, and she did not immediately demur.

'I cannot of course disclose his name to you – the more especially since moving in the highest social circles he will be known to you, and it would be impossible to avoid embarrassment when you met, should you decide against a permanent affair. But I can assure you of his perfect reticence, and that his passion for you is such that whatever your reception of his attentions he would never afterwards reveal an assignation, nor so much as with a smile acknowledge your condescension should you agree to favour him.'

My lady was clearly tempted.

'To afford you the greatest protection from embarrassment, the gentleman will consent that you should both be masked – he so that you should not discover his identity, you to spare your blushes. Nor will it be necessary for either to speak, and happily in such cases actions make words superfluous.'

Since I was already privy to my lady's sensual nature, she could not pretend to me that she was averse to the embraces of the male sex, and only a little more time must be spent in persuasion. I had rightly counted on her appetite for love being now so keen that the offer of the embraces of a gentleman of her own station was irresistible, and in the end she acquiesced, agreeing to return to the house three evenings later to make her unknown admirer happy.

I ensured that the house was empty that evening both of visitors and of our boys. The unknown admirer appeared first, brought hither by Andy in a closed carriage, and taken to a room where he could mask and don the silk gown which I had placed for him. A few minutes later Lady Chichley arrived, and I escorted her to my own bedroom where she too stripped and clad herself in a similar plain gown, before fixing upon her face a velvet mask which covered all but her lips, placing her eyes even in such shadow that they could barely be seen. I then escorted her to the main cabinet, where her would-be lover already waited, and paused only to place her hand in his.

He was – the reader will already have apprehended – none other than her husband, having been told by my brother of the beautiful woman who admired him this side of desperation and offered the encounter.

Andy and I now retired – I shame to say, but that the reader will share our curiosity – to the neighbouring cabinet with its secret view of the room and all that passed within it.

When we reached our vantage-point we found that the two were still standing hand in hand, their eyes locked together with such an intense gaze that – despite the masks – I feared for a moment that they had recognised each other only from the interchange of looks. At last Chichley let go his companion's hand to release the tie which held the cloak at his throat, so that the covering fell to his feet revealing that admirable frame which I still so keenly recollected – and the sight of which, I admit, released in me a moment's regret that I was not the creature about to receive his attentions. He had the grace of an antique statue, perfectly balanced, with broad shoulders and narrow hips, a breast like burnished armour, flat belly dinted by the central knot of his navel, shapely thighs sturdy as oaks, and between them a manhood which, as yet only gently roused, nestled within its brake of blond hair. Yet as we watched, it stirred with a faint motion, signalling a readiness to appreciate the feast in store with all the appetite of a hungry man.

Now Chichley took two steps towards his companion, and lifting his hands to her neck, loosed the ties of her gown so that it similarly fell from her, revealing her in all her beauty – at which Andy, who had never seen her, shuddered suddenly as though with the ague. In a moment I felt his hands upon my shoulders and his body pressed against mine as he bent forward to look more closely at the tableau, for Frances Chichley matched her husband as the figure of Eve matched that of Adam in the old paintings, her high breasts pointing slightly outwards, full but not heavy, firm but not angular, her broad hips poised above full thighs, strong yet unmistakably feminine, the velvet pad between them shaded darkly where lay the entrance to pleasure.

Each entranced by the sight of the other, the married lovers were in a moment drawn together as by magnetism, skin to skin, her white against his brown, hands at first merely upon each other's shoulders. But in a moment their fingers began to move, first over each other's back, then down to seize upon the buttocks, pressing their lower bodies more closely together – which had an effect perfectly predictable, for when Chichley stepped aside to lead his wife to the couch, we could see that already he was prepared for the act, his sturdy cock lifted at a sharp angle so that it almost pressed against his belly – an unmistakable sign, I have always found, of a promising virility.

This, however, was no signal that he was to be offensively demanding, for laying the lady down he now gave time to the exploration of each plane and surface of his lady's body, first with hands, then with lips, while we could not see her face as her head was thrown back with an abandon that suggested complete enjoyment.

As he paid her the compliment of caressing her nether parts, a sudden little jump of ecstasy ran through her body which seemed to indicate an arousal more than common – underlined by her now thrusting him gently away and persuading him, in turn, to lie upon the couch. Kneeling over him she played her lips and tongue over his body, finally taking his manhood between her slender fingers, supporting his cods with the other hand and drawing the skin gently back over the ridge of flesh above which the inner dome proudly rose, then running her lips, shining with liquid, over the head and sliding them . . .

But what was this? My view of the scene was interrupted by Andy's hands throwing me backward and his lips fastening upon my own while his hand thrust up beneath my skirts to find, I must admit, a certain liquidity which bespoke the impression the scene had left upon me.

From anyone else, despite the heat of the moment, such a sudden rough assault might have provoked anger, but

Andy and I had played together since childhood, and it had
been some months since we had been familiar. Moreover
though there were other men whose tributes had been more
satisfying (for he was always inclined to be too pleased with
his own prowess to be an entirely satisfactory lover,
women's preference surely always being for one who permits
them to please him more than he pleases them?) I was by no
means antagonistic to his approach, and indeed so roused
by the meeting we had jointly arranged that in no time I had
joined him in stripping as naked as our guests. Without our
even bothering to recline, I had drawn up one leg and
passed it behind and around his arse so that with a little
effort he was able, crouching slightly, to insert his cock and
with no more than two or three thrusts make both himself
and me happy (for we were evenly matched in our excitement). We had only to turn once more to be able to apply
our eyes to the aperture in the wall and discover how things
were going in the neighbour room, where our friends had
been less precipitate. Though Chichley was now happily
embraced by his lady's thighs, his handsome arse was still
moving with a regular slow motion matching the panting
cries which emanated from his wife's throat as she lay, head
still thrown back so that her magnificent bosom offered
itself to his lips.

The cry she gave as she reached the apogee of her pleasure
seemed sufficiently loud to have been heard outside the
house, and conveyed in a single spasm of sound such satisfaction and ecstasy that I unconsciously gripped poor
Andy's half-limber prick, strongly enough for him to have
to bite my shoulder to stifle his own cry, lest it be heard by
our guests. The pain of the bite was sufficient to arouse my
passion once more, whereupon we again lost sight of our
guests, and this time being less fraught to the battle took
our time in satisfying each other – and I must admit that in
the past months my friend had learned much about the art
in which previously he had been almost completely a tyro.
He now combined that freedom, that animal-like relaxation which had so drawn me to him at the time, now some
years ago, when we were both children, with a knowledge of
love-making the most impressive. And the first paroxysm
being over, he was now so in command of himself that my

best endeavours were unable to bring him to a completion
until I had myself twice been satisfied.

We lay for a time clasped in each other's arms, unconscious of anything else, and my thoughts – I confess
it – were that for all his faults there was no other man who
gave me such pleasure and comfort as my old friend. But
then once more we took ourselves to our vantage-point,
where we saw Chichley kneeling over his wife's shoulders
and ministering to her while she explored with her tongue the
delightful area of his rear, and her fingers so sensitively
played with his prick that he was clearly in an ecstasy.
Finally, as she seized upon his arse with her teeth in her own
clear delight, he erupted for what we supposed was the third
time before collapsing so that his head lay between her feet,
while she in an access of apology licked with a tender tongue
the crescent of bloody spots where her teeth had punctured
his skin.

'I think the time has come for discovery,' said Andy, holding out my skirt, into which I climbed, 'and thank you, my
dearest Sophie, for those tokens of affection' – and he
planted a kiss upon my cheek which I was pleased to return.

We entered the neighbour room without knocking, somewhat to the surprise of our guests, and indeed Chichley leapt
to his feet and was about, I think, to make a violent protest
had I not immediately apologised.

'Forgive me, my lord,' I said, 'but there is a particular
reason why we should interrupt you in order to inform you of
something while you and this lady are still together.

'This lady has no idea who you are, but she believes that
you are cognisant of her identity. I now have to admit to her
that you have no knowledge whatsoever of her.'

Lady Chichley's head came up at this, in surprise.

'No, I fear this has been a plot by my friend Andy and me; a
plot which I hope will have the result we desire. My lord, will
you kindly remove your mask?'

There was a moment's hesitation, then the viscount
reached up and slowly peeled the velvet from his face, revealing that stern, handsome but not unkind visage, well-shaped
mouth, flaring nostrils, keen eyes, and high forehead over
which a lock of hair, dampened by passion, hung.

Lady Chichley gave an immense start and a cry, and my

heart stood still, for this was surely the moment upon which all depended: would she be offended that she had been tricked into offering her husband the very body he had so disdained? But then she sat up, and slowly removed her own mask.

The two looked at each other for a long moment in complete and mutual disbelief. Then, to my great relief, Chichley slowly knelt at his wife's feet, and taking her hand kissed it with the utmost deliberation and tenderness, and looking up into her eyes in silence begged forgiveness as clearly as could be.

I touched Andy upon the shoulder, and we quietly slipped from the room – but not before the two figures were again clasped together, this time not in the throes of passion but in a mutual expression of tender recognition, apology and love.

An hour later, there came a knock upon the door of the room in which Andy and I were sharing a bottle, and, in their full dress, Lord and Lady Chichley entered. He came straight to me and gave me his hand.

'Mrs Nelham,' he said, 'I am infinitely obliged to you for showing me the error of my ways – that Frances is not the cold aristocrat I had imagined, but a lady in whom beauty of body is combined with a delightful enthusiasm for the sport. I have much to thank you for and Mr Harry Riggs – for yes, my wife has revealed to me her adventures with that gentleman, whom she admits released in her the springs of passion. If there is any way in which I can be of use to you, or to you, Mr Archer, whose part in this plot I can only, now, admire and credit . . .'

We were of course quick to assert that we were (which was true) delighted that our ruse had borne such fruit, and bade them good-night.

'Well, Sophie,' said Andy, 'Brook Street is a long way to go at this time of the evening . . .'

I smiled.

'There will always be a place for you between my sheets,' I replied, 'though after two such inspiriting encounters as you have already offered me, my bed may be a quieter place than you apprehend . . .'

But he kissed me warmly, and when we were a-bed held

me tenderly in his arms with those gestures which convey
affection rather than passion, but are no less delightful and
quite as essential to woman's happiness.

I had no idea what time it was when I was awakened by the
sound of breaking glass, but Andy and I sat bolt upright in
bed together in the darkness, and I felt his arm around me
as for a moment we waited, not knowing precisely what it
had been that had roused us. Then came another sound –
of cracking wood; someone was breaking into the house.

'Have you a weapon?' asked Andy, climbing from bed.

'Downstairs,' I replied, for alas the pistol was in the
drawer of my desk. I scrambled for the steel, and finally
managed to light the candle at my bedside, by which I saw
Andy trying to cram his legs into his trousers, the wrong
way about. We dressed hastily, but by the time we reached
the staircase there were already lights in the hall, and we
could see several dark figures moving about.

'There's the bloody whore!' came a cry from below, and
I recognised the voice of one of the two men who had
attempted to rape poor Polly. The men – there were five of
them, I now saw – began to climb the stairs. Andy stepped
in front of me, and held his hand out, though with nothing
in it.

'Climb at your peril!' he cried. 'I am armed.'

There was only a moment's pause.

'So are we!' then came the cry. There was an explosion,
and a ball whistled past us.

Throwing me aside, Andy grasped a heavy table which
stood at the side of the stair-head, and half threw, half
tipped it so that it crashed down upon the invaders, who
in turn lost their footing so that for a moment all was
confusion.

'Come on!' he said, and taking me by the arm returned to
my bedroom, where he first locked the door, then with my
help moved a tall wardrobe against it.

'I don't mind a fight,' he said, 'but unarmed, against
five . . .'

There was some muttering outside, then a cry of pain
from which I gathered that one man at least had been hurt
in the fall, the sound of a blow or two against the door, then

a shot which shattered the lock. And then more blows – but the wardrobe, now reinforced by the bed itself, which with great labour we had thrust against it, stood firm. There was more whispering, then silence. Andy placed his ear near the door.

'I can hear nothing,' he whispered, 'but it may be a ruse to persuade us to open. We can do nothing but wait,' and once more placed his arm about my shoulders to comfort me. 'I am sorry I can do no more – I fear I am not so much a man of action as to relish a naked encounter against fire-arms!' I kissed him, by way of answer.

For perhaps five minutes there was no sound; then we heard the front door slam far below us. The men had opened it, and when we crept to the window, we saw their lights – one, two, three, four, five – retreating through the garden.

It was the work of but a moment to withdraw the bed, then the wardrobe. But already there was a smell of smoke in the air, and when the door swung open, its ruined lock scraping, a red light was flickering upon the ceiling outside, growing ever more and more bright. Stepping upon the landing we saw that a fire was already mounting the stair-case, so that as we took a step forward, a great ball of flame rose up at us. Andy made to retreat but seizing him by the arm, I cried 'No!' and pulled him out and into the corridor, for the drop from my bedroom window was sheer, there being no way of descent, not even an ivy or creeper.

We felt the blast of hot air upon us as we ran past the stair-head and back down the corridor and entered the bathroom, whose window, I knew, gave onto a narrow ledge which communicated with the top of the conservatory below. As I climbed through the window, I heard a shout from below and paused, thinking it was the men returned, but then recognised the sound of Philip's voice, who upon our gingerly making the descent greeted us. Making his way back from a late assignation in town, he had met the escaping ruffians and guessed they were there for no good purpose. Being unarmed, he had concealed himself as they went by, but then saw the flames – which as we talked exploded through the roof of the house.

It was the mark of the time that the house was ruined

before anyone but we three came near. Though the river
offered plentiful water, there was no pumping apparatus
nearer than two mile, and none of us knew where to raise it,
or whom to summon. Pails of water were useless against an
inferno; all we could do was watch, Andy with fury at what
had been done, I with regret at seeing my work of a year –
and indeed much of my fortune – consumed; Philip no
doubt with keener regret at seeing the home of his past
ruined. By the time the flames began to die, a small group
of local people who had seen the light of the flames had
gathered to watch, gossip and commiserate – for though
many of them suspected our business, we had made ourselves pleasant to the local tradesmen, and were by no
means despised.

There being nothing further to be done, Andy and I set
off for Brook Street, Philip promising to remain and to
inform the boys of the business when they came the next
day, and to advise them to contact me at my brother's. I
would have first to insert a notice of the calamity in the
newspapers, informing our clients of the demise of our
project, then to consider the future.

We were silent as we walked, and then – fortunately discovering a late carriage returning from the country – rode
into town.

Was my entire fortune gone? enquired Andy.

I supposed that most of it was, I returned. Though I had
made considerable savings during the past few months
which would ensure that I would not starve, I was certainly
no longer a mistress of any considerable sum.

'But Frank will see you right,' he said – which of course
was true, but I had been happy to be my own woman, and
was sad that my independence should now be gone. But
perhaps there would be some solution, for I was ever an
optimist.

Sitting silent for a while, Andy then turned to me: 'You
know my origins, dear Sophie,' he said, 'which are not so
fine as yours. You know also that I have no fortune, though
through Frank's good offices I now also possess a certain
sum. But it occurs to me that we make an admirable partnership. Would you consider becoming my wife?'

Touched, I kissed him upon the lips, but explained that

not only was I too enamoured of my freedom, but that my observation of human nature had not so far encouraged me to believe that marriage was any guarantee of happiness, and might even divide us, for aught I knew.

'I should be sorry should that happen,' I said, 'for my affection for you is as great as for any man – but marriage is not among my plans. Do not be melancholy,' I added, for his face fell, 'I can imagine no time during which we shall not be friends, or when you will not be welcome to my bed. But marriage – no.'

There was another pause; then he took my hand and raised it to his lips.

'My very dear sister,' he said, and we rode on into the city.

Chapter Seventeen

The Adventures of Andy

I must admit to considerable pleasure in not only having captured Miss Mary Yately's affection, but having impressed myself so considerably upon her that she was willing to take me as a husband. What a future now opened before me! A fortune as vast as hers (and though I had not been able to come at the precise sum, reliable rumour put it at not much less than a quarter of a million pound) would enable me to live in a style beside which Frank's estate would seem miniscule.

I must confess that this knowledge somewhat affected my attitude to my old friend. I would of course never forget his kindness and condescension to me, but nevertheless he could not expect me to interest myself in our present business once I was married. I now began gradually to absent myself from it, taking myself more and more to Miss Yately's, where I ingratiated myself further with her aunt, and by dint of arriving at particular times contrived to meet some of her circle of friends, one or two of whom seemed to treat me with a certain disdain. Little did they know that I was soon to become the master of the house, or they would have paid more attention to their manners!

It sometimes seemed to me that dear Mary, though always happy to admit me between her sheets, and as voracious as ever in her physical requirements, was cooler to me in public than our relationship warranted. But she had insisted on my not announcing our engagement, and I believed her public attitude (which sometimes extended even to snubbing me) was adopted to put society off the scent. Nevertheless, after some weeks I became exceeding impatient, and at last, as we lay cooling ourselves after a bout, argued that the time had come when we should make public our plans.

'I think not,' she said.

'Then when may society know,' I asked, 'of our approaching nuptials?'

She seemed to smile at this, at which I became angry. 'If you are not prepared to acknowledge me at least among your friends,' I said, 'I . . .'

'You what?' she enquired.

'Well . . .' I said, and then came to a stop, for I could not think what to say next.

'You might withdraw your offer?' she enquired.

'Nothing,' I said swiftly, 'would persuade me to relinquish such a prize!' Then seeing her eyes narrow, I added, 'As your love, of course, my dear Mary!'

She seemed to consent to this, and we parted friends, if a little coolly. When I returned next day, I was surprised that the door was answered by Mrs Yately, who announced that Albert was upon a private errand, while she also on her way out, but that her niece had requested that I should go straight upstairs. Bidding her a courteous good afternoon, I proceeded to the drawing-room, and finding it empty, knew where I would find my fiancée. Making my way to the dressing room which I had adopted as my own, I unclothed, and then threw open the communicating door with my love's bedroom.

There she lay, indeed, apparently awaiting my arrival, and with a flushed face, and panting bosom (just peeping, enchantingly, from beneath the sheets) which bespoke her emotion at my arrival – except, did not the sheets of the bed seem peculiarly piled? And was not there a strange movement about her waist?

She smiled to see me looking, and as I approached threw back the sheet to disclose to my horror the naked body of a man curled about her lower parts, his head between her thighs – which, when startled he raised it, I saw to be that of none other than the missing footman, Albert!

Furiously, I stepped forward, but he raised himself from the bed at this, and he being a large and powerful man, I stepped back, for unarmed I could not hope to counter an attack.

I bowed coldly.

'Madam,' I said, 'I see you are engaged . . .'

'I am, and am not,' she said. 'I am certainly engaged with Albert, and in an encounter not one whit the less inspiriting than you can offer, Mr Archer. Engaged to you, by way of a promise to marry, I am certainly not! And no gentleman would have put the question at the time you put it, nor in the manner; nor indeed been silly enough to have interpreted my response so seriously!

'Could you really suppose,' she went on, 'that I would trust my fortune to someone born in a pigsty and raised in the kitchens?'

I was silent at this, for it was nothing but the truth, however much I had supposed my conduct to have disguised the fact. Nor could I deny that her fortune had been my chief attraction, though I cried, 'Madam, I confess all, but I hope you will believe that your fortune was not your only attraction, for indeed it was your beauty that first caught my eye, and the pleasures you have shared with me will ever remain a happy memory!'

She softened somewhat at this, and even smiled. I stepped forward, at which Albert looked menacing, but nevertheless I continued my progress, and taking her hand pressed my lips to it.

'I hope you will forgive me,' I said, 'for being what I believed you could not suspect – a fortune-hunter, and a clumsy one!'

'So clumsy,' she smiled, 'that indeed I knew it from the first. But, Andy, you have nevertheless a charm which my sex will ever find it difficult to resist, and –' (with a sigh) ' – alas, I have ever to be on the watch, which is why . . .' And she glanced sideways at the naked footman, who gravely inclined his head.

'Albert,' she said, 'I am sorry that we should have been interrupted' – and indeed his male implement, raised at full tilt when I had first entered, was now somewhat crestfallen – 'but I must make my farewells to Mr Archer.'

The man, evidently used to obeying orders, of whatever nature, bowed and left the room. And to my surprise I was beckoned to the bed, where Miss Yately kissed me first upon the lips, then applied herself in an unprecedented manner to rousing those passions which in the past two or three minutes had been completely dampened in me.

To make a long story short, we were reconciled in the best manner, and I could not resist, as her moment approached, asking whether she would not always remember me with a passionate interest, to which she gasped 'Yes! Yes!! Yes!!!' – only to dissolve immediately afterwards in a laughter which we shared.

As we talked for the last time, she freely admitted that she had met as yet no man she could not suspect of desiring her fortune more than herself. She therefore reconciled herself to satisfying her desires in the most calculated manner for, she said, she always knew where she was with servants. Nor, when she took a lover from beyond the walls of the house – as in my case – did she hope for more than bodily satisfaction, which she made sure of by simply allowing them to pleasure her.

'It has made me selfish,' she said, 'and I sometimes fear that a true lover will find me over-short in my attentions to his desires, in my habit of consulting only my own.'

I did my best to reassure her, and indeed believe that when – as must happen – she finds her true love a partnership will result which will make both happy.

I then made my final bow, and left.

So my hopes of becoming a man of means faded, at least for the time. But we parted friends, and my memories of the lady remain, even after some years, tender in respect of her person and appreciative of a keen intelligence, for she was to be no man's fool.

It was a week or so afterwards that Sophie and I engaged in the little deceit which we practised upon Lord and Lady Chichley, and which she has related in the previous chapter – culminating in the early hours of the following morning in the fire which laid waste her beautiful house at Chiswick. All I need add to her account is that the proposal which I made to her in the carriage might have been sudden but was entirely sincere, for no woman has ever meant so much in my life (nor, I dare say, ever will) as my adopted sister. Nevertheless, the moment I had made the proposal I was hoping that it would be refused, for still not twenty years of age, it was not yet really my intention to saddle myself with a wife – unless, of course, an uncommon rich one!

Upon reaching Brook Street it was still very early, and letting myself in with my key I hurried Sophie to my bedroom, where we rested for some hours before meeting a surprised Frank at breakfast, and rendering him still more astonished by an account of the destruction of Sophie's hopes.

She was by now putting a brave face upon things.

'It may be,' she said, 'that 'twas a blessing in disguise, for 'twould be early days for me to settle into so sedate a way of life, and I shall now be forced into new adventures.'

'But have you no idea of what sort?' I asked.

No, she said, but she had long wished to see more of the world than England, for her previous adventures had given her an itch for travel, and she wondered whether she might not travel in Europe.

'Of course,' she said, 'I could not go alone. Perhaps you might spare Blatchford as an attendant . . .'

I was a little surprised at this, and must have shown it, for she added, 'Do not mistake me, I do not mean as a lover, but as a servant! For lovers, I shall make my own bed, no doubt, as I have been used,' and blushed a little, for we were privy to all her adventures, and knew that her sheets, though not a public tent, had rarely been unfrequented by gentleman usually of her own choosing.

Frank nodded.

'I see no reason why not,' he said, 'but perhaps we can contrive a better scheme, for of late I have been more than a little bored. While you and brother Andy have had your adventures, I have remained sedate, seeing little more than home and university. Father's fortune was by no means fully taken up by the establishment of this house, and moreover, considerable profits from the business have further enhanced it. If I could find someone to take over, why should we not all go on the Grand Tour? You would come, of course, Andy?'

It was a wonderful notion, to which I was quick to assent.

'But who . . .?'

'Philip?' I suggested, but neither Sophie nor Frank thought that Jocelind had the qualities necessary for running the house, for while pleasant enough, he had no real interest in the business, and Aspasia had lately been expressing the desire to retire to her old way of life . . .

'But,' says Frank, 'of course I am forgetting that my girls will shortly have their own fortunes, and may well wish to relinquish the life! Why should not your boys simply come here, and carry on your business from this address? If Polly and William are to wed, you could place them in charge – perhaps with the help of Spencer, that admirable man?'

It was a notion which seemed peculiarly to suit, and we determined to put it to them all, which we did one afternoon in a few days' time, when we gathered our friends together, with Philip, at the house.

Everyone was immediately in accord. The girls, it appeared, had been discussing how and when to make it clear to us that they wished to retire. Polly was delighted at the confidence her mistress was to put in her, and was well-known enough to all Sophie's gentlemen to command their allegiance – though I believe it may be the case that the clientele of Sophie's establishment may be deprived of William's services, after their marriage.

The serious business over, the meeting was about to break up when Frank suggested that we should spend the rest of the day in relaxation, for it was surprising, he said, that his girls and Sophie's men had never met. He had taken the liberty of ordering some wine round, in which he hoped the company would drink prosperity to the continuing business!

It was true that there had been no meeting between the two establishments, and it had been amusing to see their members sitting politely at opposite sides of the drawing-room while hearing of our plans. But now they began to introduce themselves, and certainly after the consumption of a few bottles conversation began to flow without difficulty, and some of our ladies offered to show the boys the pleasures of our warm rooms which they had heard of, from Polly, but had never encountered. I was persuaded once more to bring my guitar and to play, and with wine and good food and conversation, all was soon an enjoyable familiarity, which gradually extended to a more febrile activity, as now and again a couple would disappear from the drawing-room.

How, I wondered, would the house adapt itself to the

new regime? Would the female visitors, for instance, enjoy our hot rooms as much as our gentlemen? It was something we could only guess at and taking my guitar, I strolled thither with a view to enquiring of our girls how they felt in the matter. But upon reaching the lower rooms I found it unnecessary, for all was pleasure, and though they were of course entirely familiar with the place, there was no sign of enervation or dissatisfaction among the females.

The warm room, as I passed through it, was occupied only by Ginevra and Sophie's senior gentleman, Mr Spencer Middlemas, she being mounted upon the older man as though to save him unnecessary motion. He compensated by the wildest bucking, which evidently gave her the keenest pleasure – perhaps because, as I could discern in the intervals of her rising upon her knees, his cock was sufficiently sturdy and thick to fill her own narrow and somewhat constricted parts to admiration. She tipped me a wink as I passed; he, his eyes closed, took no notice.

In the hottest room, Rose and Sally had taken refuge in the cold pool, accompanied by Ben and Tom. The gentlemen were close behind the ladies who, as they knelt with their arms over the sill of the pool, betrayed by their satisfied expressions no less than by the gentle jigging of their bodies the fact that their lower parts were in a sufficiently close proximity to those of their partners to offer considerable pleasure. Their pleasure was raised also by the sight before them, for their attention was focused upon two figures which took the centre of the room where, their bodies liberally drenched with perspiration, Xanthe and George, the negro, were performing a sort of dance the rhythm of which I was soon able to match with the strumming of my instrument.

Though George had never been outside England, it was impossible to doubt that the blood of his ancestors ran in his veins, for his firm and muscular body moved in a manner difficult of counterfeit by the white races, his torso seeming to be attached to his hips by double joints; so independent the two parts of his body seemed, it was as though his backbone was hinged at the waist. I had never seen him unclothed, and could only admire and envy the dexterity of his movements as his buttocks plunged, throwing forward a

cock which was so large as to fulfil every legend I had heard
of it (from Sophie, who had blushingly spoken of her
encounter with him upon their first meeting). Indeed, so
long and substantial was it that the movement of his hips
threw it into a positive dance of its own, clearly delighting
Xanthe, equally a stranger to him, who seemed mesmerised
– as a snake will be mesmerised by a rabbit, yet in the most
delightful way. She too danced about him, reaching out a
hand to slide over the shiny surface of his ebony skin, flicking the perspiration from a shoulder or a breast, cupping
one of the small, firm globes of his behind as she moved to
rub her own body against his back, her breasts flattening
against it and her white skin thrown into startling relief by
the darkness of his own. Finally he placed his hands upon
her shoulders and she sank to her knees, with a sigh of
delight opening her lips and taking between them as best she
could a portion of that instrument which, I fear, both Rose
and Sally envied her the possession of. However, the furious
manner in which Ben and Tom were now moving suggested
that they were receiving the full attention of such equip-
ment as they could muster, which no doubt was as formidable as that of most white men.

Xanthe's lips being unable to accommodate more than
one-third of the length of George's prick, he soon grew
impatient, and gently threw her backward upon the floor
where, with the steam weaving about them, he was careful
to drive it slowly within her so that her cries were of pleasure
rather than of pain. Wishing not to intrude longer on so
intimate a scene, I walked into the neighbouring warm
room, still empty save for Ginevra and Spencer, occupied
as they had been ten minutes before, his age and experience
clearly enabling him to contain himself; her movements had
necessarily slowed, but her enjoyment was still evident.

'Why did you not introduce me before, Mr Andy?' she
asked. 'I rise to the third wave, and still it has not broken!'
– and she continued her bucking, while he placed his hands
behind his head and smiled.

Upstairs, the bell rang as I passed through the hall, and I
admitted Philip Jocelind, who had been summoned to take
a glass. I invited him to enter the drawing-room, though – I
explained – he might well find it unoccupied, but someone

would be with him in due time. I knew that since he had spent an hour with each of our girls, he would not have come for carnal pleasure. He nodded amiably, and took a seat and a bottle, while I went on to the upper rooms.

In the first, Polly was engaged with William, and Constance with Will Pounce – two pairs of lovers, whose faith being plighted, I did not observe more closely than to notice that their sentimental attachment no whit detracted from their interest in the game, which they were playing with enthusiasm. They had clearly decided that, as being plighted each to each, they would not wish to become part of any general amorous enthusiasm, and though they lay upon the same bed, were no more in connection with each other than the occasional brushing of an arm or a leg performed.

In a second room, I was delighted to see Moll engaged in pleasuring a man who by his lithe appearance and brown, gypsy skill, could be none other, I inferred, than Harry, the most active of Sophie's men. For once he lay upon his back while his companion reclined between his legs, her head upon his belly, playing with his chief male attribute. She paid it the compliment of kisses and caresses which extended now above, now below, while her fingers smoothed and flicked and turned about it and his cods which, closely drawn up beneath, bespoke a pleasurable tension.

As I watched, indeed, he reached the point at which he must take her, and raising himself upon an elbow, turned so that she fell below him, somewhat unwillingly relinquishing her hold so that he could slide downwards and place himself between her thighs. As he lifted his buttocks and lowered them to pierce her (to her infinite glee) I was astonished to see upon the right cheek, half-hidden in the down but none the less marked, nothing less interesting than a red birthmark shaped like a triangle!

'Harry!' I cried. 'Harry Riggs!'

Startled no less by the sound of my voice than by hearing his name, he paused, while Moll's mouth dropped open in amazement. Clearly they had exchanged familiarities, but not names.

'Harry *Riggs*?' she exclaimed. '*Harry?*'

Yes, reader, 'twas her brother, who speedily withdrawing

was none the less so inspirited by her attentions that he could not refrain from spurting forth his life's essence upon the belly – not, fortunately, within the body – of his sister!

No less delighted than astonished, he held her in his arms and pressed those kisses upon her lips which were no less passionate for being, now, fraternal. Their pleasure in each other was no less great than before, though of necessity it took a different course. However, as he struggled to cover himself she could not resist leaning to give his shrinking prick a last kiss, murmuring that from a small child she had determined to capture it, and now counted the chase as concluded!

I did not longer remain to intrude upon their happiness, nor do I care to speculate in what manner their joy at reconciliation was further expressed. It was enough that I had been quick in recognising the birth-mark which identified him, and had been the instrument of their reunion.

The room next-door was occupied by Cissie and Bob Tippett, the lively lad engaging himself by demonstrating how rapidly he could change from one mode of making love to the next, so that as I watched, he first entered her from the front, then throwing her face downward upon the bed, plunged in from behind, lifting her legs so that he held them within his armpits, offering himself the clearer mark. Then, as she began to gasp with pleasure at his vigorous thrusts, he paused to persuade her to stand and, lifting her bodily, encouraged her to place her legs about his waist while he placed his hands beneath her bottom and fucked her with no other support than those. Tiring of this he lowered one of her legs to the ground while he raised his opposite leg and passed it behind her, the two standing upon one leg each, while he still contrived to remain engaged. Then lowering them both once more to the bed, he began to lap at her body voraciously with his tongue, while she cried for the mercy of a speedy deliverance from the height to which his activities had raised her . . . These rapidly changing figures reminded me of nothing so much as a book in Philip's uncle's library at Chiswick, which pictured the attitudes of certain Indian lovers, and I could not but suppose that in some manner Bob had come at it. Though his visits to Chiswick had only been in the capacity of messenger, his curiosity and quickness knew no bounds, and it would not surprise me to know that he had poked his nose into every available room there!

By this time I had had enough of observing, and was acutely uncomfortable from the efforts of my prick to escape from the confines of my breeches. Dropping my guitar I threw off my clothes, at which Tippett must have believed I was about to join him, for he lifted himself from his companion and went to make room. But I shook my head with a smile, donned the robe which hung upon the back of the door and, more comfortable, left to search for the only companion I desired.

Passing through the door, the bell rang once more, and I went down to admit none other than David Ham, whose lively eyes flashed humorously as he saw my dress. Embracing me he slipped his hand beneath to discover the state of my prick, saying that if he knew no better he would have thought I had prepared a welcome for him!

Philip, he said, had asked him to join him here – so I took him to the drawing-room, but Jocelind was no longer there.

'Never mind,' said David, 'I'll find him!' and left, while I continued my search. But the person I sought not being upon the ground floor, I took myself below, where I found Jocelind in the warm room, stretched out, unclothed and asleep upon a bench alone, while across the way Spencer and Ginevra lay quiet in a sleepy lethargy.

'Your friend has arrived,' I said, shaking him, 'have you not seen him?' – at which Philip roused himself.

'Young David?' asked Ginevra. 'He looked in some moments past, and went into the hot room.'

Passing there, we found only the three couples I had previously seen, Xanthe now curled up upon the body of George, both exhausted, but she clutching in one hand his still massive but now soft member. Not far away, Rose and Ben, Sally and Tom lay twined in each other's arms so close that it was impossible to discern which limb was which.

But now, a low laugh came from the open door which led to the room containing the fire for our boilers. Stepping to it, we saw in the ruddy light of the open grate the naked figure of Blatchford, his body running with steaks of black sweat, bending forward shovel in hand to stoke the boiler.

Immediately behind him David, who had clearly just thrown off his clothes, which lay upon the floor regardless of the dirt, reached between his legs to fondle a member less ready than the boy's own, which clearly sought a home I doubted Blatchford would be willing to provide. But we were never to find out, for Philip stepped forward and, grasping David by the shoulders, pulled him away and into his own embrace.

Blatchford, looking round, merely winked at me, and continued to place coal upon the fire – from which I gathered that, as I had suspected in the past, he regarded congress between the sexes as a strange occupation which wasted time that might more properly be spent in grooming horses or consuming small beer. This had in fact made him a most valuable member of our organisation, for he could be entirely trusted to regard all our ladies with an equally impartial eye, and was incapable of being stirred by passion or by prejudice.

Philip had now thrown David face downward upon a pile of empty coal sacks in the corner, and placing his hands upon the boy's hips, had raised his arse so that he could place his own prick in a place where David was clearly very willing to receive it, for while a grimace of pain at first crossed his face, he then grinned happily at me, and winked. Naturally, I had known of old of his preference for his own sex. As for Philip, if that was his course, then I could only allow him to pursue it; I only hoped that Sophie did not feel towards him such warmness as to be dismayed by hearing of it, for I had every intention that she should do so!

My only recourse now was the upper rooms, and making my way up past the smaller bedrooms, I came to Frank's room and my own. The door of the former standing open, I could not help but see my friend in the company of the handsome Aspasia. It had been my observation that Frank had ever enjoyed the company of older women, and this splendid lady who would never again see the age of thirty was clearly for him the *sine qua non* of delight. They lay upon the bed, in a state of nature, but not embraced – on the contrary, they were some inches apart, their heads thrown back upon the pillow. From the thread of liquid which lay upon my friend's upper thigh, I imagined that they had already enjoyed each other, and were now preparing for a second congress, for each was leisurely exploring the body of the other with a single hand. The lady's fingers were engaged upon the contours of his belly and thigh, from time to time merely brushing a tool which already began again to rise, while his hand lifted and embraced a breast which, while it had the fullness and heaviness of maturity, was from the tight button of pleasure at its middle no less a centre of delight.

Their eyes were closed, and they did not see me, nor did I stay longer than to observe and envy their pleasure, before passing on to the door of my own room. Opening it, I saw the room to be empty. I was clearly the only soul destined to be unsatisfied that evening, and closing the door reclined upon the bed, my mind playing over the engagements I had seen between my friends, so that despite myself I felt the necessity of taking my over-stimulated cock between my fingers and beginning to stroke it – when the door opened, and who should walk through it but dearest Sophie.

'I am sorry, dear Andy,' she said, 'to see you reduced to this measure. But if you would rather –' and pretended to go.

I merely smiled, for I knew she was better acquainted with me than that. Indeed, closing the door behind her, she soon unclothed herself, revealing again that body which familiarity could not make me indifferent to, with its high breasts, generous hips, arms always ready to embrace, ever-welcoming thighs.

How we amused ourselves it would be impertinent for me to report or for a reader to enquire, the delights of love being ever too private to be disclosed except by way of narrative among friends. I need only say that when we rose, an hour later, we had pleasured ourselves and each other in such a manner as I believe no two lovers have bettered. The evening ended in mutual friendly delight, the entire party gathering in the drawing-room which, crowded with satiated bodies, became for many one large bed upon which exhaustion now decreed sleep rather than further amorous pleasure. I noted, happily, that upon seeing Jocelind walk in with his arms about his lover, Sophie merely approached to embrace them both, as though to bless a union of which, she knew, she could have no part.

The marriages of William with Polly and Will Pounce with Constance took place on the same day and in the same church, with all our friends present. Mr and Mrs Pounce were particularly happy, for they received a message from Viscount Chichley that an inn which he owned in a village not far from his estate was theirs should they desire it. Of course they were delighted and immediately sent a message of thanks and acceptance, and nothing would do but that they should leave the same day – not for the proposed holiday they had planned in Worthing but for their new home, the Black Boy – there was some laughter at this, and a cordial invitation from them to their friend George to visit them at any time!

Meanwhile, Chichley's generosity did not end there, for he agreed to purchase from Sophie the land on which her house had stood, where he wished, he said, to build a mansion to which he could take his bride, the locality ever having for them a particular significance, having first been brought together there by our good offices, and he paid Sophie considerably more, it seems, than the land was worth. And more, he sent a present to me of a splendid gold watch, a gift of a hundred guineas, and the assurance of his friendship and assistance at any time I should need it.

Mr and Mrs Langrish were to take a short honeymoon at Alcovary, where Frank had sent them with instructions to use it as their own. And I imagine that they did so with style, for William had been brought up a gentleman, while Polly was quick to gather every impression and fashion, and I doubt not found it easy to play the part. They planned then to return to Brook Street and to supervise the house, for though William's family had sent messages to the effect that he should return to the cathedral close and to a living which had become available nearby, Polly was of the opinion that life as a Bishop's wife (for she was sure that in no time her William would rise to that office) was not for her, while William was of the opinion that he now had a taste for riggish behaviour which would betray itself despite the covering of the most distinguished canonicals. So we waved them off in the direction of Hertfordshire, confident that we left the business of Brook Street in good hands.

It only remained to make a few arrangements: to obtain passports for ourselves and to distribute to the girls certain small tokens of our affection and thanks. We had obtained from a silversmith's in Bond Street silver peppers and salts made in the shape of the male and female members, the salt flowing from a small aperture at the head of the phallus, while pepper sprinkled at a touch from tiny holes within the delicately-wrought hair surrounding the female part. These were indeed received with rapturous pleasure, not least by Moll, who now planned to return to the neighbourhood of her old home to live with her re-found brother Harry, reunited too with her younger brother, and she looked forward, she said, to a life of dull respectability. I doubted, myself, that it would long content her.

The house was quieter than we had ever known it when we breakfasted there for the last time before setting off on our journey. Bob Tippett had been turned away with a generous gift, and had been cheerful enough at it, regarding his time with us as a great joke with which he would regale his fellows for many years. Blatchford was to remain as a caretaker, and to continue his work – Frank left with him, in addition, plans to turn the basement from a baths to a mere set of additional cabinets, should custom and fashion require it.

And so, at eight o'clock in the morning, two carriages appeared, our trunks were hoisted upon them, and Frank, Sophie and I climbed in. And as the door of the house closed we began to rattle southwards, to the river and over it, and out towards Dover and the packet which would carry us to the continent, and no doubt to fresh adventures.

Roberta Latow

Three Rivers

A SENSATIONAL WOMAN.
A FABULOUS MAN.
TOGETHER THEY EXPLORE THE WILDER
SHORES OF LOVE . . .

Isabel and Alexis – rich, beautiful, successful – and
obsessed with each other.
This is their story.

AN INTOXICATING NOVEL THAT GOES
RIGHT TO THE HEART OF EVERY WOMAN'S
FANTASY OF EROTIC LOVE

FICTION   0-7472-3045-5   £2.50

MALEE

TIGER CLAW AND VELVET PAW

The erotic odyssey of Thai prostitute

The world of Suzie Wong . . .

The daughter of a Thai rice farmer, Malee is forced to leave
her village and enter domestic service at the age of fourteen.
Raped by her master, she flees to the nearest open door –
the local brothel.

Realising that prostitution offers her only chance of
survival, Malee becomes a showdancing star, devising erotic
spectacles of Oriental sensuality.

She moves on from the world of the American GI to the
cosmopolitan life of Bangkok and finally settles in the red
light district of Hamburg.

Explicit and touchingly honest, Malee's story explores a
sexual underworld of fantasy and compulsion exploited by
whore and punter alike.

NON-FICTION   0-7472-3047-1   £2.50

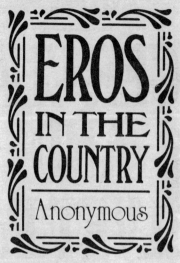

Headline books are available at your bookshop or newsagent, or can be ordered from the following address:

Headline Book Publishing PLC
Cash Sales Department
PO Box 11
Falmouth
Cornwall
TR10 9EN
England

UK customers please send cheque or postal order (no currency), allowing 60p for postage and packing for the first book, plus 25p for the second book and 15p for each additional book ordered up to a maximum charge of £1.90 in UK.

BFPO customers please allow 60p for postage and packing for the first book, plus 25p for the second book and 15p per copy for the next seven books, thereafter 9p per book.

Overseas and Eire customers please allow £1.25 for postage and packing for the first book, plus 75p for the second book and 28p for each subsequent book.